TO STREAM AN OCEAN

Arts of Substance - Novel 3

Sharon Rose

Eternarose Publishing

Book Cover by: Kirk DouPonce, DogEared Designs

Edited by: B Squared Writer Coaching

ISBN: 978-1-948160-36-0

DEDICATION

To Jude,
May you always discern the difference between the real and the fake.

CONTENTS

CHAPTER 1

The wave descended with a crash. Danivid strode farther out on the rocks, following the retreating water. He summoned the next wave to rise higher. It obeyed, then plummeted toward him. Above his head, it divided, leaving him dry from cloak to shoes. Only his streamer's gift kept the raging waters from sweeping him out into an ocean grave.

That would be the easy way out. No more grief over his brother's shortened days upon the throne. No more sorrow over the life he himself must now give up. No more dread of the heavy crown he was never meant to wear. No more worry about the questionable changes since he'd left the palace a decade ago. No more sideways looks.

Strange how tempting it could be to forsake honor in a watery grave of his own making.

Yet in the face of all this chaos, forsaking honor was the one thing Danivid could not do. Even if the hints of corruption were true. In fact, that possibility made his new duty all the more necessary. And all the more impossible.

A swelling wave leapt higher as though it could portray his suppressed—what? Was there a word for this emotion? This mix of sorrow and loss and betrayal and dread. No word that a man could speak. Could the ocean pronounce it?

Danivid reached his streaming gift into the dusky harbor, spreading his hands to mirror the silent command that he cast far and broad. The waters changed course, unified in a single current, and rushed toward him. He longed to let them come ashore. To cast boulders up the cliff. That would be fitting.

At the last moment, he reversed his own command. The current leapt from the ocean, straight up toward the sky. A tower of water. He twisted it aside and let go.

The boom rattled his bones. He embraced the depression and surge within the harbor. Demanded they stay with him and not trouble the distant ships. The energy trapped within the water demanded release, and he sent it skyward a hundred feet offshore. A raging fountain of the deep, flinging droplets high enough to catch the setting sun. For a moment they flickered like stars falling from the darkening sky. Raining down to their home, winking out as they fell, vanishing in the swell.

Yes. *That* was the word he couldn't speak. He sensed the underwater current spreading, sweeping away along the cliffs. He imagined it embodying his anger and released it to flow away.

Footfalls struck the rock behind him. "Still playing games, I see."

Danivid shut his eyes. The last voice he wanted to hear—Chief Streamer Chardomeer. Unavoidable. He turned. "I will practice my gift how I please."

"Pointlessly, in other words. Wasting it. How many times did I tell you that an ocean cannot be streamed?"

"Enough to make me avoid you. Did you have a reason for coming down here?"

The old streamer snorted. "The chief keeper demands your presence. And of course, you couldn't be found. Idiots are running all over the palace grounds looking for you. I sensed you still practicing your foolish ways, so—"

"Is this how you address your king?"

"But you aren't that yet, are you? Dally long enough, and we'll both bow to a witless child."

A comment as absurd as it was cruel. Danivid had no patience for the enigmatic ramblings Chardomeer favored. Better to go see what was happening than to waste time in question or rebuke. He strode past the chief streamer and across the natural rock to the cliffside stairway, then climbed to the colonnade.

Lights flicked on beside the garden pathways, for shadows encroached. The low sun revealed a crowd on the terrace surrounding the palace's entrance. Danivid followed the colonnade beside the garden, using the minutes to determine who gathered. The chief keeper's flowing robe and glittering sash were easy to pick out on the upper tier. So was the widowed queen's ornate cloak. A short woman, likely his sister, Allirae, and a couple other men stood with them. Those on the lower tier faced away from Danivid. One of the men pointed toward him, and the rest turned to watch his approach. Nobles and governors from the provinces who had come to the king's funeral.

Danivid's own cloak weighed heavy on his shoulders, the breeze tugging it back as he neared them. He caught sight of the young princess, hovering closer to her Aunt Allirae than to her mother, the queen. How unkind to bring Aneen into whatever this was. She didn't do well in crowds. As for the others, Meroak stood beside his wife, Allirae, and Chief Former Shevnal hovered near the queen.

Reaching the terrace, Danivid stepped between pedestals that ringed the upper tier. Their flower urns sat on the pavement next to them, replaced by bowls of burning incense. The sun's horizontal rays lingered in the rising smoke. The emerald- and diamond-studded crown of Welcia sat upon a small table beside the Chief Keeper of the Writ. Why? Who had ordered these arrangements?

Danivid addressed the chief keeper. "What is the meaning of assembling witnesses with the crown and incense? The coronation is tomorrow."

"So it is planned, Prince Danivid. Yet Queen Lenneth insisted we proceed at once."

Senseless, yet she was mourning her husband, so Danivid kept his question soft. "Why, Lenneth?"

Her lips trembled. "Tomorrow's crowd will not be good for Aneen. Better to do it with this small group and less pomp." She reached toward her daughter and sweetened her tone. "Come here, Aneen, and stand before this kind man. He has something to give you. It's very pretty."

As usual, Aneen did not respond. It was always hard to tell what she understood, for she rarely spoke and never more than a few words at a time.

"Lenneth," Danivid whispered, "why are you doing this? Do you not know what is in King Vancent's will?"

"Oh, I couldn't bear his morbid talk back then. I'm sure he has left me provided for. The will doesn't matter in this moment. Let's just finish with crowning his only child and heir, so that she may go to bed on time. Come, Aneen."

"You must realize she cannot bear the crown."

Lenneth's pitch edged higher. "She'll grow up, even if it takes her longer. You'll see. And I'll be her regent until then, so all will be well." She couldn't meet his gaze longer than a second and hurried into more words. "At least give her the chance to reach twenty before you deny her."

Just what he needed to start his reign. Lenneth was on the verge of a hysterical scene, which would drive her child into violent shudders.

Lenneth cast quick glances toward the chief former, who had no authority to participate in a royal proceeding. A fact he ignored as he took a step nearer. "Let us not delay, for it upsets both the previous and future queens." Reaching toward Aneen, he said, "Come and look at this pretty crown."

The moment his hand touched her shoulder, she yelled, "Bad man!" and flung herself against her aunt's legs.

Princess Allirae spread her cloak around the girl. "It's all right. You can stay with me."

Shevnal stepped back. "Under the circumstances, the crown can be placed on Queen Lenneth's head as proxy for Princess Aneen." He gestured Lenneth toward the crown. Her stilted approach proved that she knew this was wrong.

Why did she follow his bidding? "Enough," Danivid said. "We shall proceed, but it shall be according to protocol. Chief Former Shevnal, join your peers on the lower tier."

"Queen Lenneth requested that I support her during the ceremony."

Danivid moved to Lenneth's side and rested a hand on her shoulder. "I am the protector of my brother's widow." The people he needed stood in the small crowd. He drew Lenneth from the place she did not belong. "Your parents may come up to stand with you. Also, I summon Prime Minister Katowau of Dirklan as witness. Princess Ambassador Allirae de Noviam is the other witness." He gestured to an honor guard as he spoke. "See to it." Danivid turned his back on Shevnal.

Behind him, the stern guard said, "Precede me down the steps, sir."

Those Danivid had summoned made their way up to join him. He whispered to Lenneth, "I will help you in every way I can. For now, try to accept what must be."

Tears streaked her cheeks as she trembled. "I can't do this. I need…"

To his relief, Lenneth's mother reached her and wrapped her in an embrace. Danivid approached the chief keeper, whose rigid expression had eased a trifle. "Did you bring the will?"

He raised the paper he was clutching. "I did."

"Read the succession article, then proceed with only the necessary coronation rites. We'll save the pomp and full ceremony for tomorrow."

As the sun sank behind the horizon, Danivid—heir of the House de Noviam—pronounced his vows to serve the people of Welcia as king under the divine authority of Ellincreo. He knelt on one knee to receive the crown. Only then did he feel the tremor radiating through the stone.

For the first time in this long day, Danivid let his posture ease. The formal processions...the coronation rites...the reception with endless acknowledgements and bowing...at last they were over. Danivid strolled across the deserted palace hall into a salon. Cushions askew, empty glasses, and a trampled handkerchief made it look oddly abandoned.

Already his formal coronation seemed distant. As though he had watched the pageantry from the sidelines, even while he was the center of it all. He unbuckled the gold clasps of his royal cloak and swung the heavy garment from his shoulders and onto a chair. Its passing drew a cascade of flower petals from a nearby vase. Apparently, the flowers were also tired of the day, though they still sweetened the breeze he had stirred.

His sister followed him into the room. "Free of crowds, at last." She dropped into a chair and let her hands dangle from the armrests.

Danivid closed the door, then joined her within a cluster of chairs arranged for conversation. Sitting, he extended his legs and stretched his arms overhead. "A funeral one day, a celebration the next. Disorienting."

"Awful, isn't it? But necessary, considering the potential for chaos after..." She lowered her gaze and let her words out on a sigh. "After Vancent's untimely death." She blinked hard. "With so many unaware that he'd appointed you as successor, everyone from lords to laborers worried. You can't blame them. Bad enough to have a child crowned, far worse when she is likely to remain a child no matter how long she lives."

Danivid lifted the jewel-studded circlet from his brow. "I can guarantee she would never tolerate wearing this uncomfortable thing." He set the crown on the table beside him, then linked his hands behind his neck. "Strange how the timing worked out. Vancent tells us of his new will one week and dies the next."

She eyed him, her slow words sounding reluctant. "What are you suggesting?"

"Oh, come, Allirae. He was thirty-five and healthy. He legally documents that I am to be his successor, but before the public announcement, he dies in his sleep."

"You realize, don't you, that declaring suspicions could be disastrous? The medics have stated that they found no evidence of foul play."

"Nor could they determine the cause of death. I cannot accuse without proof, but I would like to know who was aware of the succession." He spread one hand as he shifted. "There are the obvious ones—ourselves, the witnesses of his will, and such. None of whom have anything to gain by making me king in my brother's place. And then there is Lenneth, who is most likely to have let the news slip. Yet she claims she didn't know. Do you believe her?"

Allirae smirked. "So hard to say. If she knew, it was beyond absurd to try to have Aneen crowned queen. One could claim she had a motive, since a regent has considerable power, but Lenneth has never had the least interest in governing. She is wonderful at entertaining and gracing charitable events, but she never attended even the smallest council meeting. Nothing got her out of the room faster than Vancent and me discussing matters of state."

He rubbed a fingertip across his chin. "It seemed odd that Shevnal was supporting her."

"Perhaps to you, but you haven't lived in Regissa for years. Vancent and Lenneth considered him a friend. He's at the palace way more than any other guild chief, and he's often invited to stay for lunch. Lenneth was so fragile yesterday. It's no wonder she'd want a friend at her side."

"Is he a closer friend than her parents?"

"No, but they live far and he lives near. Lenneth must always have a cluster of friends around her." Allirae tilted her head. "You don't think there was anything inappropriate between them, do you?"

He huffed. "My visits may have been infrequent, but nothing could be more obvious than the commitment between Vancent and Lenneth. Shevnal could never attract her."

"What are you getting at, then?"

"As you say, Lenneth wouldn't want to govern. She has no motive to either kill her husband or become queen regent. Who has a motive for both of those very unexpected events?"

Allirae braced her elbows on the armrests and peaked her fingertips. "I'm an advisor to you, right?"

"Of course."

"Before you get any farther into the idea that our brother was murdered, you had better think about who has the most to gain from his death. Because it's *you*."

"Bear in mind that I am the one person who is certain beyond all possibility of doubt that I did not kill my brother. Anyone who knows me at all, knows I never wanted to rule Welcia."

"You needn't convince *me*. I know how much you loved living in Dirklan. Being the royal ambassador to our belowground province suited you perfectly. But most in Regissa, or anywhere else aboveground, *don't* know you well."

"O wise sage," he quipped, "do you foresee a hanging in my future?"

She grinned. "Not at all. I'm far more worried about financial woes."

"Ominous." He said it lightly, though he'd caught hints of his brother's worries on this very matter. Not that Vancent had spoken of them. "Are there any issues in the provinces that have created ill-will?"

"There is always some small matter, but Vancent dealt with that sort of thing right away. Bonador Province is still struggling with heightened crime. The General Council approved sending more funds."

"I assume you've still been traveling the provinces regularly?" After her nod, he asked, "What are the general sentiments toward the crown?"

"Vancent was well liked. Accommodating, whenever possible. Never forcing dictates upon the local elected officials. The biggest complaint against him was that he was *too* welcoming of every new thing. He wasn't one to give much thought to ramifications."

A yip beyond the door prevented Danivid's next question.

At his raised brows, Allirae said, "That's Cam. Aneen must be looking for me."

The door latch turned, and Aneen wandered in. "Find Al'rae."

With all the grace of the Flyound breed, the dog trotted to Allirae, dropped to her haunches, and gave a satisfied yip. A dainty sound from such a large dog.

"Good Cam." Aneen patted first the white patch, then the black patch on the dog's head. That task completed, she leaned against Allirae, who wrapped an arm around her.

These dogs Vancent had acquired when Aneen finally learned to walk—such a perfect example of his common-sense kindness. Danivid would never forget his visit after Aneen's overdue achievement. Thrice in one week, the entire household scoured the palace searching for the three-year-old princess. Not only did she wander everywhere, she never answered anyone who called her name.

A warm ache filled Danivid at the memory of Vancent's response. He'd uttered no rebuke for losing the wee princess. He simply procured Flyound dogs, bred for their legendary scenting ability, and had them all trained to the command of "find Aneen." Nor had Danivid been surprised a few months later that Aneen had claimed the dog with piebald markings. She'd renamed her and even started shouting, "Cam find Aneen" whenever she wanted her pet.

Danivid silently thanked his brother for his insight into caring for a child many would have ignored. Now, she was *his* to care for. Affection, he had, for her heart was sweet. But knowledge of how to care for her...*inadequate* would be an overstatement.

Meroak, Allirae's husband, strolled into the room, doubtless keeping an eye on the princess. Danivid glanced up at his brother-in-law. "Thank you for bringing her down."

Meroak quirked a smile. "Better to thank Cam than me."

"I didn't realize she had been trained to find anyone else. What need brought that about?"

"Aneen taught her."

"Really? How?"

"Simple wisdom." Meroak sat beside his wife. "She says *find* with a name, takes Cam to the person, then gives her pats and praise."

Danivid smiled at his niece. "Aneen is clever."

Her unfocused gaze zeroed in on him, and she gripped Cam's harness. "Find Da'vid." They crossed to Danivid's chair. "Good Cam." She precisely patted the dog's head.

Curious, how he felt honored. "Thank you for teaching her about me."

She offered no response, but behind her, Allirae gave him a pointed stare. "I'm tired. I think it's time for bed."

"No bed." Aneen declared.

A hint this obvious, he could manage. "It *is* dark, and I'm tired too." He picked up his crown, then rose and gathered up his cloak. "Will you walk up the stairs with me, Aneen?"

This strategy won him an approving nod from Allirae, and they all climbed to the bedchamber floor. Aneen continued on to the nursery with her aunt and uncle.

Danivid looked toward his bedroom of many years, but that was his past. He proceeded to the king's bedchamber. His brother's dog lay outside the open door, curled up rather than in his usual commanding pose. Poor thing. "Hello, Burnie." The dog stood, though his tail didn't lift. Danivid rubbed his head. "You feel it, too, don't you, boy? Come on in."

Danivid suppressed a sigh at the sight of Yautan, his brother's personal aide, waiting in the chamber. Privacy was not yet his.

Yautan sneered at the dog, an overused expression judging by the creases in his fifty-something face. "Rather a nuisance that the beast keeps sneaking back up to this chamber. I told the kennel master to lock him up, but he is uncooperative."

"He merely understands dogs better than you. Burnie may stay."

"I believe his name is Burnswick," Yautan said. "I must warn you that he tends to challenge my presence in this chamber."

Probably because the man called him by a stuffy pedigree name. "Nothing wrong with a dog who protects his master." Danivid glanced around. His personal things lay on the dresser. He set the crown beside them. "I gather you moved everything over from my old room?"

"Yes, sir. The tailor has added royal trim to a couple of your tunics. He will come to measure you in the morning."

"You may take this cloak to wherever the state garments are kept. I need nothing more toni—"

A bang and shriek drew Danivid's head around to the side door. What was going on in the sitting room? He crossed to the door and jerked it open. The room was empty and undisturbed. On the far end, a closed door led to the queen's chamber.

Yautan edged around him and through the doorway. "Perhaps a chair tipped over, sir. I will check with the lady's maid."

Lenneth shrieked words this time. "I need it now!"

Footsteps ran down the hallway, and a woman's voice called out, "Lenneth, dear, I'm coming."

"Ah, that is Lady Emuria," Yautan said. "I'm sure the queen will be fine with her mother present."

"I think I'll sleep in my old room."

"No need, sir. I will make sure she quiets down."

Did he not comprehend grief? "You will do nothing of the sort. She has lost her husband, and she is allowed to weep." Yautan blinked. How could he look surprised?

"Ah, yes. No doubt, that is it." A moan emanated from the far door, and Yautan backed toward the corridor exit from the sitting room. "I'll just check with her maid. No need to disturb yourself in the matter. Pleasant night, sir."

Bizarre, but there seemed to be nothing for Danivid to do. He closed his own door, returning another layer of wood between him and the grieving widow. He leaned against his brother's desk and rubbed his fingertips over his brow where a headache lurked. Tears were not his way, but nonetheless, his eyes dampened.

Burnie padded over to him, then rose up and placed two paws on Danivid's shoulders.

Surprise drew a chuckle from him. "You're all legs, aren't you?" He averted his face, so the dog's wet tongue swiped only his chin. "Thanks, but licking isn't the way to my heart. Down, boy." He rubbed Burnie's neck until the dog backed away to give himself a shake. Black ears pricked up, and his tongue lolled from his slender brown snout.

"You think the world looks a little better now, do you? I hope you're right." Danivid surveyed the king's chamber, trying to grasp that it was his bedroom. Less ornate than he remembered it. Not that he'd seen it often. Maybe Vancent had replaced furniture. He took a few steps from the desk. That piece was the same. Made sense, considering what their father had shown them in their teen years.

He had no heart to check that cache yet. Especially if he might be interrupted. Lenneth had been quiet for a while now, but if she shrieked again, should he check on her himself? Would that help or harm? Was this how a woman mourned? Sure, they cried more than a man, but screaming? Yautan's strange reaction cycled through Danivid's mind. Something wasn't right.

CHAPTER 2

A flapping sound nudged Danivid from sleep. He cracked an eye. A sliver of pale light escaped the drawn curtains. Burnie completed a vigorous shake, stretched, and padded over to the door.

Ugh. He must need to go out.

The dog angled his ears to the door and nose to its crack. His tail began to wag. The handle turned, and the door stealthily opened on silent hinges. Danivid snapped wide awake.

Burnie exited as soon as there was space enough, and the door closed in complete silence.

Danivid chuckled at his fear. Not an intruder. Just someone tending the king's dog. His new role would have a few perks. Perhaps they would take the edge off...whatever it was he was facing.

Hushed footfalls reached his ears, though no voices intruded. It must be early, but his brief alarm had put an end to sleep. Might as well get up.

After a shower, he wandered into the dressing room. Beside his brother's extensive wardrobe hung the garments Danivid had hurriedly packed when the dreadful news had reached him. Most of his bore the single gold cord of a royal ambassador. On two of them, ornate gold braiding had been added to the cuffs and shoulder pieces. He preferred simple styles, but he couldn't portray himself as a reluctant king.

As he donned the embellished garb, someone knocked on the bedroom door and opened it without pause. Danivid angled his head to see who entered.

Yautan set a tall case on the small table by the door. "Pleasant morning, sir. I trust you slept well."

"Well enough." Danivid returned to the bedroom and made use of the dresser's mirror. "In the future, wait for permission to enter after you knock."

"Ah. Problematic, since waking the king is one of my duties." Yautan spread his case open on its vertical hinge, revealing a tall, sealed flask, two tins, and more tea paraphernalia than seemed necessary. "What if you were too deeply asleep to grant permission?"

Danivid adjusted his tunic. "Knock harder."

"As you please, sir." Yautan's tone indicated that *he* was not pleased. "May I make your tea?"

"Yes. I like it strong." Danivid dropped his gaze to his brother's jewel case. He set his jaw and opened it. Pins, clasps, cufflinks. Some jeweled, some sculpted or etched gold. All familiar—worn by his father and brother. He chose a gold clasp almost at random. Lighter weight than it looked, but it served to fasten the cross-over front of his tunic. He ran a hair pick through his short, dark curls to bring some order to them before they dried.

"Would you like me to assist with your hair?"

Danivid's hand froze. "No." Oh, how he missed Prentov! Could he convince his Dirklian aide to come aboveground? Probably a foolish desire, since Prentov knew nothing of the palace or Regissa City.

Yautan busied himself in the dressing room, returning a moment later. "How else may I be of service?"

Irritating, but maybe he truly intended to be useful. Danivid sought for a task of some value. Ah, information. "Who came to collect Burnie this morning?"

"That is the kennel master's duty. Did he awaken you?"

"No, Burnie did."

"Most annoying, I'm sure. I will pass on your instructions to the kennel master to keep the dog in the kennel where it belongs."

"No. Like my brother, I grew up with dogs and horses. One advantage of living aboveground is that I may enjoy them again."

"*Enjoy* isn't the word I would use."

Danivid hid a smile. "What has Burnie done to you?"

"At best, he ignores me. At worst, he growls and snaps. The queen's maid is terrified of him. Unpredictable dogs are dangerous."

"Burnie is a Flyound—a breed known for loyalty, not ferocity."

"Loyal to King Vancent, he was, but I doubt he'll transfer that to anyone else. Regardless, he is such a pest during the morning that King Vancent always kept him out of the bedchamber until he'd been exercised."

Clearly, Yautan knew dogs no better than he knew Danivid. "How is the tea coming along?"

"Should be ready, sir." He walked to the round table by the window to uncover the mug and remove the tea strainer. "Would you like your breakfast in the morning room, or would you prefer it privately in your sitting room?"

Danivid settled into one of the two wing chairs and picked up the mug. "The morning room." He savored the first few sips of the fragrant brew. Remarkably good. "Inform the royal steward that I wish to review accounts after breakfast."

"The tailor will be ready for you after breakfast, but I will tell your scheduler to set up a meeting with the steward. He brings the accounts the first week of every month."

"Did you contradict my brother this often?"

A pause preceded Yautan's answer. "King Vancent knew that I held his interests near, and he trusted me with arrangements between his many aides." Yautan opened the heavy drapes. "The crown came to you unexpectedly, sir, and you've had no time to learn the intricacies of the royal household. My only desire is to ease the transition for you."

Danivid slowed his crisp words. "*Did* you contradict him this often?"

"There was nothing to contradict. Our mutual understanding enabled us to work well together."

Work well together? Strange to phrase it as though they were peers. Despite the changes late in his father's reign, a king was still king. Easygoing, Vancent may have been, but did he really let his personal aide order everything? Danivid wouldn't, no matter how delicious his tea was. On the other hand, he didn't know who administered the details of palace affairs. Yautan knew, and he could be useful—provided he didn't overstep. "I am not the only one facing a change, Yautan. You will need to learn my ways as you once learned my brother's. Assume less. Listen more."

"Certainly, sir."

"Then I expect to see the steward this morning."

Yautan gave him a tight-lipped nod.

Danivid drained his mug and set it down. "You brew a fine cup of tea."

"Thank you, sir. I have made a study of it." Yautan gathered the tea things and carried them into the bathroom. Water sloshed, and he returned a few minutes later with a towel full of paraphernalia, which he stowed in the compartments of his elaborate tea caddy.

"You wash dishes in the bathroom?" Danivid asked.

"Just these. Allowing residue to dry in the cup or strainer causes bitterness in subsequent brews. I will only serve the finest to my king." Yautan picked up his tea caddy and opened the chamber door. He stiffened as Burnie bounded past him, then he made a hurried exit.

Burnie plopped his head onto Danivid's lap, drawing a chuckle from him. "Well, you ferocious beast, how is it that you terrify that tea connoisseur? Or did you lift a leg on his tea caddy?"

Burnie tilted his head, directing Danivid's fingers to his favorite spot for a scratch.

Dangerous? "Whatever Yautan may know about the household, he knows nothing about dogs."

Burnie angled into a different position, then sighed. When Danivid stood, the dog shook himself and waited to see what was next. Not a pest, either.

To fulfill his morning habit of reading a passage, Danivid looked around the room for a copy of the Holy Writ. Not a single book was in sight. Perhaps in the sitting room. Awkward, with the queen's bedchamber adjoining it, but it was his sitting room now. He entered it, Burnie following. At least no shrieks emanated from the far door. Hopefully, she was past the harshest moments of grief.

The room's well-stuffed chairs, rich hangings, and intricately carved furnishings seemed more in keeping with palace style than the king's bedchamber. A bookcase offered what he'd come for. He was reading the titles, when a high-pitched voice reached his ears, answered in a much lower pitch. Probably the queen's father. Their words were indistinct, but he didn't want distraction. He took a book to his chamber and read for the few minutes left before the hour chimed. His stomach agreed with the clock. Breakfast.

Burnie again followed as Danivid stepped into the corridor. The queen's door also opened, and he turned to greet her. The words stalled, for the chief former emerged and closed the door on her sobs.

He checked his first step when he caught sight of Danivid, then he cleared the expression of annoyance from his face—mostly—and approached. *Long* described every part of him, from legs to fingers to his arrogantly lifted nose.

"Shevnal," Danivid said. "An early hour for visiting. What brings you?"

He drew near and bowed. "I agree, sir. The queen summoned me to come at once. Considering her recent bereavement and my close friendship with the late king, I felt I might be able to offer her some comfort. So I decided to overlook the irregularity of the timing." He closed his eyes in a pained fashion. "A mistake I will not repeat. The lady seems hysterical. I have no idea what she wanted from me."

Footsteps hurried near, and Danivid turned to see who approached. Lady Emuria. She drove a daggered look at Shevnal and passed them without a word.

"If you will excuse me," Shevnal said, "I will depart."

Danivid inclined his head and let him pass. Lady Emuria waited with her hand on the queen's door latch, glaring at the man's back. Not until Shevnal reached the staircase did she enter the room.

Danivid followed the chief former slowly. A guard closed the hall door behind Shevnal. Danivid descended the stairs, looking over the two guards who waited below. They bowed at his approach and straightened.

"How is it that a visitor wanders unattended through the palace?"

Blanching, one bowed again. "The fault is mine, lord king."

His sleeve cord indicated that he held the highest rank, so he was at fault no matter what. He kept his eyes on the floor as he straightened.

"I asked for an explanation."

"Yes, sir." The guard's Adam's apple bobbed. "The late king and his queen permitted Chief Former Shevnal that freedom. This morning, he carried a note written in the queen's hand, so I did not question. In this, I erred."

"Who else enjoys such a permission?"

"None but Shevnal."

"That permission is withdrawn, regardless of the queen's request."

"Yes, sir. No visitor shall remain unescorted again. All guards shall be informed at once."

Danivid left them, Burnie's claws clicking on the marble floor behind him.

He arrived in the morning room and found his sister and brother-in-law already present. Allirae's back was to the door, and when he said, "Pleasant morning," she jerked her head around, eyes wide.

She dropped her gaze. "You sound so like him."

"I know." He touched her shoulder as he passed on his way to the head of the table.

"And walk like him too...with Burnie, no less. It's hard."

"The little sudden things are the worst, aren't they?" Danivid touched the gold pinned to his tunic as he sat. "Like wearing his clasp."

Meroak looked at it. "Doubtless, but it is your clasp now."

"Indeed." And the unknown woman who stepped to his side was no doubt one of his staff.

"Would you like coffee or tea, lord king?"

"Tea, please."

Burnie sniffed the air, then sat down in a corner.

Allirae adopted an arch tone. "I see that Sir Burnswick acknowledges the crown, and that you grant his accustomed rights."

Danivid chuckled. "He is certainly attentive and well-trained, though Yautan wants to be rid of him. Can anyone tell me why?"

"Not I," Allirae said, and Meroak shook his head.

The server uttered a faint *ahem*. "The dog growls at him sometimes."

"Often?" Danivid asked.

"No, sir, for Yautan tries to finish his morning duties before the dog comes in from his feed and run. Though the poor thing's been touchy for the last few days, I think he's usually just bursting with energy and longing for someone to bark at."

Meroak selected a cinnamon roll from a serving plate. "More likely, he considers himself a royal guard. There is no end to that dog's pretension."

Such mild jests smoothed over all the things they didn't want to say. But breakfast couldn't last forever. Danivid stood. "Allirae, will you join me in the study?"

"Of course." She glanced at her husband. "You'll go to Aneen, won't you?"

He gave her a faint nod and smile that seemed to indicate an extra meaning. A solid, dependable man, ready to take on a duty that should belong to someone else.

Danivid strolled beside his sister. "I feel so inadequate to be Aneen's protector. What is it that she needs at this moment?"

"One of us. Vancent used to sit with her for a while after breakfast. Aneen must have a routine. She became quite difficult for her nanny during the mornings whenever Vancent was away, so Meroak or I would always fill in."

"I suppose her mother cannot do so until she recovers her equilibrium."

Allirae didn't answer. An omission so blatant that Danivid said nothing else until they reached the study. The moment he closed the door, she said, "Lenneth cannot really take care of Aneen."

Silence stretched between them. Despite visiting only four times a year, Danivid had sensed changes in his sister-in-law. A charming hostess she had remained, but brittle moments cracked the shiny facade. "Lenneth was all joy when we first knew her. What happened?"

Allirae moved to the chairs near the window rather than the oversized desk. "Troubles, I suppose." She swept her skirt aside and sat. "Lenneth is very good at being happy, but she has no idea how to manage anything less."

Danivid sat next to his sister. "Didn't Vancent give her everything she wanted?"

"No one can give everything. A baby, for instance. It took her four years to get pregnant. She never let on that it bothered her, but the extent of her relief when it finally happened tells a different story. She was all joy again, but it turned brittle when we noticed that…Aneen wasn't progressing like most children do. So placid, but rarely smiling. Never reaching for toys. Not bothering to crawl or to walk until so very late. She didn't speak her first word until she was five. And through all of it, Lenneth pretended…said Aneen just grew a little slower, but she was fine."

"When did she figure out the truth?"

"She knew all along. That's the problem. Her world must be perfect, and she cannot bear to think her child isn't…" Allirae swung her hand. "…whatever perfect means. So she misses the joy of how sweet her daughter is and tries to get her to behave like the average seven-year-old. Some days, she tries to teach her things and scolds her for failure. Sometimes, just sits and watches in silence. Other times, she runs from the nursery, sobbing."

None of this had shown during his visits. It seemed that charming Lenneth was a mess long before she lost her husband. "What did Vancent do with all this?"

"Remained patient—perhaps to a fault. Grew firm when absolutely required."

"Firm in what way?"

"Oh, like when Lenneth hired an unsuitable tutor. Vancent dismissed him—kindly—for the poor man had no hope of pleasing Lenneth. Then he found someone who *could* teach Aneen. Only a gradual process is appropriate. If you come across a woman sitting on the floor, playing with Aneen, that is her tutor. Don't criticize her methods. They work. Slowly."

At least he didn't need to worry about that. "What does 'patient to a fault' mean?"

"Vancent gave Lenneth all the money she wanted, which she spent on ambertrop. That way, she could return to her pretend perfect world and be happy…until the effects wore off."

Danivid compressed his lips. Contention over the drug would likely never end. A pleasant diversion to some—tolerated by others. Or not. Dirklians considered it evil, so his only involvement with it had been to ensure that it was never offered in trade arrangements. "I have heard that some people crave it more than food and drink."

"Lenneth certainly does. The medics have coined a new word for the condition of excessive craving. They call it *addiction*. Be careful using that word, though. Some consider it a slur. Others claim there is no such thing—quite adamantly."

"Do the medics offer anything more useful than a word?"

She directed a stern frown at him. "Don't be harsh. If it is indeed a malady, it's a new one. Thus far, the only cure seems to be complete, enforced abstinence. Which leads to anguish for a time, but eventually sufferer returns to a normal state."

"Eventually? How long?"

"I guess that depends on how long they have used it and how much. It seems to vary quite a bit from one person to the next. Some people never become addicted, though medics will argue that point."

Danivid rubbed a fingertip beneath his mouth. Was this the reason for Lenneth's recent behavior? "She shrieked so loud last night that I almost returned to my old room. Lady Emuria went to her, and I assumed she was able to calm her."

"Not likely."

"This morning, I heard Lenneth sobbing when her door opened. Shevnal walked out of her room."

Allirae's voice squeaked. "Before breakfast?"

"Indeed."

"That man haunts the palace but never that early."

"He said the queen had summoned him, and he seemed to regret having come. Lady Emuria saw him, too, and looked ready to claw his eyes out."

Allirae huffed through her nose. "You better figure out an answer for Lenneth. She'll ask you for money soon. I hear that ambertrop costs a small fortune."

"I'm not funding drug use."

"Then she'll spend her widow's allotment on it and beg you for clothes and—"

A knock interrupted Allirae's words.

"Enter," Danivid said.

Lord Eavertin, Lenneth's father, walked through the door and closed it behind him.

He looked so troubled that Danivid omitted the normal greeting of *pleasant morning*. "Is something amiss?"

He bowed and said, "I shall not take much time, for I see that your steward has arrived."

"You may take whatever time you need—and sit down, if you like."

"Thank you." He remained standing. "There is, indeed, something very much amiss. I realize, of course, that you are the protector of your brother's widow, but...I request that you allow my wife and me to take our daughter to stay with us."

"Certainly. She may visit wherever she pleases."

"Well...no...it doesn't please her to leave Regissa City. She is unwell and should not be making her own decisions right now. So I do need your permission to take her. I hope you understand."

"Ah. I probably do, but I like plain speech."

Lord Eaverton shifted his feet. "I mean no disrespect, but it is far too easy to obtain ambertrop in the palace. In our own home, we can ensure that she receives only wholesome food and drink. Also, we will not be taking her maid with us. I suggest you cease employing her in any capacity."

"I see. I permit you to care for Lenneth at this difficult time. Aneen, however, will remain here."

"I quite agree. That is wisest."

"Write to me of Lenneth's welfare."

"I will. I must also ask...it is irregular, but please do not send any money to her."

That could cause trouble. "The funds my brother left her may be managed here. Provide what she needs, keep account of it, and you will be reimbursed from her funds."

"Thank you. That is all I needed."

Danivid stood and walked to the door with him. Resting a hand on the older man's shoulder, he murmured, "I am sorry for what you endure, and I am grateful for what you are undertaking."

Lord Eavertin gave him a close-lipped nod and left.

Allirae had followed them, though not to leave quite yet, for she pushed the door shut. "There is something you ought to know."

Danivid steeled himself.

"Vancent used ambertrop too."

CHAPTER 3

Danivid propped his elbows on the desk amid ledgers and stacks of paper. He barely prevented himself from clutching his hair. The royal finances were nothing short of appalling. Though he didn't intend to, he muttered a thought aloud. "How did it get this bad?"

"Eight years of poor management," his chief steward said.

Eight years—the length of his brother's reign. "But to sell off the lands that provide the de Noviam family's income...*why*?"

"Well," Stanton replied, "the first sale provided funds for building the private rail to the king's woodland. I do understand that a person needs restful pursuits, but the cost was rather high. Far above the original estimate, in fact, so the king sold another plot to pay it off. And then it became easier to sell whenever...expenses exceeded income. Which happened ever more often." Stanton unfolded and refolded his hands. "I did caution the king. Several times. There were *some* months when they didn't withdraw cash so excessively. He also reduced expenditures in various ways, but they were not always...shall we say..."

"Say the word you mean."

Stanton met his gaze. "They were not wise."

"For instance?"

"When I advised him that the land steward had begun to allow excessive costs and could not provide all receipts, he dismissed the man but never replaced him. That led to more problems and reduced income. He let the palace steward go to reduce staff costs here, but that means no one manages day-to-day expenses."

Stanton shuffled through a stack of papers. "Anyone may order whatever they wish. The bill comes in and must be paid." He withdrew the paper he sought. "This one, dated the day after King Vancent's death, is for an order of fabric for the new royal wardrobe."

"I did not order that."

"Yautan ordered it. He has often placed orders for the late king."

Danivid took the bill from Stanton and almost gasped at the total. "This is exorbitant, and the quantities absurd. It must be sent back."

"I assume Yautan can take care of that," Stanton said. "Then there is the issue of Queen Lenneth drawing rather large sums of cash."

"That will cease."

"Good—though there is the matter of her widow's inheritance."

Danivid cringed. Even as he explained the arrangement he'd made with Lord Eavertin, he wondered where he would find money to place in her account. A curious provision in the will now made sense. Vancent had granted her a fixed amount or a percentage of the estate—whichever was less. He'd known how unlikely it was that the royal fortune could afford a queen's inheritance.

"I believe," Stanton said, "her money should be placed in a trust. Please discuss the choice of trustees with me before finalizing anything."

He clearly knew of her ambertrop use. "Where will we get the money to place in such a trust?"

"A difficulty, it is true." Stanton rolled his lips. "I am not saying I recommend this, but you should know that an offer has been made to purchase the woodland."

"No!"

"That was King Vancent's response as well. I should point out that the woodland does not produce income. Your remaining profitable land could be sold, but then you will have *no* income."

"In other words, the House de Noviam will be bankrupt."

"Yes."

Finally, a bald word from the man. "Is there any hopeful news anywhere in the mess?"

"There is, sir. Foremost, I see that it will be easier to converse with you about finances than it was with the late king and, especially, the queen."

"I was hoping for something more tangible." Against his inclination, Danivid asked, "What is this offer for the woodland? Do they want all of it? Who wants it, by the way, and what do they intend to do with it?"

"*Who* should not be considered a 'by the way' matter. Chief Former Shevnal has offered to buy it. I'm sure he will purchase however much you are willing to sell. He has not specified the use he intends, but with all his other purchases of de Noviam land, he extended the city of Regissa. Usually, manufacturing or retail is built on it, along with some housing. That provides land-lease income, which is far more lucrative than your agricultural income. Considering the beauty and current use of the woodland, a resort might be in his mind, with some logging first."

Why must this meeting constantly make Danivid feel like a quake was shaking his world? He'd better get himself together. "I'd like a list of all purchasers of de Noviam land, including the acreage and prices paid."

"Shevnal is the only purchaser."

"The *only* one? Why does no one else invest?"

Stanton's voice grew nasal. "You see, he was the king's friend. Which is why he always offered the most generous price. Lately, buying without a public offering, so the king needn't absorb that added expense. So...very...generous of him. More cash in the king's coffers to be spent on ambertrop."

"How much was spent on that?"

"Impossible to give a precise answer. The king and queen freely withdrew cash. The uses were not specified."

"Who did they purchase ambertrop from?"

"I do not know. Nor will it be easy to learn. Despite so many claiming that ambertrop is a harmless and pleasant diversion—a form of restful savoring—suppliers prefer to remain anonymous. Isn't that odd?"

"Should I take it that you are not among those who support free use of ambertrop?" Danivid asked.

"I most definitely am not. And though I just quoted the perversion of the Holy Writ that some use, I do not need the Writ to build my case." He slapped a hand down on the stack of ledgers. "These make my case. The decisions the king issued with a lazy smile, only to be rued when the golden brew had worn off—they make my case. The stuff is vile. The ambrosia of fools."

The steward's many revelations weighed heavy as Danivid left the study. Burnie ran ahead of him and disappeared into the hall.

This palace—his childhood home, a place of beauty and good—felt so diminished. As though tragedy, both sudden and creeping, had tarnished it. He slowed as he crossed the great hall with its jewel-studded mural of wind-driven waves breaking against rock. Emblematic of the three substance gifts in all their power. The mural should be glittering, for sunlight poured through windows and doors flung wide to welcome the ocean breeze. It was still pretty, but not breathtaking. Had the mural also been neglected?

Danivid climbed the stairs to his chamber. It was time he looked in the cache.

Again, that was not to be. Someone argued in his bedchamber.

"I have told you before that I prefer to choose fabric myself," one voice snapped.

"The king must have the very best." That was Yautan at his haughtiest.

Danivid stepped through the doorway, startling them both. A middle-aged man with a tape measure around his neck bowed.

"I gather you are the tailor my brother employed?" Danivid said.

"Yes, lord king."

"Forget the past." Danivid angled a hand toward his own chest. "*This* king will have exactly what he requests and nothing more. Yautan will no longer place orders on my behalf."

The tailor inclined his head. "Very good, sir."

Danivid turned to Yautan. "I have learned that you ordered considerable fabric for a new wardrobe that you assumed I would need. Return it at once."

"I—" Yautan faltered under Danivid's gaze. "I'll see to it."

With him out of the room, Danivid turned to the tailor, who did not deserve his ill temper. "If you have made the clothing I found here, you are a fine tailor."

The man's wooden look gave way to pleasure. "Thank you, sir."

"Though position demands otherwise, I prefer simpler styles. If you can somehow combine those conflicting desires, I would appreciate it."

"Simplicity can be as beautiful as complexity. May I take your measurements, sir?" At Danivid's nod, he began. "The late king—may he rest in the joy of Ellincreo—liked what he called a calm style. Not suitable for state or formal affairs, but perfect for daily life." He paused to jot numbers in a pocket notebook.

"I noticed his clothes in the dressing room. A great plenty. Can you alter them to fit me?"

"Easily. I see that you are of similar build. If you could hold this end of the tape here at your waist, please?" He dropped to one knee. "Only an inch shorter. Alterations will be no problem."

"I will need something for riding too. Soon, please."

"Of course." He finished measuring. "I will take some garments from the dressing room to begin with."

"Through that door," Danivid said.

The tailor gave him a prim smile. "Yes, I am quite familiar with the king's dressing room." He no longer smiled when he returned, but he laid several garments on the bed. "Will these be acceptable for the initial alterations?"

"Yes." Danivid checked that a riding coat and breeches were included, then eyed the tailor's frown. "Is something wrong?"

"Well...I do not wish to speak out of place...but there used to be more clothing in the dressing room."

"Oh?"

"At least a dozen rather fine garments are missing. I suppose they could be in the laundry." He uttered that as though he doubted it. "Or perhaps stored elsewhere. Not that it is my business. I will return tomorrow to ensure the first alterations are correct."

The tailor left, and Burnie took the opportunity of an open door to slip inside.

Danivid rested a hand on his head and murmured, "What do you think? Is there a market for stolen clothing?" He looked again toward the hidden cache. Did he have time before lunch?

A knock sounded. Apparently not. "Enter."

Yautan stepped through the doorway. "Luncheon is served in the small dining room."

Danivid acknowledged with a nod. "I need to be sure what I said earlier is clear. You may no longer order or purchase *anything* without specific instructions."

"As you wish, sir, though I think you will grow rather tired of every small request."

"Have you finished sending the fabric back?"

"It is packed. I have set aside some black silk for the queen, if you please, sir."

"No, send it back. The queen is leaving for a visit to her parents."

Yautan looked startled. "I cannot imagine she would go *there*. Eavertin Province is such a backwards, intolerant place."

"Is it, indeed? Is that what you think of Dirklan Province? Backward and intolerant?"

Yautan lost a little assurance. "I have never visited there. Naturally, you have a fondness for it, since it was your home for years. I did not mean to disparage."

"I have a fondness for every province of Welcia. After seeing my sister-in-law's suffering, I have no *tolerance* for ambertrop. None of it is ever allowed in the palace again."

"As you wish, sir," Yautan said, stepping into the corridor as Danivid moved toward it. "Will there be anything else?"

"Have the palace former clean the mural in the hall."

He startled again. "Uh, why?"

Caverns, this man irritated him. "Because it's dull."

"Oh, I suppose it collected dust slowly, and we didn't notice. There is no palace former these days, but I will send a request to the Formers' Guild."

Danivid strode down the corridor. How could the man look shocked over a cleaning request?

Allirae spooned fruit salad onto her plate. "Did you know that Lenneth and her parents left an hour ago?"

The question interrupted Danivid's cycling worries. "Already? I would have thought they'd wait till morning, so they needn't stay overnight anywhere."

A smile nudged her lips. "You're too used to the open, low-speed trains of Dirklan. Only the northernmost provinces require a full day of travel.

They'll reach their home station by sundown. I'm sure her father wired a message ahead, so their cair will be waiting for them."

"I don't envy her parents." Danivid passed a plate of bread to Meroak. "If the message is lost between the relay huts, they'll have a beastly time with her in a public station."

Meroak selected from the variety of breads and passed the plate to his wife. "That's rare now that the operators have improved procedures. Also, there should be cairs for hire at the stations. Eavertin Province may resist technology, but they do accommodate decent travel."

"Ah, resist technology. The cardinal sin in these progressive days." Danivid spread butter over his bread. "I suppose Dirklan is considered the greatest sinner in that regard."

"An odd twist, isn't it," Meroak said, "since primary technology started there? Magnery. Powered machines and transportation. Wired communication. And now they push back."

"They still invent. They just pause to consider—and dare to say *no*." Meroak tilted his head. "Do they say *yes* often enough?"

Danivid considered his answer. "They said *yes* to fully lighting the tunnels, thereby revealing rock formations, colors, and crystals that few had ever seen. They *could* say *yes* to covering their train carriages, enabling them to race through the tunnels. All the beauty would become a blur in the windows. Those who objected could be told, 'We have printed pictures so people may enjoy them whenever they like.' But each picture is a travesty. Many in Dirklan, as do I, prefer to savor the original beauty during a slow ride."

"A fair answer," Meroak conceded. "Not that it will convince those who love speed more than beauty."

"Both fast and slow are useful," Allirae said. "The problem is that, once high-speed trains are implemented, slow speeds become impossible on the same rail system. Now, only Dirklan can retain a low-speed system, because theirs has a single controlled interconnection at the access tunnel. I'm glad someone keeps the treasure of *slow*."

Danivid grinned. "Dirklan's rail system was considered fast when it was first powered. Before the collapse, they were using burros to pull carriages along the rails. Welcia above didn't even have rails. Their transportation relied on horses."

"I don't disagree." Meroak winked at Allirae. "And with an ambassador wife, I wouldn't dare suggest overstepping provincial rights of decision. Nonetheless..." He turned a more serious look to Danivid. "Slow travel makes Dirklan look like a museum exhibit of a stuffed, extinct animal."

"I assure you, Dirklan is very much alive. If it is an exhibit, I wish more people would view it, for they enjoy a rich life belowground."

Meroak opened his mouth to respond, but a tremor radiated through the floor.

Silverware rattled atop the dishes. Water quivering in his glass triggered Danivid's streamer sense. He closed his eyes and extended that awareness to the harbor. Difficult to sense from within the palace, but it seemed that only the deepest water absorbed the shaking from below. The current swept it away the moment the vibration of his chair ceased. He reached farther—into the open ocean. No swelling waves—that he could sense. Either the epicenter was landbound or beyond his range in the ocean.

His companions were already commenting, though he'd missed the beginning of what they said. The tremor had lasted no more than a quarter of a minute. They both resumed eating.

"Short and low intensity," Danivid said, "but this is the second since the night I was crowned."

"Oh, you felt the one last night, too?" Meroak asked.

"No—what do you mean?"

"I got up in the night. It wasn't much, just a quiver through my bare feet. Anyone in bed wouldn't have noticed."

"I didn't," Danivid said. "The first was during that brief coronation on the terrace."

Meroak wrinkled his overly expressive face. "Are you sure?"

"I felt it," Allirae said, "but my slippers had deerskin soles. I'm surprised you felt it, Danivid."

"Only through my knee when I knelt to receive the crown." He drummed his fingers on the table. "So, there have been three little quakes in three days. Doesn't that strike you as odd?"

Allirae's brow puckered. "The only other time I remember them so frequent was when we were little. We were told to run outside if a quake shook harder, but that never happened."

"Not in Welcia," Danivid said, "but there was damage in Felverland." She looked surprised, so he added, "You were seven, but I was ten."

Suddenly, the obvious hit him. She was his heir. And there was something his heir needed to know. Perhaps even something that he did not yet know.

CHAPTER 4

Danivid would allow no more delays or interruptions. He closed his bedchamber door so fast, he almost caught Burnie's tail. "Sorry, boy." After locking his door, he strode to the desk. He pulled the top, lefthand drawer open, then tilted and wiggled it until he found the notch that released the slider from its rail. He set the wooden drawer on the desktop. Memories sparked.

The back panel of the drawer contained a hidden compartment. Not one that could be found by comparing the depth of drawers, for the panel looked identical to its counterpart. Their father had shown him and his brother on the same day—after swearing them to secrecy. He shut is eyes, fighting the pang of loss. A nudge on his hip jerked him back to the moment.

"You notice things, don't you?" He rubbed Burnie's neck and ears. "At least this secret is safe with you."

He returned to the drawer and tugged on the back panel. He squeezed and pushed. Had the parts warped? At last, he managed to slide half of the split panel up. And there, in the indentation behind it, sat the key. He slipped it into his pocket on the way to the priv, grinning despite his concerns. Whoever designed this had a sense of humor.

At the sink, Danivid felt along the mirror's frame for the two false screws that supposedly anchored it to the wall. He pushed them in and slid the mirror up the mounting rails until it came free. Rather heavy. He set it against the wall and turned to the cache above the sink.

The easy part now. He turned the key in the lock and opened it. Not much to see. An old-fashioned cloth purse, which he lifted. Heavy coins slid within it. Gold, no doubt, but it was the envelope and the words upon it that sent a quiver surging through his nerves. *To Danivid de Noviam only.*

Ominous. He took it to a wing chair in the bedroom before withdrawing the papers and unfolding the stack. The top one was a letter dated eight weeks ago. A rough scrawl with blatant mistakes.

> *My brothr, if youre reading this, I am dead. I'm so very sory. Others piled dung into the mess I made, but the fault is mine, for I am king. And husband to. much love—no sense. Poor Lenneth!*

Danivid closed his eyes and drew a steadying breath. This wasn't going to be easy. He glanced at the other pages. They were dated later and written legibly. He could endure one page.

> *I hope I can bern this letter and you'll never see it but I go from one stupid hope to the next. I draged the fortunes of House de Noviam to dust with my stupidty. My brain is too addled with ambertrop to know who to trust. I jst know that amber is worst of all my mistaks and I'll never find my way back if I can't get free of it. I told Lenneth and Yautan that Im going away alone to rest for few days. Not where thogh. They cant follow since the trail needs a horse. They both mean well but they beleve amber is fine. You'll know*

where I went. The cottage in the woodland. It's poor shape, but the only place I can think of. When I come back, I'll rite again. If I don't make it—I'm so so sorry!

Vancent

Danivid squeezed his damp eyes shut as Burnie shoved his snout into his lap. "That's not the brother I knew." He stroked the dog's long head. "Did you comfort him too? Try to, anyway?" Flipping to the next page, he read again—this one written two weeks later.

I am free of ambertrop.

Despite his determination to read through, Danivid dropped his head against the wing chair's tall back. "Well done, my brother." He took a minute to settle himself, then read again.

Those first three days without it were the worst of my life. No matter what anyone tells you, Danivid, never touch the stuff. I thought a little during the evening now and then would be no problem. It does not addict at first—at least for me. That lulls one into thinking it's fine. Then it has you. I read the first letter I wrote and started rewriting it. Then I decided to let you see the mess I had become. Enough warnings. You probably know better anyway.

I still have trouble knowing whom to trust. At this point, I exclude anyone who allows ambertrop use, even if we agree on other subjects. The bitter irony is that my wife and closest friend are within the untrusted group. That leaves

*me Allirae (who is off touring the provinces) and Stanton.
His extreme disapproval of ambertrop is abundantly clear.
If I had listened to his financial advice, we would not
be teetering on the edge of ruin. He knows most of the
three-pronged plan that I am now setting in motion.*

*The first prong is to reach out to the prime minister
of Felverland. He is reputed to oppose the production of
ambertrop. If I can halt the drug's flow into Welcia, we
have hope. I wrote to him but received no answer. I tried
a wire enquiry, asking whether he got my letter. No reply
yet. Doubtless, worry makes me impatient, but I fear that
someone intercepts my communications.*

*The second prong is to find a remedy for the financial mess.
That will take years, and I will write nothing more of it in
this letter.*

*The third prong is to make you my successor. Stanton has
found a trustworthy lawyer named Turnin, who has no
association with the inner circle of Regissa.*

An odd phrase. What did *inner circle* mean? Danivid kept reading.

*Turnin is to draft my new will. I should have done this
years ago, but I hoped for more children. The medics tell me
that children such as Aneen, passive and silent, have become
increasingly common. Families tend to hide them. Medics
cannot tell me if it is related to ambertrop, for people deny
taking it. Lenneth has no interest in being free. She takes it
at least twice a day—large doses, I suspect. I dread what a*

*child conceived in that internal poison would be like. Maybe
someday I can hope again, but for now I must name you
as my successor. If my plans don't work, please forgive me
for dragging you away from being Prince Ambassador to
Dirklan and forcing a crown upon you.*

Vancent

"I forgive you," Danivid whispered, "but why do you think you will
die?" He flipped the page. This one was dated only a week ago.

Dear Danivid,

*It may seem strange that I write to you again. I have told
you and Allirae about my new will and that you are my
successor. Everything is final. Though I haven't formally
announced it to the High Council yet, key people are aware.
Multiple copies of my will are safely stored.*

Then I told Lenneth.

*There was no end to her distress. It was as though I had
pronounced a curse on my daughter and, in that moment,
made her what she has always been. If only Lenneth
could accept the sweet affection Aneen offers and forget
about making her into some façade of a queen. If Lenneth
knew the weight of my crown, she would never want it
on our daughter's head. I love my wife, but she lives in a
make-believe world. I tried again, very gently, to urge her
toward giving up amber. She refused. I told her that the
Council would someday present me with a law to ban it*

forever and I would endorse it. She raged. I only meant to convince her to give it up sooner rather than later. A mistake. I thought I might be wiser now, but apparently not.

I went sailing yesterday. A hole opened wide in the hull, and the boat sank in minutes. An awful moment—looking down on it hovering below—taunting us. If a streamer had not been out for a walk on the cliff path, my mate and I would have drowned. She altered the current and got us to the beach. My mate insisted that such a hull failure could not have been an accident, so the streamer somehow got the craft to the dry docks. Two shipwrights agree with my mate. I thought using ambertrop would kill me. Now, I think refusing it will kill me.

It is agony to write this, but I suspect that Lenneth told her maid that I'm taking a stand against ambertrop. The woman must buy amber for Lenneth, so she would have contacts among the dealers. They would do anything to prevent a law that interferes with their lucrative trade. I don't believe Lenneth would harm me on purpose, but she spends her days flipping between drug-induced calm and desperation.

It is past two in the morning as I finish this letter. The writing of it has eased me a little, and perhaps I can sleep at last. Again, I hope to someday come out the far side of this nightmare and burn all these letters. If not, I hope that you and Allirae forgive me. You are both precious to me.

Vancent

Danivid sat still, he knew not how long, stroking Burnie's head. He sniffed and blinked at stubborn tears, grieving not for his brother's death, but for the last months of his life.

All this had gone on while he'd enjoyed the simple pleasure of Dirklan. He should have visited more often. Should have seen…Would he have seen if he'd been here? Allirae didn't know—not all of it—and she lived in the palace when she wasn't traveling. "Well, Burnie, she's going to have to know."

He took the letters back to the cache and replaced the mirror. Caverns, he looked terrible. After splashing cold water over his face, he returned the secret drawer to normal and stepped out into the corridor with his four-legged shadow. No one around. Was Allirae in her suite? "Can you find people, Burnie?"

The dog hopped a pace forward, ears erect, at the word *find*. He looked eagerly at his master.

"Find Allirae."

Burnie pranced ahead, darting looks back at Danivid as though he couldn't understand why his master wasn't running. They reached her suite, where the dog sniffed at the door of her bedroom, continued onward to sniff the study door, then sat and woofed softly.

"Aren't you polite. Good boy." Danivid knocked, and his sister bade him enter. She sat at a desk with papers scattered over it, one in her hand. "Ah, you do work," he teased.

"Very funny. What brings you to interrupt my diligence on your behalf?"

"Strange though it seems, you are my heir, first in line to be named queen. There is something you need to know."

"Not my favorite thought. You look awfully serious. Am I going to hate this?"

"You'll love the first part. It's a secret cache, known only to the king and his heir. Or did Father show you?"

That brought her from her chair in an instant. "No, he did not. Lead on!"

He soon ushered her into his chamber.

"Isn't this room a little obvious for a secret?" she asked.

"Perhaps, but few would have opportunity to search it. Left drawer of the desk."

She rolled her eyes. "Don't tell me there's a false back in the drawer. That is so obvious."

"You may open them both and measure, if it makes you happy. You won't find any difference."

She pulled the drawer open. "Stationery. Do I get hints, or do I need to look entirely on my own."

"Neither. We don't have the time." He showed her how to find the key, then put it back so she could open it with her own hands.

Allirae held the key up between two fingers. "What is this to? A safe?"

"That's the modern word, but our father called it the cache."

"Much more romantic." Her gaze traveled the walls. "Where is it?"

"In the priv."

"Oh, stop. It's not in the priv!"

"As true as I stand here. Behind the mirror above the sink."

She looked suspicious but went ahead of him.

"Pocket that key. If you drop it down the drain, we're in trouble."

"Men are silly." She plugged the sink and laid the key on a shelf of toiletries. She pointed at the water glass sitting there—iridescent cut crystal. "That's pretty. Fit for a king."

Danivid produced a quick smile, though his heart didn't feel it. He taught her how to remove the mirror. A challenge for her diminutive stature, but she got the mirror down and leaned it against the wall.

She straightened her skirt. "Why would anyone hide a safe in a priv?"

"Because it's unexpected. Also, the wall is already thick enough to enclose the water heater. No mismatch of wall thickness to give away its location."

"Fine. It's suitably clever." She opened the safe, looked into the bag of coins, then read his name on the envelope. "Did you take anything out?"

"It's as I found it. This is where the fun part ends. I've read the letters, and now you need to. Come."

She'd scrunched her mouth tight by the time he seated her in a wing chair. She unfolded the pages and frowned at the first. "I hardly think this is his hand."

"It is. Only the first is a mess."

She read, making recourse to her hanky as she did so. That embroidered scrap was soon soaked, and he gave her one of his handkerchiefs from the dresser. She covered her face with it and sobbed when she finished the final page. Burnie whined and curled up on the floor.

Allirae's voice rasped. "This is as bad as seeing him lying there in the bed all pasty-looking."

All Danivid could do was pat her shoulder and bring her a drink of water in his ornate glass.

Finally, she leaned back and mumbled, "I'm better now."

Danivid sat in the other wing chair. "We need to talk. Decide what to do."

"You were right to suspect murder." She turned her red eyes on him. "And now you are a target for murder."

"If that were to succeed, *you* would become the next target, which I cannot allow." He tried a quip. "Makes my desire to stay alive look quite unselfish, doesn't it?" That surprised her enough to give him a shaky smile.

He noticed the dog, who was still curled tight. "Come here, Burnie." He stroked the silky ears as the dog pressed against his leg. "I suppose you saw it all. If only you could tell us who did it."

After a silence, Danivid said, "Motives. Selling ambertrop is legal. The desire to keep it legal could be a motive. I wonder if that would be enough to risk murdering a king. The successful attempt coming so close after the failed one suggests a hurry that I don't understand. Is the General Council actually near to passing the law he mentioned?"

"Rumbles only...no proposed law has been written."

"What other motives can you think of?"

She leaned against an armrest. "There are some who want the monarchy done away with. The concessions late in our father's reign were not enough for them. Instead of a king, they want an elected prime minister." She wrinkled her nose. "Could that explain the timing?"

"I don't see how. Even if all copies of the will had been destroyed and Aneen had been crowned, we would still be her heirs. We might die before she does, but we are likely to produce more heirs, so the royal family remains."

Allirae widened her eyes. "Is there some lady you have been hiding in Dirklan that I should know about?"

He grimaced. "No, there is not. Though you tell me I am far too picky, I'm not old enough to be a lost cause. Even if I were, you are married. Can we go back to murder motives now?"

"I don't know any others."

He pondered again. "Money, I suppose. There is a question of de Noviam land. Vancent sold a lot of it, but lately, he refused an offer to sell the woodland." He shook his head. "Doesn't mean much. Shevnal wants it, but I think his chances of getting it would be better if Vancent were alive. The money situation is terrible, and because of it, Shevnal has bought *a lot* of our land from Vancent."

"Must you let him off the hook? I cannot stand the man's arrogance."

"Arrogance isn't exactly a hanging offense."

"Pity." She tucked stray hair behind her ear. "We aren't getting anywhere."

"Do you know if the sailboat incident was investigated?"

She shrugged. "I don't know, but our police detectives solve little." Her mournful look returned. "Murder used to be so rare. No longer, particularly in Bonador Province. The murder rate is rising here in Regissa too."

Allirae fidgeted. "Police are the king's responsibility, but Vancent's latest choice of their captain puzzled me. Even if we had someone skilled to investigate..." She folded her hands in her lap and pinned him with a stare. "You still have the greatest motive. We've been down that path. Even if we trusted our police, which I don't, we cannot call them in."

Silence stretched between them as Danivid tried to grapple with an inconceivable idea. Might the police try to pin the murder on *him*?

Finally, she said, "Vancent's letters were shocking to us. Tragic. Emotion may have led us off course. It is possible that a motive exists that we can know nothing about."

Danivid considered for a moment. "If that is true, then you and I may not be at risk." He drummed his fingers on the arm of the chair. "That's a relief, if true. I would still like to see my brother's murderer face justice."

"So would I. We will just have to pay attention. See if we can glean anything."

"Speaking of that," he said, "I need to do something about Lenneth's maid. If her loose tongue—intended or not—had something to do with the king's death, then I want her accessible for questioning."

"She's from a local family. She'd be easy to find."

"Good, for I don't want her in the palace." Danivid stood. "Let's see if you can get the mirror put back."

When Allirae had reassembled all parts of the secret, she left him. Seconds later, she reopened his door and whispered, "The maid is in Lenneth's room," then left again.

Hmm. Maybe he could get a little information from her before he let her go.

Danivid strolled down the corridor toward a pile of bed linens outside Lenneth's door. He stepped around them into the room.

The maid bent over the large bed, jerking the bottom sheet free. She wadded it, then spun and flung it at the door—where he stood. She startled badly at the sight of him. "I'm sorry—I didn't realize—I didn't mean to throw linens at you, lord king."

He'd caught the bundle. "I'm sure you didn't. All is well." He pitched it into the corridor where Burnie had shoved his nose deep in the linens. A low growl rumbled from him.

The maid paled as she backed into the bed and nearly shrieked, "The dog's not allowed in here."

Danivid shut the door. "Calm yourself." To give her a moment, he took a few steps around the room that had once belonged to his mother. The hangings and upholstery were different, but the chests and dresser were the same—off-white with gilded edges and delicately painted flowers on each panel.

He looked to the wall between the windows for the table that had fascinated him as a child. Its rich wood had been generously inlaid with a lustrous dusky gold stone. To his childish eyes, the colors had seemed to shift as he moved. His mother had called it shimmerstone and said it came from Dirklan. Now, he knew how rare it was.

The maid straightened her black skirt and belt, where a key hung from a chain. She stood with hands folded at her waist.

He pointed to the vacant space. "Where is the half-moon table that used to stand against that wall?"

Her eyes rounded as though he'd asked something alarming. "My lady...the queen...she grew tired of it."

She answered questions much like Yautan. "I see. My question was, *where* is it?"

Her eyes widened further, then she seemed to collect herself and lowered her gaze. "I don't know, sir."

A strange reaction, but she may not know where a piece of furniture had been taken. "Where did the queen keep her ambertrop?"

"I don't know what you mean, sir."

"Then you must be the only person in the palace who doesn't know she used it. From whom did you obtain it?"

"I didn't, sir."

Her knuckles whitened as he let the silence stretch. "I could name at least two people who know that you did. I will not tolerate your lies."

"My lady promised she would never tell and forbade me to ever speak of it."

"Unwise to trust your secrets to one who uses ambertrop. Now the queen craves it so helplessly that she had to leave her own home. And *you* are left to answer to the *king*." The woman trembled. "You may have one more chance. Where did she keep it?"

The maid pointed. "That drawer."

Danivid walked to the dresser and pulled out the drawer. "It is empty."

"She used it all up."

"When?"

"Um, the day of your coronation...I mean, that night, she used her last."

"Why didn't you buy her more?"

The maid looked hunted. "My lady had no more money."

"Who did you buy it from?"

Tears sprang to her eyes. "I cannot tell you."

"Lying again?"

"No, I'm not. Bad things will happen if I do." She covered her face with her hands. "Terrible things, and not just to me. I *cannot* tell."

Who terrified her so? Clearly, he would not learn the truth by demanding an answer. "Stop crying."

She gulped back a sob and wiped her eyes, darting a glance at him before staring at his shoes.

"You are no longer employed here. You will collect your belongings at once and leave the palace."

Her head snapped up. "My lady the queen employs me. She bade me stay for when she returns."

"You argue with the queen's protector and your king?"

Her mouth worked as though she sought words and found none.

"You will never serve the queen again, for you provided her with ambertrop. Give me the key to this room."

Her trembling fingers struggled with the chain looped over her belt, but she got it free and dropped it into his outstretched hand. Then she ran for the door and jerked it open, only to jump back with a whimper at the sight of Burnie, who added curled lips to his growl. "Oh, he is worse than ever!"

How tiresome. Danivid held the dog's collar until the maid ran past to the back stairs. "Stay," he said, then returned to the room. He searched it and found nothing of value or interest. All doors except the one through which he'd entered were locked. He stepped into the corridor and locked that door too.

Burnie cast an innocent look at him.

"Growling? At a woman who's afraid of dogs? And you pretend to have good manners."

Burnie stood and wagged his tail.

"I see. I could use a walk, too, but quakes concern me more than your desire to run." He strolled to his chamber. "You'll have to wait for me to write a quick letter."

Having sealed his letter, Danivid took it downstairs. For a change, Yautan was not hovering nearby. He called for a page and handed the letter to the eager young man. "Deliver this to Chief Former Shevnal."

"Yes, sir, at once."

A nice change in response. Danivid crossed the terrace and descended the central steps to the palace garden, which Burnie took as permission for a mad dash around the encircling path. That dog was fast! When he tired enough to join a stroll, Danivid followed a path through the north half of the garden, then stretched his legs with a brisk walk along the clifftop colonnade. The perfect vantage point to extend his streaming sense into the harbor waters.

Nothing could relax him more. Savoring the invisible beauty of currents brought calm clarity. Realization. He needed to look forward more than back. He had a kingdom that still needed its king, whether anyone appreciated him or not. The General Council had only existed fifteen years, its members still prone to much posturing and vying for influence. They would not address the problem of ambertrop unless it gained them favor. Too slow for a poison that embedded its hidden talons ever deeper into society. If he did not do something about it, no one would.

The sun lowered as Danivid retraced his steps. The evening murmur of converging voices rose from the nearest train station. Indistinct to him, but Ellincreo heard each voice, both spoken and silent. How many suffered as his family did? "I vowed to serve your people," Danivid murmured to Ellincreo. "This challenge is beyond me, but it is not beyond you."

Options began filtering through his mind as he returned to the palace, where the page was even now running up the steps.

"Chief Former Shevnal sent an answer, sir." The page held it out. Danivid took it with a word of thanks and opened it.

> *I regret I will be unable to visit you tomorrow afternoon as requested, since I will be in a guild meeting all day. My schedule is quite full, but I will make room to meet with you next week, first workday, 8:00 to 8:30.*

Arrogant didn't begin to describe him.

CHAPTER 5

Danivid stepped from the cair that had transported him and an aide to the Formers' Guild Hall. Since the formers could command stone into any shape they desired, it was an impressive structure. Its three domes covered the primary and two secondary chambers. The rest of it sprawled wide, housing offices, meeting rooms, and test facilities.

He hadn't been inside it since he'd accepted the ambassadorship ten years ago. He waited for the aide—armed with a notebook and pens—to hurry around the cair to his side, then climbed the steps.

Pages stood around the entry hall looking bored. The first to glance toward the door hurried to bow. The others sprang to attention as the first said, "How may I serve you, lord king?"

Danivid gestured toward the primary chamber. "Is the chief former presiding here?"

"Yes, sir. The city planners are in session. Shall I announce your arrival?"

"No need." Danivid crossed to the double doors as another page hurried over, and with a bow, opened one for him. He entered the circular room, arranged with the focal point at the low center, where those on the shallow tiers could see the broad map table.

As he'd hoped, no one looked up to see who had entered. He scanned as many faces as possible before he was recognized. The mayor of Regissa City was present and some formers Danivid recognized from earlier days. Ah, there was Rebanak, the man Dirklian formers had wanted in the position that Shevnal won. But most of the fifty-some people in the room were unknown to him. How many of them actually possessed the forming gift?

The mayor noticed him first and hastened to bow. "My lord king."

That brought heads around, leading to bows and curtsies, but it was Shevnal whom Danivid watched.

He had been standing sideways to Danivid and spun to face him when the mayor spoke. He offered his bow last. "We are honored by your presence. I wish I had known you were coming and could have presented you."

"It would have been a simple matter for you to know, so it appears you *didn't* wish to." Danivid stepped into one of the spoke-like aisles. Since all eyes faced him, he didn't proceed to the center but scanned their faces. "I wanted to see the Formers' Guild at work. To know more than just the one person who would speak for all of you—as though there is not more than one opinion in this room."

"A worthy desire," Shevnal said. "However, I'm sure you do not want us to dishonor the city council members who have waited several weeks for this meeting. I suggest you proceed to either the laborers' or artisans' hall, where those formers may have time for you today." He turned back to the table.

The mayor said, "But I don't—"

Shevnal cut him off, addressing someone else who turned his back to the king. No surprise that the chief former would have supporters ready to follow his lead. This was his turf, and the king was an unknown quantity.

Danivid had a matter of seconds to counter or be forever dismissed. "Chief Former, is city planning a higher priority than the quake reports you are required to make to the king?" He could not say *no* to this, but he could answer in several ways.

Shevnal straightened again. "Allow me to give my report now. There was a mild quake yesterday morning. Now that my report is complete, we have real work to do."

"Anyone in Regissa City could have said that. Does the chief former have nothing else to offer?"

"Must I explain that one tiny quake is not a threat?"

"There have been two other quakes since the funeral, though harder to discern."

Shevnal's pause allowed the mayor an instant to speak. "I thought you were a streamer, sir. Do you have a forming gift?"

"No," Danivid replied. "I am a streamer, as you thought. The first two tremors were faint but could be felt." Conversation Danivid could catch revealed that a few people knew of them, though Shevnal seemed unaware.

Rebanak stepped down a tier to the central floor. "There were indeed three tremors, lord king. Near sunset after the funeral, another during the following night, and the third yesterday morning. They radiated from an ocean bed source beyond my range. Based on the frequency and its spread, I believe their shared epicenter is very distant."

"Thank you," Danivid said.

"That matter being resolved," Shevnal said, turning away again, "we will resume—"

"The matter is not resolved." Danivid strolled down the aisle's broad steps. He halted near enough to Shevnal that the man could not turn away without showing disrespect too blatant even for him. "The chief former is chosen by the guild, but confirmed by the king. Since you were aware only of the quake felt by all, I must question whether *you* possess a forming gift." Danivid enjoyed the outrage a twitch of Shevnal's nostrils betrayed. Everyone in this room knew what an insult and challenge he had justifiably leveled at the chief former.

"I do possess the forming gift, as I proved before the vote and King Vancent's confirmation."

"You may now prove to me that you still do." An even greater insult, since the loss of a substance gift came only from misusing it to attack a person.

Shevnal glanced around, picked up a wax pencil from the map table, and held it out in clear view. As he looked at it, the pencil turned to dust, which cascaded to the floor. "There is your proof. Your confirmation now, please, unless you wish to defy the vote of the Formers' Guild."

"You will have to rely on King Vancent's confirmation, since only he heard the vote. Should I need anything destroyed in the future, I will be sure to contact you. However, since you are unable to determine when quake reports are needed, I request that information be provided by Former Rebanak henceforth."

Shevnal must have decided on damage control and reverted to smooth words. "A wise choice, sir. That is now his assigned duty. If—"

Danivid strolled away from Shevnal. "Rebanak, I would like a word with you." They ascended an aisle together and left the chamber, then followed the rear corridor toward a small meeting room. Hurried footsteps followed as they were entering it.

The aide caught up. "Sorry, sir. The mayor stopped me. He wants a meeting with you."

"Schedule it for this week," Danivid said. "Wait for me in the corridor."

Rebanak closed the door, then took a seat at the table opposite his king.

"It has been a long time," Danivid said. "How are you?"

"I am well. You appear to be also. I offer you my condolences."

The sentiment gave Danivid pause, for since the funeral, none seemed aware that he had suffered loss. "Thank you." He cupped his hands together on the table. "What do you think of the guild's current structure?"

The mole beside Rebanak's nose warped his sneer. "I didn't mind letting non-formers attend meetings. We work with builders and owners, after all, and their presence was sometimes convenient. But giving them voting rights was a disaster."

"I was stunned when King Vancent wrote to me about it." Danivid shook his head. "The formers of Dirklan still do not grant such a right. How did it come about here?"

"Shevnal convinced many formers that they were being overlooked because their gifts were—less impressive—than others. A distorted view, but gifts like mine are rare, so the majority fall into that so-called lesser group. They voted for him to become chief former, and his first official act was to propose a new charter that allows non-formers to vote. That cost him some favor, though not enough to vote the new charter down."

"Does he still enjoy majority support?"

"Not among the gifted. Now they understand what it *really* means to be disregarded. But he has brought so many non-formers into the guild that, yes, he does enjoy a majority. Dirklan and Eavertin were the only provinces to hold out. Since those formers defy Welcia's charter, there are fewer gifted guild members when the entire Welcian Formers' Guild meets to vote. The sum of the matter is that we can neither revoke that ill-conceived charter nor be rid of Shevnal as Welcia's chief former."

"Hmm."

"Are you thinking of...doing something about that, sir?"

Danivid smiled. "Not without grounds. Is his forming gift as trivial as the proof he offered?"

"No, he can do much more than that, but his gift alone wouldn't have gotten him the position he wanted."

"What do you think his real reason is for wanting control of the guild?"

"Power." Rebanak shrugged. "Money. He has plenty of that now. Building projects on the land that he has purchased from the crown are always top priority. Even the mayor and city council, who are rightfully concerned about the lower city, wait long for repairs or projects."

"Has the mayor tried taking his concern to the governor of Regissa Province?"

"I'm not sure, though it would do no good. One of the governor's sons has become a favorite of Shevnal. Like his patron, he flaunts his new wealth." Rebanak looked aside. "Not relevant, but I hear that the governor's other son is flirting with the ambertrop siren."

Danivid pitied the family in that regard, but worried more about Shevnal's reach.

Rebanak leaned forward. "Why did you really come here today?"

"I do wish to observe meetings of all the guilds, beginning with the substance guilds. Shevnal declined to meet with me, so I decided to...beard the bear in his own den, so to speak." He angled his head. "A risk, I admit. I'm glad you were on hand to confirm the quakes. What do you think of the results of my strategy?"

He shook his head. "You made few friends in that chamber."

Not good news. "How many of them possess the actual forming gift?"

Rebanak stared at some point on the wall, his lips moving. "I believe nine, including Shevnal and me."

So few! "That's appalling."

"The mayor brought three council members for support. The rest of them are building owners or in the construction industry." When Danivid only shook his head, Rebanak offered, "If you'd like to make friends, I'll take you to the laborers' and artisans' chambers."

Now, that was worth doing.

Danivid mulled over the mayor's complaints again as he walked from the morning room to his study on first workday. If the original portions of Regissa City were that neglected, he would need to take action. Exactly what action, he didn't know. Better to confirm the allegations first. Also difficult. It wouldn't work to ask Shevnal. Assuming he even came to the meeting.

But at the appointed time, a guard escorted Chief Former Shevnal to Danivid's study.

He offered a slight bow, but his gaze wandered the room. "Interesting. Though I met often with your brother, I didn't even realize this room existed."

Danivid gestured to the chairs across the desk from him. "Oh? Where did you meet?"

"Wherever he chose to be in that moment. Our meetings were more casual than…" He spread his hands. "…this."

"And rather frequent, I gather."

"Yes. We were friends, after all."

"Odd that a busy man such as yourself could find so much time for casual encounters, but no time to respond when a new king requested your presence."

"You see, the shock of his death, the funeral, and even the queen's needs, caused other matters to be postponed. They had become urgent and needed considerable attention. Though I could not come earlier, I did not mean to offend you."

Danivid raised his eyebrows. "Offend?" he said with an incredulous smile. "You seem to misunderstand the situation."

"I cannot drop everything and run to the palace on your whim. Meetings need to be scheduled."

"I am not given to whims. We will have a scheduled meeting each month. Three days before it, provide me with a list of the guild's projects, including location, expected duration, who requested it, who is paying for it, and who owns the property. This will allow us a meaningful discussion without wasting time. For other matters, I also prefer scheduled meetings. However..." He slowed his words. "...if I summon the Chief Former immediately, I expect you to come immediately."

"I will come as soon as I'm able, but you need to realize that many people depend on me."

"And you need to realize that many *more* people depend on *me*."

Shevnal's lips curled as though amused at Danivid's naivety. "Do they? Many things have changed over the years. A new constitution, for instance, which stripped the king of ultimate authority. I'm rather surprised you don't know."

"You may want to reread that document. You see, I listened to the entire proceedings as my father, the *king*, led negotiations between the rival parties and drafted the constitution that allows the councils and the *king* to check one another."

"And then you left—living in Dirklan for ten years, while more things changed that you seem to have missed."

"The king and his ambassadors converse far more than you realize. I assume you refer to the new charter of the Formers' Guild. While it changed internal voting rights, it still affirms that the guild operates under the authority of Ellincreo and the king."

"A nod to tradition, nothing more. The very fact that you mention Ellincreo shows that you don't understand the modern world. I mean no disrespect in this. I'm sure it is the result of living in Dirklan."

Surprisingly, Shevnal's voice drifted toward a conversational tone. As though he enjoyed the subject and was ready to expound. "The most significant changes are not written in charters or constitutions. Many come from other sources. From inventions. From contact with other countries. From philosophical advancements." He shifted in his chair. "I've meant to offer you help in navigating the changes. I admit that in the chaos following the tragedy, you and I did not start out in the most congenial manner. But now it is time to put that behind us. Please know that I stand ready to aid you in any way you desire."

"Then you may start by listing the guild's major projects."

Clearly, not what Shevnal had meant, but he listed several projects, all construction on land once owned by the crown.

When he finished, Danivid said, "You mentioned none within the original city."

"Ah, I suspect that the mayor has complained to you. There are repair projects underway in lower Regissa City, but you asked about *major* projects. The mayor and city council oppose replacement of existing structures, so new construction cannot occur there."

The mayor had defined *replacement* as demolition of history. Repairs, he claimed, were so delayed that few renewed leases in existing buildings. Shevnal droned on about the superiority of mechanized construction over the slow methods employed by formers of the past. Did he not know that Danivid had listened in a room full of formers denied work?

"Enough," Danivid said. "Slow is better than not at all. Though you deem them *old-fashioned*, send formers who are begging for work to the mayor who is begging for workers."

"Perhaps that seems like a viable solution to you," Shevnal purred, "but these matters are far more complex. I could explain the fine details, though it would be a waste of a king's time. I'd be happy to advise you on broader matters."

"Like you advised my brother? No thank you. See to the needs of the lower city. Our meeting is over." Danivid stood.

"I shall continue to do so," Shevnal said. "Now that we are finished with business, I had wanted to ask when the queen will return."

He still sat. Disrespectful to any host, grossly so to a king. Also implying that he controlled this encounter. Danivid looked down at him in impassive silence.

Shevnal shifted forward to rise. "Ah, forgive me. I am accustomed to your brother's easy manners." He stood to his full height, taller than Danivid. "Queen Lenneth—when do you expect her return?"

"I assume when she recovers. Or perhaps she will prefer to stay in her old home."

"You do realize that this looks much like an exile, do you not? Forced from her home in strange haste. Stripped of her child. For a supposed illness, that none have seen or heard of. This does not reflect well upon you."

What was he playing at now? "And yet, *you* said she was hysterical."

"That could have been managed with a little something to calm her. Here, that is. Probably not in Eavertin Province."

"A little something?" Danivid prompted.

"Ambertrop."

"I gather you are not among those who consider it an evil."

"There is no evil in someone choosing to enjoy deep calm. Nor is it evil to give simple comfort to a woman who has just lost her husband. Denying it could even be called cruelty."

"One opinion. There are others. Long-term use is not without risk."

"Doesn't Ellincreo grant us the right to decide how we wish to live our lives?"

"I thought you didn't believe in him."

"I don't, but you do—until his words contradict your chosen belief."

What incredible gall! Trying to rile him? "You presume to know much, but if that were true, you would know how little I'm interested in your opinion of ambertrop. You are dismissed."

CHAPTER 6

Loneliness haunted Danivid, despite telling himself he shouldn't feel it. Allirae was traveling to deal with an issue in one of the provinces. Not a long absence, thanks to high-speed trains, but still... Her departure spiked the truth that most of his friends were belowground and his parents and brother were dead.

Meroak, at least, remained at the palace, for Aneen's tears almost turned frantic when she heard that Allirae would be gone a few days. Understandable, considering that she'd lost her father forever and her mother for a time that no one could predict.

The two men strolled together along the colonnade one evening after they'd finally gotten the child to bed. A challenging task that kept them both silent until the evening breeze whittled the stress away. Stars sparkled beyond the big moon's sheen, while the waves of returning tide beat the cliffs below.

Eventually, Meroak said, "Thanks for helping with Aneen tonight."

Danivid huffed. "Believe me, *you* have every speck of my gratitude. I can't imagine what would have happened if you hadn't remained. You must be missing your wife too."

"True." His voice dipped. "Twice over!"

"I imagine none of this is what you envisioned when you married my sister."

"I knew what I was getting into. Not specifics, of course, but your father explained in fine detail what it meant to wed a princess ambassador."

Danivid grinned. "A fun conversation, was it?"

"Your father terrified me at first! Not all his fault, considering my nerves. *Yi!* Asking a king if I could court his daughter. He wasn't near as intimidating after I realized all his stern words meant I had a chance. Only her future husband needed to know what he spoke of."

"Which was?"

"Dozens of things. From taking on the name of de Noviam, to travel, to shouldering any upheavals that the royal family might face." Meroak's voice dipped. "Actually, he said we *would* face some. He was right about that."

"Indeed. Was it hard to give up your own family name?"

This time it was Meroak who huffed a laugh. "Skies, no! The rest of us barely remember we have a family name—unless we're elected governor, which couldn't happen for me since nobles still govern Wirthland Province. I doubt I could ask for a finer name than de Noviam, and *certainly* not for a finer wife than Allirae."

The praise of his sister warmed Danivid, but he couldn't resist teasing. "You'd better—"

The ground shook. Danivid planted his feet wide, spreading his arms for balance. Though he stood amid columns, he flung his senses to the harbor.

Meroak gasped, staggering. "Skies above!"

A rumble began on the cliff face far to the left. Danivid sensed a rock smack flat on the water's surface an instant before sound slapped his eardrums. "Ugh!" He shuffled to the cliffside railing and clutched a column, struggling to make sense of the sea's motion as the ground still lurched.

"Danivid!" Meroak careened into him, hands against his back. *"Uff!"*

Only Danivid's grip on the column saved him from pitching over. Then Meroak's fingers dug into his tunic and jerked him backward.

"Are you crazy! We have to get off the colonnade!" Meroak shoved him against the land-side railing. "Get over!"

Danivid jumped to the far side and turned.

Meroak slid over the railing on his belly and swung his feet to the ground. After a lopsided step, he fell to all fours. "Skies and caverns!" he cursed through his teeth as he crawled farther from the colonnade. "Have you forgotten what to do in a quake?"

Little remained of the tremors, but Danivid sat on the ground beside Meroak. "What was that all about? You almost knocked me over."

"I was trying to grab you away from the edge, but my ankle turned from that last lurch. What possessed you?"

Danivid's body began to mimic the quake. "I was sensing the harbor."

"Can't you do that from here?"

"Enough yelling. I get it."

Meroak rubbed his ankle, silent except for his trembling breaths. "What do belowgrounders do in a quake?"

"Squelch panic and get into a building."

"What?" Meroak hissed, shaking worse than Danivid.

"If the entire cavern roof falls, it doesn't matter where you are. If only some rock falls, you're safer inside. Quakes were rare, and nothing ever fell the entire decade I was there."

Meroak shook his head. "Next time, get away from cliffsides and structures."

He gripped Meroak's shoulder. "I will, but it's still a good idea to squelch panic. We're fine now."

Male voices reached them from a distance. "Find Da'vid." "Find 'Roak."

Danivid laughed, relief welcoming any outlet. "Sounds funny coming from a grown man." He cupped his hands to his mouth. "We're over here." He stood and rubbed his hand where he had grazed it clutching the column. Meroak started shifting to rise, so he said, "Stay put until a medic checks your ankle."

"It's not that bad. Being scared witless must have made it seem worse than it is. Skies, that was a terrible time to stumble!"

The dogs ran up to them, Burnie overjoyed to find his master, and Cam yipping around Meroak. A moment later, one of the guards reached them and offered Meroak a hand to pull him up. He barely favored his foot as they returned, but he couldn't seem to shake his horror.

Rebanak came early the next morning, and Danivid took him out along the colonnade. Burnie made tentative friends with him, then used the time to race back and forth atop the cliff.

Danivid stopped where he'd stood when the quake hit and pointed. "The rock that I noticed falling was a few hundred yards that way."

"Do you know how high it broke off?"

"No idea. I was sensing the harbor water. I heard a general rumble, then a broad flat surface struck the water hard." He shook his head. "Quite an impressive sound. You may think water is passive, but if rock demands sudden compression, rock loses."

"The battle of the elements," Rebanak said with a chuckle. "Like the child's game of rock, water, wind." His voice faded to a murmur as he grew intent in the use of his gift. "Ah, that's where it fell from...and yes, it shattered." He grew silent again, eyes half closed.

The wait lengthened, so Danivid savored the harbor water to stretch his patience.

When finished with his assessment, Rebanak said, "I checked the colonnade and palisade beneath it. All remain structurally stable."

"Good. Can you give me an idea where the quakes originate from?"

Rebanak pointed across the harbor. "Beyond the headland, veer a few degrees left and reach much farther than I can sense. Way past the islands."

Danivid nodded and extended his streaming sense to its fullest extent. Was there anything to be learned? He'd spent his teen years practicing his gift in the harbor—when Chardomeer wasn't dragging him off to this river and that—but he could sense much farther than the harbor and islands. The ocean beyond swelled, perhaps more than usual, but less than during one of the grand storms that the wind weavers steered away from their shores.

Rebanak's stomach rumbled, and Danivid grinned. "I'm hungry too. If you haven't had breakfast yet, please come in and join me."

"I would much appreciate that, sir."

They strode at a good pace toward the palace along the interconnected colonnades. As they neared it, Danivid remembered the dull mural. "I requested a former to clean the hall mural, but none ever came. I assume Shevnal couldn't be bothered. Can you send someone?"

Rebanak angled a look at him. "Shevnal told Keevan to do it."

"Who is Keevan?"

"One of the few formers among the laborers who still seek the favor of Shevnal."

"It looks the same to me," Danivid said as they crossed the upper terrace. The outside guards pulled the doors wide for them to enter. He and Rebanak paused in the hall to study the artwork. Danivid looked over his shoulder to the inside guards. "Did a former come to clean the mural?"

"Yes, lord king. Two days ago in the afternoon, while you were out. Not that he did much—not near as much as last time."

Rebanak turned to the guard. "What did he do to clean it?"

"Studied it like any former would. Some dust fell along the length of it. He drew that into a pile and left it for the staff to pick up."

Rebanak nodded and asked. "What was done last time?"

"This same former and another came. They spent two whole days, running up and down ladders, taking each gem out, and cleaning behind it."

The hall clock ticked off seconds before Rebanak asked another question. "When was that work done?"

The guard frowned for a moment. "Over a year ago, it would have been. Before the new year when the king and queen always went to visit her family in Eavertin. I remember because the travel party had already gone out to the cairs, but then Yautan came back to tell us that the king had requested formers to clean the mural while he was gone, and we were to let them in to do so."

Rebanak turned to Danivid. "Sorry—professional curiosity. Didn't mean to keep you waiting."

Whatever had caught his attention, he didn't want it discussed in the hall. Danivid led him to the morning room. A server was cleaning the table where Meroak always sat. "Bring another plate for my guest," Danivid said.

With that done, tea poured, and a covered serving dish placed between them, Danivid dismissed the young man. "What were all those questions about?"

"Uh..." Rebanak glanced at the closed door. "The gems in the mural, sir..."

He looked too serious. "Are you going to finish that sentence?"

"They're not gems. They are glass."

Heat darted up the back of Danivid's neck. He wanted to snarl out a most unsuitable oath. He steadied his voice. "I see." All desire for food had left his churning stomach. "I assume you determined that by your forming sense?"

"Yes. I delved them."

Danivid realized his friend wouldn't eat until he did, so he lifted the cover. Eggs. He wouldn't be able to swallow them, but he took a spoonful. "Your questions concerning the cleaning?" he prompted.

Rebanak served himself. "There is no reason to remove the gems to clean them. They must have been replaced with glass at that time." He didn't pick up his fork.

Danivid still could not force himself to take a bite of egg. Stupid protocol that a guest couldn't eat before him. He took a piece of bread and reached for the butter. "Please take whatever you would like. Why did you ask about the timing?"

"Have you ever seen Shevnal's house?"

"No."

"He bought two properties adjacent to the elite quarter, demolished both houses, and built himself an elaborate spread. It was finished a few years ago, but he embellishes it now and then, usually with artwork. Last summer, he added murals to the long walls of the formal dining room. They were formed in relief work and gem-studded."

Danivid took a bite of bread and forced it down his throat with a swallow of tea. "Do you think they are the stones of the palace mural?"

"Well...at the party where he first showed them off, I asked him where he obtained such fine gems. He replied, 'Don't be crass.' My question was mere curiosity. If he didn't want to be specific, he could have given a here-and-there answer."

"Mm."

"I know that proves nothing, but I attend his various events. I can inventory the gems...and the false gems in the mural. See how they match up."

"Please do, but discreetly."

Rebanak chewed and swallowed. "One way or another, someone has stolen the gems from the palace. If formers discover a theft of substitution, they are to report it to the authorities."

"Do not do so until you have documented the inventory and discussed it with me." All Danivid could think of was the ledgers Stanton had left for him to review. He turned the subject to Formers' Guild business and forced himself to eat a little more.

When Rebanak departed, Danivid strode to his study and jerked open the drawer where he had stashed the ledgers. He searched for the year he wanted, then read entries. No deposits were consistent with the value of such gems, but cash withdrawals had diminished after his brother's annual trip, gradually increasing over the following months.

Was this an indication that Vancent had sold the gems to Shevnal—and didn't want anyone to know? Too humiliating for the House de Noviam to be selling off their treasures. And for what? Ambertrop? Or could Lenneth have been involved? For that matter, it was Yautan who'd instructed the guards to let the so-called work be done—when the king and queen were absent. How was Shevnal involved? He'd sent the same former to clean the false gems, after all. But that could also mean that the man's skills were suitable for the task. Nor was it confirmed that Shevnal now possessed the mural gems.

Danivid slammed the ledger shut, no wiser than when he'd opened it. Whether his brother had agreed to the removal or not, the House de Noviam had been robbed.

Lady Zendell set her empty glass on a tray as she strolled past it, avoiding eye contact with those nearby. How much longer must she endure this tedious party? Had she known that yesterday's quake would be the sole subject of conversation, she would have stayed home. Across the ballroom, Shevnal also looked bored. He'd probably been asked the same question fifty times by now. The penalty for his powerful title of Chief Former. Annoying, but worth it, no doubt.

Governor Rikion had Shevnal's ear now, though they talked longer than the quake subject warranted. Maybe he was getting inundated with public concern too. And that would be his penalty for being Governor of Regissa Province. Also worth it, at least from his eldest son's point of view. Quite convenient to have a father who was governor.

Lively music resumed. That son approached her and asked for the dance that was starting. She placed her hand in his, knowing full well that he sought her favor for money, not love. She didn't mind. Love was an effervescent thing one couldn't count on. Besides, he must be ten years younger than she—not interested in marriage to a thirty-something widow, even if she was rich.

He faced her in the dance and said, "I trust that the quake did not disturb you too much."

"Not until it overwhelmed this party. Yes, I felt it. No, it didn't damage my house or investment properties. Nor do I feel a need to describe my sensations when it struck."

He spun her, laughing. "You tolerate the talk with less patience than Shevnal."

"It's his job, not mine. How is your new building coming along?"

That question lit his eyes, and he talked of its progress through the remainder of the dance. They ended it near his father.

"Ah, Lady Zendell," Governor Rikion said. "I'm so glad to have the opportunity to talk with you. The veranda will be cooler than the ballroom. Shall we walk?"

Was this a coincidence, or had he sent his son to collect and deliver her? No matter. She was used to these games. "That would be delightful, sir." She preceded him through the doorway, where a cool breeze carried the hint of salt behind floral fragrance. "Though I must warn you that I do no business after I've drunk from the amber flask."

He gave an automatic smile to her light words, though it didn't reach his eyes. "I've no business in mind, lady. I'm thinking more about a party that I'll be giving soon."

"Let's hope there is no quake the night before. Plan something to divert us, just in case."

He guided her past a couple standing suspiciously close together. "Would the king's presence be enough to divert you?"

"Oh, indeed! So, this will be held after his month of mourning then?"

"No, I think a day or two before. No dancing, of course. An extended dinner would be more the thing."

"Often a pleasant way to spend an evening, but why before?"

"Timing is everything. The first party will make the biggest impression. As would his first escort."

What under the skies? "Your wife, you mean?"

Governor Rikion chuckled. "For protocol's sake, she will doubtless escort him to the first table or two. However, I'm sure the king would prefer a much younger, unmarried lady at his side. Someone, for instance, as charming as yourself."

Implications spun through her mind. No matter how sweet the honeyfall, she looked for flaws. "I've never met him, though. Wouldn't it be rather awkward to suddenly shove me into her place?"

"We'll plan better than that. You are my cousin, after all, and we need not explain how many times removed when I introduce you. Of course, you and the king will be at my table for the first course, and we'll arrange the second to keep you with him. My wife will find an excuse to step away, and you may fill in for her. I'm sure you have the finesse to carry it off." He stopped their stroll, perhaps trying to read her expression in the darkness. "If you would like to, of course."

She raised her eyebrows.

"Not," he said, "that I expect you to turn down an evening with the king. Quite an opportunity. But I don't want to presume. What do you think?"

Something told her there was more to this. Her connection to Governor Rikion was so remote that they rarely exchanged more words than *pleasant evening*. Not that it would make any difference to her answer. She'd be insane to pass up this chance! "I would be delighted to help you entertain the king."

Governor Rikion soon left her, and she lingered on the veranda, trying to figure out why the man was granting her such an enormous favor. Was Shevnal involved? He often claimed to look after her interests, since he'd been such a close friend of her late husband. In truth, she'd never much cared for that friendship. Any assistance Shevnal offered her always suited his interests too. Not that she was fool enough to rebuff him. But how could Shevnal benefit from giving her an in with the king? No matter either way. She'd figure it out tomorrow.

Allirae, home from Bonador Province, sat across the desk from Danivid in his study. "The long and short of it is," she said, "that a couple of Felverland's police pursued a criminal across the border into Bonador. They were arrested, and the criminal escaped capture. The Felvarian police accused our police of aiding the criminal, which is why they were still being held. Bonador's police captain didn't take kindly to their accusations."

Danivid laughed. "Imagine that."

"Yes. I took care of the legalities. As I was seeing that they were sent across the border, I prompted conversation without the heavy-handed approach they'd already endured. One of them told me that their smuggling problems are our fault."

"Ours? Why?"

"I don't know. The other told him to 'shut it' because they needed to get back."

"How did they treat my ambassador?"

"Well enough. I gave my name, but not my title. The loudmouth didn't seem to recognize it, but the other one did and started addressing me with *ma'am*."

"That's more obscure than *shut it*."

"*Madam* or *ma'am* is their version of *lady*. Have you received any answers from their prime minister?"

"None—to either my communications or Vancent's."

"That does not look good."

"No." Danivid drummed his fingers on the desk. "There has been another murder in Regissa City. Someone we know." Her eyes widened at his grim tone. "Lenneth's maid."

Allirae gasped. "Do you think it has something to do with ambertrop...or something she knew?"

"Could be either or both. Regissa's police captain has no leads. Do try to contain your surprise."

She smirked at his derisive tone, but after a moment, said, "Even if we knew the cause for certain, a murderer is bound to cover his tracks."

"True."

"What else has gone on while I was away? The quake, I know about. Meroak told me. I've never seen him so upset."

Danivid told her of Rebanak's visit—and the revelation about the gems that were *not*. He kept that subject short. "I visited the Streamers' Guild. Chief Streamer Chardomeer is pleased with me because I do not support a movement from irrigators to alter the Guild's charter so they can vote in the chief streamer election. However, he has learned that I oppose the use of ambertrop. He berated me—in private, at least— for focusing my attention on such a negligible matter. Much like I misuse my streaming gift where it can have no lasting impact." He didn't pause, though she was shaking her head. "The Wind Weavers' Guild was delightful. No non-gifted members demanding additional rights."

She grinned at that. "It's not like there has been some mechanical innovation to control weather."

"Can't you allow me to believe they are merely sane?"

"Fine," she said, laughing. "The feistiest of all the gifted are sane. What else?"

"I've started visiting other guilds. I don't learn much, since they focus on hosting me, but it makes them happy."

"A useful first step. You see? There is good news."

He supposed she meant well. "A raindrop in the ocean, my dear. We'll be living on a pittance, Shevnal has a strange degree of wealth and influence, and the ambertrop issue eludes my grasp. The only thing that will make it worse is more quakes. No, not the only thing. Border problems can also make it worse."

Her brow puckered. "The non-responses *are* worrying."

At least she didn't offer a platitude. "I suspect a relationship between the silence and ambertrop. The mail and wires follow the same route along the coastline. I imagine that vile drug does too." He leaned forward, resting his arms on the desk. "There is one reliable way to open communication."

She lifted her brows. "Me?"

"Sorry. You're not even back a full day yet, and I talk of sending you out again. Stay home until after the weekend."

She smirked. "You know, I used to have to keep *myself* busy when Vancent was king. Now I suspect that *you* will keep me busy."

He spread his hands palm-up and shrugged to tease her.

She snorted. "Oh, innocent one, have you by chance forgotten that Dirklan is supposed to have a royal ambassador in residence? Dirklan likes to keep its traditions."

"Don't I know it." He traced his finger below his lip. "I suppose I could pull in a cousin—who won't appreciate it. Let's leave that for now. Since I left in such a hurry, I need to go below anyway. I'll do that before you set out for Felverland."

CHAPTER 7

Trellian entered the debriefing room of the Felverland-Welcia border station. The lead investigator glowered at her. Too bad. If he didn't like her presence, he could take it up with Callon. He wouldn't dare, for Felverland's prime minister had set Callon as Chief of the Ambertrop Eradication Task Force.

She jerked a chair out from the table and dropped into it. "Summary first." She slid her portfolio strap from her shoulder, deftly separating it from a lock of hair that curled around it.

The investigator tilted his head toward two men who carried a week's worth of wrinkles in their uniforms. "These are the two idiots who created the incident that makes Felverland look like the cause of border problems. Since they are unable to correlate locations on the ground with maps, and also unable to read signposts, they crossed into Welcia. Furthermore, they failed to apprehend the suspect, and the two idiots got themselves arrested by Welcian police. If that wasn't enough, they irritated the Welcian police captain so bad that their royal ambassador was summoned to the northern border, where one of these two idiots didn't—"

"Officers," Trellian said to the investigator.

"What?"

"Clearly there are two of them, and they are officers."

"Oh, ex-cuuuse me. These fine officers—"

"You are dismissed."

"What?" The investigator's spittle flew.

"I have yet to hear anything I don't already know, and you're making it unlikely that I'll learn more. Your presence is detrimental." He had yet to move, so she switched to a soft voice. "I don't repeat myself."

His teeth scraped, though not as harshly as the chair he shoved back. He exited with the loudest possible slam of the door.

She let the soundwaves fade. "There. Now, perhaps we can talk."

"Yes, ma'am," both officers murmured. Neither looked willing to do so.

Damage control first. She was as tall as most men, and she'd just driven off a lead investigator. Comfortable was not what they felt right now. She smiled and lifted an eyebrow. "Hard week?"

"Yes, ma'am," Officer Alder said, easing back in his chair.

She had a little history with Alder, who was not an idiot. Shorbet, she didn't know, but idiots didn't last in the police. "I can see," she said, "why it could have been rough in Welcia, but not why a lead investigator was on that tirade."

Shorbet squirmed in his chair. "My fault was to miss the name *de Noviam*. I didn't realize who the ambassador was."

Alder smirked. "My crime was asking for you."

"Ah," she chuckled. "I have to uphold the official stance on the border, which you shouldn't have crossed. But you know that. Was it accidental?"

Shorbet said, "It was way past midnight and far from the official crossing at road and rail. If there was a signpost, we couldn't see it in the dark."

An explanation without claiming an accident. Yet his excuse told her nothing. She looked at Alder. "Even if you might have guessed you were going too far, I think you had a reason. What was it?"

"We were closing in tight on the suspect," Alder said. "He was dodging around, like one who knows the terrain. Then he broke into a straight run. That's when we almost caught him. Next thing we know, we're surrounded by Welcian police. He runs right between them. They didn't lift a hand to *him*, but they sure grabbed us. I am certain that he knew they were there, and he planned to meet them. Once we were after him, he led us right into the pack."

Alder rubbed the side of his hand where a graze had scabbed over. "I know that amber is legal in Welcia, but their border police are supposed to check for it and turn smugglers back. I hoped their captain was an honest one, but he can't be. Said there was no sign of the man we *claimed* to be following."

"It's possible he was told that by his own people," she said. "He might trust them."

"Possible, but he interrogated us. I thought, at first, he was after information about the smugglers on our side of the border, but really, he wanted to discover how much we knew about Welcians involved in the trade. He even believed we have agents in Welcia." He stared into her eyes, maybe hoping to glean whether that were true.

"How I wish!"

"Anyway," Alder said, "he wanted names and descriptions. By then, I wouldn't have told him my cat's name! He tried forcing information from us by locking us up and refusing to go through proper channels for sending us home. Someone else must have gotten word up the chain, because it wasn't him."

"Interesting. Their local captain and some portion of their officers— what do you think they are guilty of?"

"I don't know if they sell amber themselves, or if they're paid by those who do. I just know they are *ensuring* that amber flows into Welcia."

That was no surprise. The same question always remained. What could they do about it? Nothing yet, but if that day ever came, she would have information. Trellian flipped open her portfolio. "Who were you following?"

Alder knew the drill, and she let him page through the drawings. In the same moment that he turned over one of the pages, both officers said, "That's him."

She had no name for this one, but she recorded the number and other pertinent information about the event. Then she flipped to a clean page and pulled out her pencil. "Describe the police captain who detained you."

Alder started with the shape of the face and went on to details, while she sketched. She loved working with people who paid attention and explained coherently. She soon had a decent representation.

Shorbet agreed it was very much like the man. He was the sort who noticed things like pale blue eyes, graying brown hair, and a height estimate of six foot, one. All of which she added below the drawing.

She flipped to another page. They weren't able to say much about the officers who'd arrested them in the night, so she moved on. "Describe the ambassador."

"Why do you want her likeness?" Shorbet asked.

She grinned. "Don't you wish you had known who you were talking to, even without knowing her name?"

"You have a point."

She completed the sketch and latched the portfolio. "Thanks for the information. Now, maybe you can go home and clean up."

"There's one other thing..." Alder shrugged. "It may not be significant, but it seemed odd. The ambassador mentioned their new king and seemed to be prompting us."

"Prompting?"

"Like she wondered if we knew. I told her what the papers reported— that a wire had come through to the prime minister with news of King Vancent's death and that his brother, Danivid, had been crowned king.

She asked what else we had heard, but I couldn't think of anything more to say. Are there rumors about it?"

"None that I've heard. Hmm." She leaned back. "If there's nothing else, you may go."

She sat for a few minutes after they left, considering what this meant. It smelled off. Like a pinnpear going bad though it looked fine.

News traveled fast now that wires crisscrossed so many lands. Delays and lost messages had become rare. Was there something that the king and his ambassador didn't want Felverland to know? Or was there something they should know, but didn't? Trellian hadn't been to Qualketeen in over a month. Maybe it was time she delivered a report to the capital in person.

A day later, Trellian wondered if she would regret that decision. People said she was intimidating. If so, Prime Minister Starroni was terrifying. He was a stirring speaker before crowds, but in this office, his face was immobile.

She stood in front of his desk to give her report, with only Callon to support her. At least she knew how to speak succinctly and still include what mattered. When she finished, he stared at her for a full minute. Was she exaggerating this endless moment?

"I've heard of you," the prime minister said.

She almost jumped. Was she supposed to answer?

He pointed. "That portfolio you carry—is it the one with the drawings?"

"Yes, sir."

"May I see the one of the ambassador?"

She turned to it as quickly as possible. "It's just a sketch, only as accurate as the description." She laid the portfolio open before him.

He studied it. "So I assumed. Have you drawn one of me?"

"Uh…" She struggled for a normal tone. "No, sir."

He looked up, and tiny lines crinkled around his eyes. "That was a joke. You may sit down."

His eyes smiled above a straight mouth. Unusual. She took the empty chair in front of the desk and stole a glance at Callon in the other. He wasn't easy to read either, but he didn't frown, so she must be doing fine.

"May I look at the other drawings?" the prime minister asked.

"Yes, sir."

He paged through, remarking, "You are as skilled as I was told."

"Thank you, sir."

"These drawings with finer detail—I assume they are people you witnessed yourself?"

"Yes, sir."

He stopped at one of the front pages. "This, I recognize. The drawing that sent a repeat murderer to the gallows."

That drawing had also set her on a career she'd never expected. Again, she didn't know what to say.

"How were you able to capture such detail without becoming a victim?" the PM asked.

"I have a good memory for faces," she said, "and his was interesting. The day after I saw and drew him, another murder was reported. I had seen him go into that very doorway, never having the least idea what was about to happen inside. So, I took my drawing to the police. They asked for several copies, which I made."

"From artist to officer. How did that happen?"

This was far from what she had come to report on, but she had to answer. "I'm good at noticing all sorts of details and their significance."

"Ah, yes. You mentioned that the police captain in Bonador was suspicious that we have agents in Welcia. Do we?"

"No, uh, that is…" She looked at Callon. Did they?

"We do not, sir," her chief answered for her.

"Why not?"

Even Callon must be surprised, for it took him a moment to answer. "I assume you're thinking about the suspicion I shared with you that Felvarian drug smugglers may live in Welcia. Even if we had our government's approval to place agents across the border..." This he said with a pointed look at the prime minister. "I'm not sure what they could do. It's not as though we can arrest anyone in Welcia."

"Chief Callon," Starroni said, "that wire from Welcia, informing me of the death of one king and crowning of another, was quite terse. It was not phrased in the Welcian royal manner. I sent my condolences, also by wire, and included my desire to open communications with the new king. As I have done with previous messages, I asked him to confirm that he received my wire. Never has either king done so." The PM leaned over his desk. "I don't need to arrest people in Welcia. I need to know what is going on."

CHAPTER 8

A freight train waited for Danivid on the peninsula at the entrance to Dirklan Tunnel. An odd thing by aboveground standards, looking more like a string of beads than train cars. He climbed into the passenger carriage that had been added for him and belted himself into one of the two pivot seats. Strange to be alone, now that he was always followed by an aide. That had often been true belowground, but Prentov, his Dirklian aide, was a friend of ten years. Unlike the aides above, who said "yes, sir" a lot, but never chatted.

The train pulled forward along its magnery line, curving much tighter than a train could anywhere else in Welcia, and began its descent. His seat rocked soothingly on its pivot, even when the cars ratcheted down the vertical drop.

Prime Minister Katowau met him at the belowground station, Prentov a step back from her. A crowd gathered, as well, so Danivid took a moment to address them before hopping into an open cair for the drive to Dirklan House—and much waving. The cair took a familiar turn to skirt the square with its fountain shooting high, surrounded by Dirklan's grand government buildings. So natural. So pleasant. This was a workday, but he enjoyed it like it was Savoring Day.

They arrived at Dirklan House, the imposing residence of the prime minister. That title—would he someday have to change it to *governor*? The position's authority was equivalent to that of the aboveground provincial governors or lords, but Dirklians still kept somewhat to themselves—a remnant of the long separation they had endured after the old access tunnel's collapse. They did, indeed, govern themselves differently than abovegrounders. He would be loath to interfere with their partial autonomy.

Danivid and Prentov joined the prime minister's family for lunch in the smaller dining room, where he greeted her husband and two teenage daughters. The young ladies wanted to hear about his coronation, so it was easy to keep conversation from difficult subjects. That part was for their mother's ears after lunch.

Lady Katowau led Danivid and Prentov to the second-floor salon, which she preferred to her study. "Give us a minute," she said to Prentov before they entered it.

Danivid strolled through the familiar room, decorated in cool tones and overlooking Jourendia Square with its centerpiece fountain. He paused at the window to gaze out on it, then reached his streaming gift within the spray to savor all aspects.

After a moment, he turned and discovered that Katowau was still standing. "Ah, please sit. Aboveground, a few try to skip protocol. Belowground, I wish *I* could skip it."

He settled into a chair, as she said, "I recall predictions that respect for the crown would be lost with the new constitution. Has that proven true?"

He pondered his answer. "Not while my father still reigned, nor do I believe it's a result of the constitutional changes."

"What, then?"

"I loved my brother but must admit that his reign lacked wisdom. There was less to respect."

"The merchants have begun to gossip of ambertrop in the palace."

He crimped his lips. "That's even known here?"

"So, it's true. How bad?"

"The queen is addicted. Her parents have taken her to Eavertin Province and are hoping to get her free of it. King Vancent *was* addicted, I think to a lesser degree. He got himself free a couple months before his death. After that, he began an attempt to reverse damage in the kingdom. Unfortunately, he didn't have enough time."

"So, you are left to scrape through his mistakes?"

"Indeed. It's exhausting."

Her welcoming nature showed in her face. "You can always come home when you need a break."

He let out an easy breath with his smile. "You don't know how beautiful it sounds to hear you call this my home."

"Well, it just *is*. Besides, I can't give one of the ambassador suites to some local. And since there are two of them, one will always be yours. I doubt you've had time to select a replacement, but do you plan to send us another royal ambassador? Your sister or someone else?"

"I cannot send Allirae. I absolutely require her aboveground. Some of my de Noviam cousins may be suitable, but that choice must be made with due consideration—if, indeed, you desire it."

"Hmm. Some Dirklians claim it would be a slight if we lost our royal ambassador. On the other hand, I'm not sure I want an ambassador between us when I can climb into a train carriage and go above for a chat with the king. I'll wait and see how things work out."

"Thank you. And since the king is here, tell me of Dirklan after I left in such a hurry. No, wait, I need Prentov."

He began to stand, but she waved him down. "Sit still. I'll get him."

Prentov soon balanced his notebook on an armrest and took notes while Danivid conversed with Katowau. As he'd suspected, there was little change.

After breezing through most of it, she said, "I'm sure you can guess our biggest worry."

"Quakes?"

"Of course. Chief Former Gairedon traveled above to consult with Welcia's Formers' Guild. The kingdom's chief former was utterly dismissive of his concerns."

"Shevnal sneers at my concerns too. Tell Gairedon to discuss quakes with Former Rebanak. That's where I get useful information."

She turned her head aside. "You should hear how he pronounces the name Shevnal. If scorn could be called slander, I'd have to fine him."

Danivid laughed. "Shevnal's arrogance is plain fact, so slander cannot be charged on that count."

"Well, you should know that Gairedon claims he will not be bound by dictates from 'that man' if they defy the charter of Dirklan's Formers' Guild."

"I doubt Shevnal cares what Dirklan's guild does. He is absorbed in new building projects around the western high ground of Regissa City."

She gave him her opinion of so-called progress, which Danivid had heard before, then asked for permission to leave him to attend a meeting.

How strange to have her request permission, but he gave it. When she left, Danivid said, "Please come with me, Prentov. We need to talk."

"Certainly, lord king."

That manner of address from a friend was as annoying as the friend following a step behind while they passed from the salon to the gallery. "You know that's only said once at the beginning of an encounter, right?"

In a silky tone, Prentov replied, "I do, lord king."

Danivid halted and shot a look back, then burst into laughter. "These few weeks haven't changed you."

"Nor you. At least, not at heart."

"I hope the crown never does, but there's no denying it is draped with worries."

"That was to be expected," Prentov said with his usual calm.

They continued in silence to the opposite wing of Dirklan house, which contained the ambassador's suite that he had chosen to occupy ten years ago. The door latch surprised him—locked.

"I have the key, sir." Prentov stepped forward and opened the door. "Lady Katowau bade me lock it since it still contains your things."

"Of course." They entered the sitting room, and Danivid felt a tinge of disappointment. It looked the same, but something was off. A stagnant scent, perhaps. Prentov was already opening a window. "Thank you."

"What do we need to speak of, sir?"

"I left in such a hurry, we never settled anything. Sorry if it feels like I abandoned you."

"Not quite that. There are the notes we exchanged by wire for the things you wanted sent up, and the month's pay you left me. But I'm glad you came below, because I was wondering how long you intend to pay me. Wife and children to support, you know."

"I do. In some ways, I want to keep you on my payroll in Dirklan so I can maintain my presence here. I doubt there'd be much work though, and..." Danivid dropped into a chair. "This is the hard part where it becomes strictly confidential."

"Confidential is my job."

"The truth is that I cannot afford to pay anyone belowground. King Vancent let a couple stewards go, which led to more expenses than it saved him. I have an excellent steward watching funds from a high level, but I'm desperate for someone I can trust to manage daily affairs in the palace."

"Ah, you don't need an aide, I take it?"

"There are a couple aides who take turns accompanying me around the city. Why two, I don't know. I have a scheduler. More aides manage correspondence." While Danivid spoke, Prentov's eyes widened. "I also have a personal aide who waited on the late king and now me."

"What does he do?"

"Well, he did spend money, but I've put a stop to that. He brews morning tea, which is the best I've ever tasted, and takes clothing in and out of my room. My first day as king, he offered to comb my hair."

Prentov flopped backwards in his chair and laughed so hard, he gripped his head.

Danivid grinned. "You seem to have caught that wave."

"Yeah, I'd say so." He cleared his throat to stop laughing. "A lot of aides and a tight budget—why not make one of them a steward?"

"Yautan, my personal aide, was sort of a steward. Since I will not allow him to waste money any longer, I have to approve all expenditures. He's trying to wear me down with trivia. I don't actually *know* any of them. Don't know what they do or if I need them all. Strange things happen in the palace, and I've no idea who might be involved. More than anything, I need someone I can trust. A person who could not be involved with bringing ambertrop into the palace."

"Oh, I see." Prentov frowned at the carpet.

Danivid waited a few minutes. Prentov wasn't the sort to withhold his thoughts. "What troubles you?"

"I don't much want to raise my children where ambertrop is available."

"Nor would I. No guarantees, but I'll do my utmost to outlaw it in Welcia."

"My wife won't like leaving family in Dirklan."

"Though Dirklians don't seem to know it, the trains do carry passengers up and down that tunnel."

"So I've heard." Prentov rubbed his short beard. "I won't deny that I'm going to have a hard time finding work as enjoyable as serving you. But going to a palace, in a new city, for a job I've never done, amid total strangers—it's intimidating."

"I know the feeling!" Danivid narrowed his eyes. "No, maybe I don't. I grew up in the palace. My sister still lives in it. I recognize most of the guards, and the chief steward served my father before my brother. The rest of my staff are strangers to me. The original city is familiar, the newer part, not so much. The crown—" He shook his head. "That is terribly *un*familiar."

Danivid leaned nearer to his friend. "You may have more strangeness to deal with than I, but you would know *me*. And be certain that I will always support you."

"I suppose there is a little something to having the king at my back." Danivid grinned.

"I'll talk with my wife. Can't leave her out of this decision."

"I may not be married, but even I would know better than that."

"A good thing, because I imagine you'll have to do something about that 'not married' part."

Danivid spent the remaining half-day in Dirklan's public spaces. The Tea House, the restaurant of Fountain Inn, the square—so much easier to feel approachable in all these familiar places than in Regissa. Yet he could not escape the change. It wasn't just that bows and curtsies were deeper. Nor the title change from *ambassador* to *lord king*. If anything, the smiles he received were broader. Yet there was a difference. No, two of them. Not only was he king, but he was uniquely *their* king.

The warmth of heart that lulled him to sleep that night belowground made his morning discontent almost shocking. At Katowau's breakfast table, he had to claim a headache to explain his silent frown. Escaping from her family, he arranged to arrive at the train station with only a moment to spare before climbing into the passenger carriage. Perhaps the bright blue sky above would help.

But it didn't. Surprisingly, Yautan met him, with a cair standing ready to take him to the palace.

Danivid leaned back in the closed vehicle and rubbed his forehead. "I don't recall, do I have a meeting this morning, or some place to be?"

"Not until afternoon, sir."

"Good thing. I must not have slept well or something."

"Perhaps the air of Dirklan isn't as healthy as—"

"There's nothing wrong with Dirklan," he snapped. *Yi*, he was out of sorts to be that sharp.

Yautan didn't even seem to notice. "Perhaps a touch of headache then. I daresay it will pass after you've had a short rest in your chamber."

A good idea to stay clear of everyone till he got his temper down, so Danivid followed his aide's advice and settled into a wing chair to drink the tea Yautan served him.

"I added a little of the headache powder, sir."

Danivid grunted, for the indescribable feeling wasn't a headache. Whatever it was, the tea and a half-hour of quiet helped. Still lacking energy, he sat with Aneen for a while, giving Allirae and Meroak some time together before she set out. An easy task this morning, for his niece sat on the floor with a picture book, turning the pages from front to back and back to front, over and over.

Her placid silence allowed him plenty of time to think. He had worried earlier about sending Allirae to a foreign country without advance permission to visit. Maybe he was being paranoid after his brother's death. She'd have her aide and an escort. He'd chosen a tall, broad-shouldered guard to fulfill that role. After all, why would anyone in Felverland want to harm Welcia's royal ambassador?

CHAPTER 9

Unbelievable! Trellian kept her opinion to herself, for the various men in Chief Callon's large office were voicing theirs.

"How can it be her?" one of the men asked. "Isn't the ambassador a princess? She wouldn't travel with just an aide and a single guard."

Another suggested, "Maybe she's trying to travel incognito."

"Nonsense," Callon said. "She announced her name and title at the border. An officer who met her last week has confirmed her identity."

"How could she assume that she'd be safe and welcome here?"

"She ought to be," Trellian said.

The man hmphed. "What *ought* to be isn't reality."

"We will make it a reality." The chief's stern words brought silence. "One of our own is now traveling with them as a local escort. Out-of-uniform officers stand watch at every station. She will be met by the capital guard in Qualketeen this evening, where she will receive formal escort to be greeted by Prime Minister Starroni. He has issued a statement to the papers that she is visiting, so her sudden arrival won't look quite so...unplanned. We'll need to deal with some crowd control during her visit. That's why we are having this meeting. Not to discuss the wisdom of her travel arrangements."

They got down to details for the ambassador's arrival. That settled, they moved on to departure plans, which would require more diligence. None of this was Trellian's responsibility. So, why had Callon included her? A question she kept to herself. The answer would come at the appropriate moment. For that reason, she didn't follow the others when Callon dismissed them.

He gave her a half-smile. "Still here?"

"You didn't call me in without a reason. Am I artist or officer in all of this?"

"Artist, at a minimum. You're off duty until her arrival. Buy a new portfolio and take a nap. Stay inconspicuous during whatever reception the PM gives her. We aren't going to be caught unaware of who she is again. Make a drawing and as many copies as you can produce overnight. You'll be given a room at the PM's mansion for the duration of her visit. Pack a suitcase." He tilted his head and looked at her from under his brows. "With changes of clothes."

Interesting. She'd have to stop by her parents' house and pick up the latest *perfect-for-you* clothes that her mother kept buying, notably unsuitable for a lowly officer. Trellian would let her mother bask in the knowledge of where she was staying and not mention the *changes of clothes.* "What else, sir?"

"That, we shall see. All we really know is that Welcia is breaking its long silence."

Trellian sketched far into the night until her fingers cramped. Drawing, she loved. Copying, not so much. After the first few, she'd quit writing Princess Ambassador Allirae de Noviam across the bottom. Some clerk could do that and add the blond, blue-eyed, and size description. Not that anyone would measure and weigh her, but a guess would be more polite than *tiny*.

The woman's image was fixed in her head now. Pretty, with a faint smile. Trellian tried to capture neutral expressions when the purpose was identification. That smile had never left the ambassador's face while she chatted with dignitaries the PM had summoned. Part of her role, not her feelings. Some officers claimed they could read everything they needed to know from a person's face. Trellian had studied too many faces to believe them. That, and all the times people misinterpreted her expressions.

She just wished she could have learned something during the reception. Difficult when her every move was designed to maintain obscurity. Callon had paused beside her to whisper one scrap of information. Messages between the PM and king were indeed being blocked. Confirmation rather than news.

Trellian stretched, then pulled her subtle but elegant dress over her head. Could she learn what those messages had contained? Or more important, who blocked them? Not just the flunkies, but who ordered it done.

The next day, Callon's orders kept Trellian busy creating drawings of her brother, Byerno. Just a few, but quite detailed. She even included the style of hat he would wear. It wasn't until the afternoon of the ambassador's second full day in Qualketeen, that Trellian got to meet her...under strange circumstances.

She was summoned to the PM's office, where she joined a select group of the Ambertrop Eradication Task Force.

The ambassador showed no hint of surprise during the introduction, but followed it with, "I didn't realize you employ women in your police force."

Callon let one of his subordinates answer, for he needn't fake his disapproval. "No, ma'am, we don't, properly speaking. Trellian aids us now and then, for she is a skillful artist."

Callon allowed his smile to appear as he addressed the ambassador. "You see, she only needs a reasonably coherent description of a face in order to render a recognizable drawing. That enables our police to identify suspects, to narrow the search for evidence, and thus to convict criminals. She also understands the need for *complete* discretion."

"Oh, I see," the ambassador said.

Hmm. Did she also see that no one had explained why Trellian was present?

Fading as much into the background as possible, Trellian settled in to listen. It was encouraging to hear that Welcia's new king wanted the ambertrop trade to stop. Forever. That was the crucial piece of the puzzle their task force lacked. She hoped it was true. What did the king and his ambassador actually know about smuggling and distribution? How committed were they?

As she expected, Callon dismissed the other members of the task force, then waited until the door closed.

Prime Minister Starroni clasped his hands on his desk and regarded his guest. "Ambassador of the House de Noviam, are you satisfied with our agreements?"

Tiny though she was, the ambassador responded with all the confidence demanded by such a title. "I am. I can assure you that King Danivid will be pleased also."

He kept his lips closed, his eyes slightly narrowed.

The ambassador took up the silent challenge. "Are *you* satisfied, Prime Minister?"

"Not to the extent that you are."

"What lacks?"

He took his time answering. "You have come into Felverland, met with me, with members of my government, with our task force—all of us determined to stop the lucrative flow of ambertrop into Welcia. But I have met *one* person from Welcia telling me you want it stopped." He angled his head in a conceding gesture. "Granted, a royal ambassador who came at considerable risk. Sister of the king. You have excellent credentials, but you are still only one person. I have seen nothing of the circumstances in your land. Perhaps even worse, you are telling me what I want to believe. Have you ever heard the proverb, 'Doubt the messenger who brings you perfect tidings'?"

She nodded. "I have, and I recognize the element of truth in it. Yet it would be a shame to reject what is good, simply because it's not bad enough."

She let that irony settle for a moment. "My initial purpose was to see if we could work together toward a common goal of ridding ourselves of this curse. You have given me more hope than the king or I expected on such short acquaintance. But the truth is, we are going to face challenges in convincing many people that ambertrop is far more dangerous than they believe. The tidings are not perfect."

"In that case," Starroni said, "I can see two steps forward—one that I need and one that you need."

"I'm listening."

"You need someone who can explain the long-term effects of this drug. I need someone who can witness firsthand what the situation is in Welcia, and more specifically, with the king. I believe we can accomplish both with one person."

Trellian suppressed a gasp.

"Who do you have in mind?" the ambassador asked.

"Trellian." Starroni lifted his brows as he turned to her. "I suppose I should have asked whether you are willing first."

How best to phrase this? "I am committed to the goal of eradicating ambertrop and to your orders, sir."

"Thank you." He turned back to the ambassador, but her look gave him pause. "Is something wrong?"

"I...gathered from what was said earlier, that she is not part of the, uh, Ambertrop Eradication Task Force." She shook her head. "That is such a mouthful."

The corners of Callon's mouth dipped. "Some shorten it to AETF."

Trellian allowed herself a chuckle. "My brother, whom you may meet on your journey, calls it the Amberforce."

"Speaking of that," Callon said, "Ambassador Allirae is departing early tomorrow morning. She will have an escort from here until she changes trains. Please tell your brother that he is to take over escorting her at the first change."

"I will see to it." Trellian opened her portfolio and released the fasteners at a certain page. "I will join your traveling party later in the trip. My brother, who keeps his identity quite secret, will not be in uniform. The guard from here may not even recognize him." She removed a drawing and handed it to the ambassador. "This is he, right down to the details of the hat he will be wearing. Study it in private, please. Though you may show it to your staff who are traveling with you, show no one else. Not even your escort from our capital."

She frowned at it. "Somewhat ordinary, even with the mustache and hat. I could mistake him in a crowd."

"You needn't find him. He will watch your luggage transfer and then enter your train car. I only showed you this so you would recognize him and not be alarmed when an otherwise unknown man joins you. Also, we have been told that our eyes are identical, so you may recognize that trait too. Please return the drawing to him when the train sets out."

"Is this much secrecy necessary?"

"This and more."

"What more?"

"May I search your luggage, ma'am?"

"*My* luggage?"

Well, that spiked her indignation. "Yours and those who travel with you."

"You think I have come here to smuggle ambertrop?"

"Outrage will not deter me or my brother," Trellian said. "We share another trait. Neither of us will sugarcoat anything. You may have perfect intentions, but baggage handlers are another matter. If you hope to fight drug smuggling, you and every Welcian better get used to inspections."

The ambassador licked her lips. "I see."

"We may as well get the unpleasant part over with. When you crossed the border, you disrupted some people who were going to a lot of trouble to prevent communication. They could have killed you. The suddenness of your trip may have saved you. Once we knew you were on our soil, we put non-uniformed guards in the train stations you passed through. Now, potential enemies have had a few days to prepare for your return. Stay with me or my brother. Do exactly what we tell you. We know whom to trust. You do not."

Her cheeks had lost their bloom. "Oh."

"We will get you across the border before nightfall. Are you planning to stop for the night?"

"Yes, an inn near the border is holding rooms for me."

Proof that she was more naive than brave. "That just became the most dangerous place in Welcia for you to sleep. Let's bypass that one."

"I suppose so." The ambassador was looking more thoughtful now, less intimidated. "The king selected members of the palace guard to be stationed along the route. The guard with me knows where, and how to contact them. They will return with us as we travel."

"Good. Just so I know all risks and opportunities—can you or your guard make sure we have a train car to ourselves in Welcia?"

"That is already arranged."

"Will we need to change trains between the border and our destination?"

"No."

"If we had to travel through the night, could we?"

"Yes, there are two unidirectional rails on that route. If a train needs to stop, it is shunted off to a side rail. The journey would be quite tiring, though. It's a twelve-hour run from the border to the palace."

"Better tired than dead."

CHAPTER 10

Byerno let the suede travel bag swing in sync with his long stride. His soft-soled shoes added little to the many thumps on the wooden walkway. He stopped to check a schedule board, then continued on, checking platform numbers and looking all around. Like a traveler unfamiliar with the station. In reality, he checked faces.

The cool morning breeze penetrated the short hair at the back of his head. A pity that he couldn't wear a full hat this far into summer. The station wasn't too crowded this early. Made it easy to watch the baggage handlers from far off. They'd be hustling later, but took their time now. Byerno spotted the ambassador's twin suitcases—two-toned green with the reinforced corners of expensive luggage. They were placed inside with care. The aide's and guard's smaller cases were tossed in, then his sister's. Hers was plain, but he'd recognize it anywhere. At the moment, it was tagged with the aide's name and destination.

He checked the clock suspended from the walkway's tilted canopy. Time to get closer to his target.

A baggage handler shouted to someone, "Loading complete!"

The ambassador's personal guard lingered on the platform beside the car that she and her aide had already entered. He said something to the occupants, then swept another slow look around the platform and walkway. Their gazes connected for a split second, before his eyes continued past.

The bell rang, and a voice called out, "Final boarding!"

The guard stepped into the car and slid the door partway shut.

Byerno sauntered past it and nearly kept pace with the train as it began to move. The moment that open door reached him, he grabbed the bar and jumped within, then spun to close it. The guard, only inches from him, latched it. Good. He paid attention.

Byerno gave the ambassador a crisp nod. "Ma'am."

"Your sister's drawing is very like," she said.

"Always." He looked at the woman next to her.

"This is my aide, Brenlie, and my guard, Gordin."

"Give me a moment," Byerno said, and walked the length of the luxury car, inspecting every seat, rack, and the priv. He returned forward to the small galley and opened the food cabinets. An exact match to Trellian's order. He latched them shut again and turned to the three who watched him. "Your suitcases were not disturbed during the luggage transfer."

"Did you expect them to be?" the ambassador asked.

"Unlikely before now. Moreso as we near the border. You three must stay in this car, but I will be off at each station…" He transferred his gaze to the guard. "…then back on in similar manner."

The man gave him a single nod, shifting with the sway of the train.

Byerno returned to the ambassador and extended a hand. "The drawing of me, please."

She reached into her bag as she studied him. How much would she notice? She withdrew the folded paper and gave it to him. "As I consider the arrangements, I cannot help but wonder why your sister is not with us."

"She is on the train but does not wish to be seen yet."

"Why not?"

"Because some know her and will do nothing wrong if she is present."

The guard's voice ground. "We would prefer that."

"*We,*" Byerno said, "would prefer to catch criminals in the act."

"The princess ambassador is not bait for your trap," Gordin snapped.

Byerno directed his response to the ambassador instead of her guard. "You made yourself bait when you set out to visit us. That is not our doing. My job is to make sure the trap does not harm you, if or when it springs. Pay attention and do what I say. Instantly."

The guard stepped nearer, scowling. "You will—"

"Leave it." Though the ambassador's words were quick, they were calm. "We work as a team, even if he's rude."

The guard gave her a slight bow. "Yes, lady."

Interesting exchange. "I'll spare you more of my objectionable words," Byerno said, tossing his travel bag onto one of the side seats, away from the table and couches the ambassador and her aide occupied. "Besides, I predict a sleepless night ahead." He sat opposite his bag, propped his feet up, then leaned back and closed his eyes. He longed to peek—to cull a little amusement from the looks they would be exchanging.

After Byerno's first exit from the car and return, Gordin confronted him. "Your travel bag contains woman's clothing and no shaving kit. Care to explain that?"

Was this it? Not if he could help it. "Trellian doesn't shave. Did you need to dig in her bag to figure that out?"

"Why do you have her bag?"

Time to look disgusted. "Obviously, she wouldn't want to bother with it while she's keeping out of sight. Why would I need a bag when I'm leaving you midway?"

It was the ambassador who answered him. "Her suitcase is with our luggage. You are the one who actually needs a travel bag."

He made a mock bow. "Thanks for the non-compliment. I am more resourceful than that. And by the way, Trellian would never leave her portfolios in a suitcase that could be tampered with. Did you rifle through her drawings as well as her clothes?"

"No rifling was done, just a quick glance into the bag." The ambassador arched a brow at him. "Considering how you inspect, I wouldn't think you'd find it so odd that we'd look in your bag."

He snorted and returned to his seat, where he made a show of checking the bag's contents and closing it before faking sleep again.

They lunched between the next two stations. The trip grew tedious, with little talk inside and nothing happening on his walks past the unmoved luggage. Until the second-to-last station on Felverland soil.

He returned from his walk along the platform toward the ambassador's car. Oh, now this was interesting. A woman with a cart was passing covered dishes into the car. He scanned the surroundings as he strolled nearer but couldn't pick out anyone who seemed interested in the delivery.

He reached her just as she finished handing boxes from the bottom shelf to Gordin. Byerno smiled at her. "This is a nice touch. Who ordered it for us?"

She looked him over. "I wouldn't know. I just do deliveries. There's a card with it, so if it's any business of yours, read that." She swung her empty cart around and headed toward the building.

He hopped into the car as the ambassador's aide lifted one of the lids from a covered plate. "Oh my, it smells just lovely."

"Of course, it does," he snarled, taking the cover from her and snapping it back down on the plate. "Where is this card that came with it?"

The ambassador stood in the aisle a few feet from the delivery, holding an open envelope and gilt-edged card. She handed it to him. "What do you think of that?"

He read it. "An order wired from the prime minister's office, is it? He knows full well that the Amberforce supplied all the food we need for the trip. No one eats any of this."

"How unfortunate." The aide sighed, giving the food cabinets a disparaging look. "Are you sure that's necessary?"

Idiot. "If we eat food laced with amber..." He strode down the aisle and dug in his bag as he spoke. "...we'll all be blissfully ignorant when we must disembark to board a Welcian train." He returned to the food delivery with a corked vial and opened one of the boxes. "Let's see what else we have."

"What are you looking for?" Gordin asked.

"Something to test, preferably without herbs. Some of them will react the same as amber."

"Anything cooked," the ambassador said, "may be seasoned with herbs."

"Dressings and sauces, too. Even this bread is flecked with something green." Byerno dropped it back into the box and opened another. "Ah, cheesecake, which always has a faint golden hue." He pinched off a bit and dropped it in the vial. Before he even had time to swish it, foam oozed out the top.

Byerno compressed his lips. "If all the food is this contaminated, the intent may have been murder rather than drugging."

Shocked silence. The ambassador broke it. "I've never heard of it being fatal."

"It's unusual if one is choosing their own dose. They'll fall asleep before they consume enough to die."

"Are you going to test the rest of it?" Gordin asked.

"No point. Pack it up." He returned to his bag as the train lurched into motion. He pulled out a portfolio again. The ambassador followed him. Better start with words. He wrote, *Female—delivered A. contam. food to railcar—*

"What are you doing?" she asked.

"We'll leave the food with the police at the next station. They'll want details to trace the source." He jotted a description.

"Why bother with delivery staff?"

He added location and time to the notes. "Teens run deliveries to trains. That woman looked thirtyish." He met the ambassador's gaze. "Rude, too, which isn't a good way for a runner to keep her job. Now, I must sketch her—and since I'm not as good at it as Trellian—please don't look over my shoulder."

That rid him of her scrutiny. How suspicious was she? He made two sketches. They'd only see one and it would seem like he was slow. Besides, it gave him time to plan.

Danivid found Yautan in his chamber laying out clothes for the dinner party.

"I took the liberty of choosing a few that would be appropriate for this evening. Which do you prefer?"

Six was a few? Danivid pointed to the blue so dark it was almost black. "That one." The gold braid over shoulders and cuffs minimized within a couple inches to gold embroidery, then wove into the fabric itself.

"An elegant choice," Yautan said, "with an appropriate hint of mourning. The invitation didn't mention dancing, but music is likely. These parties that end the work week often include some revelry. Couples may choose to dance, but that won't be expected of you yet."

Danivid slipped his shoes off. "Do you think I've forgotten the protocol lessons drilled into me in this very palace?"

"Not at all, sir. I was merely trying to hint that there could be more revelry then would have occurred when...say...your father would have attended a dinner party." He hung the coat Danivid had selected on the door hook of the dressing room. "To be honest, I'm trying to lead into a change in recent years that you may not have seen. And won't like."

Danivid tossed his daywear tunic onto a chair and paused beside the priv door. "What is that?"

"Beverages are still served in clear flasks, so one can see if they contain water, seasoned juice, or wine. It is not unusual now for ambertrop infusions to be served. The concentration would be light and difficult to see. Such a beverage is always served in an amber-hued flask. Understanding your opinion on the matter, I wouldn't want you to take it without realizing." Yautan lowered his gaze.

Danivid forced his tight-drawn lips apart. "Thank you. That is the sort of information I appreciate hearing."

Cleaning up gave him a much-needed moment of privacy—including an opportunity to wad up his undershirt and hurl it at the innocent hamper. Behind the mirror he now stared into, lay the letters that revealed his brother's torment. Soon, Danivid would have to watch others consume that pleasurable poison.

Should he object? Follow the law or follow his morals? Easy choice for himself—harder if he applied his morals to others. Or should he use this event to learn? He scowled, for half his brain shouted that he was making an excuse, while the other half pointed out that he didn't yet know how to recognize the signs of someone under the influence of ambertrop. The longer he thought of it, the more ignorant he felt. He'd heard it was like having a glass of wine, but without undesirable effects like slurred speech or awkward motion. He sighed and pulled on the fresh undershirt that Yautan always placed on the priv shelf for him.

In the dressing room, his worries shifted to Allirae, his usual preoccupation every evening this week. She had sent a brief wire that she'd arrived in Qualketeen, but he'd heard nothing more. He picked up the pale blue silk shirt that hung on the garment stand and pulled it on. Perhaps she had set out for home by now, but she couldn't have crossed into Welcia yet. That, he would have heard. Maybe tomorrow evening he could welcome her home.

Yautan waited for him in his chamber, ready to hold his coat, while Danivid slipped his arms into it. According to prevailing style, the coat crossed in the front, the hemline sloping only a little toward the back. A hint of the long-tailed coats his ancestors had worn, but not enough to make sitting down an annoyance.

He opened his jewelry case and found the set of sapphire coat clasps. "Yautan, I've been wondering—who supplied the late king with ambertrop?"

"Hard to say. He probably sampled it while visiting, at first. Perhaps brought some home from parties. I was never sure how much he used, for he didn't take it in my presence. For the past year or so, his use may have increased, but as to his supplier, it's impossible to say who he—or *she*—might have been."

Why had he emphasized that? Danivid closed the clasp in its ornate loop. "She?"

"Well, it's bad form, of course, to accuse the dead, but I'm fairly sure that the queen's maid supplied her mistress. Obviously, the king and queen spent time together." Yautan walked behind Danivid with a clothing brush and took a few swipes along his back. "That should take care of the dog hair."

Danivid squelched the desire to laugh but couldn't help smiling. "Tomorrow morning, I'll want my riding clothes. Which I intend to bring home with both horse and dog hair."

"I hope the rain clears. I'll send a message to the stables."

Byerno sat at the table with the three Welcians when a jolt indicated that the train was starting its deceleration. At least he had convinced them that they were in as much danger in Welcia as Felverland, even if they didn't believe it was a single organization operating on both sides of the border.

"If I trust a police officer," Byerno said to Gordin, "I'll give him the picture. Either way, I'll leave to start my normal walk and return. You do the talking."

"Agreed. I'll tell whatever police I see that we suspected a food delivery, tested it, and found it contained ambertrop. I'll let them take it, whoever they might be."

"Right. Make as much fuss over it as you like and keep the focus there instead of on the luggage. It will have to be moved when they separate the cars. That's when I expect tampering."

Once again, the door slid open. From a window, Byerno recognized the lead officer who approached. "Motion him inside."

Out of view from the platform, he slipped the drawing into the officer's hand, said, "Guard will explain," then jumped down to the platform.

For most of the train, this was the final destination. Byerno joined disembarking passengers as though waiting for luggage, then faded into the shadows, watching. Ah, there it was, just as he'd suspected.

He returned to the ambassador's car. Inside, he said, "They've tampered with your luggage, ma'am. Give me time to record."

None of the three bothered him this time. He hurried, two faces to draw—not sure if one or both were involved. He was close to blowing his cover, but the ambassador made no attempt to view his work. He joined Gordin near the open door. He recognized a few officers that the Amberforce had proven loyal. He indicated the lead officer and whispered to Gordin. "Summon him to come in again."

When he entered, Byerno passed him the drawings. "I believe only the ambassador's suitcases were tampered with. We'll verify later."

"Right."

"Are we about ready to continue?"

"They're taking their own sweet time," the officer said, "but it shouldn't be long. I'll keep this guard informed."

When he returned, it was to report a delay. Some of the station's staff had believed the train was not continuing and left—including the engineer. At the next report, the engineer had returned, and they were ready to set out. Then, a rail switch was found to be jammed, so their short train could not leave the platform's shunt rail. They lost another half-hour in the repair.

The lead officer returned to the car to confer. "We are again clear for departure, Ambassador, but you'll be arriving in the dark." He included Gordin and Byerno in a worried glance. "We can escort you all to the station hotel, but after that contaminated delivery at the last station, and the repeat delays here, I do not consider that wise."

Byerno said, "Ma'am, I recommend continuous movement to get you across the border and well beyond it."

"Agreed." Gordin said to her. "I want you in Welcia, surrounded by as many of the king's guard as possible."

She addressed the lead officer. "Get us moving."

"Yes, ma'am."

He exited, and they latched the door.

Only the aide had sat down. Gordin and Byerno stood on either side of the ambassador, keeping her separated from the windows.

The aide looked out her window. "Someone is out there, staring at me."

"Lie down sideways on the couch," Byerno said.

She did so. "Am I just being paranoid?"

"You may be the safest person in this car, but there's no need to sit in plain view."

They waited for the muffled bell, which finally rang. Gordin grabbed hold of a grip and offered his other arm to the ambassador. At last, movement caused them to sway.

More than one breathy sigh eased out as they picked up speed.

CHAPTER II

T he Felvarian border master met their train. Police from the last station jumped down from the lead car. Brilliant magnery lights illuminated the gate and the paved path through it, glossy from recent rain. Byerno slung his travel bag over his shoulder and jogged back to the rear car, where he joined the two officers who waited with the luggage. It was lined up on the floor instead of in the rack. "What do you see?"

"The seals on the green cases are clean. The other three are nicked or twisted."

Byerno grinned. "I was a trifle messy with all five seals when I pre-inspected." He glanced across them. "These three look like mine, but inspect anyway and be quick. It was the green ones that were shoved around and obscured at the last station."

Byerno opened one of the ambassador's cases. "Take note of the seal here. Confirm that the original was broken and covered." As the officer confirmed his words, Byerno slipped his hands into the front side of the case and felt the dense weave of smuggling bags. "They were planning for a quick pull." He withdrew two flat bags, their folded ends stitched down, and so tightly packed they thudded when he tossed them on the floor. He ran his hands through the rest of the case's contents and found nothing more. The other case held another two bags in the same position.

"Nothing unusual in these three," one of the officers said.

"Reseal them all." Byerno stood and nudged a smuggling bag with his foot. "You'll have to take charge of these. I'll report four bags in your custody. Get the suitcases out before the delay is any more obvious. Once they're in view, no rush."

Byerno sauntered back to the ambassador's car and leaned in. Only she and the aide were there. Brusque as ever, he said, "I need to talk with Trellian. Give us ten minutes."

He strode to the building, where the border master watched Gordin talk with guards on the other side of the gate, in the same uniform as he. The man passed him a drawing. Byerno took a quick look to confirm it was a drawing of himself, before crumpling it. "What's going on at the gate?"

"Supposedly," the border master drawled, "the wires are damaged some ways south of here. The guards didn't like it, and they sent some extra men up to the gate."

Not good. Byerno pulled out his latest sketches and handed them over. "I left four amber bags with the officers in the rear car. I believe they were added at the last station, and these are the ID drawings. I'm done with my part. I'll send Trellian out. Don't let them cross the border without her."

He went inside and found the room he needed. Time to transform.

Trellian walked from the building with her bag hanging at her side. Its two-tone weave made an attractive contrast with the knee-length brown dress she wore over warm leggings. She kept her stride lady-like, though only Gordin watched her approach. By the time she reached the car, the ambassador stepped down from it. "Good evening, ma'am."

"I'm glad to finally see you. I hope you don't mind night travel."

"My brother told me of the need. Shall we cross at once?"

"Absolutely."

Encircled by officers, they started toward the gate with Gordin in the lead. Trellian glanced toward the luggage and did a double-take. "Why is there a shipping case with your luggage?"

"To pack the remaining food from the galley," the ambassador said. "Your brother has me feeling quite paranoid."

"Wise choice."

The gate opened with no delay. Luggage passed from Felvarian officers to Welcian guards, who closed in behind the three women as they crossed over. The Welcian side had a less secure layout. The pavement stretched a hundred feet, then met a covered boardwalk that parallelled a row of cairs, doubtless with a thin magnery line beneath.

A pointy-nosed man in a glitzy tunic and hat ignored the guard. "Welcome home, Princess Ambassador." He spread his arm to guide her. "We have cairs ready to take you to the inn."

"No, thank you. We'll take the evening train."

"But...b—" He hastened out of the way of a guard who refused to alter course, then darted within the group and kept pace at the ambassador's side. "But, my lady, the evening train has already left."

The man's persistence grated on Trellian's nerves. They didn't have much light here. Broken plans in unfamiliar dim territory made her muscles clench.

"Why did it leave?" the ambassador asked.

"Well...past sunset...and we assured them that we are prepared for your arrival. If you'll just follow me to—"

"Get back to your cairs," Gordin ordered the fellow. "Stationmaster!"

A man stood some way ahead with his mouth open. He closed it and hurried toward them. He began a bow to the ambassador, but Gordin grabbed his arm and forced him to walk along with them. "Why was the train allowed to depart when I had wired to have it held for the ambassador?"

"I held it at first, sir, but then the other wire came through that said to let it go." Being dragged along by a guard at least six inches taller than he didn't help his dignity. "I did hold the state carriages here, sir, and—"

"What is that train on the rail up ahead?"

"The first morning freight train."

They had reached some sort of office area with a broad opening and counter. Trellian scanned inside without showing interest.

Gordin released the stationmaster. "You will summon the engineer and have the state carriages hooked to the freight train. It will set out immediately. Ring the bell."

The man grabbed a lever and gave it two hard pulls. Sharp peals rang above the canopied walkway. Squares of light angled over the damp ground, and thumps of running footsteps soon followed. The stationmaster barked orders, and the hum of magnery powering up soon joined clangs and thuds.

A burly individual stomped into view, shouting, "Is a wind weaver blowin' your brains around, man? Does anyone in this station know what they want? Who ordered this latest switch?"

The ambassador spoke with sublime calm. "I have ordered it."

He leaned sideways to peer between guards. Gordin said, "You stand before Princess Ambassador Allirae de Noviam."

"Ah." He bowed and spoke with far more civility than Trellian would have thought possible. "Happy to be of service to the crown, lady. We'll have you on your way in no time."

It took a little longer than no time, but they waited inside, out of the wind—and whatever threat the darkness might hide—until the guards escorted the ladies into the middle one of three passenger cars. Luxurious. A galley, a spacious lounge with well-cushioned seats, and compartments at the rear.

This time, it was Gordin who inspected the car, and Trellian got a glimpse of four made-up beds in sleeping berths stacked two on each side. A guard finished stowing suitcases under the aide's direction, then opened a narrow door at the far end. Wind surprised Trellian, blowing through the door before he closed it behind him.

"Where does that go?"

Gordin closed and latched the side door. "The state carriages have walkways over the connections. My men will be in the cars on both ends." He turned to the ambassador. "Where do you want me tonight?"

"Once we are in motion, I don't feel the need for a guard, so this will be the ladies' carriage tonight."

"There will be stops." He pointed to the side door. "Promise me you won't unlatch that door."

A jolt made them sway, and the ambassador gripped a seat back. "I promise. Take a little something from our food stash. Can I assume that the king's guards will have provided for themselves?"

"A safe bet. Either way, we won't eat from the galley stocked here."

She nodded, and he departed through the forward door. "Sit with me here, Trellian," the ambassador said. "Brenlie, find us a snack and something warm to drink."

Trellian sat, pulled out a portfolio, and started sketching.

"Who are you drawing, this time?"

"That fellow by the cairs. Far too insistent. That may be his job, though, so I'm not accusing. You should know that four bags of amber were hidden in the front of your suitcases. I'm interested in anyone who wants access to your luggage."

That brought a serious look to her face. After a moment, the ambassador said, "My luggage is in here and won't be removed until the palace station."

"Yes. Disappointing, but your safety is more important than my drawings of questionable luggage handlers. I noticed people calling you *lady*. How do the titles work here?"

"We don't use *ma'am* or *madam*. Simply replace it with *lady*. We use *sir* the same as you do."

"When I meet the king, do I need to use *highness* or *majesty* or something?"

"Those are obsolete. *Lord king* is used at first encounter, and *sir* thereafter."

Trellian sketched as the ambassador described titles for nobles and elected officials. Somewhat complex, since not all provinces were governed in the same manner. "If I'm in doubt," she asked, "can I just use *lady* or *sir*?"

"Yes. It's considered bad form to show superiority over one's title, so no one will take issue if you make a mistake. Speaking of titles, we need some way to indicate your role. I don't think *Officer Trellian* is a good idea."

"A horrible one!"

"*Ambassador* is a possibility, but that implies you have negotiation authority."

Trellian shook her head. She should have discussed this with the PM. "How can we say that I just want to learn about your culture?"

The ambassador tilted her head. "I think we should introduce you as Lady Trellian. If anyone inquires further, we will say you are like an ambassador but merely sent by the prime minister to learn of our culture."

"All right." She hid a smirk, thinking of how much her mother would approve. "Can you tell me the members of the royal family?"

Trellian jotted names down, as Allirae explained relationships, and Brenlie served herbal tea and biscuits.

Brenlie sank into a seat and wrapped her hands around her steaming cup. "Skies, it's been a long day."

"What does *skies* mean?" Trellian asked, setting aside her portfolio.

Brenlie blinked her eyes wide, and it was the ambassador who answered. "Emphasis of any sort. It comes from an old expression of *skies above and caverns below.* It's rare to hear the entire thing now. *Skies and caverns* gives double emphasis. And if you happen to go belowground while you visit, *caverns* is the preferred expression."

"Do you really have people living underground?"

"Yes, but you'll want to say that as *belowground.* Underground means buried. Belowground is the Welcian province of Dirklan. They are alive and well in a vast network of caverns."

Trellian set her cup down. "I learned about it when I was a little girl in school. I'm afraid I doubted it, and frustrated my teacher with questions like 'why would anyone live there?'" She put enough childish accent into the question to draw smiles from the women.

The ambassador said, "It started hundreds of years ago with a gaping hole in the side of a mountain. Miners would travel in and out. They traded the ores from near the opening at first, but there are always some who love to explore. The caverns they discovered led them to many more metals and gems. Eventually, it took more than a full day to walk out, so of course, they built places to live. They laid the first rails of Welcia, although the early carts were pulled by burros. Later, the Dirklians discovered magnery."

"That must have been a relief, to have light down there."

"They have light from above. Natural crystal formations brought light into some of the original caverns. The formers took a cue from that and created purified light shafts. It's quite amazing, what they accomplished. Forming has always been the predominant substance gift belowground, and it's not hard to understand why. They construct almost everything they need from rock, and their economy is based on the export of mined products."

"It's still hard to imagine that sleeping in a cave could be comfortable."

"You have the wrong image. They sleep in beds, that are in houses, that are in cities, that are in caverns. Every building has a rooftop garden, and some caverns contain fields and orchards."

Trellian could only shake her head.

"Maybe I should warn you that King Danivid lived in Dirklan for ten years as royal ambassador. He has quite a fondness for it."

"Ah. I will keep that in mind." Trellian dusted crumbs from her fingers. "Amazing what one can learn by asking the meaning of a single expression. How often do people have their brains blown around by wind weavers?"

Both women burst into such laughter that Trellian couldn't help but smile.

The ambassador wagged a finger. "I don't think you want to repeat that colorful tidbit. If you need a negative expression, use the word *quakes*."

That sobered her. "Quakes, indeed. How has Welcia fared during the recent ones?"

"We have felt some in Regissa, though not severe. Have they troubled Felverland too?"

"Near the coast," Trellian said with a nod. "The papers report on them. Most are insignificant, but one took a life."

"Sad," Brenlie murmured, standing to pick up their dishes.

The ambassador frowned. "I've heard nothing of quakes in Felverland. The news across our borders has dwindled so much over the years. Unacceptable." She turned to her aide. "Brenlie, if you'll just get out my night things, please, and then you can go to bed."

She wanted a private talk, did she? Trellian picked up her portfolio again and added more detail to her latest drawing.

Silence reigned until Brenlie pulled the partition of her sleeping berth closed.

The ambassador leaned over the table between them. "I noticed that you turned your reversible bag."

"Naturally. You can't expect someone like Byerno to carry a lady's bag."

"I also noticed that it is much thinner."

Oh, this was too funny to stop. "Did you?"

"And you are wearing the clothes that were in it."

"Well, you see, when I was traveling behind the luggage car, a woman with a baby sat next to me. Can you believe that dear sweet little thing threw up all over me?"

The ambassador narrowed her eyes. "I have been longing to pull your hair to see if it's a wig."

"I won't put you to the trouble." Trellian gathered her tresses back. "I have very thick hair, and every summer I trim off the underside." She turned her head sideways to reveal the nape of her neck. "It looks quite manly when I must wear a summer hat. Also, that part is darker than the sunny side of my hair. The perfect color from which to make a mustache." She tilted her head. "Oh, don't scowl at me! I would have told you anyway—right about now."

"Why not from the beginning?"

"Because I didn't know whether you were any good at hiding a secret. Or willing to. Your guard or aide, even less so. Who saw into my bag?"

"Not Brenlie. Gordin looked over my shoulder, but I'm the only one who touched things."

"Mm. I've always kept Byerno in the background—never in close proximity to anyone for hours together. What else gave me away?"

"I don't know if I would have been suspicious if I hadn't seen inside the bag. While we talked here, you seemed very different in manner, but then *he* hardly spoke." The divots beside her nose deepened. "I assume his surliness was to ensure that."

"Yes. While I can drop my voice very low..." She did so with a few words. "...my throat gets sore after a while. My one worry is that you will equate his rudeness with my attitude. That is not me."

"Says the woman who demanded to search my luggage and declared that she and her brother would sugarcoat nothing."

"That part is true. I pretty much *have* to say what I mean."

"Is that so?"

"Yes. Apparently, my face contradicts me. Those who know me, give my words more weight than my expressions."

"So, you never lie?"

"Let's not push it *that* far. I would lie to an amber smuggler any minute. Fictitious baby vomit aside, I won't lie to you."

The ambassador leaned forward again. "Why not?"

Trellian mirrored her motion. "Because, if we don't stop *both* the supply *and* the demand for amber, it will never end. As far as I can tell, you and the new king are the only hope for that."

CHAPTER 12

Danivid awakened early, his worries over Allirae having followed him through the night. A storm hadn't made sleep any easier. He almost decided to stay at the palace in hopes of news from her, but by the time he'd finished the tea Yautan made him, the sun came out and tempted him. So did the riding clothes laid out on the bed, embellished with minimal gold braid across the shoulders and all other gold thread woven into the tan cloth of the coat. He rocked, remembering the sway of a saddle. He should take his pleasure while he could.

He went down to the morning room and was almost done with breakfast when his brother-in-law sauntered in.

"Look who's up before me," Meroak said. "We must record this momentous event."

"I'm going riding today."

Meroak directed a nod toward his garb. "So I deduced, clever sort that I am." He served himself and ate a few mouthfuls before he spoke again. "I checked for wires from Allirae. Nothing yet."

So somber. Danivid countered with a light tone. "She isn't actually late yet. Come riding with me."

Meroak threw him a low-browed look. "No thanks."

Danivid drained his teacup and set it down. "I'm just trying to get your mind off it—cheer you up."

He smiled—sort of. "Horses aren't my favorite path to good cheer."

"Everyone takes a toss at least once in their life. You just need to carry on."

"I'll leave that to you. See that you stay on your horse."

Danivid couldn't resist a tease as he stood. "I'm good at that."

He strolled through the hall and left the palace through the rear doors, where a guard waited beside a cair to take him the short distance to the private rail. No delay there. Though the rail connected to the public station, which provided the magnery to power it, no train car but his glass-fronted carriage sailed across the city and up the hill. The forest ahead—sublime beauty.

Silly of Meroak to have turned down the ride. Joking aside, he could manage a horse well enough. Besides, Allirae couldn't be any nearer than the border, or they'd have heard. She wouldn't reach the palace until sunset.

He disembarked on the little platform, where the hillside leveled enough for stables, groom quarters, and some long pastures.

The head groom, who had taught him to ride years ago, jogged over, all smiles. "My lord king!" He pulled his tweed cap off as he bowed.

Lots of gray on that head now. "Good to see you, Jonger. How have you been?"

They walked side-by-side. "Doing well, sir. You're getting your tan back, I see."

Danivid laughed. "I'll never compete with yours."

"'Course not! Wouldn't be proper. I told the lads to turn out your horse into the corral." They strolled along the side of the stable. "I suspect that's him we hear mouthing off right now. I'll get him saddled up for you quick."

They rounded the corner of the building. One of the young grooms stood by the gate and bowed at sight of the king. A horse, already saddled, trotted around the perimeter of the corral. A beautiful tan with black socks and mane.

A pang hit Danivid. "Ah. My brother's horse."

The young man's face fell. "The...the message said...the king's horse... and I..." He straightened, though he looked at the ground. "I beg your pardon, sir. I should have realized. It's just that we call the roan the prince's horse."

In the corral, the horse had stopped and angled his ears at Danivid. Did a horse grieve for an absent master?

"Understandable mistake. Since they are both mine now, I will have to be clearer." His brother had let him try the paces of his horse a couple years ago. As smooth as his pedigree. The creature deigned to approach as though the mud were a carpet laid for him. To Jonger, Danivid said, "You've been exercising him, I assume."

"Myself, sir," Jonger replied. He nodded toward a distant riding enclosure. "I don't let the young ones ride him."

Danivid craned his neck. Teens and children sat on horseback within the enclosure. "Young, indeed. Who are they?"

"The ones who care enough to learn everything, right down to mucking a stall. I don't allow the ones who just want to ride, for they'll never be fit to work here."

Work here. Jonger knew what it cost to staff the stable and feed so many horses, but he had no idea that the crown couldn't afford that expense. His brother's horse decided to thrust his head over the fence and allow Danivid to stroke his nose. He couldn't sell this horse. Nor his own, nor Allirae's. Several noble families still made much of riding with the king, and his brother had extended that privilege to any of the governors' families who were interested. Wouldn't happen if he couldn't provide mounts. How could he sell off even the old horses, at pasture now? For they had once served his parents. He remembered his brother rubbing this horse between the ears and did the same.

"Do you want me to send a lad for your roan?" Jonger asked.

"Next time. You say that some want to learn to ride but not share in the work. How common is that?"

"Hard to say. A week doesn't go by that at least a few don't come to hang on the fences and watch lessons."

"If they don't want to work, they can always pay for their lessons."

"Sir?"

"No point in training future grooms if no one else in the city learns how to ride. Give some thought to offering classes with the staff you have. Classes that can turn a profit. Maybe guided excursions too. We'll talk about it next time I'm out."

Danivid walked toward the gate. The young groom opened it, then pulled it shut after he'd entered the corral. He stroked the horse's neck until its fidgets eased and it stilled for mounting. Taking the reins from the saddle clip, he put a booted foot in the stirrup and swung his other leg over. As his weight shifted across the saddle, the horse went mad.

It launched Danivid from the saddle. He flipped in midair and landed on his back in the mud. For several seconds, all he knew was that hooves pounded beside him. One landed inches from his head, and his senses returned. He rolled sideways, slipping and scrambling to find his feet. Hands gripped him and helped him stand upright. People were shouting and running, while the horse bucked.

It was Jonger who clutched him, hustling him to the fence. "My lord, my lord, are you all right? Please answer me."

Danivid gripped a rail and made the mistake of licking his lips. Ugh! He spat. "I'm standing, aren't I?" He raised a hand to wipe his face, but it was filthy.

"Are you injured, though?" Jonger shook out a large handkerchief and shoved it into Danivid's hand.

He wiped his face as best he could. "Nothing obvious. Get the saddle off that horse."

Some grooms had managed to catch the reins and were guiding the horse toward the gate's hinge post while avoiding flailing hooves. They got a clip on his halter, then slowly swung the gate around to contain the horse between it and the fence. Only then could one release the girth and another, standing on a fence rung, lift the saddle off. He tossed it onto the fence beam and lifted the blanket. His open lips twisted in a puzzled fashion. The horse finally quit screaming his fury.

"Can you tell what hurt him?" Jonger demanded. "Is there blood?"

The groom poked at the underside of the blanket. "No blood." He sounded shocked. "It looks like a *burn*."

Burn? How could— Danivid looked around. "Where is the groom who was here with him?"

Everyone else looked too. A dozen people stood around, their hands spread or shoulders lifted.

Jonger barked orders while Danivid breathed through his mouth, trying to avoid the stench that clung to him. His initial tension had already subsided.

His old groom turned back to him. "My lord, are you sure you're not injured?"

"Nothing hurts. Not even my pride. What could be under a saddle that could burn?"

"Makes no sense, but I'll find the scoundrel who saddled him. First, I have to get you back to the palace."

"Forget that! Get me to a shower!"

Jonger uttered an uncertain laugh and fell into step beside Danivid as they sloshed from the corral and set off toward the buildings. "You *seem* fit. Gotta admit, you shake this off better'n I do!"

"You'll have to excuse my haste. Rain isn't the only thing in corral mud."

At the door to the head groom's cottage, Jonger knelt to pull off Danivid's boots. "I'll have these cleaned. Not worthy of you, but I offer you a loan of my clothes. We're not that different in size."

"Quite worthy enough for me. I'm riding, after all. Have my roan brought in."

With wet hair, borrowed clothes, and a far more pleasant scent, Danivid helped himself to the tea set out on the table.

Footsteps approached, then Jonger pushed the screen door open. His other hand was clenched. He paused to scrutinize Danivid. A mistake, for a fly buzzed past him. He strode to the table, where he opened his fist and released tissue balls onto the wood surface.

"What are..." Danivid stared at them, as childhood memories surfaced—flinging the little balls onto the paved terrace so they would spark and pop. "Bangers."

"Yep. We found these stuck in hair under the saddle."

This only half made sense. "We used to fling them on the ground to make them explode." Danivid remembered the restriction that adults be present. Were bangers more dangerous than his boyhood mind had grasped?

Jonger placed one on the stone floor and ground it with the sole of his boot. A muffled pop sounded, and ash remained when he lifted his foot. "They're sold by the pouch, and few were caught in the horsehair. If many were close together, they would trigger each other and be enough to burn. Not a deep or serious burn, but enough to make a horse believe he was being attacked."

"Why didn't they explode when I put my weight in the stirrup?"

"That wouldn't be your full weight, for we all jump from the other foot. Frankly, I'm surprised that mounting set them off. I would have thought it would take a jump or trot. And if so, you would have been alone on the trail somewhere. There's no saying how you might have landed amid rock and trees. Being thrown in the corral was either lucky or the protection of Ellincreo."

Danivid couldn't help but laugh at those final words. "I hope he chooses something other than manure and mud the next time he protects me."

Jonger braced his fists on the table. "This is serious!"

"I know." Danivid stood and clapped a hand on his friend's shoulder. "A fall in the woods *could* have killed me, but we must admit it's not certain. Nonetheless, the incident should be investigated."

"That, we've already started. The groom who saddled your horse is named Durki. He did it in the corral. An unusual place for saddling, but the one who saw him assumed I must have ordered it. I did not. Durki's not where he should be. I've still got men searching for him, but I checked his room. His clothes are gone."

"Send for the police then. Has my roan been brought in?"

"Yes, sir, but...surely you're not still going to ride."

"The culprit has run. You needn't worry. Since I'm off to a late start, could you spare me some bread and cheese?"

Jonger shook his head, but grabbed a sack and began filling it with more than requested.

Danivid leaned against a counter and folded his arms. "What sort is Durki?"

"Middlin', I guess. Been here a few years. Diligent mostly. Bit of a slug on his own time."

They went out to the stable, where a groom checked the hooves of his roan. Danivid got a warm greeting from his favorite horse and watched Jonger inspect the blanket and saddle before lifting them on.

The other groom looked familiar, though Danivid didn't know his name. Still, it couldn't hurt to get another opinion. "I assume you worked with Durki?"

"Yes, sir."

"What did you think of him?"

"On the quiet side, but he did his share of the work—as long as you didn't need him in the evening. He liked ambertrop, so that accounts for it."

"Do many of the men use it?"

"Skies, no! A family man can't afford it. Durki is single, but even he spent every payday returning money he borrowed the week before."

Jonger tightened the girth. "B'sides that, no one's allowed that stuff nor strong drink during their shift. They're out in a minute if I catch 'em."

"A rule that shall now be extended." Danivid mounted. "I have forbidden ambertrop in the palace. I don't want it here either. Those who wish to use it, must do so elsewhere and not return till it has cleared from their system."

"I'll pass that along, sir. Enjoy your ride."

Danivid set out along a familiar trail up the hillside. He let his horse walk the incline, pondering. These few weeks had held so many problems that questions over his brother's death had slipped to the bottom. This morning's incident...should he think of it as a murder attempt? Sloppy, if that's what it was. It didn't seem that Durki could benefit from it. Who could?

CHAPTER 13

Danivid's unanswerable question faded as birdsong and dappled sunlight joined the steady thud of hooves and the blissful sway of the saddle. How he had missed this! Out here, one could think without distraction. Though what he thought of, he couldn't have described a couple hours later when he reached the brook.

This was one of the maintained stops. A flat stretch here allowed horses to drink and be tied. Leveled stones led up to a rustic table and firepit near the top of a short cascade. Room for a tent, too, though the cottage farther ahead was more comfortable.

Danivid dismounted, tended to his horse, then took his lunch sack up the stone steps. He halted, for someone sat at the table with a lunch of his own.

The man nodded to him. "Pleasant day."

The absence of his title or a bow surprised Danivid for only a second. He was wearing the groom's clothing. Unrecognized. He returned the greeting and stepped over the opposite bench to sit down.

They commented on the perfect turn of the weather and, between bites of his sandwich, Danivid took note of the substantial hiking pack leaning against a tree. The two parts of a trigger-spring crossbow stuck out of the side pockets. Danivid chided himself for wondering how quickly it could be assembled and what sort of bolts the pack held.

The man looked fit, but not young. Maybe sixtyish. He finished eating first and was chatty enough to carry the conversation. Danivid soon learned that he'd grown up in Regissa City, spent thirty years running a resort on the far side of Mount Estelle, and moved back last year for family reasons. Danivid slipped in a leading question to find out what he thought of recent changes.

"Gotta admit," the man said, "it's a little hard adjusting to the city again. We visited often, so we knew it grew, but faster than ever as the years passed. We'd hoped we could bring our horses back with us, but there's a train station where we used to board and pasture them."

Danivid wondered where that was. "We?" he asked.

"My wife and I. We used to ride in here on the weekends. Taught our children to ride too. So many good times. A pity that's lost to most these days."

"I've been gone a while, too, but now that you mention it, we'd meet a lot more people when I rode here as a child."

"I'm sure you did. With all the boarding stables pushed farther out into the country, no one can ride in from the public entrance. I had to start at dawn to hike this far." He scanned the campsite. "It's not the same without my wife."

Oh, no. "Ah, forgive me for being obtuse. Is she..."

The man turned back to him. "Oh, nothing tragic. She can still manage a couple hours of hiking with me, but this far is too much for her." He made a rueful twist of his mouth. "I suspect I've found the end of my current range, but it's a fine spot to camp and rest up. I can walk out tomorrow afternoon."

"It sounds like you've done a lot of hiking over the years."

"Sure have. I started out as the trail guide at Starmount Resort and taught small game hunting too. Even when we were managing the place, my wife and I used to lead a hike every week or two."

Danivid angled his head toward the pack. "I saw your bow. Do you plan on rabbit or squirrel for dinner?"

He half laughed. "Naw, I'm just the sort who believes in being prepared for the unexpected. Cleaning game isn't my favorite pastime, but I'll do a little target practice. Keeps me sharp in case I can find a way to use my mountain skills here in the city." He nodded—to himself, it seemed, for his gaze lowered. "I miss it. I do, indeed."

Danivid thought of Stanton's mention of a resort. He'd grown so cynical over the past few weeks that he wondered if this fellow was sent here by Shevnal to scout out locations. "What if a resort could be built here? Would you like to manage it?"

"I'd rather be buried alive in a quake!"

Danivid drew back, lowering the apple he was about to bite into. He considered the man's scowl for a moment. "Did something go terribly wrong at the resort you used to manage?"

"Oh, no. I loved the work. We left because our daughter needed us here. But everyone knows that Shevnal fellow gets all the land now." He'd snarled the name. "I've heard rumors he's after the king's woodland. I'd bet any money he'll close off the public entrance first thing. If he let a resort be built, it would only be for the wealthy. All his lease agreements charge a flat fee *and* a percentage of profits, you know. He wants those profits high."

"What if someone else owned the land?"

"No one else will get it. I can't imagine how he has enough money to win every bid, but he does. That, and I've attended community meetings where he and his cronies push their agenda through. I've seen people scowling while they vote in his favor." His face mirrored the looks he described.

"How does he make that happen?" Danivid asked.

"If I knew that..." The man shook his head. "I don't know what I'd do. The General Council pays no attention, nor does Governor Rikion, and the old king didn't care. Some say the new king is different, but he hasn't shown it yet." He shrugged in concession. "Early days yet, of course." He tilted his head in the direction of the horse. "You must have ridden up from his stable, so I gather you're a groom there. Have you met the king? Do you know much about him?"

So much for incognito. "Perhaps I should explain that the first horse I mounted this morning threw me into the mud. After a shower and borrowing clothes from my head groom, I mounted another one of my horses and started my delayed ride."

The man gripped the table's edge. "Skies above," he murmured.

"I do know much about King Danivid, for I am he."

The man was already on his feet, and he managed a bow despite the fixed bench that made it awkward. "Lord king. I beg pardon for—"

Danivid stopped him with a raised hand. "No, I won't even let you apologize. Sit down." Danivid smiled wryly, hoping to dispel the serious gaze that now confronted him. "I knew you didn't recognize me and could have introduced myself. It wasn't my goal to deceive, only to have an ordinary conversation. Which is rather hard to come by in gilded clothes."

"I imagine so."

"Now that you know my name, may I know yours?"

"Burdock, sir."

"A pleasure to meet you, Burdock. I hope our conversation remains candid."

"I don't know. I suppose I shouldn't have said King Vancent didn't care."

"I understand why you believe it. My brother realized far too late what damage he had allowed and laid plans to turn things around. Then, he died before he could implement them."

Burdock made a sound in his throat, eyes still fixed on Danivid's. "What I said about Shevnal is far worse. Is he a friend of yours like he was of the late king?"

Danivid pressed a hand to his chest and adopted a tone of great sadness. "Alas, Shevnal does not like me."

It had the desired effect. Burdock snorted a laugh.

"What does he think of you?" Danivid asked.

"He doesn't notice me. My wife and I aren't nearly rich enough to be worthy of Shevnal's attention."

Interesting. Also, Burdock had yet to use Shevnal's much-loved title of *chief former*. Did Shevnal enjoy approval only in certain settings? "If there ever was a resort here—not owned by Shevnal or his like—what would it need to succeed?"

"Well..." Burdock fiddled with his lunch pack. "This close to the city, it shouldn't duplicate what is already found in Regissa's hotels. It should offer a unique experience that cannot be found anywhere nearby. Starmount Resort offers stargazing, rock climbing, mountain hiking, and an aerial lift. That's what draws people in from far away. Here, horses could be part of the attraction. Perhaps a place to escape speed and machines." He tilted his head toward the eastern branch of the trail. "The open ocean views ahead are unique, and the power of the crashing waves is incredible. There might even be possibilities of walking the descent into Dirklan."

"That is *not* easy!"

Burdock laughed. "No, but I did it once and survived. There is still a breed who do things *because* they are hard. The rest can ride the train down." He smirked. "Good food and friendly staff can never be overlooked, of course. Lodging should fit in with the sort of experience people come for. Here, it should blend with the forest. Such a resort needs an owner who understands and loves the land, or it will be ruined." He lifted an eyebrow. "Is this useful?"

"It is." Danivid leaned a little nearer. "And it is *most* useful if it does not spread before its time."

"Are you...actually thinking of some such endeavor?"

"I wasn't before meeting you, but I do think it's a shame that so few people are able to enjoy Regissa's unfettered land." Danivid pushed himself up from the table, causing his new acquaintance to rise also. Danivid grabbed his sack and the apple core he'd left on the table. "Come down and meet my horse, if you like."

"I would indeed."

The roan consumed the apple core and soon permitted Burdock's touch. His familiar manner with the horse demonstrated the truth of his earlier words.

Danivid retightened the saddle girth. "Thank you for your company over lunch."

"It was my pleasure, sir."

Danivid mounted. "You should bring your wife to the palace in a week or two. You may take my rail carriage up to the stable and borrow a couple horses."

Burdock's jaw dropped. "I...uh...sir...I don't know what to say!"

Danivid shrugged. "It won't trouble my horses to do a little work in between eating. I'd also like my steward to hear your thoughts on a resort. Pleasant day!" He guided his horse to the trail that skirted the campsite.

"Pleasant day, sir—and *thank you*!" Burdock called after him.

Danivid continued on his way east, riding fast enough to put substantial distance between himself and anyone on foot. Interesting, the conversation had been, but it must be past noon now. He couldn't help second-guessing his decision to leave when his sister might be nearing home. Yet the purpose he'd conceived last night urged him on.

Might the cottage tell him anything about his brother's last days—or even his death? He should have come before now, and if these early weeks were any indication, there was no saying when he'd get another chance. It wasn't much farther.

He urged his horse to canter and soon reached the cottage. The ocean breeze was stronger here. Trees grew tilted from the wind. Danivid tied his horse on the lee side of the cottage, under an extension of the roof, and walked around to the front. Paint was long overdue.

He crossed the small porch and entered. It was a simple structure, much as he remembered, though it smelled like stale sweat. A spider scurried up a dangling strand of silk that fluttered away from the open door. Danivid raised a side window to let the breeze through. Running water—though cold and slow—was the cottage's one feeble claim to civilized living, for magnery had never been installed.

The fireplace, cooking area, and necessities took up the back wall. The sitting area and bed faced broad windows with a view of the ocean. A curtain could be pulled around the sleeping area, not that there was a particular need for privacy in a cottage meant for one or two people. Two wooden chairs by the table, a small couch facing the fireplace, and a thick quilt on the bed provided basic comforts.

The strike of Danivid's boots on the stone floor sounded lonely. He checked the cupboards. Dishes but no food. A stack of clean towels. The bedlinens appeared to have been laundered since their last use. At first, there seemed to be no sign of his brother's stay, but the wood box was empty and the lamp oil low.

Danivid braced himself against the back of the couch and folded his arms. "What happened here, Vancent?" he murmured. "What happened afterward? After you set things in motion?" He rubbed his chin. "Yeah, you died, but *why*? How?"

Talking to himself now. Perhaps the result of being pitched from a horse. By intent, no doubt. He could have broken his neck or been trampled to death. Or survived unscathed, obviously. He wished he could talk through it with someone he trusted. Not many such people existed, and Allirae was...where? He should have stayed at the palace.

A steady clop pierced his thoughts. He glanced out the side window. No one on the trail by which he'd arrived. He crossed to the other side. Nor on the trail that continued east along the bare peninsula. So, someone approached from the rear trail. Strange. Who? Someone as harmless as Burdock or someone who wanted to finish what Durki bungled? All at once, it seemed foolhardy to be out here alone.

A horse whinnied, and another answered. Whoever was out there would guess someone was in the cottage. Whether they meant ill or good, they might come to see who. Danivid stepped to the hearth, giving himself maximum separation from the door, plus access to the poker near his right hand.

CHAPTER 14

Footsteps reached the porch, and a woman stepped through the door. Good thing Danivid wasn't holding the poker like a weapon. She wore a split dress over her leggings—ordinary riding clothes. A long, thick braid lay over one shoulder. Wind had teased some of the brown hair from its restraint, and freckles stood out dark against her tan. Her frank gaze turned puzzled.

"Pleasant day," Danivid said.

"It is," she murmured, scanning his clothes then back to his face. "Do you know that you look very much like King Vancent?"

"I should. I am his brother." He gestured to his garb. "Obliged to borrow clothes after an unfortunate toss from my horse."

She curtsied, not flustered in the least. "That explains it."

"And you are?"

"Velzain. I'm the wind weaver assigned to the peninsula."

"Ah. I haven't been out to World's End in years."

"*Pff.* I wouldn't think a streamer like you would misname it any more than I would."

He chuckled. "I take it you prefer the name Land's End."

"Former's nonsense to call it more than that. As though wind and water are not more of the world than land is."

"True."

"I've heard that you are like the de Noviam streamers of old. Like the kings who could open the whirlpool and lift vessels out of Passage Lake."

"I imagine I could have, though the dome of the lake has long been sealed."

"I sometimes wondered why King Vancent didn't possess the streaming gift."

"How do you know he didn't?"

"He told me."

This unconventional woman knew his brother? Danivid strolled to the table, then made an inviting gesture to the chair nearest her while pulling out the other for himself. "In days of old, the crown needed to fulfill a covenant obligation, which required that gift. Streaming is less useful for a king now."

She scoffed as she sat down. "I've heard far too much about gifts being obsolete in our modern age. Fortunately, the Wind Weavers' Guild doesn't have to put up with that absurdity. Ellincreo help us if anyone ever devises an artificial way to control the wind."

She clasped her hands and looked at them. "Even King Vancent repeated that drivel about obsolete substance gifts." She met Danivid's gaze. "Though, in his defense, he was enduring a horrible day when he said it."

That statement, from one who lived on the peninsula—She had to know more. "How did you meet my brother?"

"I met him here."

"When?"

"A few months ago. I spend winters in Regissa City, but, eh, such crowds." She flicked her hand as though flinging all crowds into the wind. "I'd returned to Land's End the week before and was just going down early in the morning to fetch some more things. I saw the horse standing out back, saddled and...well, I could tell it had been standing there in its filth all night. The girth hadn't even been loosened. I came inside, ready to tell whoever took such poor care of an animal exactly what I thought. But I found the king."

She'd interlaced her fingers again, but they wouldn't rest. Her gaze flitted around the cottage, anywhere except on him. "And then?" he prompted.

"One is not to disparage a king. Nor is it kindness to add tragedy to one who mourns already."

Another of the rare people who understood that a king also grieved. Danivid gentled his tone to reassure her. "I know—from my brother's own hand—at least part of what he faced. I know why he came here, and that the days were grueling. But I would like to know more. What state did you find him in?"

"He was lying on the bed." Her eyes widened a trifle. "Uh, not indecent or anything—dressed except for his boots and the fine riding coat he'd left hanging on the chair. The bed looked like he must have thrashed all night, but he was asleep at that moment. Sort of, anyway. He was shaking."

"Cold?"

"Perhaps. The fire had been lit, but it was dead. I was so shocked that I backed out and shut the door. I just had no idea what to do!"

"Understandable."

She let her shoulders relax. "I went and took care of the horse. That might seem backwards, but I needed time to think, for I ought not to see the king in disarray, nor be with him alone. But he looked so ill. How could I neglect anyone, the king especially, if he was in need?" She straightened. "So, I returned and lit the fire. Filled the kettle to heat. He had an open pack on the table with some food in it. A dirty plate and glass beside it. I figured he must have come sometime the day before. After a bit, he started to moan and clutch his head. I got him to drink a little water. The first words out of his mouth were, 'I need ambertrop.'"

She looked down. "I must admit, that shocked me, and I'm afraid I sounded quite disgusted."

His sense of humor perked up. "What did you say?"

She looked sideways. "'Driven bats, I thought you were ill.'"

Danivid's lips twitched. "I gather you were born in Dirklan."

"Yes. I came aboveground to train, and since my range proved unusually long, never returned except to visit."

"Not surprising for one assigned to the peninsula. How did my brother respond to such a polite remark?" For the first time, he got a smile from her, though short-lived.

"He finally got his eyes all the way open and sat up. He looked around like he was confused, then asked who I was. We covered the basics, and I got him to eat a little toasted bread. By the time breakfast was over, he'd told me that he had come up here to get free of ambertrop, and I had promised never to tell."

She sniffed. "Yeah, I know. I just told you, but I haven't told another soul, and I won't. Did you know he used it?"

"I found out after he died—mostly from some letters he left for me. I know he stopped using it, but I don't know what *stopping* entails."

Velzain bit her lip. "He shook the whole time. Kept asking for tea. I don't know how he got a pack of food together, or why he didn't put some tea in it if he liked it so much. I was just certain he wasn't going to get through the day on his own. He'd pace around this tiny space, looking outside, clenching and opening his fists. He didn't have enough supplies for more than a day, but I was pretty sure he'd bolt back to the palace if I left to get them.

"So..." She gave Danivid a look—half guilty, half pleading. "I temporarily stole his horse and took it out to my stable at Land's End. Then I loaded up some food and tea, and hurried back. Found a good spot for my horse in the woods, and hand-carried my supplies from there to the cottage." She shook her head. "Oh, he was a mess. I've never taken that curst ambertrop myself, but I'd heard that giving it up is awful and the second day is the worst."

She stopped talking. Danivid waited. Perhaps she needed a moment, but she didn't resume. "Was it the worst?"

"Yes."

He waited again, without success. "Velzain, the people I talk with in Regissa tell me that ambertrop is merely pleasant, without the side effects of wine."

"They're lying."

"At first usage, I think their words are true, so they may lie through ignorance. They will not tell me what it's like to break the addiction. They may not even know. Will you tell me?"

She let out a loud breath. "I already feel bad about what I've said so far. Besides that, I have siblings, too, and this is the last thing I'd want to hear if one of them died from that vile stuff!"

"Died from it? What do you mean?"

"Well...when I heard he died in his sleep, I assumed he went back to it...that it killed him."

Was there any chance that could be true? He considered. "No. I'm quite sure he stayed away from it. Letters aside, he took several actions. Difficult ones that he would have avoided if he was hiding from the truth with a drug." Danivid rested a hand over hers. "Actions that make me proud to call him brother. Be assured, what you witnessed of him here did not consume his final days."

She leaned back, drawing her hands to her lap. "I'm glad of that. Guess my effort wasn't wasted, after all."

"Not in the least. Tell me now, please."

"Well, in a way it was like I already said, except very much worse. By that evening, the shaking wracked his entire body, and it made his muscles cramp up. It almost looked like convulsions, though I don't think it was. All night long and the next day, it went on. He'd clutch his head or wrap his arms around himself...grip his torso or shoulders till I think he must have bruised himself. Maybe he was trying to stop the shaking, but I fancied he was losing himself and trying to hang on."

She blinked hard, looking away. "He sweated like a horse. It streamed from him so bad that I'd wipe him with towels. He guzzled tea, which I had to hold for him, but I could barely get him to accept food. He didn't say much beyond asking for tea. Toward evening, the shaking began to wane at times. I realized that if I could get him to talk during his better moments, it distracted him from the agony. Not much relief, but better than none.

"He fell asleep, and I went out to walk my horse and find her a new spot to tear bushes apart. When I came back, he was awake. Said he couldn't stand it anymore and wanted to know where his horse was. I refused to tell him. He tried everything from begging to threatening. Fortunately for him, I'm stubborn and the sun set while we argued. I convinced him that he couldn't go stumbling around in the dark."

She huffed. "He was so desperate, he actually intended that. In the morning, I tried convincing him the worst was over, which he didn't believe, but I persuaded him to stay one more day. It only worked because I pointed out that he was better while we argued. So he stayed. Arguing being rather tedious, I set myself to discover some other interest, then more or less coerced him through a day-long summary of Welcian history." Impish creases formed beside her eyes. "I gather princes are required to study that in detail."

Danivid forced a smile, hoping the rest of this would be more tolerable. "We are indeed. I trust that it was more interesting than argument."

"Far better." Her rather gloating smile accented her words. "Especially when I insisted on a thorough discussion of the substance gift histories from Dirklan. You know what I mean, right? About Devron and Fanteal saving Dirklan with their forming and wind weaving gifts?" When Danivid nodded, she continued. "It was only fair after he told me substance gifts were obsolete."

Danivid's mind flitted to the many derogatory remarks Chardomeer had flung at him, but he wouldn't allow the distraction. "Tell me the rest about my brother."

"There isn't much more to tell, for he improved from then on. Once he sounded rational and could get his own water and food, I spent nights in my own house. Obviously, I brought his horse back. When his dog arrived—a beautiful creature named Burnie—he said that meant people were looking for him. Lest things appear improper, we loaded everything I had brought onto my horse, and I hurried away to Land's End. That is the last I saw of him." She scrunched her nose. "Did rumors leak out that he'd been here with a woman?"

"I think not. I haven't heard a breath of it. You have my gratitude for tending his needs during such hard days."

"My duty and pleasure," she said in the customary manner. "You changed the subject when I talked about substance gifts."

She was bold. He couldn't help a smile. "On the contrary, *you* were changing the subject before finishing the first."

She lifted her chin and huffed.

"But now, O wind weaver, you may choose the subject."

"Do you think the forming and streaming gifts are obsolete?"

"No."

"What value do *you* see in them? I'm not asking about the fine detail gifts. Medics use those all the time, and artists do too. I mean the ability to search from afar. To alter. To move without machines and pumps."

She was asking more than what she fit into words—of that, he was sure. "Their *necessity* lies in the fact that machines fail. When they do, it is the gifted we turn to—those who remember how to care for and make use of our physical world."

He stroked a finger over his chin. "*Value,* however, goes beyond need. It is inherent within the gift itself. My gift is unusual, and while I find it pleasurable, I cannot deny that its purpose remains obscure. Yet I will never say that it has little or no value. To do so would be to set myself as a judge of Ellincreo, and declare his gifts flawed. But I must carry this a little farther, for Ellincreo also bestows life gifts, and some of them are inventive. I cannot call that gift flawed either. Thus, we will have machines. We might as well admit that we enjoy their benefits a great deal."

"Hmm. All true, and I don't hate machines and such. Trust me, I was *longing* for magnery here when all I had was an open fire for cooking and heat." He chuckled at her emphasis, but she continued. "Do you know what really bothers me?"

He shook his head.

"With the substance gifts...they're so powerful that, if any of us use our gift to harm someone, Ellincreo withdraws it. Gone forever. The life gifts can harm too. In fact, I think their capacity to harm is increasing. But the unscrupulous retain their gift. They can keep harming, over and over. Even if they realize their error and stop their part in it, whatever they invented, or discovered, or created, or set in motion..." She spread her hands wide. "Whatever the thing is—it goes on harming."

Her thoughts were as broad as her gift. "A valid observation," he said. "It doesn't make life easy, but we are responsible for what we allow."

"So the Holy Writ says. That is much easier to implement on the individual level. Much harder for society as a whole. There always seems to be some who say the bad stuff is good."

How rare to find someone who would delve into a subject like she did. It hadn't happened at the governor's party yesterday! "Are you talking about ambertrop?" he asked.

"That's one example. I'd never even heard of it as a child, and now it's out of control. But it's not always a *thing*."

"What do you mean?"

"It's hard to describe." She swayed her shoulders. "Like the formers and streamers allowing non-gifted into their guilds. And worse, Shevnal as the chief former, warping the guild's purpose. It's said that he rarely uses his gift. Instead, he is grasping up farmland. Of course, he has the right to buy, but the Growers' Guild is *furious* that they have no voice in the matter. Moreso, since the streamers diverted a canal to serve the buildings going up on his land." She tilted her head. "You look surprised."

It galled him to admit such, for he shouldn't be. "I meet with the guild chiefs, but they do not mention these concerns."

"Imagine that. I wonder what benefit they get from catering to Shevnal."

That was quite an accusation! "What is your source of information?"

"Wind weavers get around." She shrugged. "Not I—crowds, you know—but Chief Wind Weaver Cinnawa does. I do attend my own guild's meetings. That crowd welcomes, and we know how to talk."

How quickly her voice changed from discomfort to pleasure. "Does that mean you're going to talk about me?" he asked.

She held up her palms. "Hey, I know how to be discreet. I never said a word about your brother." She pushed her chair back. "But now that you mention it, I would *love* to say I felt your gift."

"Ah. You can sense gifts other than weaving?"

"I can. Will you indulge me? Reach into the ocean as I reach over it?"

He stood, realizing that an opportunity lay before him. "Of course. I want to sense the ocean from this angle anyway."

They walked out onto the porch. She leaned against a corner support and slipped an arm around it. Instantly, she went rapt. He may as well have vanished, but he didn't doubt she was waiting for him out there.

He slipped into his own gift, slicing his awareness through layers beneath the surface but also teasing the waves to brush the air she sensed.

Her laugh burst out like the wind. "There you are. Reach far, my lord king."

They continued for a few minutes. "This is the last of where I can flick the waves," he said, "but I'm still sensing."

"Yes," she murmured. "You're faint now. This is so unlike a streamer in a river—much wider."

"And deeper."

"How do you compare with Chief Former Chardomeer?"

"I can reach farther in a river, but he won't try a comparison for breadth and depth in the ocean."

"Is he afraid you'll best him?"

"No, he believes it's folly." Danivid altered his voice to repeat the chief streamer's words. "You cannot stream an ocean."

She laughed. "That sounds like him."

"A question for you," he said. "Have you felt the recent quakes on the peninsula?"

"Sure."

"Do you sense the wind over the ocean when the quakes occur?"

Her voice dropped. "I have, indeed."

"What did you notice?"

"Something dirties the air. Very broad and faint at first. I wasn't at all sure that it was even related to the quakes. But you know that last one…?" He nodded for her to continue. "There was a plume far out to sea. A lot of steam, but filthy with the kind of gases that come from a volcano."

"Did you report it?"

"I sent a wire to our guild hall. Chief Weaver Cinnawa is traveling, but I'm sure they relayed it on to her. Don't worry. It dispersed and wasn't even heading toward land. I'd send it away if it ever did."

The breeze had shifted, perhaps because of what she'd been doing, and she drew a breath into her nose. She pointed to the western trail. "Horses are coming."

Once again, worry hit. Friend or foe? If they were his own people searching for him, they would have brought Burnie. "Do me a favor and waft my scent toward them."

Seconds later, a distant *wa-woof* reached them.

"Is that your brother's dog?" she asked.

"The king's dog, yes. But I need to know something before they reach us. Where did the plume rise from?"

"Dip into the water. I'll show you."

He did so and sensed a trough she made with a whirlwind dancing above it. She kept it small, but sent it racing away in a straight line.

"You can feel this, right?"

"Absolutely." After a moment, he frowned. "I'm losing you. How much farther?"

"Hmm. I'll guess that you reached about ninety percent of the way. Hard to put a number on it though."

He spread out, reaching for shore to triangulate off the harbor headlands. There. "At least I will know where to look if we have another quake."

Burnie raced into sight and let out his success bark, then bounded onto the porch to rise and plop his dirty paws on Danivid's shoulders.

"Down, Burnie. We've discussed this. It hasn't been that many hours since you last saw me."

A moment later, the horses arrived, Meroak mounted on the first, with guards following.

Danivid smirked. "Ah, you decided to ride, after all."

"Not for pleasure." Meroak dismounted. His eyes flicked between Danivid and his companion.

"Meroak, are you acquainted with Wind Weaver Velzain?"

"No. Pleased to meet you, Velzain."

"This is my brother-in-law, Meroak."

"Sir Meroak." She turned to Danivid and curtsied. "I must be going, sir."

"I suppose. If you notice anything else concurrent with the quakes, send me word."

"Of course, sir." She hurried around the corner of the cottage.

Meroak pulled a pack from his horse. "I brought you a change of clothes."

"You rode all this way for that?"

Meroak crossed the porch and strode inside. "I came to make sure you were still alive. Also, you are needed at the palace. You have a guest." He threw the pack on the bed.

Danivid followed him and shut the door. "Who?"

"Lady Trellian of Felverland arrived with Allirae, right when a groom was explaining to me how you'd been thrown."

"That must have been awkward."

"Confoundedly!" Meroak untied the blind near the bed and let it drop. "Will you please get changed so we can leave?"

Danivid began pulling the curtain around the bed area, but Meroak took over, saying, "Allirae is beside herself with worry, you know."

"Fine. I'm hurrying." Danivid shrugged the borrowed coat off. Through the curtain, he asked, "Did you ever get a wire that she—they— were on their way?"

"Late and abbreviated. An hour before she arrived, but it only mentioned her. It wasn't the original text."

Danivid sneered. "So much for improved procedures at the relay huts."

"There's a lot more to it than that, but Allirae was so frantic to look for you, I didn't get details."

Danivid pulled on a fresh pair of riding breeches. "You don't mean Allirae is riding around searching for me, do you?"

"Not quite that bad, but she and Lady Trellian did ride the rail up to the stable. Don't worry. That guard you appointed, Gordin, won't budge from attendance on them. He and a few others. There are guards and stable hands on every trail in the woodland. We gave Burnie the scent from your horse's stall. He headed east, which was no surprise. I met a fellow who said you lunched with him, though I barely had time to hear that. Burnie isn't what you'd call patient when he's on a scent. Burnie, get down."

Meroak ran water, and a moment later the sound was replaced by Burnie's slurping. Danivid pushed the curtain aside and, buttoning his shirt, strode to the cottage's one small mirror for a quick look at his face and hair. Meroak closed the window, then picked up the ornate riding coat and held it open.

Danivid cocked an eyebrow before he turned to slide his arms into it. "Well, thanks, but you don't need to fill in for Yautan, you know."

"You might see more of me for a while. Apparently, my wife thinks I did a terrible job taking care of you today."

"Nonsense. What did she say?"

"It was more the tilted head and rounded eyes thing. I'm not sure if she is more upset that you *weren't* there or that I *was* there when you weren't."

"I'll let you know," Danivid said drily, "if I ever assign you the role of bodyguard."

Meroak shoved the discarded clothes into the pack. "After today, you had better assign a few men to that role. Whatever was under that saddle, it didn't get there by accident. But off you go, riding alone. Allirae may be *over*reacting, but you are *under*reacting."

Trellian stared Police Captain Narwick down. It only made him bluster more and repeat that the king was safe. "Yes," she murmured. "I see you are protecting him quite well."

A nasty glint flickered in his eye for a second, but he opted to ignore her. "Lady Allirae, I assure you there is—"

"Oh, stop assuring me. I'll believe you when you capture that Durki creature. Which seems unlikely, since you waited hours to arrive and still have not initiated a search. Be about your business." She started toward the stable. "Jonger, come with me."

"Yes, lady."

Allirae waited until she was out of hearing range of any police. "Take us to Durki's quarters."

Exactly what Trellian wanted.

His room was above the stable, facing the wooded hills. They traversed a covered walkway that passed several windows and doors. Jonger stopped at one and inserted a key into the lock. Smart enough to take simple precautions.

"Has anyone been inside since Durki disappeared?" Trellian asked.

"Just me," Jonger said. "I showed the police captain, but he didn't do more than glance around from the doorway and say it looked like the man had left. Clever fellow, aye?"

Trellian's chest shook. "Clever at playing the fool, perhaps."

Jonger pointed to the floor under the table. "There's sawdust in the corners. Bangers are packed in it, although we do have a wood pile. He could have tracked it in on his boots if he didn't leave them outside like usual. It looks to me like he swept before he left."

"Not everywhere," Allirae murmured, lifting a sheet to peer under the bed.

Trellian bent and picked up a scrap of something. Stiff wood but almost as thin as paper. "What's this?"

"Wood wafer," Jonger said. "Folks who like whittling trim them off waste wood. Children build models and such from them. Decent kindling too." He nodded toward the magnery heater. "Though he wouldn't need that in here."

Insignificant. "He didn't leave us obvious clues," Trellian said. "Let's look behind the furniture, shall we?"

The dresser and bed yielded nothing, but where a table leg pressed against a wall, another wood wafer had stuck between them. And this one had a burn mark.

"Ah." Jonger took it to inspect closer. "Looks to me like he might have tested how he could get them bangers to pop. I've been wondering about that, since horsehair and a blanket didn't seem to give the right sort of friction."

Trellian pulled a blank sheet of paper from her portfolio and swept the dust from behind the table legs unto it. She sniffed. A powdery, chemical smell almost made her sneeze. She added the wafers to the paper and folded it to contain the material. Not the best way to hide her expertise, but she couldn't leave evidence.

"Riders are coming down the hill," Allirae said from the doorway, providing a fortunate distraction. She stood on tiptoe and craned her neck. Her pitch rose. "Oh, yes. There they are."

That joyous lilt couldn't be for just any riders. Trellian stepped outside to join her on the walkway, while Jonger locked up and strode off. Two uniformed guards rode well in the lead. Of the next two men, she recognized Meroak's clothes. "Is that the king with your husband?"

"Yes." Allirae pressed a hand to her chest. "Oh, I'm so relieved!"

Odd. It seemed improbable that another attempt could have been planned already. Perhaps losing her eldest brother a month ago made her too anxious. Or was there something else that she hadn't revealed to Trellian? From the corner of her eye, she noticed Allirae turn to her.

"Why do you watch so intently. What are you thinking?"

Trellian remembered to smile. "The king is a fine rider. Oh, there's the dog. You were right about his tracking abilities."

T rellian's introduction to the king was not what she had expected. Granted, they were in a stable yard instead of the palace. The king's ornate riding coat failed to make up for it. Wasn't a king supposed to have some grandeur in his bearing? Not that anything was wrong with it, but he carried himself like any fit man. He responded to the greeting she'd practiced, then apologized for being away when she arrived.

Kings apologized for that? "Uh, no matter. I gather something went wrong with the wires."

"We'll hope that's all it is," he said drily, then gestured for her to walk with him. "Do you ride, lady, or is this just a smelly barn to you?"

"Yes, I do ride—and enjoy it enough to forgive the horses for their odor."

"I must make amends with a certain horse. Would you like to accompany me inside?"

"Please."

The thudding hooves of a horse being led through the stable held all the beauty of a drummer on parade. Trellian preferred that mellow beat to brassy instruments. There were few horses within, but Burnie ran ahead to a stall and stood up with one forepaw on the half door. A nose appeared above it, and the dog licked it.

"Now, there is an unusual friendship," Trellian said.

The king chuckled. "Not entirely. They are known as the king's horse and the king's dog. My brother's before mine, so they have shared many trails. That is the first horse I mounted this morning. Did you hear what happened?"

"That something was placed under the saddle, which burned for an instant, causing him to throw you."

"Not very pleasant for either of us," he said. "I fear he'll blame me, and don't want to put off a gentle touch."

"Nor would I." She waited a couple yards away as he used his voice, and the shared friendliness with Burnie, to woo the horse back to the half door.

With his goal accomplished, the king returned to escort her from the stable. "My thanks for your patience." They left through the door opposite where they'd entered, and he glanced westward. "Time we were heading down."

Meroak had an arm around Allirae, whose smile was quite different from the polished expression she'd used in Felverland. A relief that her tension was forgotten. Plenty of guards stood around, anyway. The king showed Trellian to a forward seat in the glass-fronted rail car, which afforded her stunning views during the descent to Regissa City and the palace. She couldn't drag her eyes from the sparkling water. "The ocean is magnificent!"

"Indeed. This portion is the harbor." He pointed. "Along the shore there, is the port." He told her the headland names, and with sweeping gestures, described where the easternmost strip of land poked into the ocean. "Called either Land's End or World's End, depending on your persuasion."

"Land's End would be the most accurate," she replied. "I understand there is a tunnel to Dirklan nearby. Where is that?"

He pointed again. "About halfway along the peninsula."

"Is that where you were riding?"

"I was in the woodland, which dwindles to the bare rock of the peninsula."

"Must one ride to reach the tunnel?"

"Oh, no. There is a rail spur to it, with a different sort of rail for the steep parts within the tunnel. It mostly carries imports and exports, though passenger carriages are available."

"I am quite intrigued about how you accomplish underground, er, *below*ground living. Allirae described it, but she tells me I still don't have the right image."

"I will take you to visit, if you like."

"I would."

They reached the palace, and this arrival fit Trellian's expectations more than her first entrance. She had time to take in the stunning mural in the grand hall, and the staff hostess waited to show her to her room.

As Trellian began mounting the stairs, the king said, "Allirae, a moment in my study."

Danivid closed the door. "Who is Lady Trellian, and why is she here?"

Allirae pressed stiff fingers to the side of her head. "Oh, what a week it has been." She frowned through a moment of thought. "I'll start with my arrival in Qualketeen City." She launched into a rapid-fire summary as she settled into her favorite chair.

Danivid joined her near the window, listening intently. Provided she was given a moment to collect her thoughts, Allirae could report concise detail with far more clarity than most. He soon had the gist of the tentative agreement reached with Prime Minister Starroni, the ambertrop smuggling issues, and the dangers at the border.

He slid his finger back and forth below his lip. "They think we are the primary cause of ambertrop traffic, and we think they are. Only a mutual effort will stop it, but before they commit, they want one of their own people to confirm we are serious about stopping it."

"Yes."

He let his tone convey disbelief. "So...they sent a police officer instead of an ambassador?"

"Detective may be a more accurate description. Perhaps there is more to the prime minister's reason for assigning her. We talked half the night on our journey home, but I would be surprised if I've gotten to the bottom of her goals." She glanced at the clock. "Nearly dinner."

"I know. I agree that—"

A tap on the door preceded Yautan's entrance. "Forgive me for interrupting, sir, but there is very little time for you to change before dinner."

"I will be up soon." Danivid waited for the door to close. "I agree that we should describe Trellian's visit only as reopening diplomatic relations with Felverland. Nothing else is to be said in the presence of anyone but ourselves."

"You don't mean I should hide it from Meroak, do you?"

"No, of course not."

"My aide knows," Allirae said, "but she will never tell. Gordin has already promised secrecy. The other guards are aware that we took precautions on the journey, but they've been told not to discuss even that much."

"The group who knows seems small enough." He stood. "I *might* discuss it with Stanton, if necessary."

She rose and strolled across the room at his side. "Why him?"

"A puzzling imbalance of money."

CHAPTER 16

Danivid chanced to leave his room at about the same moment that the staff directed Trellian toward the staircase. Since she approached it opposite him, he had an excellent view of her. The dress she wore reached her ankles in back, with an overlapping cutaway in front. She carried herself with rare grace, but her stride was longer than most women's. It seemed to portray an extra aura of confidence. Perhaps nothing more than long legs.

He waited for her atop the stairs, looking almost straight into her eyes, as he would a man. He tried to imagine her in trousers and a hat, as Allirae had described the so-called brother. Difficult. Trellian wore her hair down, draping in gentle waves past her shoulders. Lighter shades emphasized the warmth of her brown locks. A rare trait, and therefore, much admired.

He smiled a welcome and offered his arm. "May I escort you downstairs?"

"Thank you." She slid her hand onto his arm.

Thus began their entrance to the dining room and a formal dinner. None in the foursome went near discussing matters of state, so his staff would have nothing more interesting to report than Felverland's geography and popular entertainments.

On the way to the salon afterward, Allirae said, "Danivid, I heard you had a dinner engagement while I was gone."

"Ah, the subtle messaging within palace walls."

She chuckled as her husband opened the salon door for the ladies. "My source didn't know where. Who hosted it?"

"Governor and Lady Rikion." To Trellian, he added, "He is the governor of Regissa Province."

"I thought that was the name of the city."

Danivid sat down facing the brocade couch. "Welcia's capital city and the province share that name."

"I suppose," Allirae said, taking a place on the couch, "he had to be first, squeezing it in right before our month of formal mourning ended. Did he manage to keep it proper?"

"Quite. The guest list included nobles and elected officials. Dinner was served in the extended style."

Trellian settled into a satin-covered chair. "Does that mean something other than long?"

"The meal is the entertainment," Danivid explained. "The courses are spread out through the evening. The dining tables are small, and one switches tables between courses." He turned an ironic smile toward Allirae. "The governor even provided me with an escort—other than his wife."

"So...not quite proper then?"

"Close. His wife started as my escort, while the governor had a cousin at his side—who was soon at *my* side instead of Lady Rikion. Someone named Lady Zendell. She's such a close cousin that I'd never met her at the entertainments the Rikions hosted while I visited aboveground. I understand her husband died a couple years ago."

"Ah, yes." Allirae flashed a teasing smile at him. "A beautiful, wealthy widow for you. How convenient that she happens to be one of his cousins—somehow or another—and not *too* much older than you."

"Blatant." Meroak joined his wife on the couch. "She and Shevnal invariably find time to chat at parties."

"True for years," Allirae replied, "but Shevnal makes the round of everyone rich or influential at such events. Joking aside, Danivid—Lady Zendell is eligible."

"You are mistaken, dear sister. She served herself from the ambertrop flask."

His sister made a noise in her throat, but Trellian straightened. "What do you mean?"

"A recent change," Danivid said, adding dryly to Allirae and Meroak, "which I only discovered an hour before I left for the party, thanks to Yautan."

Allirae covered her mouth with her hand, and Meroak said, "Didn't you know? I'm sure you've attended parties here in the past year or so."

Allirae laid a hand on his arm. "Oh, but not everyone serves it, dear." Her gaze on Danivid couldn't have been more earnest and worried. "They are to *say* something, though—make it clear what the beverage contains."

"My hostess did mention it at the first table. Thereafter, the amber-colored flask was passed around the table without comment."

"Are you saying," Trellian demanded, "that an ambertrop beverage is served at parties?"

"At some," Danivid replied. "Two provinces forbid it, but Regissa is not one of them. Those who disapprove would not serve it, and I imagine that only the wealthy could afford to do so at a large gathering."

"And you tolerate this?"

He held his gaze steady on her. "While it is *legal*, I will tolerate it." He let those words hang for a moment. "I will not drink of it myself, but I will observe who does. That is useful information, for it tells me who will oppose my efforts to rid Welcia of this curse."

Though she didn't reply, the veiled look of her eyes revealed a hint of her opinion.

"Why did you come here, Lady Trellian?"

"Didn't your ambassador tell you?"

"I want to hear it from you."

She tilted her head. "To see what *I* could learn, and to see what *you* need to learn."

"Succinct." Apparently, she took that as a compliment, for she acknowledged with a nod, interrupted by his next word. "Vague." Was that humor in her still face? She was hard to read.

"The context," she said, "is amber."

"You shorten the word, I gather?"

"Yes. You see, *ambertrop* sounds much like *amber trap*, an alteration that was used when my people began fighting its incursion into our society. Those who resisted started using only the gem portion of the word."

"You do too, it seems."

"The term is still apt. The gem amber is created when plant resin solidifies over time. Some rare specimens contain an insect that was trapped within the resin and forever bound in its precious coffin."

An evocative word picture. "It's a gem not found in our mines. What are its properties?"

"A golden hue. Not suitable for cutting, but fine specimens are clear when polished. Not that it has anything to do with the drug. *Trop* is an old word for *plant*. Ambertrop literally means *yellow plant*."

"Ironically benign. Is this plant the source of the drug?"

"Yes, from the dried leaves."

He grimaced. "Does this mean that the plant could be grown here if Felverland ceased providing it?"

"No." She glanced around their three intent faces. "I assume you know our land stretches far north. Amber only grows at the farthest reaches. Our agriculturalists have proven not only that the seeds need a long, hard freeze before they sprout, but also that strong sunlight kills the plants. Our northern reaches get only weak sun between frequent summer fogs."

"At least that much is good news," Meroak said.

Danivid thought further. "Limited supply increases the price."

"Indeed," Trellian replied. "When Felverland outlawed it, the supply was further limited. Having also lost much of their demand, dealers focused on the newer demand in Welcia. We had asked your predecessor to close your border to it, sir. The initial ascent was not followed by action. That wasn't you, of course, but I hope you understand our doubts of Welcia's current assertions."

"I don't see any point in discussing who was at fault in the past. The current situation is a high-priced product in short supply. Yet ample enough for willing hosts to serve it as freely as wine. How is that possible?"

"What they serve is mostly fruit juice," Allirae said. "I believe it contains very little ambertrop. Not enough to taste or smell, which is why it's served in a gold-toned flask and is to be clearly identified."

"Even if it was a high dose," Trellian said, "you wouldn't notice. Amber has no taste or scent."

"None at all?" Danivid asked.

She shrugged. "None to a human. The few creatures who live up north leave it alone. I don't know how they identify it."

"Allirae told me you have a substance to test food for ambertrop."

"Yes, but of limited value. It will froth up for too many plants. Even fresh pinnpear. If we relied on that, our food supply would become terribly limited and bland."

Danivid propped an elbow on the armrest. "I still believe the dose was weak at that party. One thing I watched for was a change in behavior in those who used it. Granted, I do not know them well, but I could discern no hint that they were on anything I would call a drug."

"What would you call a drug?"

"Oh...some stuff a medic gave me when I dislocated a shoulder. It eased the pain and made me groggy. I slept like a rock and woke with a headache."

She smiled. "I think I had some of that drug once. Doesn't tempt you to use more, though, does it?"

"Not at all."

"Amber isn't like that. It induces calm. One can still speak clearly and think, though judgment is skewed. Life becomes a gentle pleasure, and it is impossible to worry. No danger would disturb. Temporary, of course, but quite alluring."

"Have you used it?"

"No. However, I cultivated a few friendships with people who did. At the time, it was still legal and—technically—we were adults." Her low voice dipped further. "Not old enough to spare me once my parents found out." She seemed to shake off a bad memory. "I only associated with them to learn what I was about to fight. It wasn't likely to entice me, for I would rather charge into a fray than doze through fake bliss." She shifted in the chair again. "Not that my mother was any happier to hear that I was leaving art studies and, in particular, which fight I was joining."

"To get rid of ambertrop, you mean?" Allirae asked.

"Yes. Abstaining, she required. Active fighting was too much for her."

"Why?"

Trellian looked at Allirae for a moment. "It's people like me who get killed by the dealers."

"Not just your sort," Danivid said. "The queen's maid was killed after she was dismissed."

Trellian's brows rose. "More information, please."

Danivid considered her. She already knew some of their troubles from Allirae. It had been necessary to account for past mistakes if they were going to get help from Felverland. But how far did he want to take it? If what she said was true, she could be a great asset. If she hid something...what could it be? Her prime minister trusted her. He could think of nothing Felverland would gain by betraying Welcian trust. One thing was true. There seemed to be no way she could be involved in the corruption plaguing Regissa. Cooperating with her seemed less risky than not cooperating.

Danivid lowered his fingertip from his chin. "She purchased ambertrop on behalf of the queen. She may have supplied the late king, too. The queen's parents took their daughter home, where she cannot obtain the drug. Her father wanted me to permanently dismiss the maid. Which I did, after questioning her. Not that I learned much, for she was terrified of her supplier. Next thing I heard of her, she was dead. The police have no leads to a killer."

A hint of contempt crept into her words. "Would this be the same police who are investigating your so-called accident this morning?"

"They don't impress you either?"

A huff escaped her thin nose. "What else have they failed to discover?"

"Who sabotaged a small sailing vessel my brother used for pleasure."

She straightened. "Is that how he died?"

"No. A streamer chanced to see the boat sink. She got the occupants to shore, and then the vessel itself. Intentional damage, no arrest. My brother died in his sleep a couple days later.

"Any possibility that he died of a natural cause?"

"He was thirty-five, in robust health. He'd been free of ambertrop for two months. There was no sign of a struggle. Medics couldn't determine the cause of death."

"How has this been investigated?"

"*Pff,*" Allirae scoffed. "Nothing beyond asking the medics their opinion!"

Trellian spread her hands. "Wait. Was this led by that Captain Narwick I met today?"

"It was," Danivid said. "Obviously, I intend to get rid of him, but other members of the police are suspect. I cannot risk replacing him with another corrupt officer. Despite their failures, I doubt the police are the primary source of the problem."

"Who do you think is primary?"

"Those who benefit from the import of ambertrop."

"And who is that?"

"Several people have a great deal more money than seems accountable. There are few people I trust, but fortunately, my steward is one of them. He is trying to ferret out some financial information for me." He toyed for a moment with telling her of his own family's losses. Maybe someday, but not tonight.

After a moment, Trellian said, "This is an interesting puzzle. I wasn't expecting police work, at least not of this sort."

"What sort did you expect?"

"I was hoping to glimpse smugglers. Either to capture likenesses of Welcian smugglers or to recognize Felvarians in your country." She shrugged. "The risks associated with reaching the palace alive outweighed my desire to watch luggage handlers on the Welcian side."

She glanced around their faces again. "I have to admit, I find some things strange about the probable murder of a king—which wasn't investigated. Would you mind if I ask some questions?"

Danivid smirked at his sister before he answered Trellian. "What? Do you want our alibis?"

"We can start there, before we discuss motives." She tilted her head, and a rare smile appeared. "I have to ask, but yes, I do see both the awkwardness and the humor."

Interesting. "I was in Dirklan the night he died," Danivid said. "I was here the week before, so if you suspect an accomplice, I could have arranged it then."

"Oh? With whom?"

"I have no idea."

"Figured as much." She turned to the couch. "How about you two?"

"We were here," Allirae said. "Asleep in our suite. We are one another's alibi. Does that make us both suspect?"

"Can either of you sneak out of bed without waking the other?"

Meroak smirked. "I can. My wife has no idea how often I sneak off for a clandestine trip to the priv."

Allirae produced a fake shudder. "Ominous."

"You may want all the attention, Meroak," Danivid said, "but I have a far better motive." To Trellian, he said, "My brother summoned me to the palace a week before he died, so he could tell Allirae and me of his new will. He had designated me as his successor."

"Your one mistake, though," she countered, "is trying to kill yourself after you killed your brother to get his crown."

He uttered a bitter laugh. If she knew what a mess Vancent had left him, that might look like suicide. He snarked, "Oh quakes, I've gone and ruined my story!" He let the mirth he didn't feel slide. "We'll quit the nonsense. The three of us know that Vancent, Allirae, and I have always loved one another, as well as being good friends. None of us would kill the other. All the drama in our family came from Lenneth, but she couldn't inherit the crown. I absolutely did not want to become king, but we must talk about that will."

"Do tell."

"In normal circumstances, the crown is inherited by the king's eldest child. Has Allirae told you about Vancent and Lenneth's daughter?"

Trellian nodded. "A silent child."

"Pardon?"

"That's what they are called in Felverland. Born to amber users far more often than to non-users."

Danivid looked at her from beneath lowered brows. "Is there proof that the condition is *caused* by ambertrop?"

"There may be other, rarer, causes, but amber is involved in most cases."

Allirae moaned. "Ugh, may Lenneth never hear such a thing. It would absolutely crush her."

Trellian's lips tightened. "Let's not tell anyone. We wouldn't want to make them *feel* bad. Far better to let ignorance injure more children."

"I didn't say *that*," Allirae snapped.

Trellian didn't flinch. "I have lived through a contentious change that lurks in your future. Pursue it, and you will be accused of 'making people feel guilty.' Here is the fact. Guilt pursues the foolish. They hide from it inside lies, and they hate those who speak truth."

"Great," Danivid said. "I'll be hated. Do you want to hear about the will or not?"

She brought her gaze back to his face and answered in her straightforward manner. "Yes."

"When Vancent got free of his own lies, he acknowledged that Aneen would never be fit to rule, and that his chances of a normal child were slim. He appointed me as successor in his new will. Key people knew of this, but he had not yet made the formal announcement to the High Council when he died."

"Who specifically knew?"

"We three." He flipped a hand toward his sister and brother-in-law. "To my knowledge, the lawyer who drafted the will, the steward I mentioned, and the Chief Keeper of the Writ, who also held one copy of the will. Also, Lenneth, though she denied knowing it."

"Did—"

He stopped her question with a raised hand. "Uncertainty in the crown causes turmoil. Hence, Allirae and I decided to hold my coronation the day after our brother's funeral. On the evening between the funeral and my coronation, Queen Lenneth ordered arrangements to crown her daughter on the terrace here. Before you assume this indicates a motive for murdering King Vancent, you should know that she loved her husband and hates nothing more than matters of state. She cannot handle difficult circumstances, and it is *unimaginable* that she could murder her husband."

"Yet she could order coronation arrangements the night of his funeral?"

He shrugged. "If she had someone to lean on, yes. Shevnal, in this case. I had stepped away for a private moment. Allirae and the chief keeper were delaying matters. When I arrived, I tried to calm Lenneth. Her words were not entirely rational—as though the next day's coronation was for Aneen. She said crowds are bad for her—true—and that it would be better to crown the child there with fewer witnesses. When I mentioned the will, she acted as though she didn't know its contents, but I know from my brother that she did."

"I gather you convinced her to stop the coronation?"

"There was no reasoning with her. The Chief Keeper of the Writ had brought his copy of the will. I had him read the succession article aloud, then he crowned me before the assembled witnesses. We still held the public coronation the next day, because the realm needed certainty."

"The name Shevnal has been mentioned twice. Who is he?"

"The Chief Former of Welcia."

Surprise flavored Trellian's voice. "There is a chief former for the entire country?"

"Yes, the provincial chief formers answer to him."

"Provincial chiefs, too? We don't have a layered hierarchy for the substance gifts in Felverland. How significant is that here?"

"Very." Danivid said. "The top position is powerful for all three substance guilds."

"Enough so that he could be part of coronation proceedings?"

"No, but he has long been a friend to both Vancent and Lenneth."

Meroak snorted. "Don't leave out that he is presumptuous and arrogant."

"In the extreme!" Danivid said with lifted brows. "By law, he is under the authority of Ellincreo and the king. He doesn't acknowledge

Ellincreo's existence, and when Aneen hid in Allirae's cloak, Shevnal urged Lenneth to be crowned as proxy for her daughter."

"You realize, I assume, that if he can control Lenneth, he has a motive for murder."

"I despise the man," Danivid said, "for personal and political reasons, but I must point out the flaws in that theory."

"I'm listening."

"Shevnal had undue influence over my brother. He continued it with ease while Vancent was alive, but he lost it all the night Vancent died."

Trellian took only a second to counter. "If he believed the child was heir to the throne, he may not have considered it lost. Or Lenneth, perhaps. They may have worked together, for similar or different reasons."

Danivid shook his head. "I still cannot imagine Lenneth in the role of murderer. Shevnal had too much freedom in the palace, but he wouldn't have been here overnight. The morning after the coronation, Lenneth summoned him. He left on bad terms with her. He seemed to regret having come at all."

Trellian considered for a moment. "Allirae told me that the queen's parents took her to their home, and they hope to free her from amber. That rarely works if a person is unwilling. Do you know how she fares?"

Discomfort wormed through him. The unresolvable conflict between her right to choose destruction and his concern for her true wellbeing. "Her father writes me every week. Abstaining caused her intense anguish for a week. She is physically stable now, but longs for the drug amid mourning her husband." He sighed. "In case it sounds like she's awful, in truth, she is a kind and charming woman when life doesn't hand her a disaster."

Trellian didn't respond. She watched Allirae, who looked miserable while Meroak rubbed her hand. Aneen's dog yipped outside the door. Allirae straightened and achieved a faint smile. "I suspect I've been *found*."

The door opened, and Aneen walked in clutching Cam's harness as they completed the find command and praise. Burnie rose to greet Cam, and Allirae hugged Aneen. "I'm so happy to be home and see you again."

Aneen remained pressed against her aunt's side, eyeing Trellian.

"We have a guest," Allirae said. "Her name is Trellian. She will stay with us for a while. Lady Trellian, this is Aneen."

"Hello," Trellian said. Aneen stared at her, which bothered some, but Trellian showed no discomfort. "You have a pretty dog."

Aneen stared a moment longer, then tugged on her aunt's hand. "Al'rae come. Bed."

"Yes, dear, I'll come and tuck you in."

Meroak followed them from the room, and Burnie returned to Danivid's side.

"These dogs," Trellian said, "are remarkably well trained."

"The urge to search is inherent in the Flyound breed. King Vancent bought some breeding stock because Aneen can be very hard to keep track of." He smiled. "The irony is that Aneen chose one for herself and taught it to find everyone she likes."

"There is often debate about the silent children. They know more than they speak, but no one is ever sure how much more."

"Probably varies with every child." He drew a breath and steeled himself for the answer he didn't want to hear. "I assume you have experience of older silent children. Do they ever grow out of it?"

She shook her head. "Sorry, no."

"It didn't seem likely."

"May I ask another question?"

"Haven't you dragged out enough dirt for one night?"

"It's not dirty. Who is your heir?"

"Allirae—until I have a child. Hence the reason for her tease. I must marry and shall doubtless be invited to a great many parties, now that the formal month of mourning has ended. Are you planning to accuse my sister of plotting to kill me?"

"I find her alibi for the horse incident quite convincing."

He chuckled. "I imagine so."

"Who inherits after your sister?"

"A cousin. I have several of them. They came for the funeral and coronation, but not for the murder—if that's what it was."

"You are correct that it's not proven. Would you allow me to see where your brother died?"

"Do you realize that you just asked to search *my* bedchamber?"

"I was afraid of that."

He laughed again. "But you're not withdrawing the request. Come with me, then." He led her upstairs, and when they reached the bedroom floor, he said, "There are multiple ways into the king's bedroom." He tapped a door as he passed it. "This one is to my dressing room. It's kept locked." He opened the next door, motioned her into the room, then leaned against the door frame. "Dressing room and priv to the right. The door on the left is to a sitting room that adjoins the queen's bedroom."

"If I may just peek into the rooms?"

"Of course." She kept her look into the dressing room and priv brief. By the time she returned, Danivid had retrieved keys from the desk.

She addressed Burnie, who had cocked his ears. "Oh, stop staring at me. I'm not being indiscreet."

Danivid hid a grin as he turned a thumb lock on the sitting room door and passed through it. "I believe my brother and his wife used this room frequently." Strolling across it, he pointed to the corridor entrance. "I keep that door locked." She checked the handle as she passed it, but he continued to the queen's door and turned the key in the lock. Depressing to step inside.

Trellian followed him. "It has a deserted feel."

"I've kept this locked since the day I dismissed the maid. She was in here stripping the bed. After I sent her away, I searched but found nothing unusual."

Burnie must disagree, for his nose was in the air. He sniffed the bed.

"Looking for his mistress?" Trellian asked.

"I doubt it. Lenneth likes people far more than animals. The maid was afraid of dogs, and Burnie was never allowed in here." Burnie trotted to the dresser, sniffed along the edges of a drawer, and growled deep in his throat. "Well, isn't that interesting."

"What?"

"One thing I did learn from the maid was where Lenneth stored ambertrop. The drawer Burnie is sniffing." He pulled the drawer open. Still empty, but Burnie started barking. Wow. "Calm down, boy." He held Burnie's collar and stroked his head. "That's how he acted when the maid tried to leave the room. I had to hold onto him to let her out. Of course, dogs know who doesn't like them and tend to reciprocate."

"True." Trellian looked over the rest of the suite and checked the locked doors.

They left, and Danivid relocked the sitting room doors. In his own room again, he asked, "Any observations?"

"The suite seems designed to allow easy access for a murderer."

"Oddly enough," he said with brittle irony, "there isn't a single such event in the House de Noviam's history."

"Strange. The constant vying for the throne was what brought about the downfall of Felverland's monarchy."

"Welcia's monarchy was never totalitarian. That could have saved us some bloodshed."

"Mm. I know the layout now, but nothing else. What did *you* notice about these rooms after your brother died?"

Burnie stood erect, ears cocked to the door, and a whistle reached them. "Go," Danivid said. The dog shot from the room. Danivid glanced at Trellian's surprised expression and said, "The kennel master tends to him at morning and evening."

"Ah."

"To answer your question, there was nothing obvious when I arrived and viewed my brother's body. That was late morning, so some hours had passed since his death. Later, I went through the room in more detail. The desk contained a few letters written to him, and plenty of blank paper and pens, but nothing written in his hand. He used to jot rough notes when he read anything extensive or while he was thinking through an issue."

"Did he always save them?"

"Only while they still mattered. Not so much as a list remains."

"Hmm. As for letters he wrote, wouldn't he have mailed them?"

"His aides would have copied most and mailed the originals. They do have such records. But I know for certain that he wrote at least one letter to your prime minister. I doubt he would have entrusted that to an aide. He would absolutely have kept a copy. None exists here. No aide admits to knowledge of such a letter."

"I wondered," she said, "if his death could be related to his new stance on amber. That now seems more probable."

"I—" A tremor interrupted him. "Another quake. Do I not have enough to worry about!" He strode to a window and opened it. "Excuse me, please. I must focus on the ocean."

She hurried to the door but must have turned back in the corridor. "Aren't you...don't we need to go outside?"

"You are welcome to do so." Already the tremor subsided, but still he reached toward the epicenter that Velzain had shown him. The deep water carried vibration, which ceased, but was there a higher surge? It took several minutes before he felt it. Nothing threatening, but it spread toward Welcia. He studied it all the way to the surface. Was Velzain sensing? No doubt. The memory of her nudged a smile to his lips.

There was nothing much left for him to sense now, so he drew his awareness inward to the immediate surroundings. Someone stood in the corridor—he sensed the flowing blood. He turned—Trellian lingered beyond his door. "Decided to brave the quake indoors?"

"The tremor ceased...that and the fact that you found no need to leave."

"I needed to confirm something I learned today, which is nigh impossible while running through a palace. The epicenter is in the ocean basin, and I wanted to study how it affected water movement. True, this quake wasn't much, but I should warn you that I may not be the best person to copy. My brother-in-law thinks I'm foolhardy."

"Oh? How so?"

"We were walking one evening along the clifftop colonnade when a quake hit. Worse than this one. I went nearer to the cliff edge as I sensed the ocean. Which Meroak found quite appalling!"

"Were you at risk of falling?"

"Only because the quake made him stumble into me. That was a tense moment, but I had an arm around one of the columns, so no harm done. He dragged me away, then ranted at me for lingering within the colonnade."

She stared at him so long that he felt uncomfortable. Did she think him stupid for trusting Meroak? Or was that his own guilt for those few seconds when he hadn't? Absurd. "Did you have other questions?"

"No. Not tonight, anyway."

CHAPTER 17

Trellian went down to the dining room for breakfast, pleased with herself for finding it without help. It was empty. As in, no sign of preparation or of a finished meal. Ugh.

Footsteps approached in the corridor. She would have to ask, after all.

A staff member stepped into view and gave her a polite smile. "Are you looking for breakfast?"

"I am."

"It's served in the morning room. I'll show you."

The woman led the way to the opposite side of the palace, where she gestured to an open door before departing. Trellian entered to find her three hosts already present. Naturally. This rabbit warren was familiar to them.

"Pleasant morning," the king said. He sat sideways to the windows, in the shade of a heavy curtain, half closed to block the sunlight that bathed most of the room.

"Good morning," she replied in the Felvarian style. "Sorry I'm late."

"You're not." Allirae wiped her fingertips on a napkin. "Breakfast is served informally, whenever it's convenient for you to come down."

Informal? A full place-setting of elegant porcelain, including glasses of juice and milk, herbed butter beside a bread plate, and a dainty cream and sugar set beside her cup. Trellian sat across from Meroak, as a server asked her, "Would you like coffee or tea, lady?"

"Coffee, please."

Allirae and Meroak appeared to be finished, but the king was still consuming meat and eggs. That seemed rather heavy, but there was a fruit plate, plus baskets of bread—some coiled, some sliced and toasted.

This being Savoring Day, the relaxed conversation wove around how to enjoy it, though the king contributed little. Would their customs be similar to Felverland's? As for the morning, set aside to honor Ellincreo, there seemed to be two options. Either a public gathering or meeting with smaller groups of family and friends.

Allirae gave her brother an odd look when he said he'd skip the public gathering. "Is it because of what happened while riding yesterday?" she asked.

He stared at her for a moment, then laughed. "Oh, that. Not at all."

Someone brought in an envelope, which he presented to the king. "This just arrived from Former Rebanak, sir."

The king pointed to the table. The man placed it there and left as the king cut another bite of meat. After swallowing his food, he asked about Aneen.

"She always slips right back into her routine after I return." Allirae's brow kept twitching with slight frowns. "Aren't you going to read that?"

"It doesn't matter."

Allirae leaned back and cleared her frown as she addressed the server. "Thank you. We won't need anything else. You may leave for the day." The young man departed, closing the door behind him. "*Now*, will you read it?"

Her brother reached for some butter. "Read what?"

"The note from Rebanak."

"I'm sure it's just the formers' report on the quake last evening."

She stared at him again. A look of realization coalesced on her features, her eyes widening in horror. "Danivid!" she hissed. "You're using ambertrop."

His knife stilled against the toast he held, and he laughed in a puzzled fashion.

She slapped the table. "How could you?"

"Allie, did you leave your mind in Felverland?"

"My mind is perfectly fine. Where is yours?"

Meroak, looking as surprised as the king, though more concerned, laid a hand on her arm. "My dear, calm down. I really don't think—"

"How can you not see this?" she snapped, turning on him. "He has zero interest in what we do today. He doesn't want to attend service. He's forgotten that his life has been threatened. He has no interest in a quake report."

Though Meroak seemed to be trying to grasp something illusive, the king dropped the bread and knife onto his plate and leaned back in his chair. "Allie, I would never, not for any reason, put that vile stuff in my mouth."

Tears slipped from her eyes. "Look at you. Listen to yourself. I just accused you of taking ambertrop, and you sit there like I uttered some triviality."

"This is breakfast. A day of rest. Why should I get upset over sheer nonsense?"

The changing expressions on Meroak's face told Trellian more than their ongoing argument. He'd paled. His eyes darted to-and-fro as though he sought something hidden on the tablecloth. He clutched the table, and for a second, Trellian thought he was about to leap up and run. Though he eased back, his frown deepened. What was he trying to figure out—or concoct?

"It...must have...happened gradually," Meroak murmured behind Allirae's rant.

He still seemed to be reassembling pieces. Of what, though? Trellian had only known the king for a matter of hours. He *was* different than last night...yet some people did start off slow in the morning.

"But, Danivid," Meroak said, interrupting the exchange between brother and sister, "you *are* acting different than...than when you first returned."

"You mean the day my brother died? You consider *that* my normal behavior?"

"No. I'm just saying that I see what Allirae means. You've been changing very slowly. I'm here every day, but she has had two weeks away in the past month. That could explain why it's more noticeable to her."

"What, exactly, is noticeable?"

"Wait a minute." Trellian stood. "There's a better way." She stepped to the door and jerked it open. Good, no one listening outside. She closed it and faced the king. "No matter how certain you are that you haven't taken amber, it is still possible that you ingested it unknowingly. If two people who know you well see a change in your behavior, then wouldn't you want to check if amber is in your system?"

He sighed like he was giving in to absurdity. "How would I do that?"

"Look away from the window." She walked past his chair and began pulling one of the drapes farther across the windows. "First, we need it as dark as possible." Meroak joined her on the opposite side, and they met in the middle. Not complete darkness, but enough. She turned back to the king. "When a person has recently consumed amber, their eyes adjust more slowly to light. Take a few minutes to get used to the dark. Then I'll watch your eyes as we open the curtains."

"This is ridiculous."

No point in arguing—especially since he didn't sound remotely like a man who *was* arguing.

"Consider the past week, then," Meroak said. "Every evening that Allirae was gone, you worried about her. And every morning, you assured me she was fine. Not once did you have a single care when you finally managed to come down for breakfast."

"Calm is wiser than worry, you know."

Allirae sobbed and covered her face.

"Can we get this over with," the king said to Trellian, "so we can silence Allirae's fears? Though none of you may believe it, I don't like to see my sister cry."

This may have been long enough. "Come over here, then. Meroak, be ready to pull the curtain." She turned her back to the window. "Face me, please, sir. Blink a few times, then use your fingers to hold your eyelid open on at least one eye."

The instant he did so, she motioned to Meroak and he jerked the curtain wide. The king cringed but kept one eye open. Her stomach sank. "That's enough."

He turned away, toward the still shadowed side of the room, and scrunched his eyes shut for a moment. She shifted so he could see her without the window's backlighting.

"Well?" he asked.

She waited for him to look at her. "You have amber in your system. The dose is *not* tiny."

He shook his head and licked his lips, while Allirae sobbed harder. Finally, he said, "But it is still true that I haven't taken any."

"I imagine that *is* true," Trellian said. "Let's sit down, shall we?" She returned to her chair.

"I don't want to eat anymore," the king said.

He didn't get it. People in this state needed a lot of direction. "No, I don't think you should, sir, but please sit down anyway."

Meroak bent over his wife, wrapped an arm around her shoulder, and murmured something that didn't help.

"Meroak, please sit down," Trellian said. "Allirae, it's time to stop crying."

Her flat delivery earned her a glare from the woman. Better than tears. She turned to the king. "Do you believe me yet?"

He pushed his plate toward the center of the table. "The main reason I believe you is because a portion of my brain knows that this is terrible...and another portion is unconcerned."

"Allirae," Trellian said firmly. Ugh! Though the king's sister wiped tears with her napkin, she still seemed to be crying. Trellian tried again. "Your brother needs *rational* thought from you right now. What is most likely—that he chooses to take amber or someone is putting it in his food or drink without his knowledge?"

Allirae met her brother's gaze across the table. "Oh, it just *has* to be without your knowledge. I did tell you about the food that was brought to our train car—contaminated with ambertrop. But..." She scanned the table. "Oh, quakes..." her voice trailed off.

"Some dishes are shared," Trellian said, "others not. Do you always sit in the same places?"

They murmured *yes* or nodded, eyeing their elaborate place settings.

At last, they got it. "How many people have access to the food and beverages?"

"Several," Allirae replied. "Servers here, plus the kitchen staff."

"Is the table fully set before any of you come into the room?"

"Yes," Meroak said. "I'm usually first to come down. The server and a helper might be setting out the hot foods, but everything is ready."

First to come down...that included him in the list of suspects. And then there was the odd mix of expressions she'd seen on his face when Allirae first declared her realization. Some police in her own country would have him under rigorous questioning with just this much to go on. There was also that incident when he'd stumbled into the king atop a cliff. Not that the king thought it was incriminating. He trusted his brother-in-law, but should he?

Allirae had been listing the food service staff and their lengths of service. "What do you think?" she asked Trellian.

"Long service to the family inspires more trust than those hired later by the queen, but all remain suspect." She looked at the king. "It sounds like you barely know your kitchen staff. If they're carrying out the deed, their motivation could be anything from greed to fear of someone else. We must do more than catch the perpetrator. We need to question them and learn who is behind this. Yet we should not let anyone realize we are suspicious." He appeared to be paying attention, but she needed to be sure. "Do you perceive why?"

"The queen's maid was murdered," he said. "Someone didn't want us to know who she feared. We don't want that to happen again."

"Right. You still have some logic, even if you sound like you couldn't care less."

"Thanks." He picked up the envelope, opened it, pulled out the paper, and began reading. He reached for his teacup as he read. Meroak clutched his wrist. The king merely glanced at it, said, "Oh," and released the cup's handle.

"Let's go to the salon," Meroak said.

"First, I want to check your eyes." Trellian returned to the window and closed the one open drape. "If you are both free of the drug, we can assume the common dishes are safe." She was sure already that Allirae was free of it, but this gave her a chance to check Meroak without singling him out. Their pupils responded normally to the light. Not that it cleared Meroak, but at least he had no addiction that demanded feeding.

Allirae opened the morning room door, and Burnie bounced inside, his tail proclaiming his joy at being reunited with Danivid. He was the only one without restraint as they followed a corridor to the salon.

"I don't understand how we're going to eat," Allirae said. "As soon as we start guarding his food, the culprit will know we are aware."

"They will know sometime tomorrow, anyway," the king said, "for if I'm addicted, I will start shaking."

Trellian cringed within at that off-hand remark. He must know something about withdrawal, but not all. "I would rather let the amber wear off before we discuss this further."

"Let me keep thinking about it until I get worried, you mean?" He gave the words a humorous lilt.

No way could she joke. "Why don't you show me how you do a family Savoring Day service."

"Good idea," Allirae said. "I'll get the Writ."

She left and returned several minutes later with a volume from the Holy Writ. They began by sharing gratitudes, then Allirae read a passage. She chose a long one, detailing an ancient struggle against adversity and ultimate triumph.

The king suggested a stroll, which Trellian stretched longer by traversing every path on both sides of the garden and the central walkway down to the palace dock, before allowing the others to lead her onto the colonnade. They climbed steps cut into the cliff, emerging between columns where the salty breeze swept her long hair aside.

Trellian suggested that Allirae and Meroak lead along the cliffside, then limited her own pace to be even slower than Allirae's. Difficult, but she created space enough for a private conversation. "Could you show me, sir, where you almost fell during the quake?"

"This area," the king said. "Maybe half a dozen columns ahead."

She considered it as they strolled. The columns looked like they'd stood many a year. Joined by entablature on both sides, with decorative arches spanning the walkway. A structure built for looks. Maybe with a little thought for safety, since a stone railing spanned the distance between columns, but some shade would have been nice in this heat.

"Does the sunlight bother you as much as it did at breakfast?" she asked.

"Not much, though it's always intense out here when the sky is clear and the harbor reflects a million tiny suns. Are you trying to determine whether the drug's effect is fading?"

"Pretty much. I would guess that you have until this evening to make plans. The sooner we start figuring things out, the better."

"Then, let's catch up with the others."

"I don't think that's wise just yet." She slipped a hand around his arm and drew back enough to stop him.

CHAPTER 18

Danivid turned to look at Trellian. The sun revealed a reddish tint in her brown hair, more so in the lighter streaks. Pretty, but not enough to distract him from the seriousness of her dark gray eyes. "Why would that not be wise?"

"How much do you trust Meroak?"

That surprised him enough to draw a laugh, but the mere fact that she asked did uncomfortable things to his stomach. "A great deal, if that's not already obvious."

"It is, but I'm going to ask you to reconsider. Show me how you stood the night of the quake."

He wanted to grind his teeth, yet he had brought this up last night, so the fault was his. He turned to the harbor, bracing his thighs against the harbor-side railing and one arm around a column. Strange how insecure he now felt. Enough to reach his gift into the harbor lest he need a wave to catch him.

From a yard away, she looked over the setting of the event. "What did you feel?"

He may as well tell her. "The ground was quivering, then Meroak's hands hit my back. I shifted, like so, from the pressure." He mimicked the movement. "But there wasn't enough force to push me over. Then his fingers dug in, almost to the point of gouging, but it was only my tunic that he got a hold of."

Danivid enacted the rest as he spoke. "He dragged me back, turning me, then pushed me toward the land-side railing. I leapt over, like so. He followed me, bracing his chest on the railing and lowering himself, for he had turned his ankle. We moved far enough that stone couldn't hit us if the quake toppled any columns." As he acted this out, Burnie followed him, enjoying the game.

Trellian leaned against the land-side railing, looking it all over.

"It was dark," he added. "We couldn't see as much as you can, but we're both familiar with the area."

"You were out of sight? Alone?"

"Yes, though my guards knew we'd come out here. They used the dogs to look for us, but I heard their commands and called out to them."

"Burnie wasn't with you?"

"No. The kennel master tends to him every morning and evening." Danivid returned and lifted a foot to the walkway, gripped the railing to pull himself up, then swung his legs over to rejoin her. Burnie accomplished the maneuver with a single leap.

"Did a medic confirm Meroak's injury?"

"No, he walked it off."

"For even one second, did you question what happened?"

His irritation flowed out on a breath. "Yes. *One* second—when I felt his hands against my back and reacted to prevent my fall. But he pulled me *away* from the cliff, yelling at me the whole time because I wasn't protecting myself during a quake."

"You do seem rather careless. I'm trained in a certain style of fighting. If I took you off guard, even from this position, I could propel you over the cliff side of the colonnade."

The ambertrop must be fading indeed, for his ire rose sharply. He summoned water with his streaming gift. She turned her head toward the thunderous rush as the wave leapt up the cliffside higher than the top of the colonnade. He was tempted to drench her and stand dry beside her, but he flung the crest outward. "Pitching a streamer like me into the ocean isn't certain death, you know."

Her mouth stretched into the biggest smile he'd seen on her. "Wow! That's amazing!"

Not intimidated. "I could have drenched you."

"Nonsense. I already know you're a gentleman."

He laughed, despite himself.

"Oh, no," she said. "You got their attention, and they're heading back. I need to impress upon you that Meroak has a motive to get rid of you—if he can do so without suspicion. Making use of a natural disaster could achieve that. Another method would be to discredit you or kill you by means of ambertrop. In that way, starting an addiction could serve his ends. Since he comes to breakfast before you, he had the opportunity to add it to your drink."

"Tell me," Danivid said, "what is this motive you perceive?"

"His wife crowned queen...and his future child reigning after her. Even if he cannot rule directly, a spouse has influence."

Danivid hated—*hated*—that he must admit the validity of such a motive. There had to be a way to refute her. But how? Ah! "Yesterday morning, I rose early and was first to breakfast by a good while. I woke up worrying about Allirae, but I had no concerns by the time Meroak entered the morning room. I cannot tell when the effect comes over me, but it must have had me before he arrived. And if he intended to push me over this cliff, he should have jerked my wrist from the column before he pushed." She was back to the unreadable expression again. "I know him. You don't."

She tilted her head. "You may well be right, but I had to test the theory. We'll leave it for now."

She had to, for Allirae and Meroak drew near. She spoke a little louder. "We need to make some plans. What about food for the rest of the day?"

"The staff is off on Savoring Day," he said, "so we'll see to our own food. Only breakfast is served hot, then they leave."

"I saw guards on duty. In fact, one is in view of us right now."

"A few remain for critical services. They take turns to work Savoring Day."

Rejoining them, with her hand resting on Meroak's arm, Allirae said, "Are you hungry? There will be cold food in the kitchen for us."

"Perfect," Trellian said. "I'll get a chance to inspect the kitchen."

"Do you ever stop police work?" Danivid asked.

"Not when someone's at risk. Since this affects a nation, I shall remain all the more vigilant."

Despite his irritation, he had to admire her. This wasn't even her country. He motioned for Allirae and Meroak to precede them along the colonnade.

As they retraced their steps toward the palace, Allirae said, "I suppose that tomorrow I'll have to watch over everything done with Danivid's food."

"No," he said. "The more I think of this, the more I'm certain we must keep it secret. Whoever is responsible, they will try to make others believe I became addicted by my own actions. That can be used to discredit me and weaken my ability to stand against ambertrop before the councils."

"You don't realize," Trellian said, "how difficult the withdrawal will be."

"Perhaps not, but I realize enough to know that I cannot keep it secret in the palace. I must leave."

Allirae turned her head and frowned at him. "You mean like Vancent did? All alone?"

Trellian spoke before Danivid could. "Are you saying that he went through withdrawal *alone*?"

"Yes," she replied.

"No," Danivid said to Allirae. "He didn't write everything. I found out more yesterday when I visited the cottage." For Trellian's benefit, he added, "It's in the woodland, and he went there alone because he didn't trust anyone in the palace. He had no idea what he was about to experience. Someone found him and helped him—even hid his horse so he couldn't go back."

"Is that where you intend to go?" she asked.

He shook his head. "It's not private enough, and we'd need horses. I'm not even sure how Vancent managed to sneak away. Discovery is too likely."

"I cannot imagine anywhere else you could go," Allirae said.

He chuckled, for it was obvious to him. "Dirklan, of course."

Her brow lifted, and she stretched the word *oh*.

Trellian asked, "How does that help?"

"For one thing," Danivid said, "no ambertrop is allowed into Dirklan. Also, there is a large house with a section dedicated to the ambassador—*me,* until a month ago. Those rooms will give me adequate privacy. My Dirklian aide is a friend of ten years. He can provide food and, uh, company."

"I assume he has no experience of amber withdrawal—and you will know how to leave. To be frank, family and close friends are not the best attendants during withdrawal. It's a good thing you already have a reason for me to go with you."

"Do I?"

"You said you'd take me there."

"I would rather," he said dryly, "do that under pleasant circumstances."

"You can always add an extra day to our absence to show me... whatever is down there."

He suppressed a shudder. Could anything above or below be more awkward than this? "Does it occur to you that I may not want the ambassador of another country to watch me go through withdrawal?"

"I'm not an ambassador. The single part of that role I'm good at is discretion. No one will ever know what I saw. If we want to guarantee your success, the only choice is me. That, or sending for a knowledgeable attendant from Felverland."

"We don't have time for that." Allirae spun to face them, stopping their progress along the colonnade. "Besides, it would mean advertising the problem in Felverland, which is detrimental to future relations. Though I appreciate your offer, Trellian, it's not appropriate." She focused on Danivid. "I will go belowground with you."

The moment she gave him an out, he realized he couldn't take it. He grimaced, and a breath escaped between his teeth. That fast, Allirae and Meroak each grabbed one of his arms.

Allirae gasped. "Is it starting?"

He caught Trellian's eye roll. "No, it's not starting," he snapped, "and you just proved Trellian's point."

"But—"

"No, Allirae. You are my heir, and we are having quakes. The last place we should be together is belowground. Besides that, leaving within a day of your arrival is bad for Aneen. You should be in the palace taking care of anything that may go wrong while I am unavailable. I could list several more reasons, if those aren't enough."

Allirae and Meroak had both drawn back in the face of his firmness. Meroak rubbed the back of his neck. "Well...should...do you want me to..."

Before Trellian could interfere and make *this* awkward, Danivid put a hand on his shoulder. "I'm not separating you from your wife again. I'd rather you take care of her and Aneen." He gestured toward the palace, to get everyone moving again. "I'm going to have to cancel meetings for next week, and I need to provide some sort of reason for my sudden disappearance."

"I have an idea for that," Trellian said.

"I'm listening."

"You could say that you have grown ill and suspect poison. Considering your brother's recent death, going to Dirklan for recovery would be logical. Also, you *will* be ill, and if you only relied on the knowledge typically available here, you wouldn't know why."

"Ah, I like that." He pondered for a moment longer. "I won't tell my scheduler to cancel meetings until tomorrow. I think, however, that I must meet with Stanton this evening."

"Who is Stanton?"

"My chief steward. He is involved with some other troubling matters, and he needs to know some information I received from Shevnal a few days ago. By the way, Allirae, my first meeting tomorrow is with Shevnal. You might have to deal with him."

"I'll just get rid of him. I doubt he *wants* to meet with you."

He wouldn't if he knew the questions Danivid had for him. "I will need to know his reaction." Oops. That brought Trellian's eyes back to him, and he didn't want to bare his financial issues. Time for a distraction. "On the matter of food, I just remembered how Burnie acted when he might have caught a whiff of ambertrop. Let's take him into the kitchen."

That worked. Though Burnie licked his chops during an inspection of the kitchen and their food, he never growled. Whined a little, but Danivid tossed him a scrap of meat.

When they finished eating, Danivid sent a note to Stanton's home. He told the guard in the hall to send the captain of the guard to him when he returned, and to have the kennel master come to him rather than whistling for Burnie.

He headed toward his study, but Allirae said, "Uh-uh," and dragged him into the salon off the hall. The others followed, Meroak closing the door. Allirae said, "You, my pensive brother, seem to be formulating a great many plans."

"Just trying to make the most of what may be my last rational day out of the next several." Of Trellian, he asked, "Can you estimate how long it will take before I'm fit to function?"

"It's hard to say, for amber withdrawal affects people in varied ways. A small minority experience little to no symptoms. The longest I've heard is ten days, but that only happens after years of use. Do you know how long you've been ingesting it?"

"No earlier than when I returned to Regissa—a month ago. Yet I cannot say when it started, for I have never noticed the effects of it come over me."

"That is typical—just a sense of well-being that grows and fades gradually. Whoever is feeding you amber understands how it works. They would have started with a small dose and increased it a little every day. Based on that assumption, perhaps three days of withdrawal, though it could be one to five days."

He nodded, careful to hide the dread that had begun to worm through his insides. "Allirae, plan a reception about a week from now, so we can properly welcome Trellian to Regissa."

Trellian blinked. "That is really not necessary."

"Oh, but it is," Allirae said.

For once, Trellian betrayed an unsettled side. He wanted to smirk but tamed it to a gentle smile. "I think you'll enjoy it. We'll make sure that anyone who might wish me harm is present."

She let out a low-pitched laugh. "Delightful. That will make it far more interesting."

Allirae's eyebrows rose. "Who are these people you want invited?"

"Nobility, governors, mayor, etc. Include the three substance guild chiefs. And most important, anyone notable for their rising wealth or influence. If I don't have time to give you the list, Stanton can tell you who they are."

"How many of these people," Trellian asked, "do you suspect of wishing you harm?"

He smiled. "That was mostly jest. None of them have direct access to the palace. However, some in the latter group are getting rich at a surprising rate."

"Ah," she purred. "An indication that they may be involved with amber trade."

"Perhaps. Or it may have more to do with Chief Former Shevnal misusing his position."

She acknowledged this with a nod. "You've summoned the captain of the palace guard. How long has he held that position?"

"I assume you are asking about who I trust and why. The captain was appointed by my father, not my brother. Much of the current guard entered it while we were growing up. The vetting process for new guards is quite thorough and administered by the captain. While I don't know all of them, I trust them more than the household staff that Lenneth brought in on any whim."

Danivid glanced around the three faces. "And now, if I've satisfied enough curiosity, I have some things to write." This time, he made it to his study with only Burnie following.

CHAPTER 19

With most of the staff away, Trellian took the opportunity to give herself a tour of the palace. Too bad only corridors and rooms with open doors were available. Despite her attempt to keep her wandering unremarkable, a guard approached her.

"What are you doing?"

She produced a smile and gave the answer she'd prepared. "Just trying to get familiar with the layout. I'd rather avoid another embarrassment like getting lost on the way to breakfast."

"I see." Whether he did or not, he didn't move.

"On my own, of course, there's only so much I can learn of the purpose for all these rooms. If you have time or inclination, I wouldn't turn down a guided tour."

"You are most likely to need the ground-floor rooms," he said. "I will show you those."

She suspected that he agreed so he could keep an eye on her, but he opened doors and announced room names. Various salons, a ballroom, a music room, an enormous formal dining room, and one area that puzzled her.

"The High Council chamber," he said.

She entered the ornate room, her footsteps echoing. Pale green satin draped tall windows, and a darker shade padded the seats and armrests of the many carved wood chairs. Several tables were arranged in an elongated ring. She rested a hand on one of the chairs placed around the outer sides of the tables, all facing the center of the room. "What is this used for?"

"Meetings of the High Council." He said it like he'd already told her.

"Please remember I'm not Welcian. What do you mean by *high* council?"

"The upper echelon of the General Council. That is, lords and ladies if the province is still governed by nobility, or governors of the other provinces, and the prime minister of Dirklan Province."

"Dirklan has a prime minister?"

"Yes. Some of the governors want that title changed, for she is elected like the provincial governors are and has the same level of authority." He cracked a smile. "Myself, I think it's jealousy that Dirklan's primary office has a higher-sounding title than theirs."

Trellian shook her head. "Ah, politics." They returned to the hall, and she angled her steps toward the one corridor they had yet to explore.

"We won't be going down there. It's the king's study, which is private, and the library."

She considered pushing to see the library, but she recognized an inflexible stance when she saw one. "Then I think I'll just run up to get my sketchpad and go out to the garden for a while."

That rid her of this stern shadow and gave her time to sketch a couple diagrams—the layout of the ground floor and the harbor-side face of the palace. When a layer of sweat made her dress cling, she took refuge in the dense shade on the terrace and sketched a view of the harbor for the sheer pleasure of it.

The heat was enough to cause the guards to open the double doors of the palace wide on both sides of the hall. Murmurs of conversation reached her as staff returned to the palace through the opposite doors.

When might the chef return? Only one way to know. She closed her portfolio and slipped the strap over her shoulder. Time to haunt the kitchen.

When she entered it, a balding man was flipping the neck strap of a white apron over his clothes. He checked for an instant when he caught sight of her, then finished tying it. "You must be Lady Trellian."

"I am, indeed. And you are...?"

"Chef Perkett." He filled a utility teapot with water and set it on one of the magnery coils. "I was wondering how I'd go about finding a chance to talk with you." He selected mugs and plates from one cupboard. "I daresay you came for a snack—which I'm happy to serve—but it's information I'm after."

He wanted information? Too funny—that was her job. What could he possibly want to know, and how could she weave her own questions into it?

He lifted a large tin from the shelf and brought everything to a table with stools. "Have a seat, lady. I can offer you a cool lemon tea or steep something fresh if you prefer."

"Cool sounds wonderful."

With practiced speed, he retrieved a clear pitcher and poured for them both. Prying the lid off the tin, he presented it and asked, "Do you like scones?"

"I do." She took one and set it on her plate.

He finished bustling and sat opposite her. "And now for the important information, lady. What do you enjoy eating?"

She almost laughed. No careful hiding of sensitive matters, then. She listed several Felvarian dishes, giving brief descriptions while she nibbled her way through the scone. Time to start a subtle change of subject. "I hadn't thought of it before, but it must be complicated figuring out menus when people from all over the country come to a dinner here."

"Oh, I'm used to that. A little harder, though, when we have guests from another country. I was an undercook the last time we had visitors from Felverland. Back in the days of the old king—the father of Kings Vancent and Danivid, you understand. Been a long time. One way or another, I treasure any creative spark. Queen Lenneth loves to entertain, and she always wants something new on the table."

"That must keep things both interesting and challenging," she said. He nodded portentously, and she hurried on before he could expound. "I suppose there will be parties again, and I have no idea what they are like here. Please tell me of your most recent dinner party."

"That was a month ago." He leaned forward. "The evening before King Vancent died."

Perfect. "Ah, it must have been. What did you serve?"

He gave her more detail than she needed about every dish, but she let him talk.

"Was it frightful the next morning? With his death so sudden, I imagine there must have been questions about everything."

"Well, the police were down here. I suppose because they have to be diligent in questioning, but whatever killed the king couldn't have come in his food."

"Why not?"

"The undercooks all taste whatever dish they are making, and I taste all of them before the serving dishes are filled. None of us, nor any of the guests, were sick in the least."

"Do you oversee the serving too?"

"That's up to the table steward. The police asked about what's at the individual place settings, but it all comes out of the same bowls or pitchers. Nor could anything be added, for a dozen people sat down to dinner, and there would have been several servers in the dining room from preparation until cleanup."

"Such a mystery. Was there nothing at all that seemed unusual?"

"Not until hours later."

"What was that?"

He sniffed. "I told the police about it. The head fellow said I was meddling and wasting their time, since it couldn't have a thing to do with the king's death."

Probably that idiotic captain. Trellian smiled. "I have plenty of time to listen."

"Well, it is true that it couldn't kill anyone. It was just bread and butter. Yautan came down after the guests had left. Long after, in fact. I was the only one here, tending to a morning pastry dough that needed to be rerolled and folded."

Not more cooking details. "But why did Yautan come down?"

"He said the king's stomach was troubling him and he wanted some bread. So, of course, I cut off part of a loaf and scooped butter onto the plate. But the strange thing was..." He leaned closer. "Yautan took one of the saltshakers with him when he left. The late king would snack on bread and butter now and then, but I've never known him to ask for *salt* with it."

Salt? Curious.

Danivid leaned against the back of his desk chair. Quivery exhaustion crept through his entire being. Was it somehow related to the drug he'd been ingesting? Even though he had revealed the truth to these few people he'd summoned to his study, he didn't want to fall to pieces in front of them. Especially Turnin, for he'd only met the lawyer the week before he'd become king. "I think that is enough for tonight," he said to Stanton and Turnin. "I thank you for giving the last hours of your Savoring Day to my issues."

"The cause is worthy," Stanton said. He looked over the papers on the desk. "So much information here, and the culprits still unidentified."

"I understand your concern. That's one of the reasons I included the captain of the guard in this meeting." He tilted his head toward Koriak. "While I am in Dirklan, this study will remain locked." He gathered papers into a drawer as he spoke. "Also, this desk will be locked. Allirae will hold the keys." He glanced across the desk at her, where she sat with the lawyer and steward.

She nodded, and Koriak replied, "I will see that all access points remain under the eyes of a guard."

Turnin tapped a sheaf of his papers on the desk to align them. Tucking them into his portfolio, he said, "If you don't mind, sir, I would like to meet Lady Trellian."

"I suppose you should at least know each other by sight, but I've had enough discussion for one day. Koriak, send someone to find the lady and request that she join us."

"She was in the hall sketching the mural when I came in. I'll get her." He strode to the door.

Danivid exchanged a faint smile with Allirae. Doubtless, Trellian's true focus was on who came and went from the palace. He finished stowing his papers and turned the key in the lock. It caught as he tried to pull it out, for his hand was trembling. Why? Too soon for withdrawal. Was it the dread of tomorrow that made him shake? He masked it with movement—pocketing the key, standing to introduce Trellian when she entered, giving Burnie a rub behind the ears. Allirae seemed to notice his tension, for she orchestrated small talk between the new acquaintances while they got their things together and strolled into the hall.

Danivid locked the study door, then followed his guests. He lingered with Koriak at the fringe. The kennel master was waiting by the entrance, and Danivid motioned him near as the others left. "Tomorrow, don't give Burnie his morning exercise. I want him brought back to me as soon as he's eaten and relieved himself. I may be up quite early."

"Just as you please, sir." He patted Burnie and took him outside.

To Koriak, Danivid murmured, "Both tonight and tomorrow morning, let Burnie into my bedchamber *while* Yautan is there with me. Don't even knock. Just open the door to let him in."

Koriak said, "I will have guards in movement—not too obvious, but the corridor outside your chamber will always be in view. Whoever is there will make sure that the dog is in the right place at the right time."

Danivid nodded, and with a quick murmur of "Pleasant night," in the ladies' direction, went up to his chamber. Continuous tension quivered in his chest. Why did he feel this way? If he was ingesting ambertrop in the mornings, then he shouldn't feel withdrawal until tomorrow. He'd been suppressing dread half the day, but was that enough to make it manifest early? Regardless, this combination of exhaustion and high energy was awful.

Yautan's characteristic double-tap knock struck the door.

"Enter."

He came in with his tea caddy, and as always, set it on the small table beside the door. He took out the hot water flask and a decorative tin. Painted leaves surrounded a scroll with the word *Chamomile*.

According to him, it aided sleep, though Danivid usually opted for plain water in the evening. He rolled his stiff shoulders, eyeing the empty mug that sat, so innocent and ominous, on the small table between the wing chairs. The same one he drank tea from every morning.

Danivid hadn't responded to Yautan's greeting, which drew a questioning look from him. "Is something wrong, sir?"

"I'm just tired."

"Probably goes along with healing muscles after your accident yesterday. Would you like me to add a pain relief powder to your tea?"

"No." Danivid shed his tunic and tossed it on the bed. The remaining thin shirt granted a welcome coolness, and he went to brush his teeth. Finished, he refilled his ornate glass with water and took it into the bedroom, where he set it beside the mug of steeping tea.

As usual, Yautan began listing the appointments scheduled for the next day. Danivid stood in the gentle breeze of the open window and stared at the moonlit garden below, uttering an occasional, "Mm-hmm," as though he cared. The drone of Yautan's voice merged with the sounds of him moving around the room in his routine of turning down the bed, straining the tea, and tidying.

Danivid strolled to a wing chair and sank into it. Would rest calm the hurry of his heartbeat? If only he trusted that tea, for its warmth would be soothing. He stirred it, then forced himself to release the spoon and lean back in his chair.

Yautan picked up the tunic from the bed and headed toward the dressing room. Then the door latch turned.

Yautan jumped. "What—*no*—don't let that—"

Burnie barked and charged Danivid. Or rather, the table. His chest thumped its edge. If Danivid hadn't rested his arm atop it, the whole thing may have gone over. Even now, the dog kept his head on the surface, growling at the tea mug.

Yautan berated the guard for opening the door without permission and demanded that he remove the beast.

"Yautan," Danivid said. He waited for the man to turn and look at him. "Why is Burnie growling at the mug of tea?"

"I don't know. I told you that dog is unpredictable. He is not safe. If you won't put him down, at least have him caged."

"On the contrary." Danivid stood. "He *predictably* growls at the scent of ambertrop."

Yautan blanched. "No. No, he...he growls at anything."

"In the queen's chamber, for instance? At the queen's maid?" Taking Burnie's collar, he pulled the dog around to face Yautan. Still, he growled. "And at you."

"Sometimes yes, sometimes no. There is neither rhyme nor reason to his fits."

"But there is. You always clean up so thoroughly—flushing the tea leaves, washing the mug and your hands. But you haven't washed them yet, have you? He smells the ambertrop on you."

Yautan looked at the guard, whose broad stance filled the doorway. His breath came fast. "If the tea leaves are tainted, it wasn't me who—" He dropped the tunic and bolted through the dressing room door.

The guard stepped into the corridor and strode toward the far door. "Seize Yautan!" he ordered.

Danivid followed him, holding Burnie's collar, and watched two guards tackle Yautan to the floor. He didn't quit struggling until they tied his hands behind his back.

Beyond them, Trellian watched with an expression that Danivid could only describe as professional interest. When the struggle ceased, she walked past the men and didn't speak until she stood near enough to whisper. "What happened?"

"Burnie took issue with the smell of my tea. Yautan found my comments about ambertrop difficult to answer and bolted." She craned her neck to see into his room, and Danivid said, "You may enter."

She stopped just inside the doorway, turning her head to survey the entire room.

Koriak conferred with the guard who'd brought Burnie, then approached.

Danivid gestured to the opposite side of the corridor. "Hold him in one of these rooms temporarily."

Koriak returned to his men. "Find a suitable chair and tie him to it."

Trellian distracted Danivid with another whisper. "How are you doing?"

"Far more tense than I ought to be." He licked his lips and whispered, more from loathing than secrecy, "And I'm convinced that drinking a cup of tea would make me feel so much better." He gritted his teeth, exhaling through his nose. "This doesn't fit. He has just recently started bringing me chamomile tea in the evenings. I don't even always drink it."

"Hold that thought."

Koriak returned as Yautan was lifted to his feet and forced into one of the rooms.

Trellian spoke before either of them could. "Bear with me a moment, please." She waited for the door to slam on Yautan's temporary prison. "I want no one to enter the king's chamber while I get my test kit. Will you two stay right here in the corridor and wait for me?"

"Yes," Danivid said.

Koriak scowled after her as she hurried away.

"She has a reason," Danivid assured him. "Don't be angry with her. Did Yautan say anything?"

"Only that he has done nothing wrong, but he will go quietly with the police and cooperate with any investigations they make."

Danivid laughed. Sarcastic though it was, it gave him a scrap of relief.

Koriak's voice ground. "I am still the person with the least information. I cannot serve you without it."

"As far as facts go, Burnie growled at the tea Yautan made for me. When I implied that it contained ambertrop, Yautan ran."

Tilting his head in the direction Trellian had gone, Koriak asked, "What is this *reason* of hers?"

"I imagine she doesn't want you to let me go in there and drink that tea, which part of me longs for."

"Oh." His scowl faded. "That, I will forgive, but I'm not going to take orders from her."

"Certainly not. You know what she means by her test kit, right?"

"Gordin told me about it."

"I'd like the results of that first. Then we question Yautan. I doubt he will tell us what I want to know, so while I am in Dirklan, he will wait in the cells here."

"You mean in the foundation level? They haven't been used in years."

Danivid smirked. "Dirty, are they?"

CHAPTER 20

Trellian retraced her steps. Even in that plain white shirt, the king's stance held a subtle presence. Why hadn't she noticed that before? A guard listening to the captain gave a crisp nod and strode toward the back stairs. When she reached the two remaining men, the king motioned her into his chamber, and they followed her in.

Burnie trotted to the table that held the mug and glass. By the way he growled at them, they'd fear for their lives if they had any.

She pointed to the open case on the table by the door. "This wasn't here before."

"It's Yautan's tea caddy." Danivid picked up the tunic lying on the floor. "He brings it in every morning and evening." Slipping the tunic on, he said to Koriak, "Relock the dressing room door. Wouldn't hurt to check the others." He stroked the dog's head. "Good boy. Calm down."

The caddy was taller than wide, with a handle on top and a vertical hinge. The larger side had compartments for a heat flask and tea tins. The smaller had a wire mesh pocket for paraphernalia. Fabric stretched across the upper portion, with an elastic band to hold rubber-topped bottles in place. Trellian lifted one. It was labeled *mint*. She was about to open it for a sniff, when she realized what Danivid was doing.

Twice now, he had moved Burnie to a new location and said, "Find amber." Then he walked the dog back to let him growl at the mug, followed by praise.

"How long will it take to train him?" she asked.

"Not long. He knows the *find* command already. We just need to teach him to associate the word *amber* with the drug's scent. I'll have the kennel master work on it while I'm in Dirklan."

"Let's confirm content." She set her kit on the dresser, opened it, and removed a vial. "If you don't mind, sir, would you tell me every detail of what you and Yautan did in this room tonight?"

As he began, she tested the dry tea from the tin. It produced a moderate reaction, which she noted on the test result pad.

Koriak returned and watched her. He pointed at the vial. "What does that mean?"

"Not much. Only that it *could* contain ambertrop, not that it *does*. Some other plants react in the same way."

"What's the point, then?"

"If it didn't react, I would have been sure that it contained no amber. Elimination can be useful."

Danivid also watched. "Whatever you do, don't spill anything contaminated on my carpet."

She grinned at Burnie, whose shifting revealed how hard it was for him to stay where his master had commanded him to sit. "I suppose he would never forgive me. But please continue what you were telling me."

He did so, moving the mug and strainer from the table to the dresser while he spoke. She tested the steeped tea from the mug as she listened. No surprise that it frothed like the dry tea.

While she noted the results, a guard showed up with three more tins. "We found these in our search of Yautan's room, sir."

Two were large with vendor labels. Another, small enough to fit in the tea caddy, was labeled *morning blend*. The king pointed to his dresser, and the guard set them down and left.

"We'll let Burnie run the first tests." He opened one tin at a time for the dog. The two largest warranted only a disinterested sniff. At the morning blend, Burnie growled.

"Good boy." The king rubbed Burnie's ears, then took the dog with him to sit at his desk. "Please see if you can confirm his results."

He waited for her work in silence. Though she focused on the tests, she kept the king in her peripheral view. Twitching shoulders. Continuous shifting. He never stopped petting his dog, perhaps an outlet for restless fingers.

She completed her notes and reported, "Only the vendor cannister of black tea gives no result. The vendor's chamomile gives a very slight result, which could be from another substance, since it reacts less than Yautan's small tin of chamomile."

"We'll test and compare Burnie's reactions," Koriak said.

"How does one do that?" Trellian asked. Not that she couldn't figure it out, but Koriak's undercurrent of resistance was not lost on her. Requesting guidance might help.

"By scattering samples." The king opened a desk drawer. "You may use the dressing room and sitting room to spread things out." He lifted a sheaf of blank papers from the drawer and held them out to her. "Set the tea leaves on these."

"Perfect. I can label them *and* leave no mess." She and Koriak placed them strategically, ensuring that Burnie would have to pass uncontaminated scents to find what she believed contained amber. She returned to the bedroom. "All set."

The king stood, still showing tired eyes and jittery movements. "Burnie, find amber." The dog started around the bed, paused to growl at the mug on the dresser, then accused the table between the chairs.

"Hmm." The king patted Burnie. "I suppose it's possible that some drips spilled here and that's what he smells." He directed the dog toward the other rooms and repeated his command.

Burnie trotted around, correctly identifying everything that Trellian believed contained amber. "He keeps bypassing the vendors' chamomile and black tea." She clicked her tongue. "When we get back, I'd like to set up some more stringent tests to confirm it, but I suspect he is better at avoiding false positives than my chemical test."

"A pity we cannot bottle his detector," Koriak said.

She watched the dog again growl at the table. "It's odd how he goes back to that location."

"Indeed." The king urged Burnie to find the mug of tea again, praised him, and commanded, "Sit." He crossed the room and moved the water glass to his nightstand, then stretched out on his bed. Propping himself on one elbow, he picked up the water glass and brought it toward his lips.

Burnie nigh exploded with barking. In a flash, he was inches from his master's hand, teeth bared, growling like he'd rip someone apart.

The king's calm response showed no fear that it would be him. "Good boy. Down." He set the glass on the nightstand. "Test that, Trellian." He swung his legs to the floor and rubbed Burnie's neck.

She had already grabbed a fresh vial and pipette from her kit. Moving a wing chair to keep it between herself and Burnie, she drew a sample from the glass and dropped it into her vial. It frothed. She stared at it.

"Ambertrop?" the king asked.

"Yes. Didn't you say you filled this yourself from the sink?"

"I did."

She straightened. "Show me your movements. Uh, please, sir."

His lips twitched. He went into the priv, flicked the water on for a second, came out with his fingers curled around an imaginary glass, which he set on the table. "Yautan started listing tomorrow's meetings. He does so every night." The king rounded one of the wing chairs and faced a window. "I was trying to hide how on edge I felt, so I stood here and looked out into the garden while he talked."

"Could you tell what he was doing?"

"He moved around like he always does, tidying and such. I wasn't really paying attention."

"He didn't tidy, though. Your tunic was still on the floor."

"I don't throw my clothes on the floor." How funny that the king sounded offended. "Yautan had picked it up from the bed, oh, about the time Burnie was let into the room. He dropped it when he ran. But if your real question is whether he had time to put something in the water—yes." He looked down into the glass and swirled it a little, as Burnie growled again. "I don't see anything floating in it, though. I rarely drink the tea he makes me at night, but often sip water before bed. I would notice if ground up tea leaves were in it."

She stared at the tea caddy. "He has liquid flavorings in there." The king followed her to it, Burnie keeping to his heels. She pulled one out—yellow tinted glass—and read the label. "Lemon." She unscrewed the cap and lifted out the dropper.

Since Koriak was maintaining a position in the doorway, he was as near as the king. His eyebrows shot up. "Wouldn't want much of that in my tea."

"He never added more than a drop if I asked for it," the king said. "I assume they are concentrated for ease of carrying."

Trellian put it back and took out a green one. "Mint." When she opened it, Burnie averted his head. "Guess he doesn't like that one." She took out a clear bottle with very tiny letters for a word she didn't recognize. "A-mare-toe?"

The hint of a laugh snuck into the king's voice. "Amaretto."

She unscrewed it. "Mm. I like that. Smells nothing like a mare." She put it back and pulled out the brown bottle. "Vanilla." She unscrewed it and barely lifted the dropper.

Burnie went mad, growling, heaving up on his hind legs like he was going to snatch it from her.

She quickly screwed it tight as the king got the dog to sit again. "Did either of you smell any vanilla?" she asked.

They shook their heads. She sidestepped to the dresser and grabbed another vial from her kit. "I'm testing this one at the sink."

"Hold Burnie," the king said to Koriak, then hurried after her.

She set the brown bottle on the shelf and squeezed the rubber top to draw up fluid into the dropper. "That is quite yellow."

"What color is vanilla supposed to be?"

She smirked. "Brown. I take it you skipped culinary classes."

"That's not covered in prince school."

"Shocking." She held her vial over the sink and squeezed in a single drop. Froth surged from it and flowed down over her fingers. "*Fwoh!*"

"What does that word mean?"

"Um, maybe 'skies and caverns.' This is *highly* concentrated ambertrop. Worth quite a sum."

He stared at the dripping foam, then met her eyes in the mirror. "Enough to kill?"

"Not that amount." She slipped the dropper back into the bottle, then lifted it to catch the light. Almost full. "The whole bottle would be."

He closed his lips, but they kept moving despite his effort to clench them. He reached over and turned on the water. "Wash your hands. Burnie could smell it on Yautan after he made my tea—and poisoned water. He won't like you if you carry that scent."

She began to scrub. "Why did you lie down on the bed just now?"

"Testing a theory."

She waited, watching him in the mirror.

"I couldn't figure out why Burnie growls for ambertrop. The Flyound dogs are trained to give a single bark when they find their target. Not a threatening sound or behavior. But Burnie growled at it before anyone trained him to even search for it." His fidgety fingers picked up a comb to turn over and over. "It's not just that he doesn't like the smell. He associates it with something—*bad.*"

She rinsed her hands, sealed the vials, then lathered up again to remove external traces from them. "And lying down?"

"My brother died in that bed. I cannot help but wonder if he smelled of ambertrop." He grunted. "Before I slept here, the mattress and linens were replaced—at Yautan's order. Seemed normal at the time."

"I would think so too. Was the dog with King Vancent when he died?"

"I don't know. He would have been near. He was still returning to guard the closed door of the king's chamber days after Vancent died."

"A dog trait, either way." She shrugged. "He is useful for future protection, but not as evidence—and that is what we need. Would Yautan have been with the king that evening?"

"I imagine so. He was my brother's personal aide for years." Danivid slapped the comb down on the sink. "The only reason I accepted him in that role was because I couldn't bring my own aide up from Dirklan." He handed Trellian a towel. "I will have to change that. Let's go see if Burnie thinks you washed well enough."

Fortunately, she passed inspection.

Koriak was folding one of the scent samples into a neat packet. "Burnie is stir-crazy with all this stuff around." Trellian's eyes darted to the packets he'd already wrapped. "Don't worry. You aren't the only one who knows how to label evidence."

"Sorry," she murmured. "Force of habit." She put the test vial into the numbered slot on her kit and jotted more records, then noticed the king staring at the mug of tea. "I will just wash these." She picked it up and strode to the nightstand to collect the glass.

"Wait."

"*No*—lord king." Good to have a long stride, which got her to the sink for a satisfying whoosh down the drain. As she washed the dishes, her mind darted ahead.

She finished and stomped back into the room. He was sitting at his desk. "We are going to have a problem in Dirklan. You will demand to leave, and I will demand that you stay. No one there knows me *at all*."

He held out a piece of paper to her.

Puzzled, she took it and read. Addressed to Prime Minister Katowau... granting authority for Lady Trellian to decide his care...with his signature below. She folded the letter. "Thank you." She kept her eyes on it. "Um, I forget at times to curb my bluntness. I apologize for—"

His chuckle stopped her. "Oh, come, you managed to squeeze in *lord king*."

She narrowed her eyes at him, but he only chuckled again as he stood. "It so happens that I prefer direct speech," he said. "Pack up your kit. I need to question Yautan and finish plans."

At least she hadn't ruined everything. She turned back to the dresser but halted her first step. "Where is the bottle of amber I put there?"

Koriak reopened the tea caddy, which was latched. "Here." He pointed at a twist of paper, with the word *poison* written on it, that stuck out of the cloth pouch. It was fat enough to be wrapped around the bottle, but she never left anything unconfirmed. When she reached for it, Koriak snapped the caddy shut. "If my king trusts me, why should I tolerate your mistrust?"

She stepped back and gripped her hands at her waist. "Sorry. It's not that. It's just—at home we always double confirm everything we can. It strengthens the evidence."

"You think the king and I are not adequate confirmation?"

She straightened her shoulders. "I did not say that or think it." His straight-lipped silence demanded more. "I miss having a team to work with—people I know. It makes me feel like I have to do everything myself."

"Well, you don't have to," the king said, "though I admit our team is small. I'm going to question Yautan. You may listen from the corridor."

She wanted to argue that she should be in the room, but maybe this was a test to see if she would follow orders. Why did that make her feel so off?

Danivid waited with Trellian while Koriak sent the two guards who watched Yautan to opposite ends of the corridor. Then he and his captain entered, leaving the door ajar. How was he supposed to act confident while shaking?

Before he had a chance to speak, Yautan snarled, "This is an outrage! After all that—"

Koriak grabbed him below the jaw and forced his head back. "Shut up." Yautan's knuckles went white on the armrests that his wrists were tied to. "The only words you will speak are to answer the king." Koriak held him a moment longer, then stepped aside.

Danivid asked, "How long have you been giving me ambertrop?"

"All I do is serve you the tea you ask for."

Of course he would answer like this. "I expressly forbade any ambertrop in the palace. My request for tea was *only* that, not a request for the drug I forbade. Stop wasting my time and tell me when you started adding ambertrop to my morning tea."

"Drug," he scoffed. "The smidge I put in was just to see if you liked your tea that way. And like it, you did!"

"*When* did you start?"

"When did you start liking it?" Yautan countered.

"I believe I first complimented your tea the day after my coronation, so you just admitted to a full month of drugging me. When did you begin putting it in my evening tea?"

"What? A little chamomile because you can't sleep after all the worries you've heaped upon yourself. A crazy dog growls, and you dare accuse *me*, when I do nothing but serve you."

"When I accepted the crown, you knew more about ambertrop than I did, but the tables have turned. I have found both the truth and the *proof* of it. Proof that will stand in court. Stop spouting nonsense and tell me when you started drugging my evening tea."

He snorted. "If you think you have proof, send for the police. I'll cooperate with their investigation."

Danivid smiled. "The one kindness I will grant you is *not* sending for the police. They will either kill you themselves or release you for someone else to do it. Either way, you will be murdered." He shrugged. "You may deserve death or merely long imprisonment, but you will stand trial, and a judge will decide that. Bear in mind that sentences are more stringent when the accused refuses to answer questions." Danivid allowed a few seconds for him to consider. "Who provided you with the condensed ambertrop in the bottle labeled *vanilla* in your tea caddy?"

"I have nothing to say to your wild accusations. What are you going to do? Keep me tied up in a guest room?"

"That would be inconvenient. There are cells in the foundation level. You will stay there."

"What?"

"I haven't seen them since I was a boy. Could be thick with cobwebs by now, but you may clean them."

Though his face contorted, Yautan found no words to rant.

"I'm going to Dirklan for a few days, where I can trust that no one will poison me. Do you really think I will be more tolerant after I endure withdrawal?"

Danivid waited, then said, "So silent now? Last chance to cooperate. Who pays you to get me addicted to ambertrop?"

"That's insane!"

"Yes, Yautan, you are quite insane to trust him. Enjoy your stay— underground."

CHAPTER 21

The night and morning merged into a battle with ambertrop on both sides—the longing for it and the hatred of it. Danivid told himself that he was the king—failure wasn't an option. Then he wondered why. Random memories slipped in and out of existence. Fitful sleep. Food that Allirae brought him before dawn. Had he eaten any of it? She'd told him something about how she would explain his absence. What it was, eluded him. Then he'd been in a cair...Allirae and Koriak took him and Trellian to Dirklan Tunnel. Someone must have gotten him into a passenger carriage with Trellian, for the rocking of it made him feel even more ill than before. She wouldn't let him strip his tunic off. Why not?

Prentov met him at Jourendia's deserted station. For some reason, the man explained that he was the king's aide. Who didn't know that? Oh, Trellian. Prentov drove the cair—Why? He wasn't a driver—while Danivid slid down enough on the rear seat to lean his head on the backrest.

He didn't remember going to the ambassador's suite, but he must have, for he was on the bed...and at last that hot tunic was off. And his throat was parched. "Tea," he croaked and sat up unsteadily.

"I have some water here." Prentov held the glass to his lips, but Danivid made the mistake of trying to grasp it. His violent trembling sloshed water down his chin onto the shirt that already clung to his skin.

Caverns, he was reduced to a quivering mass. "Tea," he said, cringing inside. He knew what he was asking for—and mustn't. "Not that. Any tea."

"I'll make some chilled mint tea for you," Prentov said. "Lie down, sir, and rest. Lady Trellian will stay with you while I'm gone."

Lying on his back, he heard the door close. He cracked one eye open. Trellian was there. "Is this the worst, or does it get even...more...uh, worse?"

"Don't bother about the future. Just know that you are surviving this moment."

"Are you sure I'm surviving?"

"Yes," she said. "You are brave. I have seen it. Every time another bout threatens to overwhelm, you turn your head and steel yourself again. You will conquer this."

That was the first of many encouragements—each one stated with matter-of-fact calm. If only any snatch of hope would stay with him longer than five minutes. Or one minute.

During a moment of—comparative—stillness, he told Prentov to summon Prime Minister Katowau.

"Why, sir?"

"I need to explain what's going on. I can't let her think I've gotten into this state by my own choice."

"I gave her the letter Ambassador Allirae wrote. She does not expect to meet with you until you've recovered."

Had he known about the letter? "I can't remember. What's in the letter?"

"It explained that a staff member aboveground has been poisoning you. That you came here—where you know you are safe—to recover. It also introduced Lady Trellian."

That seemed logical for a few seconds, then he wondered why she needed an introduction. The confusion heralded another round of violent shaking. Somewhere in the midst of it, conversation again registered.

Prentov asked Trellian, "What's going on with his memory?"

"While he's in the throes of it, a fit turns everything to confusion, so he doesn't remember that part. Today, patience means that you will calmly repeat yourself however many times you need to."

"Will there be permanent damage to his memory?"

"No." The hint of confident dismissal in her tone brought a stream of relief to Danivid. "His memory of withdrawal," she continued, "may be sketchy, but I count that as a blessing."

The tremor subsided enough for him to speak. "Why does it grip me so hard? It's only been a month."

"Everyone reacts differently," she said. "In your case, the frequency plus daily increases in the dose may have heightened the addiction."

"Not...your most encouraging statement," he mumbled.

"The good side is that withdrawal may be shorter, even though it feels intense."

In the end, he couldn't grasp how long it lasted. He was aware of nighttime only because the window was dark and Trellian was gone. Prentov endured the night watch with him. Feeding him water, tea, juice, or broth every time Danivid begged him for tea. Now he understood what Velzain had not—the reason Vancent had brought no tea with him but repeatedly asked for it.

Sometimes there was daylight, and it was Trellian who wiped him and coaxed more fluid into him so he could sweat it out again. But all of this blended into the haze of shaking, fevered spasms, and pounding heart. Whether it spanned one night or two, he didn't know. Only that it felt endless.

At last, he awakened *without* the onset of another fit of shaking. Simply awake...after sleep...which must have been longer than a few minutes. He dared open his eyes. Trellian leaned sideways in his favorite chair, her eyes tracking back and forth over the book in her hands. "What—" His voice cracked, and he cleared his throat. "What are you reading?"

"A history of Dirklan. Last year's required text for the prime minister's youngest daughter."

Danivid tried for a smile. "Couldn't she give you an adult version?"

Trellian laid it aside and stood. "I preferred something I could follow despite frequent interruptions." She poured from a flask. "You sound better. Sit up, and I'll shift the pillows for you."

He did so. "I have a bad feeling that you've been forced into unsuitable labor."

"*I* will decide what is suitable for me."

He drank the water she handed him. "I don't think I'm up to arguing that point."

"I wouldn't let you win the argument even if you were in prime condition."

He chuckled weakly. Oh, it felt good to laugh, even though his hand trembled as he gave the empty glass back to her. She pushed the bell lever, and he asked, "Are you summoning Prentov?"

"No, he could use a few more hours of sleep. A single ring means I want food brought up. May I feel your pulse?"

He permitted it, and a moment later, she said, "Yes, much better. In case you haven't realized it, the worst is all in your past."

"Kind of hoped that's what this meant." He cleared his throat again. "Have I been, uh, rude to you?"

She laughed. "Don't worry about it. You always apologized after the snarls."

He cringed. "Ugh, I'm so sorry."

"Yeah, I've heard plenty of that, so let this be the last one. I know that not a single snap was your considered opinion or any reflection of your character."

He didn't know what to say. How could someone who had known him a matter of days be willing to see him through such trauma and forgive his surliness?

Tremors swept through him, but nothing like the earlier violent ones. He was able to eat the bland food that soon arrived, though the effort was tiring. Then he found himself waking again, and Prentov was back.

Danivid sat up. "Where is Trellian?"

"At lunch with Lady Katowau. Would you like to clean up before I bring your own lunch?"

"That bad, huh?" Danivid didn't wait for an answer. A hot shower did wonders for his aching muscles, and the bed had fresh sheets when he returned. He opted for the wing chair, hoping that wouldn't be a mistake. "Is that oyster chowder I smell?"

"Indeed, sir." Prentov pushed a side table in front of his chair and set the tray on it. He began gathering up used linens and clothes, as Danivid lifted the lid from the bowl.

He inhaled the steam. No one could make chowder like the Jourendians. Greens accompanied it, with a piquant dressing, bread, and a generous portion of river grapes. What a pleasure to enjoy food again.

Prentov finished tossing laundry out the door, pushed the bell lever, then sat down and waited.

Danivid finished the chowder and salad before he slowed down. "This is wonderful, simple though it is. There is nothing quite like ordinary pleasure in the company of a friend."

"I doubt they'll ever make decent chowder aboveground, but the friend, you'll see more of. I don't know if you remember what I told you, but my family and I will join you aboveground."

Warmth flowed through Danivid, more comforting than chowder, by far. "It seems I know that, though I don't remember you telling me. I missed you before—and all the more on the evening I discovered Yautan's betrayal. You will have some aide tasks, after all."

"I'm sure. We can figure out the details when we reach the palace. Lady Trellian told me a little about this Yautan fellow, but she cannot know all. Will you fill me in?"

Danivid did so, popping grapes into his mouth between sentences. Only once did he have to pause while another bout of tremors swept through him. He had just reached the part about Yautan meeting him at the top of Dirklan Tunnel after his earlier trip, when Trellian rejoined them. Her unreadable expression changed as her eyes rested on him. Relief, perhaps, but she said nothing.

He backed up a little so she could hear of the malady that had puzzled him and of Yautan's behavior. Finished, he said, "The strange tension I experienced that morning in Dirklan didn't pass until I drank the tea Yautan made for me in my bedchamber. Now it's obvious what was happening—the onset of withdrawal. I could kick myself for not realizing something was amiss."

She shrugged. "I'm not sure how you could have. I doubt there is anyone alive who hasn't felt *off* at one time or another. It's usually nothing."

"Besides," Prentov said, his voice grinding, "you *ought* to have been able to trust a man in Yautan's position."

"*Ought*, yes," Danivid conceded. "On the other hand, I have never fully trusted him. He was the last person with access to King Vancent, who died under mysterious circumstances." Danivid recognized the quickening rhythm of his heart, and half-groaned. "Here comes another."

"Now that you're stable," Trellian said, "try walking it off. Give all that energy an outlet."

"I'm quite tired of this bedroom, anyway." He strode to the sitting room, the largest chamber of the ambassador's suite, with space enough to circle the couch and chairs arranged around a low table.

They followed him and took seats while he paced. Trellian said, "Speaking of the king's death, Captain Koriak asked among his guards about Burnie's location at the time. He was in the corridor outside the bedchamber door all night until the kennel master took him outside. I gather, that wasn't unusual."

Prentov raised his brows. "Really? How fascinating." Danivid laughed at his deadpan delivery, but Prentov continued. "Who is Burnie?"

"Sir Burnswick," Danivid replied, "who enjoys the title of *the king's dog*."

"Oh, I see. What a relief that he has a good alibi."

This time, Trellian joined Danivid's laughter. His shakes seemed to ease with this particular medicine. "I take it that you didn't tell Prentov about our suspicions," he said to Trellian.

"Of course not. I didn't have your permission to do so."

Trustworthy. "I appreciate your discretion. Now that I permit, will you be so kind as to summarize for him?"

She nodded and paused for a moment. "King Danivid and his sister suspect that King Vancent was murdered, but there was no one with adequate motive or an opportunity to kill him in a manner that left no evidence. This past Savoring Day, we learned that someone was dosing King Danivid with ambertrop in a gradual, strategic manner. At a minimum, there is clear intent to get him addicted, possibly with future murder in mind. In the evening, the king—" Her lips twitched. "—and Burnie—caught Yautan poisoning his tea and a glass of water. I should mention that ambertrop has no taste or scent to a human, but the dog can smell it."

"Ah!"

Trellian resumed. "After Yautan ran and was captured by the palace guard, we discovered that he had a vial with enough ambertrop to kill a man. Assuming that he had access to that much in the past, he could have killed King Vancent."

She looked at Danivid. "I haven't had a chance to tell you something I learned from the palace chef, Perkett. The night your brother died,

Yautan fetched bread, butter, and oddly, a *saltshaker* from the kitchen for the king. Perkett told the police this, but was reprimanded for speaking of it."

She tilted her head in a conceding fashion. "It did seem irrelevant, but it's still folly to reprimand someone who gives all possible evidence. I didn't see the significance until I knew how much amber Yautan possessed. The problem would be to get the victim to drink it fast enough to consume a lethal dose before falling asleep. Mixing extra salt with the butter might have made the king thirsty enough to consume a glass of water all at once. Also, the glass in the king's chamber is tinted enough to hide the hue of the poisoned water."

"So..." Prentov said, "he had opportunity. Does he have a motive?"

Danivid finished his pacing and sat on the couch. "None that is clear. Money, perhaps."

"You mean, doing it for someone else who pays him?"

"That could be." Danivid slid a finger across his chin. "Or he could have made money by selling ambertrop. We knew that the queen's maid provided her with the drug, but not where she obtained it. After she was murdered, Yau—"

"Wait. Who was murdered?"

"Not the queen," Danivid said hurriedly. "Her maid was found dead after I dismissed her. The police have done nothing to find her murderer. But as I was saying, after she died, Yautan implied that the maid also supplied ambertrop to King Vancent. Easy to blame her when she is forever silent. I now think it more probable that Yautan supplied the king and the queen, as well, through her maid."

Danivid drew a breath. Did he really want to say this? Not at all. Still, if Trellian was as good as she appeared at solving a crime, she needed all the information. "There is a great deal of money missing from the royal coffers. King Vancent hadn't used ambertrop in two months and was initiating a movement to outlaw it in Welcia."

"So," Trellian murmured, "if Yautan is an amber dealer, he would lose that income when amber is outlawed." She tapped a finger on the armrest. "On the other hand, putting you on the throne only perpetuated the problem."

"True, but he probably thought that the crown would go to Aneen, with her mother as regent. That would guarantee a market for the amber trade." Memory of the evening scene outside the palace played through Danivid's mind. "There was a brief attempt to get Aneen crowned, but Yautan was not involved."

Prentov straightened. "Who was involved?"

"Queen Lenneth and Chief Former Shevnal."

"Shevnal?" Prentov obviously caught the oddity.

Cocking her head, Trellian said, "But you and your sister were adamant that Queen Lenneth would never have wanted to be regent."

"She wouldn't."

"If it was the only way to get amber, I assure you *she would*! You ought to understand the drive by now."

Did he? Danivid understood the craving, but he deemed that craving loathsome. Lenneth might see the opposite. "Only in part. Lenneth did not *want* to be free of the drug. I hope by now, she does, but she didn't that night."

Trellian shook her head. "Perhaps you have some affection for her, but you need to acknowledge that she is a suspect."

"More than affection, Trellian. By law and by my brother's will, I am her protector. But you are missing the point. I was present at this event, and you were not."

Her mouth tightened. "Point taken."

He smiled. "Not that one. The point is that Lenneth was...nervous, reluctant, doing what she was told, and not doing it very well."

"Told by whom?"

"Shevnal."

Her brow puckered. "Is there any connection between Yautan and Shevnal?"

"None that I ever heard of."

"I don't understand that part," Prentov said. "He's power hungry where the Formers' Guild is concerned, but he has no say at all in the monarchy."

"It's true that he didn't belong there." Danivid pursed his lips. "His claim for involvement was a long-standing friendship with the late king and the queen. It's possible she asked him to help her. Equally possible he was manipulating her."

"If he was manipulating, why?" Prentov asked.

"A valid question, but I don't have a full answer. This, I do know. Shevnal has obtained great wealth. Enough to buy much of the property that was owned by the House de Noviam. It's not clear how he amassed enough funds to buy so much land. My chief steward, Stanton, has been researching this, but the answer is much harder to discover than it ought to be. Valuable objects are also missing from the palace, without any documentation of their sale."

Trellian clicked her tongue. "How were the land purchases made? There must be a record of that."

"At first, through public auction, which Shevnal always won. Later, he purchased directly from my brother. Whether public or private, the advice to sell came from Shevnal."

She stared at the opposite wall. "Could he have a motive for murder?" Her finger tapped all the harder. "Perhaps he obtained his initial wealth through amber trade. Can I assume ownership of the land will provide considerable future income?"

"Yes. Also, he's leveraging control of the Formers' Guild to maximize that."

"Sounds like an awful man, but I still cannot connect the dots."

Prentov jerked from deep thought. "Dots?"

Danivid started to laugh, but Trellian looked annoyed. Her hands fluttered. "The pieces of the puzzle. The facts. They don't give a full picture yet."

"What does that have to do with dots?"

"Forget the dots." Danivid curbed his laughter. "We are talking about a possible motive for Shevnal to commit murder."

"Or have others commit it on his behalf," Trellian added. "There is also the matter of the staged accident with your horse the day I arrived."

"What?" Prentov squawked.

So many distractions! Danivid gave a quick recap, and Prentov braced his head on his fingertips.

"You're not going to like this," Trellian said. "I certainly don't. But we may have more than one plot afoot." Her eyes rounded. "I mean more than one plot going on. Nothing to do with feet."

Danivid's chest shook but he got it under control. "I have always thought of Shevnal as a separate problem." His lips twitched. "You did say it's folly not to listen to all possible evidence."

He got a full smile out of her and a chuckle. "So I did. Let's look from the other side. Can you give me a reason why we should *not* suspect Shevnal of murder?"

"Even if he got rich through ambertrop," Danivid said, "or obtained my family's land illicitly, he has it now. The land income alone will keep him swimming in wealth. Why murder *after* he got rich?"

Trellian hmphed like she was disappointed. "Fine. Can you think of a connection between Yautan and Durki?"

"Who?" Danivid asked.

"The missing groom who saddled your horse."

"Oh, him." He shrugged. "Amber craving, perhaps, for motive. For opportunity, I told Yautan the night before that I would ride in the morning. He wired a message to the stable. That's his job, though. Not much of a connection."

"Actually, if Yautan wanted you injured in such a way, he either shouldn't have given you amber that morning, or should have convinced you to ride in the afternoon. Injuries are less severe if you fall while relaxed." She shrugged. "Though he may not have known that."

Morning? Something teased at Danivid's memory, then slipped away. He shook his head and pressed a hand to his forehead. "I once asked Yautan where Vancent got ambertrop. He might have worried I was suspicious of him. If my death were an accident unlike Vancent's death, that may have seemed desirable." He fingered his chin. "That's a stretch, though, and the perpetrator wasn't as clever as he thought."

"The police actions will be revealing," Trellian said. "If they do nothing, they are likely complicit. If they arrest Durki and get him to talk, we may find the clues we need."

"With the king's life in danger," Prentov declared, "they must be forced to act. We do not have time to wait for developments."

Trellian pinned him with a stern gaze. "Time? You will notice that it moves regardless of our desires. Pressuring them is no guarantee of success, and it could cost us useful information." She turned her attention to Danivid. "I do, of course, suggest caution in your activities."

"Fair advice, but easier said than done. Burnie can check my food and drink in the palace, but nowhere else. Whoever is behind this will not repeat the same sort of attempts."

"That is true. If Yautan was acting on his own behalf, locking him up protects you. But if he acts for another, his absence will alert that person. They'll realize that something has been uncovered." She brushed a stray lock of hair back. "Allirae intends to reveal nothing of Yautan's whereabouts, while keeping track of who asks about him. I hope this Shevnal character hears of your absence in person rather than in a message. I would love to know how he reacts."

"I don't like him, but you've never met him. What sparks your interest?"

"That his name keeps coming up without a clear connection. Why do you dislike him?"

"He doesn't belong in the role of chief former. Not even at a local level, much less for all of Welcia."

"Oh. I know little of Welcia's other issues. Does that matter so much?"

Danivid nodded. "He allows building only on the land he owns, but the greatest concern is the quakes. They are small, but they do not stop. He refuses to acknowledge that a problem even exists. The Formers' Guild plans no mitigation."

"Ours does," Prentov said.

"Of that, I was already sure. The quake epicenter is in the ocean. Regissa City is at greater risk than Dirklan. Some plans for seaside barrier walls would be wise."

"Oh." Trellian's brow creased. "But if it's water that poses the risk, aren't the streamers the ones who should be planning?"

"They aren't interested either. Not many of them could do more than manage the flood waters as they recede. I'm the only streamer with the ability to control an ocean current."

"Is it...all right...that you are belowground?"

He grinned. "Don't worry. The chances of an ocean surge are quite low, and I do have a warning system. The wind weavers will be first to know of a serious problem, because it would affect the air as well as the ocean. They'll wire a message to me, and that sort of priority *will* get through. If it happens while I'm here, I must get to the top of the tunnel. I can work from there."

She stared at him in her inscrutable way. "That first night I was in Regissa...what were you doing after the quake?"

"Monitoring the ocean currents. I look for any changes—for direction and speed of an unusual flow."

She still frowned. "I don't get it. I've never lived near a coast."

"Disruption on the ocean floor can displace a tremendous amount of water. It must *go* somewhere. In the open ocean, that's not a problem. A ship on the surface would hardly be affected. But if a surge enters the harbor, it has no exit. Any ships in the port could be smashed. Much of the harbor is surrounded by high cliffs, so most of the water will be funneled into the lowest gap. That puts the palace and the port structures at greatest risk. If they are hit, lower Regissa City will also flood."

"That's terrible. Why would they not prepare?"

He used his most soothing voice. "I didn't mean to alarm you. I was only making the point that Shevnal is not fit for his job. The likelihood of disaster is small, and *I* am paying attention."

"If there is such an event, how much notice will you have before you must act?"

"Some number of hours. I don't know how many."

CHAPTER 22

"We need to talk," Katowau said to Danivid as they left the dining room. "Are you up to it now, or do you prefer tomorrow morning?"

No point in putting it off. He'd had a normal night and day to rest. He walked a few steps before answering, to give space for her husband to take the girls another direction. Trellian hovered like she wasn't sure which way she should go. "Subject?" he asked the prime minister.

"Plans. The current situation aboveground can no longer be tolerated."

"Let's go up to the garden," he said. "Lady Trellian, will you join us?"

They climbed to the third floor, then to the roof level. The view was nothing like a sunset, but a breeze wafted past his cheek. He glanced at Trellian to see her reaction.

Her gaze lifted to the cavern ceiling and swept over the light shafts. "It's like a solid, crystal-studded sky." So matter of fact. "I didn't expect the pinkish color."

He began strolling with her along one of the walkways between raised beds. "That hue shows only at dawn and dusk."

At his side, she turned her head in a broad sweep, taking in the vegetable garden. "I'm glad," she said, "that I was able to read some history before seeing this. To understand the reasons and appreciate the ingenuity."

Ingenuity? Her eyes had found no beauty, but she did find a compliment. "Are you sure no hint of an ambassador lies hidden within you?"

That earned him a sideways look. "What do you mean?"

"Never mind. There are chairs among those trellises up ahead." He led her into that small flower garden, where space had been set aside to feed the eyes instead of the stomach. He pulled out an enameled, wrought iron chair for her.

She sat, then swept her fingers over the matching table. "This design is so beautifully intricate." Her gaze wandered over the trellises, alive with blooms of violet, white, and blue. "You've created a restful charm here, Lady Katowau."

"Thank you, though I always feel a little awkward accepting such a compliment when it is Ellincreo who created the flowers."

"Ah, but you have arranged the blooms to give something more. To enhance the calm and peace they offer."

A pity Danivid couldn't feel that aspect. Perhaps the lingering effect of that hateful drug.

Katowau had tugged her chair into a position where she faced them both. "I received an invitation, sir, from you and Princess Allirae, that was most peculiar."

"Why? Because I was here when it was sent?"

"Oh, that was merely ironic." She waved it away with a flip of her hand. "No, it was the duplication. Sent by wire, plus hand delivery of a letter. And that letter included instructions to bring both the copy of the wire and the letter to the palace."

"The same was sent to all members of the High Council. Communication to and from Felverland has been disrupted, even before my brother died, though the suspicions have just been confirmed a few days ago. I want to see if it is only wires to Bonador Province that are blocked, or if other provinces are affected."

Katowau looked less than satisfied. "The reception's purpose is obvious, of course. Not so much for the High Council meeting the following day."

"Allirae wrote the summons according to my hurried instruction. Didn't she state the reason?"

Katowau altered her voice to indicate a quote. "'To inform High Council members of diplomatic relations with Felverland, discuss ramifications, and consider appropriate actions for an emergency situation.' I doubt it could have been more vague."

He chuckled. "Good. I wanted it vague. Mentioning Felverland is enough to worry whoever is blocking messages. Words like *action* and *emergency* should worry them all the more. They will block it, and records on either side will reveal the relay where that occurs, and hopefully, which individual did it."

"Fine. But Felverland is not our biggest concern. Our *king* has been attacked! That must be the first matter of business."

He grinned at her. "Nice to know I'm valued."

She angled her head down and looked at him beneath her brows. "Joke with me if you like, but don't think I'll let you pass it off as trivial before the High Council."

"I'm counting on your support to show that it is a serious issue. But it is actually the same matter as Felverland and ambertrop."

"No. Both the crown and the bearer of it are the highest priority."

"Ambertrop is the motive for the attack. If you want to protect the crown and my life, ambertrop must be outlawed."

"I agree with that, in any case," she said. "You may as well tell me what approach you're planning before I reiterate that your safety must come first."

"I'll start with declaring that Vancent was murdered and I have been slowly poisoned for the last month. Shock value, you understand.

Then I'll go into the root cause—ambertrop—and enumerate the other ills it has brought to our country. Increased crime—including murder, addiction with painful withdrawal, theft by drugging the victim, treason, strained relations with our neighbor, permanent damage to children, criminal control of the wire system, corruption of the police—that sort of thing."

Trellian's face lit up. He couldn't help himself. "Next time I want to get a smile out of you, I'll list the evils of amber."

She uttered a little snort, made playful by the smile that accompanied it. "You missed. It's the action you're taking that makes me smile. You forgot to mention Yautan."

"What I say about him will depend on what he is willing to say to me when I return."

"Makes sense." She wiggled like a schoolgirl. "Will I be allowed to attend the High Council meeting, sir?"

"Certainly. Are you willing to speak at it?"

Her face returned to unreadable. "What do you want me to say?"

"At a minimum, they need to hear what your people have learned about the longer-term effects of ambertrop. You could describe the problems that Welcia's ambertrop trade causes Felverland. Approach it as high-level knowledge, rather than as a participant with the police. You may include suspicion that Welcian police are protecting Felvarian criminals, and Allirae can back you up. Or we might have her bring it up, and you can confirm that Felvarian police have suspected it. We'll go over all these details with her, for she is good at conveying information strategically."

Trellian responded with her serious nod.

"Does speaking to our High Council make you uncomfortable?" Katowau asked.

"That makes no difference. It is necessary."

Again, Danivid admired her. "Necessity aside, in what way does it make you uncomfortable?"

She narrowed her eyes at him. "Fine. I'm not afraid to speak up, but it's a little worrying when I don't know them or the ways of your councils. Will these actions be enough to outlaw amber immediately?"

"Sorry, no. The General Council must vote on a law that is being drafted. However, the foundation is crucial. That is what we will build with the High Council. I also want to arrange a meeting of the Medics' Guild, where you may share your knowledge of the physical effects of amber and how to care for those in withdrawal. I'd prefer we have that aspect ready as soon as possible. Those who already prefer to be free need not wait for a law. The medics will also help us sway opinions of council members who teeter on the edge of decision."

Trellian surprised him with a sudden exclamation. "This is a good day!"

The childlike passion touched him. "Quite—though I think so because I'm on the safe side of the chasm. Why does it delight you?"

"For the first time, I see what I came for. Something tangible stirring below the hope." Color filled her cheeks. Was it more than the ruddy light of dusk? "Don't take me wrong," she said. "I know you couldn't have given me this before today, but it is still a joy."

"Worth savoring, indeed," Katowau said. "Maybe we can finally get you out of the house tomorrow. It'd be a shame to visit and see nothing of Dirklan."

"What?" Danivid asked. "Did you not take her out even a little while I recovered?"

She raised her hands, palms outward. "Not my fault. Couldn't pry her out of the house."

The light shaft straight above them took its regular turn to wink out. "Oh, my," Trellian said, looking away. "How quickly the light fades."

"Tomorrow," he said, "*I* will pry you out of the house, and let you see the daylight of Dirklan."

"*Now* I would enjoy that. And to see Passage Lake, if we can."

"Of course."

"Will you go to Crysalan?" Katowau asked.

He wanted to. Desperately. He'd felt so separate from Ellincreo this past month. Maybe some time to ponder before the vision wall would give him that sense of closeness he missed—and urgently needed. The road ahead had more treacherous pits than he'd shared with Trellian. She'd be bound to enjoy seeing the lustrous gold, too. But that would add at least a full day to his stay belowground, a day better spent on preparations. Worse, it would take him close to a day's journey from the top of the tunnel—and he'd felt yet another tremor this morning. "I'd love to, but it cannot be this week." He stood in the deepening shadow. "Take my arm, Lady Trellian. I'll guide you to the stairs."

Soon after breakfast, Danivid escorted Trellian to Passage Lake. They stepped from the cair near the short tunnel to the lake cavern. He led her through it, showing her the gates that she'd read about in the history book. A strange ache settled in his chest. The echoing swish of the lake that always called to him stirred nothing.

Trellian scrutinized every detail. Unlike the typical stares of most newcomers, hers was a methodical study. "Is it permitted to close one of the gates?" she asked.

He pushed the lever for the inner gate down, and the two panels glided along their track. "It's usually closed twice a year, out of tradition rather than necessity." The panels met and joined with a seam so perfect it was hard to see.

She slid a hand over the joint. "Is this the workmanship of Devron, or has it been modified?"

He raised the lever to reverse the motion. "Primarily his. I'm not sure if it has needed adjustment. Formers tell me that even rock moves over time." They stepped through the widening gap. "And here, lady, is Passage Lake."

The cavern rebounded his words, blending them with lapping wavelets.

The vast dome drew a gasp from Trellian. As her eyes devoured it, her lips parted in an awed smile. "It's so much bigger than I pictured. And the carving!"

At least *she* could enjoy the beauty. He focused on keeping the dullness from his voice. "Surprising, isn't it?"

"How much has it changed since Devron formed the dome?"

"Not much. It's preserved to convey history, as well as being the source of Jourendia's famed oysters, and a pleasant place to relax at day's end." Would he feel that pleasure again someday? Better keep talking. "The dome is sealed, but in theory, it could be reopened. In reality, that's problematic because of sediment, but Dirklians value tradition." With a guiding hand, he drew her aside from the lake to walk along the platform that skirted it. "One change is that sections of the wall have been clarified. Here, you can see into the equipment room that houses the gate works."

He paused to let her stare at the enormous gears, chains, and motors, then moved on to show her the vessels once used to lift passengers to the harbor above, also on display in their permanent berths behind clear stone. Beyond that, stood a model of the dome. He opened it for her.

She gasped. "Is this the one Devron made?"

"No. That is in his house, which is a museum. Formers in training sometimes make a new model that children are allowed to play with here. Touch and activity are often the best means of learning."

"True." She worked the sliding dome panels of the model open and closed a few times before turning back to survey the chamber. "Thank you so much for bringing me here. That book didn't do it justice at all."

"Written for those who live here, no doubt. They've seen it since childhood and only need to learn of the people and their actions."

She licked her lips and tilted her head in her suggestive mannerism. "I still can't imagine the whirlpool."

He laughed. "Are you hoping for a demonstration?"

"That would be lovely."

"It's not possible with the dome closed, but I can do a little for you." He walked to the platform's edge, his streaming sense diving through the lake. How ready it was to obey him—sneaking past his apathy as it waited for command. He set the swirl in motion, angling streams up to the higher drain channels, while keeping the platform dry.

Low, exultant laughter rumbled from Trellian. She'd come to the water's edge, right at his side. An inherent sort of trust that did his heart good.

"This," he explained, "is the gifted method of lowering the water level for oyster harvesting. I won't take it all the way down, though." He leveled the swirling mass, so it no longer climbed the walls, then drew it up at the center. "And *that* is sort of an upside-down version of the vortex that once descended. You'll have to imagine the monstrosity that used to thrash here."

"Amazing!"

It was—but that was something he knew rather than felt. In silence, he brought the lake to rest. He gestured to the bench protruding from the wall. "Shall we sit?"

She walked with him. "A moment ago, you mentioned the *gifted* method for lowering the lake. Is there another?"

"Mechanical pumps. Such means are used less here than aboveground. Local streamers are still required to learn how to drain without disturbing the oysters." He settled onto the hard bench, its seat and back formed to accommodate human structure.

"Why both?" she asked. "In case of pump failure?"

"I could give you the pros and cons of each, but to my mind, that is not the real reason."

"What is?"

"Some people are gifted to invent. Some are gifted to perform. Both add value to our lives. There is no need to debate which one is better and allow just that."

"Mm." She stared over the water for a thoughtful moment. "I like that answer."

He responded only with a smile, hoping it didn't look as forced as it felt. The echoey hush of the lake sounded inane instead of soothing. Where had the peace of this refuge gone? Maybe he *should* go to the sacred chamber in Crysalan. A portion of him begged for the comfort that eluded him. But what if he couldn't find it there either?

"Are you all right?"

Trellian's voice startled him. "Yes. Does silence trouble you?" That came out too brusque.

"No. You're breathing heavy, so you may as well tell me what is troubling *you*."

He blew a measured breath out, intentionally emptying his lungs. "I thought I would feel normal after the withdrawal. But I don't."

"Recovery may not yet be complete. What *do* you feel?"

"Hard to describe what is not there. A dullness. I'm fine when I talk—or listen—or act—have something to distract me. But the moment I pause, there is nothing where there used to be something."

"Hmm. I don't know many people who've been through this, so I can't tell you if that is common. It may be that you need a little time for normal to return."

When he didn't answer, she laid a hand over the back of his. "Remember that hope is a tenacious force. It would be a shame to let it go before it finishes its job."

Unusual words. Wavelets lapped at the shore. "I've never heard anyone describe hope as a force."

"No...most don't. People say, 'I hope so,' and they often sound like they wish it would happen but don't believe it will. That doesn't make sense when the Holy Writ conjoins faith, hope, and love. The three things that endure forever." She swept her hair over her shoulder and met his eyes. "I think it means that hope sinks its talons in and hangs on to what love decided and faith will create."

Something surged within him. Not the thing he missed...not yet. But something new.

CHAPTER 23

When Danivid and Trellian stepped into the hall of Dirklan House, he discovered someone was waiting for him.

Gairedon hurried forward and bowed. "Pleasant morning, lord king."

"Pleasant, indeed, for it allows an introduction. Chief Former Gairedon, this is Lady Trellian of Felverland."

Danivid waited for them to exchange greetings, then asked Gairedon, "What brings you?"

"I understand you must leave today, and I don't get many chances to talk with you."

"True enough."

Trellian murmured, "I have a few things to take care of," and left them.

Danivid guided Gairedon into a salon. "Are you concerned about the quakes?"

"I don't believe they threaten Dirklan, so I wouldn't worry if..." He shut the door of the salon. "...if you didn't have Shevnal as Welcia's chief former. He is *not* qualified!"

"I know."

"I'm not just talking about his mediocre forming gift. The man is an idiot!"

"Ah, but a clever idiot. That makes him hard to get rid of."

Gairedon snorted. "Clever how?"

"He is good at amassing money and influence."

"Then let him manage a bank. Not the Formers' Guild."

"I wouldn't trust him with a bank any more than I trust him with even a sliver of our planet. Yet a previous king did, so I must have provable cause to remove him."

Gairedon ground his teeth, but Danivid cut in to prevent a prolonged rant. "I'm working on it, so you may consider who would be a good replacement and advise me in the future. For now, tell me of the stability of Jourendia. What if a vast wave suddenly headed toward Welcia?"

Gairedon blinked at the switch from political to practical. "Uh...well, I would think Regissa would be the biggest concern—lower-lying than any other oceanside province."

"Yes, I know that, but if a wave were big enough to trouble Regissa City, it would pass over the dome of the lake cavern. Granted, it is always submerged, but the dynamic will be different."

Gairedon sucked in the corners of his mouth like he always did when he pondered. "It gets plenty of variation when the two moons swing the half-year tides, but the dome never shifts. Still, we could close the lake cavern gates. They were supposed to protect against a dome failure, after all. Would you have time to wire me if such a wave were coming?"

"Yes, and of course, I would warn you. The sort of wave I'm thinking of will not just enter the harbor. It will hit the peninsula too. If I asked Shevnal, he would look down his nose and tell me the peninsula is ipenrock and too tall to be surmounted by any wave. But you and I know that the ipenrock was pierced for drainage when Dirklan Tunnel was excavated." He tried to lighten the gloom with a little humor. "Rain being a real thing aboveground."

Gairedon's brow furrowed. "Yes, pierced for airflow, too, before the lower end was opened. Are you thinking that a wave would drive water into all those gaps?"

"Possible, but I doubt such inflow would be more than an inconvenience. My concern is what everyone knows but always forgets. Water is heavy and dense. The ocean's momentum is an unstoppable force. If too much of it hits the peninsula in one blow, could it shatter even a portion of the tunnel area?"

"Well...I suppose that depends on how much and how fast it's moving. Let me guess. You cannot know until it happens."

"You got that part right. The one comfort I can give is that the waves will not last. But if the tunnel is breached, only a few waves could be devastating to Jourendia."

"Huh." Gairedon was quiet for a moment. "This requires thought. Planning."

"Yes." Danivid rested a hand on his shoulder. "At least here, I can leave it to you."

"Indeed. If you'll excuse me, sir, I think I'll run off and summon the Formers' Guild."

"Please do."

Crowds lined the streets just after lunch to give Danivid and his entourage a warm sendoff. Curious they may be over why he'd come and stayed almost invisible, but it didn't cause them to hold back. Oh, how he missed living among friends!

Prime Minister Katowau accompanied them to the station, saw him and Trellian into a passenger carriage, and parted from them with the words, "See you in a few days."

Prentov's young family took a little longer to get aboard two other carriages, but soon the train skirted the city cavern and started the ascent through Dirklan Tunnel.

Trellian seemed to be looking at everything through the clear carriage walls. Perhaps she'd been too distracted to notice much on the trip down. When they reached the vertical climb, she said, "I never would have imagined this. Trains are supposed to glide, but first we're pulled up a steep slope, and now it feels like the train is climbing a ladder!"

"It is." She narrowed her eyes at him, and he grinned. "Sort of a ladder."

She shook her head. "I thought a king would be all dignified, but you tease. And then there is Prentov, who was dead serious while caring for you, but the moment you're past the hellish part, he starts spouting the strangest jokes. I cannot figure out how to take him."

"He does have his own sense of humor."

"But carrying on about dots?"

Danivid laughed. "I don't know what connecting dots means either."

"What? It seemed that you did."

"Nope. I just wanted to keep the discussion on track."

"You know, like the dot-to-dot pictures that children do."

"Never heard of such a thing."

"Oh! Well, I'll make one and show you." She cocked her head. "I suppose I'll have to make at least four."

"Why four?" he asked.

"Prentov's three children and Aneen. I bet she'll enjoy having other children around."

Would she? "We might need to take that slow." As usual, he felt that he didn't know what the child needed—other than patient love.

Before long, they emerged from the tunnel onto the peninsula, where the aboveground version of cairs waited to take them to the palace. One of his guards opened the carriage door. One of several guards, in fact. Danivid assigned another to escort Prentov's family and belongings, then set out with Trellian. They soon reached the palace, still flanked by guards. Captain Koriak had made changes.

Within the hall, Allirae hurried down the stairs to greet him, Meroak and Aneen following her. Danivid had just squatted to greet Aneen when Burnie erupted into the hall, beside himself with joy. Danivid barely managed to avoid being knocked over. "Sit, Burnie."

Aneen laughed and patted his head. "Good Burnie."

The regular guards and Koriak were soon joined by two aides, the scheduler, the staff hostess, and a server who offered refreshments. Into this scene Prentov brought his family, which necessitated introductions. Since Danivid had wired notice of their arrival, Allirae had made arrangements, but by the time Prentov had met the aides, their gazes had searched the crowd and grew mystified.

"Uh, sir," one of them said, "Isn't…Yautan with you?"

"No."

"Oh! Uh, we assumed he'd accompanied you belowground. Unless you gave him leave, I fear he has gone missing, sir."

"Yautan," Danivid said, "is quite out of favor. Prentov will assume his duties, along with others we'll discuss later. For now, we'll let him settle his family." He turned his back on their gaping stares and strolled into the salon.

The chaos ebbed. Aneen took the center position on the couch as he sat down at one end. Trellian took the opposite end, with her portfolio and pencil in hand, as they had been during much of the train ride. A server placed a tray of fruit and cheese on the low table alongside glasses and a pitcher of minted water.

Allirae thanked the server and motioned her out. Meroak and Koriak joined them as she left, then closed the door.

"Was it the common belief," Danivid asked his sister, "that Yautan was with me belowground?"

"I believe so. He traveled with Vancent, so that would seem normal. He'd always come in ahead of the king and queen and send people scurrying with orders."

"So very important, he was," Meroak drawled, "and now conspicuously absent."

"Did no one ask about him, then, while I was gone?"

Allirae gave him an acidic smile. "Only one. Shevnal."

Beside him, Aneen whispered, "Bad man."

"Shevnal?" Danivid murmured. "When and how?"

"He came for the scheduled meeting the morning you left. I told him you were unwell and couldn't meet with him. He tried prying out what *unwell* meant, and I told him he was presumptuous. Then he asked to see Yautan, and I asked him why. He spewed some nonsense about understanding a sister's reticence, and that the king's health was better discussed between men."

Trellian uttered a derisive grunt.

Danivid subdued his twitching lips. "What had you to say to that, my sweet sister?"

She struck a pose. "'You are dismissed.'" Relaxing, she said, "He decided to leave."

"How about word around town?"

"There was some conjecture, but it became known that you and I had sent invitations for Lady Trellian's reception. Thus, it was assumed that your malady was slight."

Danivid looked to Koriak. "How does Yautan enjoy his stay?"

"He ranted at length about his rights being violated, so I explained the law regarding treason. He is now surly and uncommunicative. He is moved to a new cell each day. He may either clean it or sleep in filth. He cleans."

Danivid laughed, though he shouldn't. "I never knew I was vindictive. Have you questioned him?"

"No, though I told him he could send for me if he had anything useful to say. He has not."

On a sigh, Danivid said, "I shall have to talk with him." He picked up a glass of mint water. "How annoying."

"We have learned a little that could make it more interesting," Koriak said. "Would you like a report now or later?"

"Now, please."

"The dogs have learned to identify ambertrop. We can place it anywhere on the grounds, and they'll find it."

"Excellent."

"We had Burnie and another dog search the palace. They both found some we didn't know of in the room of one of the cleaning staff." He relaxed his stance a trifle. "Mostly, I'm delighted by this because it proves how little ambertrop is in the palace. As for the one culprit, she was quite petrified and answered questions at once. She admitted it was ambertrop. She claims she obtained it before you became king, and had not yet tried it. She planned to take it with her on her next holiday and not bring any back. She says she bought it from Yautan."

"That's useful," Danivid said. "What have you done with her?"

Allirae answered. "That part was easy. We didn't want her in the cells where Yautan could influence her. She has heard that Lenneth's maid was murdered and begged us not to send her away. She is too terrified to speak of ambertrop, so we let her stay in her room, though she is not allowed to work in the palace."

Aneen interrupted his next thought, for she twisted around to kneel on the couch, facing Trellian, to whom she had never yet spoken. He glanced aside to see why.

Trellian angled her portfolio toward the child as she sketched a simple line drawing on a page with scattered dots. Her pencil point passed through each in turn.

"Ah, so that's a dot-to-dot picture," he said.

"Dot to dot," Aneen murmured.

Trellian just smiled and brought her pencil through the final details at the bottom of what was now a drawing of a seated dog.

"Cam," Aneen said.

The dog sat up from her snooze beside the couch, and Trellian asked, "Should I add some black patches?"

"Yes."

Everything else remained suspended as Trellian's pencil swished in shading. Aneen began pointing where the patches belonged, without even turning to look at her dog. Trellian took quick glances, but Aneen knew every spot by memory.

Aneen stared at the finished product, then lifted her shoulders high and let out an ecstatic sound. "Cam!"

The dog stood and shoved her head into Aneen's lap, wagging.

Aneen gazed at Trellian. "Cam likes. Aneen likes."

He felt like whispering, *Da'vid likes it too.* Then it got better.

Trellian removed the drawing from her portfolio and another paper behind it. More dots. "You may have the picture. Would you like to try drawing one?" Aneen pumped her hands, which Trellian interpreted as *yes.* "Just sit down again, and we'll set this on your lap so you can draw." Trellian got things positioned, gave Aneen the pencil, and pointed at a dot. "Start here, and draw a line up to this dot...and to this one..."

Aneen stopped and handed Trellian's finished picture to Danivid. "Hold." He didn't catch on to what she meant until she positioned his hands. She wanted it held up—and didn't want to be told which dot came next. She used it as a guide, looking up and down to follow the dots on her own drawing.

Trellian had made the two dot-to-dots identical. Wise choice, but even she looked stunned by the result, her lips parted in delight. Danivid glanced at the other faces, enjoying their surprise. Even Koriak looked pleased, though he seemed stunned by Trellian.

Aneen finished the dots, smiled profoundly, and set to work on the patches.

Danivid said, "Aneen, you are so clever with drawing." Perhaps her nod was simple agreement, or perhaps it was the fluid extension of her smile. Either way, warmth flowed through him. He couldn't help but see this as an enormous breakthrough. A way for her to communicate, though fluent speech was denied her.

Following a satisfactory meeting with his steward and lawyer, Danivid took the lawyer and Prentov down to the foundation level. Koriak had prepared by cuffing Yautan's wrists to the bars of his cell.

Danivid strolled the wide aisle, looking over barred cells on either side, while Yautan glared at him. "I see you have learned a new skill. Just as well, since cleaning cells is the most illustrious work you will ever be allowed in the future."

"I'll be released after my trial. Why did you even bother to come down here?"

"To let you see the extent of your failure." Danivid gestured to the lawyer. "I assume you know Turnin already. He will read the statement of charges to you in due course. This is Prentov, my aide from Dirklan, who has now joined me aboveground. He will record your answers to my questions."

"Good," Yautan snarled.

Koriak walked a few paces away and picked up a mop that leaned against an empty cell.

Danivid began questioning. "Are you ready to admit that you put ambertrop in my tea?"

"I gave you exactly what you asked for. Exactly what you—"
Koriak drove the mop handle into Yautan's ribs.

He grunted hard, clamping his jaw and eyes shut, then cringed on his first breath.

Danivid said to Prentov, "Whenever he speaks something other than a direct answer, note down the word *evasion*. You need not document his blather."

Yautan wheezed, "Confession under torture doesn't stand in court."

"That was for disrespect," Koriak said. "I'll not touch you if you answer questions." His voice developed an edge. "Did you put ambertrop in his tea?"

Yautan glared at Danivid. "I have nothing to say."

"Impressive. Succinct words. They don't matter, because I already have ample proof that you did. I even have proof that you sell ambertrop to others."

"It's legal to—"

"Shut up." Danivid used a conversational tone. "Who supplies you with ambertrop?"

"I don't have to tell you anything."

"You," Turnin said sternly, "are ignorant of the law. You *are* required to answer the king. Were it a trivial matter, you would only be fined for non-compliance. But this is far from trivial. A suspect's refusal to answer questions is deemed an admission of guilt. The charges against you—at the moment—include murder of King Vancent, murder of the queen's maid, theft of royal property, and poisoning of King Danivid with treasonous intent. Further charges under consideration include collusion with other parties to commit treason and the murder of King Danivid. If you believed that your dealing of ambertrop was legal, you would tell us who supplied you. Either state the name of any and all suppliers or decline to answer."

Yautan's color faded. "You have no proof!" he hissed. Perhaps he considered that unwise, for he added, "You can't have proof because it's not true."

Koriak angled the mop handle toward him again. "The name of your supplier."

"I..." Yautan spread his hands pleadingly toward Danivid. His fingers trembled. "They don't reveal their identities. Even though it's legal, some people are so judgmental about ambertrop. It's not worth the bother of people finding out."

Koriak growled. "You know who it is, though, don't you?"

"Lord king, please. I cannot tell you what I don't know."

"Obvious, though irrelevant. Even in brief, you skirt the question. Who else is part of the plot to get me addicted to ambertrop?"

"Sir, there is no such plot."

"Blatant lie. Who else?"

"I have no answer I can give you."

"That's a shame," Danivid said, his voice like silk, "for all the blame and all the punishment will fall to your lot. Since no sane judge will believe you are acting alone, you will have to bear the punishment of your co-conspirators. Don't think they will step forward to shield you. They have you where they want you—positioned to take full blame for their deeds if you failed in your part. Thus far, you show yourself fool enough to shield those who will destroy you." Danivid motioned to the lawyer. "Turnin, give the formal reading of charges."

While Turnin intoned condemning words, Danivid watched Yautan. He gripped the bars. For support? To still his shaking hands? He said nothing in response. Not even when Turnin reminded him he would be considered complicit in further assaults on the king, since he would not name his co-conspirators.

"The case against you," Danivid said, "will be discussed at the High Council meeting scheduled for second workday. A high judge will conduct your trial."

CHAPTER 24

Danivid paused where the colonnade ended, overlooking a hillside. Crumbling columns stood atop the far hill, the last hint that an ancient structure had been toppled by a quake. The steps leading to it lay in disrepair. That hilltop offered a fine view of Mount Estelle, but he shouldn't wander around ruins. Not in his current frame of mind.

He turned and strolled toward the harbor, glad to be spared the city's clatter now that the work week had ended. As he neared the cliff, a small structure jutting from the colonnade came into view. An open-air chapel. Or it had been. The mysterious golden columns that had fascinated him as a child were no more. Likewise, the fire gems no longer waited to burn incense in the stone-cold brazier.

His brother's explanation came to mind. *No one offers prayers with incense anymore, and I didn't want them stolen.*

Sure—sell them to buy ambertrop, Danivid snarled inside. Theft would have been better!

Danivid entered the vacant chapel and leaned against the rail, looking out over his beloved harbor. It sparkled in the sunlight. Burnie scouted the mosaic floor but grew bored and stretched out for a rest in the shade.

Silence—the living sort nature offered, with birds singing to the accompaniment of distant waves and wind. But the musical hush of nature wasn't peace. "Where are you, Ellincreo?"

Only wind whispered among the columns.

"You've spoken to kings and queens here before. Why do you hover so far distant? Do I not need you more as a king than I did as an ambassador? You wrapped me in comfort then. Why not now?" He hadn't meant to complain. Silly to do so, anyway, but an ache in his chest drove more words out. "I felt you with me the night I vowed to serve as king. Is it not by your authority that I reign? But ever since, I've felt such...*nothing*, when I need respite."

Still, the breeze filled in the silence. Was it his fault somehow? Perhaps his lack of focus when he read the Holy Writ. Only now did it occur to him that he had been under the influence of that cursed drug while he read each morning. "You know I never meant to take that. Do I deserve to be shunned because of it?"

You are not shunned. I didn't go anywhere.

Of course, he knew that Ellincreo was everywhere. That pretty much made it impossible for him to leave. But that didn't answer the aching question. "Fine. You are not gone, but why do I no longer sense your presence?"

I am found by those who seek me. You got used to a deadening calm and no longer sought my enlivening calm.

"How much seeking do I have to do?"

It almost seemed that he could see Ellincreo raise his eyebrows in gentle irony. *Have you noticed that we are conversing?*

"Yeah, I just..." Danivid closed his eyes in frustration—not knowing which words to use. What was he even trying to express?

Amid the uncertainty, he realized the words no longer mattered. For he stood within the calm he sought. The calm that enabled perception. Enabled decision and action. How different it was. How strong. Compared to this, the ambertrop version of calm was blatantly weak. Pathetically so! He understood now—in a way that he could never have grasped until he'd felt both the real and the false calm. A valuable understanding. Not that he would recommend this method of learning, for the risk of the trap was too great.

Suddenly, Burnie jerked up from the floor. Seconds later, Danivid felt the tremor. He'd lost count of how many there had been. All the quakes that Shevnal ignored.

"Lord of gifts, why did you bestow the forming gift on Shevnal, when he stewards it so badly?"

I bestow gifts on everyone. What each does with the gift is their own choice.

"Some suffer because of the choices of a poor steward."

True, but the alternative is to control your actions. I love all of you too much to deprive anyone of free will. The risk is great, but I am here to warn the unwary and to restore those who are hurt.

Not an unfamiliar answer. Suffering could come from free will. And while Danivid would never give up his own right to free will, it was no easier to tolerate the harm that came from another person's choices. Yautan's, for instance. "I sure could have used an advance warning on that!" he muttered.

You mean like the oddity you noticed when he went to calm Lenneth? Or a dog that objected to Lenneth's known supplier—and Yautan. Or your brother's letters, which did not include Yautan among those he trusted? Do you want me to continue?

Danivid clenched his teeth. This was what came of criticizing the one who could see everything. Judging one's own creator never worked well. "Fine. I had...indications...that I overlooked. And yes, you have restored me, for which I am grateful."

Before he could form his next words, an image of Trellian soothing him through a bout of agony filled his memory. "And thank you for sending Trellian to us." That seemed inadequate. "I doubt I even know yet the extent of...all that she...will come to mean before this is over. I remember the passage in the Writ about you bringing good out of our worst disasters, so I'll thank you now, even though I can't see it yet."

Some good is already evident.

Was it? He felt dense. "Uh, what?"

Had you not suffered through the counterfeit, would you ever have understood its subtlety? Would you have enough empathy to help those who have yet to recover?

Danivid pondered. No, he would never have imagined how deceptive and seductive it was. As for empathy…he'd just thought the users of it were fools. Not the sort of viewpoint to generate compassion for those in his kingdom who were trapped. Those who needed help to get free. Help they would not find unless *he* made sure it was provided. "Convincing point," he said. "While we're talking, I still don't know who's at the bottom of all this."

He felt a smile from Ellincreo. *You will.*

D anivid returned to the palace. He ought to spend some time with Aneen. This being Family Day, her tutor would be away, and he never felt right about leaving too much of her care to Allirae and Meroak.

He paused in the hall and asked a guard, "Do you happen to know where Aneen is?"

With a grin, the guard pointed aside. "In the salon, sir."

Why the grin? He went to the salon, where the answer must lie. And there on the floor, sat Aneen—and Trellian—surrounded by papers. "What's all this?"

"Da'vid look." He'd never heard the child sound so excited. "I drew." She rose onto her knees to grab his hand and pull him downward.

His manners urged him to help Trellian up from the floor, but Aneen held a paper in front of his eyes. A drawing of her dog—not complex but better than the skill of a seven-year-old. Nor was there any sign of guiding dots. He took it to study closer. Despite what she'd already said, he asked, "Did you draw this?"

"I drew," she declared.

Oh, no. Was he going to have to figure out how to explain lying? "All by yourself?"

"Trell..." Aneen uttered one of her frustrated grunts as her hands stiffened and began to shake.

Trellian spoke, her calm voice emphasizing certain words. "I *showed* her *how* to get the proportions right, then she drew several pictures."

"Showed...how," Aneen whispered, frowning.

Trellian smiled at her. "*Trell showed how* would be a good way to say that."

Pointing at various papers, Aneen said, "Trell showed how. I drew."

Had she ever used those words before? Did she truly understand them? Perhaps that didn't matter, for the drawings were amazing. He felt like he had just witnessed the bestowal of a gift. Inside, he thanked Ellincreo. Aloud, he said, "Aneen, you draw very well. You draw better than I do."

She laughed. "Da'vid draw water."

Trellian grinned at him. "We'll have to see about buying you some watercolor paints."

He started to shake his head, but Aneen looked hard at Trellian. "Water...color...?"

What, next, would come of this?

He was still wondering an hour later. Aneen drew her dog in five more positions. Perhaps it would just become one of her obsessions. She only stopped when Cam went to the door and whined to be let out. Trellian took Aneen and all the drawings to a table by the window, where she explained light and shadow in simple terms, then demonstrated shading.

Trellian stood behind the child and watched her try shading for a few minutes, then silently rejoined Danivid. "That should keep her busy a while," she whispered.

He ushered her to the couch and whispered even softer, "She either leaves her companions nothing to do or requires full attention."

"Since I showed her that first dot-to-dot, it's been full attention every time she sees me."

"Overwhelming?" he asked, still hushed.

She sat a little sideways to face him. With a shake of her head, she replied, "Endearing. I've never had a child warm up to me like she does." She quirked her lips. "I'm told I'm intimidating."

"Not to her." He grinned. "Do you cultivate intimidation?"

"Not really." The corners of her mouth twitched. "But I will admit that maintaining a cold expression can be useful while questioning suspects." Despite suppressing the urge to laugh, his chest shook, as she continued. "Don't worry, though. I will be polite at the reception."

"Ah! Lull them into complacency. Good strategy."

This time, *she* laughed. "Nonsense. I just want to know them a little before I address the High Council." She flipped to a back page in her ever-present portfolio. "Allirae told me about the key guests—that is, who is part of the High Council, and who is...locally influential." She pointed to the lower list, with only the word *local* for the heading. "Is anyone missing that you deem significant?"

He scanned the list. Some names were followed by titles, such as guild chief, mayor, or captain. Others had no designation. "That looks complete." He swept a finger down the list. "I'll give you formal introductions to the High Council members and at least these locals."

She pointed to the group he omitted. "Who are these people?"

"Those who have come into wealth over the past several years. Many of them own the buildings being constructed on de Noviam land that is now owned by Shevnal."

At the table by the window, Aneen muttered, "Bad man."

Not the first time she'd suddenly revealed that she listened while others talked. Nor the first time she'd said that of Shevnal. She understood more words than she spoke. How much more?

He rose and went to the table where she drew. He squatted to place himself at eye level with her. "Aneen, has Shevnal hurt you?"

She didn't look at him. Beneath a deep frown, her mouth contorted. "Bad man."

Maybe the best she could do, but he needed more than that. Yet he mustn't put words in her mouth, for though she could repeat them, he wouldn't know if she understood them. How could he help her speak? Danivid glanced at Trellian, searching for any ideas.

She was as intent as he. When their eyes met, she stood and approached, calmly sitting in the other chair at the table. "Why is Shevnal bad?" she asked Aneen.

Her pencil went still on the paper, her fingertips whitening from her tight squeeze. She scowled. "Makes Mama cry. Makes Mama go-way."

Strange. Shevnal had not made Lenneth leave—not directly, anyway. Aneen wouldn't know how the decision was made. What was the connection in her mind? That morning when Shevnal visited Lenneth—could Aneen have been in the room? Danivid asked, "Why did Mama cry?"

Her mouth contorted again, and the pencil lead broke. Her frustration over words was so tangible, his chest hurt. She blurted out, "No money, no...a'ber."

Opposite him, Trellian mouthed the word *amber*.

That was certainly what it sounded like, but they used the full word in Welcia. Not that Aneen could pronounce *ambertrop*. Nor did he know how she'd heard this. "Who said that?"

"Shevnal." She spat his name. "Mama cry." She sniffed noisily. "Mama gone. Dada gone." She threw her pencil and beat her fists on the table. "Don't—like—gone!"

She turned her wide eyes and wet cheeks to him on the final word. It sounded like anger, but he saw a plea. He wrapped his arms around her, and she melted against his chest, sobbing onto his shoulder. He murmured into her hair, "I don't like gone either."

Caverns, it was hard not to cry! Poor, broken-hearted child. Blinking back tears, he looked at Trellian, who was rubbing Aneen's back. Her eyes were wet too.

They comforted Aneen until she cried out her last tear, her breath grew even, and she muttered, "Aneen tired." The poor dear was spent.

"Maybe a nap would be good today," Danivid said. "I'll carry you to bed."

She lifted her head and rubbed her palms across her wet cheeks, smearing everything worse. "I'm big. No carry."

Somehow, those infantile words held grown-up determination. He pulled his handkerchief out and gave it to her. She wiped her eyes and blew her nose. Trellian smoothed Aneen's mussed hair and refastened it in its clasp. Then Aneen took a firm hold on his hand and said, "Bed."

Once the child was asleep and Danivid explained the situation to his sister, Allirae and Meroak returned to the salon with him. Trellian still lingered there, and they recounted what they'd learned. He hid a smile when Trellian showed him her documentation of the exact words Aneen had spoken and asked for his confirmation. If only his own police were as precise.

"I just wish," he said, "we could have discovered this without subjecting poor Aneen to more trauma."

"You didn't, though," Allirae said. "In all this time since her father died, she's had bouts of temper but never a solid cry. She needed a chance to let the trauma *out*, so I'm glad it happened."

He hoped she was right. At least, it was a better way to look at it than feeling guilty.

Meroak looked up from the drawing he was studying. "I'm not quite sure how we can use the information. Even if she were an ordinary seven-year-old, her words wouldn't be considered evidence."

"No." Danivid picked up the pencil she'd thrown. "It simply reveals a possibility—that Shevnal is the supplier behind Yautan."

"Is there any other evidence of it?" Trellian asked.

Danivid spun the pencil between his fingertips. "Not that I've noticed, though he doesn't visit me as he did my brother. Allirae?"

She settled into a chair, her gaze distant. "I've seen him talk to Yautan a few times, but that's hardly surprising. Vancent gave Yautan more to do than you did." She rocked her shoulders. "There's the letter Vancent wrote after getting free of addiction. He referred to not trusting his closest friend, which must have been Shevnal." She shrugged. "He was here often enough to do pretty much anything."

Suddenly, it clicked. "Here when?" At her surprised look, he added, "I mean what time of day did he come?"

"Mornings."

"Always?"

"Mostly. He was often invited to dinners and evening parties too."

His expression must have given away his thoughts, for Trellian demanded, "What is it?"

"The connection. Between Vancent and me. Between Shevnal and Yautan."

Her eyes begged for more.

"I know from my scheduler," he said, "that it's nearly impossible to get an afternoon meeting with Shevnal. The day is never an issue. Only the time. It must be early."

She frowned. "Yautan drugged your morning tea. Maybe your brother's, too, but is there proof of that?"

Allirae replied, "He has certainly carried that same tea caddy for years. But don't forget, Vancent took ambertrop willingly."

Danivid paced. "Either way, morning is the easiest time to drug by means of tea. Yautan knows the king's schedule. Whether Vancent requested ambertrop or not, Yautan could have made sure he had it, or had extra when Shevnal was expected."

Trellian murmured, "Those two months when your brother had stopped using...he stayed free, so Yautan was complying with his decision. Perhaps waiting him out, hoping pressures might drive him back to amber. The likelihood of ambertrop being outlawed would be too much. Thus, the motive for murder."

"It could also have been harder to drug him," Meroak said. "Vancent had an absolute aversion to tea the last couple months."

"That could have been due to his withdrawal experience." Danivid tapped Aneen's pencil against his palm. "Whether it involved Shevnal or not, Yautan may have believed he could continue stripping wealth from the royal family through Lenneth as regent. When that failed, he needed to get me addicted."

Trellian tilted her head. "What about the staged accident with your horse?"

"My death would still suit him—or them—if they didn't think I'd written my will."

"Shouldn't you make that clear?"

"I will at the High Council meeting. That is where succession plans are formally announced. I haven't even given a copy to the Chief Keeper of the Writ as Vancent did."

"Do you not trust the chief keeper?" Trellian asked.

"I do, but when he urged me to write my will at once, I was noncommittal and told him to let me know if anyone inquired about it. I admit it's a bit of a stretch, but I'm desperate for evidence. Whoever killed Vancent couldn't have known that the chief keeper had a copy of

Vancent's will. Now they would likely check that. If someone asks about my will, that could be a useful lead."

Trellian exhaled audibly. "Your lack of care for your own skin is quite appalling!"

Danivid stopped pacing. "If I cannot get to the bottom of this, I will have to fear murder for the rest of my life. Better a risk now than a lifetime of paranoia."

She shook her head, not looking at him.

Meroak smirked at her reaction, but he turned to Danivid. "I cannot imagine Shevnal approaching the keepers with that or any other question."

"It's still not certain whether Shevnal is involved in murder," Danivid said. "He is so rich and powerful already that there is little left for him to gain. Whoever might want me dead would use a tool. Though that is a risk, too, since the person may reveal who wanted to know. I can only hope that the murder or disappearance of such tools makes others less eager to follow. Speaking of which, our worthless police captain has yet to find that suspect groom, any leads on the murder of Lenneth's maid, or any information about the sinking of Vancent's sailboat."

He stopped fiddling with the pencil and set it on the table. "I authorized Stanton to review all files that the king's aides maintain. There is only one document pertaining to Police Captain Narwick—his appointment a few years ago, signed by Vancent. No request for applications, no candidates, no qualification checks, no letters of recommendation. Allirae, do you remember anything from when he was chosen?"

"No, I was in one of the provinces at the time—and Meroak was with me. I knew the previous captain was retiring, but the replacement was selected before I returned." She shifted in her chair. "I'm not excusing him, but Vancent simply wasn't as methodical as our father." She rocked her shoulders again. "Sometimes, but not always. Less so as the years passed. We could say that's because of ambertrop—but equally say it was his personality."

"True." Danivid sat down. "There is another little problem with Captain Narwick."

Trellian zeroed in on him again, waiting.

Danivid hid a smile. "He owns a share in one of the buildings on land that Shevnal acquired from Vancent."

Allirae digested that. "A connection. Certainly not illegal."

"No," Danivid conceded, "but if he harms Shevnal's interests, he harms himself. This is true of quite a large number of those enjoying new wealth. I asked Shevnal to provide the owners of all building projects that the Formers' Guild is working on. Some are individuals, or families, or small investor groups who don't hide their identities. Others are company names. Turnin has identified the members of most of these companies, though in many cases they were difficult to discover. The police captain was among those whose names were concealed."

"Mm, well...interesting," Allirae murmured. Her expression said more.

Trellian huffed. "Let me guess. That is something else that is legal."

"Irregular," Danivid said, "but not illegal, unless hiding identity allows a crime. The king, however, has a right to demand answers when he deems it necessary." He stretched his legs out and leaned back. "I'm going to enjoy my next meeting with Shevnal."

Trellian ground her voice so low, she sounded like a man. "I do hope you can enjoy it without giving him reason to arrange your immediate murder."

He grinned at her. "Don't worry. I won't bring up ambertrop poisoning."

CHAPTER 25

At Trellian's request, Danivid allowed her to join him early on first workday while he waited for Shevnal in the small salon, which was more cozy than formal. The same one Vancent had often used for visits with the man he once considered a friend.

She promised to leave after an introduction—and to show Danivid the drawing she would produce. He was curious to see how close she could get based on a glimpse of no more than a few minutes.

Right on time, a guard admitted Shevnal, then closed the door behind him.

Danivid lounged in a chair facing the door, lazily watching as Shevnal entered and checked for an instant on seeing an unknown face. He refocused and bowed. "Pleasant to greet you, lord king."

"Pleasant morning," Danivid replied. "Lady Trellian of Felverland, this is Shevnal, Chief Former of Welcia."

She stood as he introduced her, and Shevnal inclined his head toward her. "Ah, I heard of your arrival, Lady Trellian. It is a delight to meet you."

"Thank you. I've heard of you too. Perhaps we can find time to converse this evening at the reception. I will leave you to your meeting with the king." She strolled to the door, as unhurried as her smooth words.

Shevnal watched her leave. When the door closed, he said, "That was a rather quick exit after an introduction."

"She was only bearing me company while I waited for you."

"Ah. Quite a tall and lanky young woman."

Says he, who is tall and narrow. Danivid let the irony pass. "That is not how I would describe her."

"Oh?" Shevnal sat opposite him. "Do you find her attractive?"

"I find her knowledgeable and intelligent." Though the words held reproof, Danivid delivered them with such unconcern that Shevnal could be excused for not noticing. The stiff formality left his expression. Good...assuming it meant he believed Danivid's act.

Shevnal leaned back. "I was concerned when I heard you were ill, but I'm glad to see that you've recovered."

"Thank you."

"No lingering effects, I trust?"

So, he wanted to probe, did he? Danivid hid his amusement. "None."

"There was considerable speculation amid rumor, but I never did hear what ailment troubled you."

"Why should you? Even a king is entitled to some privacy."

"Of course. I did hear that you went to Dirklan to recover." He produced a smile that must have been intended as humor. "How did Yautan deal with going belowground?"

Danivid raised his brows. "Pardon?"

"Oh, it's just that Vancent used to joke about Yautan's, shall we say, misinformed attitude regarding that province."

"I suppose he remains misinformed, then. He did not accompany me."

"Oh!"

Danivid raised his brows again. "Why should he?"

"Well, your personal aide...naturally, I assumed...though, I suppose I'm thinking more of the past, since I saw him often. Vancent used to send messages to me through him."

"Did he? Yautan as a page? What an improbable image that creates."

"Well...perhaps only to me. We were such close friends, after all—your brother and I, that is—and Yautan so trustworthy that privacy was assured."

"Curious," Danivid drawled, "that Vancent had need to send you private messages."

This time, Shevnal chose not to elaborate.

Danivid slouched onto one armrest. "I've yet to notice any particular trustworthiness. About the only thing Yautan is good at is making a delicious cup of tea."

Subtle tension eased from Shevnal. With a faint smile, he said, "A useful skill in a personal aide, though how we got on this subject, I don't know. What did—"

"You brought it up," Danivid said in a rambling fashion. "I don't recall ever mentioning Yautan. How do you happen to know he is my personal aide?"

Shevnal waved a hand sideways. "Assumption, since he was Vancent's. But I'm sure you had other things you wanted to discuss."

Danivid gazed toward the ceiling. "Oh, yes, there was. Uh, something about land. I'll think of it in a moment."

Shevnal looked positively benign. "Are you thinking of the woodland, perhaps?"

"Oh, that. I was curious why you want to buy it. What would you build there?"

"That would depend on the builder who wanted to invest. I only offered because...you understand, I was in your brother's confidence and knew of his financial difficulties. Which you have inherited. It would suit us best to be candid. I can help you with funds. I'd be happy to advise you as I did your dear brother. My offer will be quite generous for however much of the woodland you wish to sell."

"Your generosity is appreciated, but I don't want to sell. I want to build on it."

"Ah. I'm not sure if you have considered. Building costs a great deal."

Danivid shrugged. "Small matter. It will provide income when complete, and in the meantime, you have promised to be generous."

After a split-second, Shevnal said, "We were speaking of the purchase. There is more to building than you realize. I'm sure it will take longer than you envision, and the Formers' Guild is quite involved in many projects. Even the architect won't be available for quite some time, and that's only the planning stage. I doubt completion will be soon enough to cover your needs."

"What I *need* is consistent income."

"Understandable. I'd be happy to advise you on a mutually beneficial option."

Danivid laughed.

"Sir?"

"Shevnal, I am not an early riser, but no matter how sleepy I am, it is quite obvious that all of your previous *mutually beneficial options* have enriched you while impoverishing the House de Noviam." He stretched his arm out to a table and picked up the papers that lay upon it. "I have the proof of that here." He tilted the papers so Shevnal could see the top one. "I'm sure you recognize the report you sent me."

"Of course. And that report shows that many people own the buildings, but I own none. Many residents of Regissa are benefiting from the projects."

"True, but you own all the land. Considering the money involved, I think it's rather odd that you don't own any of the buildings."

"Not at all. I'm—"

"I wish you woodland stop going off on tangents. We are discussing who these owners are, for your report was quite sketchy."

"It is accurate, sir."

"Some individuals and families are named. The rest are company names, rather than people."

"That is how the agreements are structured."

"But it is not the information I requested. Fortunately, my own staff pays better attention to their king than you do. They've discovered who owns these companies." He flipped pages and ran his eyes down them, then looked over the top of the papers. "You are familiar, I assume, with the significance of a king's request?"

"Of course. Since you have the information you desired, it seems my response was adequate."

"Not entirely. There is this odd reference to R.E. I'm sure you are familiar with that entity, since R.E. owns the most elaborate building of all, which spans more land than any other and rises to twice the height of its many neighbors. Quite an impressive centerpiece." Danivid wrinkled his brow. "Yet no such company seems to exist. No accounts at any bank. No record of it anywhere."

"It is a privately held and funded entity."

"Held by whom?"

"Lord king, I'm sure you realize that some people enjoy the fame wealth brings them, and that others dislike fame. R.E. is among the latter."

"What does R.E. stand for?"

"Regissa Enterprise."

"Just as vague. Who owns it, Shevnal?"

"I'm afraid I cannot reveal their identity."

"Their? Is it more than one person or are you hiding even their gender?"

"As a matter of honor, I cannot reveal their identity."

As though he possessed honor. Danivid tossed the papers back on the table and shrugged. "No matter. I'm sure *they* will reveal it."

"I assure you, they absolutely will not."

Danivid smiled. "Now, that is pleasant to hear."

It took Shevnal a moment to respond. "How so?"

"The only way you can be so certain is if *they* are dead. Like my brother. Vancent would have wanted a property that could provide him long-term income. And since I am my brother's heir, that means—*I* own the building."

Shevnal eased back in his chair. "You are mistaken. Vancent never had anything to do with R.E."

"Queen Lenneth is another possibility. And you were seen trying to get my crown on her head."

"Forgive me, sir, but you are mistaken in that as well. I acted on her wishes that night. Nor has she ever had any part in R.E."

"Then you are the next obvious choice." Danivid held up a hand. "Don't bother answering, for you *must* deny it. There have already been complaints that you use your position as chief former for your own benefit via ownership of the land. If it were discovered that you own the largest structure upon all that land, you know what would happen. The chief former title and guild's current charter will come crashing down around you...and...all...of the owners and builders you have shoved into the guild. All...gone...in one moment. And then, there will be the lawsuit."

Shevnal held up both hands. "Sir, please stop. I do not own R.E."

"This game is tiresome," Danivid said, not even needing to fake his unconcern. "This so-called R.E. positively reeks of fraud. The crown will seize it, and if an actual person owns it, they will step forward to claim it. I hope they are ready to explain their strange dealings with you, *Chief Former*. You, of course, will still end up in court." Danivid swayed one hand. "Defying the king, complicit in fraud, etc., etc."

Shevnal's mouth pressed into a thin white line. His gaze locked somewhere below Danivid's face.

Danivid waited. Would he reveal the truth or produce a lie?

Shevnal licked his lips. "R.E. is owned by a lady who does not wish to be married for her wealth. You are a gentleman. Please do not harm her by dragging her into public accusations when all she wants is privacy—and happiness."

Quakes! Could that be true? Or manipulation? Danivid responded drily. "How touching."

"It would be devastating to her, but if you are not a gentleman, after all, consider your own interests. So many are waiting to see your true colors. Making a spectacle of the poor lady, who has done nothing wrong, would damage your own reputation beyond repair."

"I think they might be looking at *your* true colors. Imagine how black your colors will look when you marry her yourself."

Shevnal's startlement was actually believable. "Oh, no, sir. There is no chance of that. I'm too old for her, and she has no such interest in me." He seemed to try to regroup his thoughts. "I wish you could believe that I do have your best interests at heart. I make every allowance for your doubts. Perhaps it is grief. Perhaps you think your brother's spendthrift ways are my fault, but in truth, they are not." He raised earnest eyes to meet Danivid's. "I *will* help you out of this financial quandary."

"You created the quandary. Why would I trust you to help me out of it?"

"You don't even have to. Not a single coin will pass between us, nor an inch of land, nor any document. But you can very soon have all the money you could possibly need. I do know the solution, but it was not mine to share. At least not yet."

"What are you babbling about, this time?"

He opened and closed his mouth. "The lady...I believe...*you* could marry her."

Danivid's brows shot up so high they could snarl in his curls. He let a slow chuckle build. "I thought she didn't want to be married for her money."

Shevnal closed his eyes in apparent pain. "I wish you would not force me to betray what a lady said to me in confidence."

"It's just so hard to imagine a lady telling you anything about her marriage interests."

Shevnal glared. "Quite a large number of people consider me a friend."

"Obviously. You have a *large* amount of money. At the moment."

He clenched his teeth, then rearranged his expression and spoke calmly. "Nonetheless, the lady has known me many years and does trust me. She told me of her hopes because *she* fancies *you*, but she made a fatal mistake without realizing it. She wanted my advice on how to correct the misconception she had unwittingly created."

"Words, words, words. Would you get to the point?"

"She was at the governor's dinner party. She didn't realize how adamantly you object to ambertrop. Knowing that the dose was very mild, she filled her glass from that pitcher. She rarely uses it and would not mind giving it up entirely. But now she feels you will have misjudged her, and she doesn't know how to set it right."

Danivid stretched his legs out and leaned back. "All of this could be true or false, but none of it answers my question. Who owns R.E.?"

"Would you at least give me time to talk with her and obtain her permission to tell you?"

"No. Who owns R.E.? Answer me this time, or I will charge you with contempt and summon guards."

Shevnal drew a shaky breath. "Lady Zendell."

That name was no surprise at this point. The wealthy widow who had already shown her interest in him. She'd even invited him to brunch later this week. Danivid held a faint smile in place as he studied Shevnal. His hand was trembling. Why? Fear over what he had revealed—whether true or false? Did he fear repercussions? From the owner or from Danivid?

Oh, caverns! Danivid had pushed farther than he'd intended. Shevnal now had a reason to get rid of him fast. Nor could he have the man arrested. Yet. But his grip on Shevnal was tight, and the man would lose everything if he didn't satisfy Danivid.

Suddenly, the puzzle pieces slid into place. Danivid recognized the trap. If he gained that building by marriage, Shevnal would have a grip on him through his ownership of the land the building stood upon. Then, there was the lady herself to consider. She could be hand-in-glove with Shevnal—or innocent. He needed to let Shevnal think his plan was working...at least until the High Council met. And if possible, he needed to glean some information from Lady Zendell. And find out if she'd had enough money to finance that building herself.

"I do not believe," Danivid said, "that Lady Zendell was invited to the reception. You may bring her as your guest."

"An excellent suggestion," Shevnal said, then made a dignified departure.

Danivid hurried to his study, where Stanton awaited him, and closed the door with a snap. "Shevnal claims that R.E.—Regissa Enterprise—is owned by Lady Zendell."

"Hmm." Stanton pushed his lower lip forward. "Wealthy, but I wouldn't have thought she could supply adequate funds on her own."

"Find out for sure. After Shevnal denied owning it himself, he fabricated nonsense to avoid revealing the owner."

"What sort of nonsense?"

"That the owner wanted privacy because 'they' don't like fame—don't want to be married for their money."

That surprised a chuckle from the dour steward. "He said that about *Lady Zendell*?"

"He didn't get to her name until later. It's possible she owns part of it, but all his evasion tells me that he must own a significant share. And if so..." Danivid clenched a fist. "I have him."

Lady Zendell turned a jeweled bracelet on her slender wrist. What ailed Shevnal that he must bring all this veiled tension into her elegant receiving room? Maybe some would see nothing unusual, but she'd known him ever since she married her late husband. Shevnal's urbane polish seemed like a spired façade, rising from the deep cushions of her satin-covered chairs, piercing the wispy blues and whites she'd chosen to lend a calm atmosphere.

Of course, everyone had a façade. Even her husband had. Though he'd welcomed her shrewdness in most of his affairs, he'd also had business dealings he refused to explain. That realization had shattered her youthful naivety. No matter. She'd had enough to do with managing their ever-increasing wealth. Where it came from had not seemed important—nor had the reasons for his private meetings with Shevnal. A mystery she had allowed to fade—though a faint worry lingered.

Shevnal's odd discomfort didn't suggest anything she wanted to hear. Nor did his strange manner of inviting her to this evening's reception at the palace.

She pursed her lips. "So, you're saying the king invites me, even though he didn't invite me, but actually, *you* are inviting me. Why all these contortions for a simple matter?"

His thin-lipped smile looked more fake than usual. "An issue came up at my meeting with him. Something you would have preferred to not have mentioned."

What could he mean? She tilted her head in silent question.

Shevnal continued after a moment. "He wanted to know who owns R.E. I thought I could avoid revealing it by claiming a lady's right to privacy...hinting that the lady didn't want others pursuing her for her money. Yet I couldn't let him think that the lady would be indifferent to him...for I would never jeopardize your interests in that regard."

Her stomach tightened. If he'd expressed himself this poorly to the king, he may have ruined her chances. "This is business, Shevnal. I need the details of what was said—as exact as possible."

She listened with all the care this delicate situation required. It didn't seem that he had jeopardized her chances with the king, but he kept referring to her ownership of R.E. Ah! That explained his tension. No need for *her* to worry. Much need for *him* to. This could be pleasant, after all. She let him talk himself out.

"I hope you can see that I tried to keep your name out of it," he said, "but in the end, I couldn't refuse to answer him."

"No, indeed. Don't let it bother you. I don't mind him knowing about my ownership." She waited for a hint of relief on his face, then said, "My *portion* of ownership, that is. I only agreed to the extreme privacy because you wanted your sixty percent ownership kept secret."

"That stipulation in our agreement is still necessary."

"Then it's a pity you broke it."

He shook his head. "No, I didn't mention my part. We'll let him assume you own it in full."

"But now you are asking me to lie to the king. Worse, a lie that is certain to be found out in the future."

"Simply don't speak of it. You had agreed not to mention that property until after the marriage you hope for."

He had reverted to his calm negotiation voice. She smiled. "*We* hope for."

He chuckled, though no smile reached his eyes. "I'm not planning to marry the king."

"I'm not going to let you pretend, you know. This is business. It has been ever since I found out you gave Governor Rikion the idea that I should escort the king at his party."

Shevnal said nothing.

"People complain about your arrogance, but that's not your real problem. It's greed."

He let his eyes roll under veiling lids. "I don't need a sermon from the Writ."

"You probably do, but I won't be giving it to you." She shook her head. "You started with little, then became the richest person in Welcia. But it was never enough. You had to own the controlling share of the most elaborate building in the country. But you knew you shouldn't, so you hid it."

He looked down his nose. "You also reach high. You want to be queen."

"And you, Chief Former Shevnal, want to hold onto your title and all that it guarantees. Which, in truth, is the ability to control the value of land in Regissa—and beyond." He still had that smirk on his face, so she didn't let up. "I know all about conflict of interest. I know why you needed to stuff the guild full of people who depend on you to construct for them, while *not* constructing or repairing for others. You support them, and they support you. *Their* ownership of buildings is the veil concealing how you line your own pockets."

She smiled at his persistent sneer. "But you got too greedy and kept the biggest and best for yourself. Once it's known..." She waved her hand in a descending spiral with each point. "...the other owners will doubt you...the king has cause to revoke your position...and the high judge will agree." Her hand dangled toward the floor.

His nostrils quivered. "Fine. You know so much, you should know that your investment is also at risk."

"Oh, no!" She tried to hide her smile, but it wouldn't be denied. "My investment is set to grow, with no strings attached."

"How so?"

"You told the king I own it, and you want me to perpetuate that lie. If I am successful in marrying him, he would hate me the moment he found out that I betrayed him into your control. The only way I will say that I own the entire building—is if I *do* own the entire building and the land it stands upon."

He swallowed but achieved a shrug. "That's an expensive jewel. What are you offering for it?"

"Not a single coin."

He laughed, his surprise almost making it sound like mirth. "Then you will not own a single rug from the floor."

"Not so. I will own it all, for no matter its value, it is worth far less to you than everything else you stand to lose. You had better get the deed placed entirely in my name before I have occasion to talk with the king."

Shevnal snorted, but she held her poise, for sweat beaded on his brow.

"Are you sure you want to cross me?" he purred. "Don't you realize how hard this decision will bite you?"

"Lying to the king would bite much worse. You are the one who tried to force me into that position. You poured out this bitter medicine, so you are the one who will drink it."

Tight-lipped, he rose and trod a dignified path to the door. A moment later, the street door opened and closed.

She strolled to the window and watched from behind a sheer drapery as he climbed into the back of a cair and sped from her sight. His threat was real, assuming he deeded the property to her. He would send a counteroffer. Perhaps controlling interest in the building but none of the land. Which she would refuse, with a demand for all or nothing. He'd be forced to accept her terms. And then he would make good on his threat—attempt to make her pay or suffer a greater loss. She pondered...turning over options for countermeasures.

The best of them involved the king. If she could tell him tonight that she owned the most lucrative structure in Regissa, right down to the land it stood upon, then her chances of marrying him had mounted to the sky. At least on the financial side. He had principles too. A pity that he was set against ambertrop. She enjoyed it now and then, but she'd give it up for a crown. She must convince him she was switching to his side. How best to do that?

CHAPTER 26

Danivid reviewed the latest version of his motion for presentation at tomorrow's High Council meeting. He had the feeling that Prentov was holding his breath. "Yes, I believe this covers it." A good thing, for it still needed to be copied before tomorrow. Why couldn't the inventors come up with some kind of simplified printing press, so his staff didn't have to slave over hand copying?

He handed the paper across the desk to Prentov and smiled. "Thank you for the long hours you've put in, especially since they came right on top of moving your family."

"My hours are no longer than yours, sir, and with the reception and meeting so close at hand, I don't see how we could have done it any other way." They both stood. "I'll get the aides started on copying this, and I'll be up to your room in half an hour."

Danivid grimaced. "A half-hour reprieve for me before days of nonstop politics."

Prentov grinned as they walked to the door. "Sneak off where your latest houseguests cannot see you. I happen to know that the musicians are practicing in the ballroom, and I believe ladies Allirae and Trellian are there."

That did sound tempting. They parted in the hall, and Danivid followed strains of music to the ballroom. A bit echoey, since much of the room was empty. Magnery chandeliers reflected from the glossy floor and gilded marble walls. The vast room had space enough for many dancers and still allowed chairs around the edges and dozens of little tables, soon to be loaded with hors d'oeuvres and beverages. Yet it was the woman who watched a dancing couple that interested him.

Lady Trellian spared him only a quick glance as his footsteps gave away his approach. Her attention was fixed on Allirae and Meroak.

"Is this the opening number?" he asked.

"Oh, Danivid." Allirae twisted her head to look at him as she turned in the dance. "I'm so glad you've come. They don't do this dance in Felverland."

"Well, something similar," Trellian murmured, "though not with the promenade steps. Allirae says I'm expected, um…"

She sounded uncertain. Such a rare tone in her voice, that it drew gentle chivalry from him. "My dear sister had better not have dictated what I plan to request. May I have the first dance with you, Lady Trellian?"

She caught the humor and relaxed. "I'd be honored, of course." She added a whisper. "But enjoy it more if I knew the steps."

"Easily accomplished." He held out his hand, palm down, so she could rest hers atop it. She did so—Allirae must have explained that part. "This rather awkward formal escort position is only used in the first dance of royal events," he said, placing his other hand on her waist to guide her.

She followed his steps with ease while they faced one another. "It's the transitions that worry me. I don't know when to step back."

"As I release your waist on this faint rising trill." He lifted her hand as they switched to side-by-side movement. "Good. Unfortunately, this is the final promenade, so we'll end with the bow and curtsy." They bent to match the words. "Not enough practice, for me. Will you join me in the full dance, lady?"

She smiled at his implication that *he* needed the practice. "Please."

Through the open windows, the bustle of yet another arrival reached them. Allirae glanced toward the sound. "Another interruption, but never mind. We'll greet them for you." She and Meroak headed to the door, which she closed on her way out.

The leader of the musicians looked questioningly at Danivid. "Repeat the opening piece," he said, then led Trellian through the entire dance. All thought of the politics that lay ahead slid from his mind. She mastered the transitions, and he could soon add more complex twirls. Such a pleasure to dance with a graceful partner, especially one with stamina for this lengthy dance.

Rising from the final bow, he took both her hands. "It has just dawned on me that I am going to enjoy this evening far more than I expected."

The whisper of a chuckle emerged with her answering smile.

Arrayed in a coat of deepest green, with copious gold trim, Danivid settled his emerald- and diamond-studded crown upon his brow. It no longer annoyed him, for Rebanak had re-formed the interior to a precise fit. Leaving his chamber, he strode to the staircase, then stopped to savor Trellian's approach.

Her gown of seafoam green would complement his traditional colors this evening, though her embellishment was daintier. A gathered fall of lace around the back and shoulders tapered in the front to meet the V neckline. A matched set of jade necklace, earrings, and bracelet added understated polish. Rather than the complex twisting styles of hair that Welcian ladies wore to parties, Trellian had only drawn the sides back, allowing her waving locks to cascade over the lace. She would be less elaborate than many of his guests, but in his opinion, the most elegant.

Atop the stairs, Danivid offered his arm. "You look lovely."

She accepted his escort and the compliment with a quivering smile and soft, "Thank you," as they descended to the hall.

The murmur of many voices reached them—the governors and nobles who had arrived from their provinces and now waited in the salon for dinner to begin. Nonetheless, Danivid paused at the bottom of the stairs and waited for Koriak to approach, then asked, "Has the party from Eavertin arrived yet?"

"No, sir. However, I've received wires from all remaining stationmasters acknowledging your orders to grant priority. Their train is about an hour from Regissa station."

Considering the number of dignitaries coming to the palace, perhaps it was too much to expect that all travel plans would run smoothly. But Lord Eavertin would be a strong supporter of Danivid's agenda. He couldn't help but be suspicious of the myriad delays that had plagued their journey.

His tight lips must have shown his displeasure, for the staff hostess drew nearer and dropped a curtsy. "We have prepared for their late arrival, lord king, and will provide all that they require."

"Thank you." He strolled across the hall with Trellian.

"What's the issue?" she whispered.

"A broken rail, and no former could be found to repair it. Which could have prevented Lord Eavertin's attendance at the High Council." He had no time to say more. He slipped his hand beneath hers and lifted it for formal escort into the broad drawing room.

Introductions galore, followed by dinner in the state dining room, and a brief interlude for his houseguests to refresh themselves before the local guests began to arrive.

Fortunately, the Eavertin party reached the palace before the throng. Danivid stepped into the street-side vestibule of the hall to greet them, his focus on Queen Lenneth. She looked better than he had dared hope, though not strong. He took both her hands in a tight clasp. "Lenneth, my dear sister, how are you?"

That question may have been poorly chosen, for no sound came out with the first movement of her lips. She tried again. "Exhausted."

"No doubt. From what I've heard, you've had an awful trip."

Lenneth smiled at the staff hostess who curtsied to her. "We did," she said, "though I can be easy now. I hope Lady Trellian will understand if I don't come to meet her tonight. I'm just so worn, and I want to see Aneen."

"Naturally. No one will be surprised." He released her hands, about to greet her parents.

Lenneth touched his arm, and he turned back to her. "Danivid, I… well, there isn't time to talk now, but…I want you to know I'm not angry with you, even though I was at first."

Warmth flowed into his words. "Thank you, Lenneth. Tomorrow will be hectic, but we will find time to talk, for I do realize that much needs to be said."

He welcomed Lord and Lady Eavertin before sending them on to their delayed dinner.

Moments later, he began greeting a steady flow of guests, introducing Lady Trellian over and over. She handled the tiresome ordeal as though born to it. There was more to this woman than police officer.

In due course, the musicians began a prelude and Danivid led Trellian to the floor to open the dance. Her grace was flawless as they circled one another, and her transitions perfect. After the first promenade, Allirae and Meroak twirled onto the floor to signal others that they may join in as well.

A fact Danivid barely noticed while Trellian smiled at him. Perhaps it was the setting, but her staid expression was only a memory. "I didn't realize how much you enjoy dancing," he said.

"Who says I do?"

"Your smile, your energy, your grace."

The corners of her mouth quivered. "Hmm, well then, I will admit that some dances are more enjoyable than others."

"I quite agree. And this one just might be my favorite of all time."

"Ah, but it is only the first of the night."

"Trust me, I've danced with most of the ladies here. Obligatory for a prince, you know. None of them stirred this much pleasure, even before they were married."

"Oh, poor prince."

He chuckled at her mock sympathy. "Then you must take pity on me and save the last dance, so we may end the evening with a memory to savor."

Lady Zendell watched while sipping daintily from a cut crystal glass. Since gentlemen gave the first dance to the lady they escorted, she was without a partner. Even if Shevnal didn't have the worst sense of rhythm in the province, his anger would have turned awkwardness to torture. Her promise to help him get the woodland—once she was married to the king—had dulled the knife edge of his fury enough that she didn't bleed from his glance. But the less time she spent with him tonight, the better.

No matter. She wouldn't want for a partner. Her charm and wealth guaranteed her favor would be sought. She let her complacent smile grow. And that was just the wealth they knew about. Once she was queen...

Her gaze returned to the king as the circling dance brought him into her view. A fine-looking man, especially with that smile. Courteous, too, attentive only to his partner. Lady Trellian, of course, since she was the visiting dignitary. She danced well. Not surprising, considering her role.

The king twirled her out and drew her back in, sharing first a smile, and then a laugh as she made some quip.

Quaking caverns, what was that lighting up their faces? Zendell took firm control of her expression. She must reveal nothing. For if what she saw was true, this would *not* be a relaxed evening. She viewed them from a dozen angles, and not one glimpse told her she'd been mistaken. Nor did her later glances, as she shared the dance floor with them. They remained pleasant and courteous to future partners, but none of their smiles went beyond polite.

This required strategy, for she might not have as much time as she'd thought to engage the king's interest. He would not dance with her until he'd honored the ladies of the High Council. But her chance would come—and she would be ready. Know her rival first—if rival Trellian was.

A good thing Zendell knew how these particular musicians liked to space their brief intermissions. She maneuvered so as to end a dance near Trellian at a moment when conversation would replace dancing. Ignoring a governor who was advancing toward the guest of honor, Zendell said, "Ah, Lady Trellian, you dance quite charmingly."

"T hank you, Lady Zendell," Trellian replied, and watched to see the reaction.

Zendell raised her brows to match her increasing smile. "An impressive memory, despite I know not how many introductions. Will you join me for a glass? I've been hoping we could find a moment to talk."

The lady had already begun moving, urging Trellian toward one of the small tables. This was no chance meeting. Zendell had a goal. They each took a glass and moved clear of the small crowd converging on the beverage table. Rather than sitting, Zendell found a nook between two enormous flower arrangements and maneuvered them into it in such a way that it would be awkward for anyone else to join them. Amusing. What could she want?

With the look of an insider, Zendell said, "This will be comfortable. I do so hate to be jostled. Don't you?"

"I suppose. Though empty preambles are worse. What do you wish to discuss?"

Zendell's brows arched up again. "I wouldn't exactly call it *discuss*. More of a simple chat."

"Then what would you like to chat about?"

"You are quite direct—though I admit I've never been to Felverland, so I don't know your native style of conversation. A gradual approach is more common in Welcia."

Zendell used such flowing gestures and expressions that Trellian accommodated her with a smile and friendly tone. "And yet the King of Welcia prefers direct conversation. Interesting."

"Ah, you must have the king's ear."

What? Some sort of cliché? Trellian's inner artist rendered the mental image so absurdly that she had to choke back a laugh. "We talk frequently, if that's what you mean."

"Yes, naturally you would." Zendell may have realized she wasn't doing well. She used a sip from her glass to create a pause. "Since you like it direct, I'll dive into what could be an awkward topic. Ambertrop, in fact."

"Oh. It's not awkward to me." Trellian smiled. "Unless you're offering to sell me some. *That* would be awkward!"

Zendell tittered. "Quakes, no! I've never had much interest in it myself. The little I tried left me wondering why such a fuss was made about it. But the fuss is turning into an uproar, and..." She assumed a serious expression. "...one must acknowledge that it has caused serious difficulties for some people. It's just hard to separate facts from emotion—on either side of the touchy opinions. I wondered about

your view of the matter. I gather Felverland has a longer history with it."
She ended on a prompting note.

"True." Trellian sampled her own tangy juice. Danivid had demanded
secrecy about the motion to outlaw ambertrop that he would present
tomorrow. Even the content of the speech she had practiced before
him and Allirae was to remain unknown until she gave it. She needed
to be careful in what she said. And yet, public opinion didn't change
because politicians debated behind closed doors. Both approaches were
needed. In her opinion, winning over the masses was most important.
It was necessary that she be deemed approachable—reasonable. But also
necessary she didn't ruin what Danivid was doing. How could she cover
both needs?

Trellian swallowed her slow sip. "What prompts you to ask?"

"Well...I thought I knew what made sense. But if my judgment was
based on ignorance, I'd like the chance to correct it."

A reasonable response. Questioning further would be
counterproductive. "We've had about twenty-five years to see the
long-term effects in Felverland. I understand why Welcia initially
considered it harmless. We did too. In fact, medics were the first to
introduce it—to calm patients during difficult procedures. Now medics
are the most vehement adversaries."

"Why?"

"Because they are called upon to treat those harmed by it. There is no
easy way to break the addiction—which can sometimes occur following
only a few uses of the drug. Repeated use was never the medics' idea,
and it nearly always leads to addiction. We don't have time here to go
into all the problems it causes. Damage to children, impaired judgment,
increased crime, etc. But there is a truth that Welcians should already be
able to recognize. The ambertrop dealers hide their identities—a strong
indication that they, at least, know how harmful it is."

Zendell shrugged. "That point is the easiest to contradict. The Keepers of the Writ condemn the use of ambertrop. Dealers just want to avoid the stigma that they feel is unfair."

Trellian tilted her head. "It's an interesting conundrum. Do the keepers *cause* the condemnation? Or do the dealers bring condemnation on themselves by harming others for their own gain?"

"The keepers are quite vocal about it! Offensively so."

"What is worse? To offend those who cause harm, or to be silent and allow many others to be harmed?"

"This is the point where the argument becomes circular," Zendell said, "because the dealers say they are helping, not harming."

"Do you know many dealers?"

It took Zendell an extra second to answer. "Perhaps, for I know many people. I wouldn't be aware of that part of their, uh, business dealings."

"Then where have you heard the argument you just conveyed to me?"

"I attend many social events. It comes up now and then, and the general idea is repeated."

"Repeated from where?"

"You don't give up, do you? The one concrete example I can give you is that the papers printed an article some years back. A Keeper of the Writ publicly challenged a known dealer, and their argument grew heated enough to attract a crowd. And an agent of the press. That is the angst I want to avoid, which is why I asked for facts."

"You're not the only one who wants to know." Gentle strains of music indicated that the musicians were beginning another set. "For now, I will just tell you that the dangers of ambertrop are worse than Welcians realize."

Stepping away from their flowery alcove, Trellian hoped her words were vague enough to avoid immediate and deadly repercussions. They may have been heard, for a gentleman stood near enough to ask her for the next dance and another escorted Zendell to the floor.

Trellian's new partner was the son of Regissa Province's governor. The dance kept them in one area of the floor, facing each other as they rotated with the steps. Trellian asked about the new construction in the upper city to see where it would lead. His face lit up, and he launched into a description of the building he owned and the high-quality tenants he was attracting.

Bragging, in fact. This sort was always scattered among society at any level. Tiresome, but harmless.

His expression changed to one of distaste. "Every way I turn, there's a guard propping up a wall and staring down our fun. Two of them even have *dogs*!"

She couldn't resist asking, "Why are guards surprising? This is the palace, and the king is present."

"King Vancent never had guards hovering over his parties," he grumbled.

"Doesn't that rather hint at the reason?"

"What do you mean?"

Unbelievable. "King Vancent died young, without known cause."

Her partner lost track of his steps and almost tripped her before recovering his place in the dance. "Well, that...that has nothing to do with guards at parties." He looked everywhere but at her. "And I don't want it to spoil your fun."

Pathetic. She replied cheerfully. "It doesn't bother me at all." The dance ended after another moment. A good thing, for he hadn't come up with another word to say.

A few dances later, Trellian chanced to spot Danivid approaching Zendell. Whatever words they exchanged, they did not join the dancers. Instead, they turned toward the garden doors. Not good. Trellian nearly made an excuse to the gentleman who was about to lead her onto the floor, but Captain Koriak moved around the ballroom toward those same doors. His job, not hers. A fact that did nothing to get her mind off Danivid.

CHAPTER 27

Lady Zendell smiled up at the king. He'd made it so easy, including an option in his invitation. "A cool garden breeze is far more tempting than a dance," she said.

"The garden it is, then." He drew her hand onto his arm and strolled with her through the open doors.

They traversed the paved walk and descended the steps. Torch-style magnery lamps cast an unnatural mix of light and shadow over bushes and flowerbeds. She glanced at the king. Below the golden glint of his crown, half of his intent face lay in mystery. He seemed to gaze neither at the garden nor the starry sky. "What are you looking at?"

"The harbor," he said. "Sensing it more than looking."

"Oh, of course, the royal streaming gift. Perhaps you were always meant to be king."

Though his brow lowered, he didn't respond.

A little gust from the harbor provided her with a quick change of subject. She spread her hands wide to take full advantage. "The breeze is such a delicious relief. I pity you with those long sleeves."

He released his frown. "No need. My tailor comprehends both fabric and summer. I noticed that you found a moment to talk with Lady Trellian."

"Indeed. An interesting conversation."

"Oh? About what?"

"Ambertrop." She tilted her head. "My choice of topic. I've begun to doubt the prevailing opinion and wanted a view based on longer experience. And less rant."

"Then you chose a good source. Her speech is refreshingly clear—and free of rant."

"Do you think she is accurate?"

"Yes—more than anyone in Welcia. For, as you noted, Felverland has the long view. Do you care to share your thoughts on the matter?"

"I shall let the amber flasks pass by me in the future. Though I never used much, it doesn't seem worth the risks."

"If you don't mind my asking, where did you buy it?"

"Oh, I've never bought any myself. My late husband kept some available, but I've just had a little at parties. I won't miss it."

"Did he use it often?"

"Only in the evening. The one danger he warned me of was that a person should never make decisions for several hours after taking it." She lifted her brows in dainty displeasure. "I can also vouch for its ability to induce sleep." Hopefully, he would catch what she couldn't say—that her husband caused their childless union. "I will admit, as I began to think of my future family, I was already disinclined to consider marriage with any man who uses ambertrop."

"Or anyone who pursues you for your money?" His tone matched the ironic lift of one eyebrow.

"*Pff*. Shevnal told me what he said to you. So silly! As though people in our station can marry *without* considering money."

He faced her with a teasing grin. "So, you *do* want to be pursued for your money."

Not the normal way to play the game of flirtation, but humor was a good sign. She laughed softly. "There is more to marriage than money."

"So I have heard. I gather that love has something to do with it."

His tone remained teasing, but...there was no denying that he was talking of marriage. This seemed too good to be true. Her innate negotiating sense waved a warning flag. But if he favored direct discussion, he might think her disinterested if she evaded.

She granted his words a thoughtful look. "I prefer the sort of love that grows out of truly knowing someone. Mutual respect and kindness are more trustworthy foundations than the flowery sort of love that naive youths put their faith in." She had the satisfaction of watching his expression change to genuine interest. "But I suppose you know this as well as I do."

"It sounds like something my father once said, though I lack your first-hand experience. So—money and slowly nurtured love. What else is there in marriage?"

She shrugged in an off-hand fashion. "Whatever the parties bring, for we all have our own gifts. For instance, my late husband knew I had learned business savvy from my parents. That was more significant than the investments I brought to our union." She tilted her head playfully. "So, you see? I don't in the least mind being married for tangible benefits in addition to respect and love."

Wow. She followed Danivid's bait better than he wanted. At this rate, *she* would propose to *him*! But it was worth it, for he could now ask what he wanted to know. Get the corroborating evidence to lock in an accusation against Shevnal. "Doubtless, then," he said, "you will find a husband soon. I hear you are even more wealthy than most people realize. Regissa Enterprise is no small thing. How much of it do you own?"

She inched nearer, her voice turning to silk. "All of it. Even the land."

His lungs morphed into rock. This couldn't be! Stanton had found a registered document...and only one. Near proof that she couldn't own it all. But if she did—Shevnal was as secure as ever. Keeping fury from his face took supreme effort.

Zendell turned to him, for he had stopped on the path. "I imagine that land must be especially dear to you."

Caverns and skies, what was she playing at? He needed time to think. He choked out a non-answer. "Oh?"

A hint of surprise flickered in her shadowed eyes. "It's part of the de Noviam land."

"That Shevnal bought from my brother?"

"Yes, but now—"

"Are you lying to me?"

Her shoulders dropped. "No! Of course not. I would never!" When he didn't budge, she added, "Besides being illegal, it would be stupid beyond anything."

Revealing reasons. Honor was not among them. He held a level tone. "After I discovered the hidden owner of Regissa Enterprise, it was not difficult to find your investment document of record—executed by you and Shevnal. You exchanged a substantial sum for forty percent ownership of a proposed building. Land was not included. In fact, there is not a single record of him selling any land, ever. How is it that you now tell me you own all of it, land included?"

Her smile returned. Like she held a tantalizing secret. She took another step nearer. "I acquired it." She rested her hand against his chest. "For you," she purred.

He had never understood how a man could hurt a woman, but the temptation to shove her away swept over him. He let his voice deal the blow. "Lady Zendell, maintain a proper distance."

She nearly stumbled backwards at his rebuke. Her voice squeaked, "I thought you'd be—"

"When did you acquire it, and how? Where is the document of record?"

"I don't understand you at all." She straightened her shoulders and drew a breath, easing back into her customary poise. "It was a private business arrangement. I hold the deed, which I will soon have recorded. But you sound so angry that I think you have misunderstood. I obtained it for *you*. I thought sure you would be pleased."

"Are you saying that my name is on the deed?"

She uttered a dry laugh. "Well, no, even *I* couldn't have negotiated that out of Shevnal. But don't you see?" She swayed gracefully. "It can be yours."

He held his tongue, willing her to let something slip.

She ducked her head. "I see that I was too forward. I never intended that, but somehow, we got onto the subject of marriage, and I mistook what you meant." Her eyes lifted to his with a soulful look. "But even still, I got that land for you. I know your brother sold too much, and you must marry someone who can bring wealth to the match. Which I can, even without this land. I have the skill to restore the fortunes of the House de Noviam. But I thought..." she folded her hands at her waist. "...if I could get that building free of Shevnal's grip—if I could get that land—then I could give you a wedding gift that is deeply meaningful to you."

"Let's test the truth of that statement. If I marry someone else, will you deed the land to me as a wedding gift?"

She blinked at him, then smiled. "Ah, you can negotiate shrewdly. No, it is too valuable to be a wedding gift to anyone except a spouse. I will deed it to you when we are wed."

"In other words, you are trying to coerce me into marriage with an offer of land."

"What coercion? You are free to marry anyone. If you want this particular piece of land, I will either sell it to you or exchange it for some other parcel of similar value."

"What did you pay for it?"

The split-second she took to answer was telling. "It was a mutually beneficial arrangement of a private nature."

"That sounds as coercive as your offer to me. With no transfer of ownership on record, I must wonder what is going on—much as I suspected fraud when I learned that Regissa Enterprise hid its ownership."

"Sir, why do you take this tone with me? I cannot understand it at all. I got this land away from Shevnal for *you*. I was so sure you would be delighted."

"I would think someone with your business savvy would ensure that all parties of the deal are willing participants." Though she gasped, he continued. "My affairs are matters of state. They are not, and never will be, for your personal gain."

She held herself very erect, with her eyes veiled. "Unintentional though it was, I apologize for my error, sir." Anger vibrated under the contrition she seemed to be trying for.

"I acknowledge the apology, but it cannot protect you. Who, besides you and Shevnal, knows of your acquisition?"

She glared at him before answering. "No one." Her compressed lips wouldn't rest, so he waited her out. "Both copies of the deed are written in his own hand," she said. "He normally has an aide write up documents."

"If you hope to spare yourself avoidable damages, I recommend that you speak of this to no one. Not even to Shevnal. You would be wise to bring the deed to me."

Her nostrils flared. "That is not—" she clamped her lips on whatever folly she was about to speak.

"If I am occupied," Danivid said, "you may give the deed into the hand of Stanton, my chief steward."

Perhaps her silence meant surrender. Or battle. He resumed the tone of a courteous host. "You may enjoy the garden as long as you like." He left her there and strolled back into the ballroom.

Danivid sank into a chair in the drawing room adjacent to the dining room. "The one thing I dislike about hosting parties is that I must always be the last to leave." Burnie lay down beside him, rested his head on his paws, and sighed his agreement.

Allirae wandered in from the dining room, a glass in her hand. "You're the king. You can leave anytime you want."

He shook his head at her, as Prentov said, "The high cost of good manners. May I get you something, sir, before the staff clears away the buffet?"

By the clinking of dishes, they must already be at it. "Something to drink—whatever you can find that I would like." Trellian had followed Allirae, also with a glass in one hand and a crisped cake in the other. She bit into it, and Danivid's mouth watered. "And some of those cakes," he said to Prentov's back.

Danivid gave Trellian a moment to chew, then asked, "Did you enjoy your reception?"

"It was quite interesting." She sat beside Allirae on the couch facing Danivid. "By the way, I got to meet Queen Lenneth's father, who shared conversation with me instead of a dance. He wanted to hear about amber—and wasn't the only one to bring up the subject."

"I understand that Lady Zendell talked with you about it too."

"Yes. I wondered why, despite her giving a reason."

"To make a point, I imagine. She told me she never used much and is now giving it up entirely. Also, that she wouldn't marry a man who used it."

"Aligning with your views," Allirae said. "That is a good thing."

"Strategic," Danivid said, as Prentov returned with a tray and closed the door to the dining room. "Nothing more." He took the glass from the tray and selected one of the cakes surrounding it.

Prentov set the tray on the low central table and went to close the opposite door to the corridor.

"I know you are skeptical," Allirae said, "but I don't see why."

"If you'd heard our conversation in the garden, you would." He motioned Prentov toward a chair.

Allirae clicked her tongue. "You can't just leave us hanging like that."

"She says she owns *all* of Regissa Enterprise." The heat he'd suppressed through half the party returned to scorch his chest.

Allirae pursed her lips.

"All of it?" Prentov murmured. "With no documentation?"

"She *acquired* it, to use her term, from Shevnal quite recently. Both the monstrous structure and the land it stands upon. Land that she will give me—provided I marry her."

"Oh," Allirae said flatly. "Was she that crass, or are you shortening it?"

"I skipped her...I suppose she considered it *alluring* behavior. I wasn't in the mood. Not after she *ruined* my case against Shevnal. Land that the crown could have legally seized is now owned by Lady Zendell, who will use it to force me into marriage." His lips tightened more with every word. "She expected me to be pleased."

"Oh dear." Allirae adjusted a fold of her full skirt. "But in fairness, Danivid, she wouldn't have known your plans. She is the most eligible woman of your age. I'm not sure you should blame her for trying to bring de Noviam land back into the family—not when she didn't know what she was ruining."

"She knows something. She could never have gotten both the land and his sixty percent share of the building away from Shevnal unless she understood his need to get rid of it fast. Whether her motives are good or otherwise, I will not marry a woman who schemes with Shevnal in order to wed me." He'd better tone it down. Trellian's fingers were rather tight around the glass she held atop her thigh.

"If the land was just transferred to her," Prentov asked, "can the crown still seize it?"

"I don't know." Danivid took a sip from his glass. His abstracted gaze settled on the tray of cakes. An almond peeked from the thin crust of one. "Taking property from Lady Zendell is a very different thing than taking it from Shevnal. It doesn't accomplish the primary goal of proving he misused his position as chief former. Even if he transferred that property to her today, as I suspect, that deed is bound to have an earlier date." Preoccupied, he leaned forward to take the almond cake, unaware that Trellian was also reaching for it.

She sucked a breath in, jerking her hand back.

"Ah, forgive me," he said. "I wasn't paying attention."

"That's fine, I—"

"It's yours." He took one with a dollop of yellow frosting and smiled to diffuse any embarrassment she might feel. "I like the lemon ones just as well."

She murmured something that sounded like thanks, looking almost shy. Or at least what might pass for shyness on her serious face. Taking the almond cake, she asked, "Will this change the proceedings tomorrow?"

"Not the beginning, nor the discussion of ambertrop."

CHAPTER 28

Danivid tried to ignore the crown's weight. Why did it feel heavier this morning? He watched the faces of the High Council members as Turnin read the succession article, naming Princess Allirae as his heir. Not one showed surprise, nor did they have any say in the matter.

Governor Rikion merely commented, "It is good to have that clarified."

"Yes," Danivid said. "With that formality out of the way, we will begin a discussion of ambertrop. I have asked Lady Trellian to address you on the subject because her people have more experience of it than Welcians."

Now they shifted, showing hints of concern or skepticism. Aides rustled papers, and the few agents from the presses, whom Danivid had allowed to attend, poised their pens above notebooks, eyes keen with the hope of news more exciting than a succession announcement.

Trellian spoke with her natural assurance, explaining Felverland's early belief that ambertrop was harmless and mounting evidence to the contrary. Then she enumerated the types of damage caused by the drug. She closed her speech with a request from Felverland's prime minister that Welcia assist in the eradication of ambertrop.

She had not even returned to her chair when Governor Bayalkor said, "I must take issue with—"

"Hold your comments," Danivid said. "We will now hear from Chief Medic Fivian on this subject."

She delivered her speech with greater passion than Trellian, corroborating the physical ills suffered in Welcia, the damage to children in the womb, proof of addiction, and the suffering of those who dared to fight through withdrawal. In one sentence, she chanced to say the words *find* and *ambertrop* rather close together, bringing Burnie to his feet. Danivid settled him before the fervent medic noticed the interruption. She closed with a demand that the government take decisive action to rid Welcia of this heinous poison.

Governor Bayalkor again began to speak, but it was movement that stopped him as much as Danivid's repeated order to hold comments. Danivid turned, knowing who had waited beyond the corner door.

Queen Lenneth entered the High Council chamber and proceeded with royal dignity to a vacant chair beside her father. Those seated around the ring of tables bowed from the waist, acknowledging her. "Members of the High Council," she said, "though I have no vote among you, I have chosen to attend in order that I might confirm the truth of what you have just heard."

"Difficult," Governor Bayalkor said, "since you were not present to hear it."

Lenneth sat erect. "I knew what they intended to say. It is a subject quite painful to me because of my personal experiences." A tremor crept into her voice, and a tear spilled from each eye. She made no attempt to wipe them away, nor did she pause her determined words. "The king permitted me to listen from outside the chamber. I wanted Lady Trellian and Chief Medic Fivian to speak candidly without hindrance from my presence. Let it be recorded that I assert that their words are true. If anything, they have understated the severity of the suffering caused by ambertrop." She leaned back, deflating in her chair as though her statement had taken all the energy she possessed.

Even Governor Bayalkor didn't have the audacity to jump in with his derisive tone.

Danivid addressed his sister-in-law. "I thank you, Queen Lenneth, for addressing this difficult issue on behalf of the people of Welcia." He turned to Koriak. "Bring in Police Captain Narwick."

As Koriak obeyed, Danivid interlaced his fingers on the table before him. "Lady Trellian spoke of both physical and criminal aspects of ambertrop in Felverland. Since Fivian is Chief Medic, she could only speak of the physical suffering here. I will now address the criminal activity in Welcia related to ambertrop."

Koriak escorted Captain Narwick into the chamber and bade him stand a few feet from the double doors of the entrance.

Danivid resumed. "Certain crimes that will be discussed in this chamber are under investigation. The details cannot yet be made public. Agents of the press and aides of the High Council members will now leave."

A few gasps greeted his unprecedented order. Those identified closed their gaping mouths and began shuffling toward the exit. Still, too many people remained seated.

Danivid looked straight at the two sons of Regissa's Governor Rikion. "This includes family of the High Council."

They weren't the only family members present, but they were the most concerning. Sure enough, one objected. "Insulting! As though we cannot be trus—"

"Obey the king!" his father snapped.

Somewhat surprising, but the man looked oddly pale. Danivid said, "Voting members of the High Council may remain, along with Queen Lenneth, Princess Allirae, Lady Trellian, the lawyer Turnin, my aide Prentov who is scribing, Captain of the King's Guard Koriak, and for now, Police Captain Narwick."

"This is most irregular," one of the High Council members complained.

"A great many things are far more irregular than you realize," Danivid said. Let them chew on that until the room cleared.

Koriak closed the door behind the last individual as Governor Varanaw griped, "You send out more than half the attendees, and keep a *dog* with you?"

Danivid allowed a hint of ironic humor to lighten his voice. "He has witnessed some of the crimes, so there is no need to exclude him."

A few people granted that a huff of amusement.

"Doubtless," Danivid said, "you noticed dogs at the reception too. You see, one of the several crimes that I will soon enumerate is defiance of my order that no ambertrop is allowed in the palace. Fortunately, dogs can smell it, so I was able to determine who was poisoning me with it."

A whisper of gasps filled the room.

Danivid swept his gaze around each face. "Members of the High Council, I know that most of you allow ambertrop in your provinces and may be disinclined to change that. I have heard too many times that everyone should be free to choose for themselves whether they will use it. Yet those who become addicted are no longer free to choose. Not only are the addicted preyed upon by dealers, but those who stand against the drug are attacked. *I* was certainly not allowed to choose while it was being slipped into my beverages. Crime and corruption are running rampant in both Regissa and Bonador provinces and spreading into others. We must address this *now*. Delay will only cost more lives."

Governor Bayalkor cleared his throat. "There can be many causes of crime and corruption. If we blame it on ambertrop when it's caused by something else, we only make matters worse. We must have facts and proof."

"That is true," Danivid said. "Today, I will present you with instances of treason, murder, and corruption that are directly related to ambertrop. A small number of people know that a few months ago,

King Vancent decided to initiate action to outlaw that drug. These events followed his decision. The first was sabotage of the king's sailboat. A clear attempted murder. He was only saved because a streamer happened to see the boat sink. Captain Narwick has found no leads in that case, and it is unclear whether he investigated."

Narwick uttered a sound, but Danivid granted no pause for him to speak. "After surviving the so-called boating accident, King Vancent was murdered with a high dose of ambertrop."

This time, it was Lenneth who gasped. Though every face revealed shock, Danivid continued. "Narwick pretended to investigate, suppressed the testimony of a witness, and dropped the investigation with no result."

Danivid held up a hand to halt the interruptions. "After I was crowned king, I made it clear that I oppose ambertrop. Within days, Queen Lenneth's maid was murdered. She had been delivering ambertrop to the queen but was too terrified to say who supplied it to her. It is also possible that she knew who murdered the king and how. Narwick has not found any leads in her murder case."

The council members were staring back and forth between their king and the police captain, who had gone pale, then red, and was now white around his tense lips.

He sputtered, "This is—"

"Silence!" Koriak snapped.

Danivid continued. "An attempt was made against *my* life when a groom tampered with the saddle of my horse, causing it to throw me." Judging by expressions, the repeating shocks were having the desired effect. "It is nearly miraculous that I survived without serious injury. Narwick delayed arriving to investigate. The perpetrator is an ambertrop user who did not earn enough money to support his addiction. He is likely a tool coerced into attempted murder or injury. His identity is known, but he has not been apprehended by the police, so he cannot be questioned."

Lord Eavertin banged his fist on the table. "This is even worse than I thought. Is there no indication of who is behind all of it?"

"I assume that Narwick knows," Danivid said. "He has, we will say, *interesting* business associations that may give him a motive to conceal certain facts. Before we go into that, there is another crime to discuss." Danivid curled his lip with a glance toward Narwick. "Since our police captain is either inept or complicit, I did not report this crime or the capture of the perpetrator to the police."

Narwick practically vibrated as he shouted, "This is one-sided hearsay. I demand a chance to defend myself."

"Of course." Danivid leaned back. "You will have a trial after the full investigation is complete. For now, you must be prevented from causing further harm." He signaled with a flick of his finger toward Koriak, who stated the arrest, bound Narwick's hands, and took him away.

"I should mention," Danivid said, "that the King's Guard has taken possession of police headquarters and detained officers temporarily, pending investigation. I have appointed a member of my guard, Gordin, as the new police captain."

Danivid picked up the water glass that sat in front of him. He turned it, staring into the clear liquid. "When I discovered a week ago that ambertrop was in my system, I could not eat or drink anything without wondering whether it contained that drug."

He looked around their somber faces. "That first day was difficult. Fortunately, I discovered some important things about this dog at my feet. Burnie was my brother's dog. He can smell ambertrop—and associates that smell with King Vancent's death. I had a suspicion as to who had been gradually poisoning me, so I had the dog let into the room while that man was in the act of serving me drugged tea."

"Who did it?" Dirklan's prime minister demanded.

Danivid nodded to her. "Katowau already knows of this crime, because I went to Dirklan to recover from the poison."

"You mean, when you said you were ill?" Governor Rikion looked rather sick himself. "It was really…"

"I was being poisoned with ambertrop." Danivid gestured to his side. "I have Lady Trellian to thank for determining which substance was used. That is why I include her now as a witness. She also helped me recover from the addiction, for the poisoning had started right after my coronation."

"How much longer must we wait for the name?" Lord Eavertin asked.

"Yautan—personal aide to King Vancent for many years, and then personal aide to me." Danivid continued to sweep his gaze around their faces. He avoided fixing on Lenneth but noticed her pallor. "Yautan served me tea every morning, tainted with ever-increasing doses of the drug I specifically forbade. I'm sure he also gave it to my brother. Whether King Vancent knew of the morning doses, I cannot say. I do know that he was manipulated into making decisions in the mornings, and that those decisions have led to an unprecedented transfer of wealth."

Lord Eavertin leaned forward. "Do you think Yautan is the primary driver behind all of this?"

"Doubtful, though I'm certain he knows who is. He refuses to tell. Many treasures have also been stolen from the palace. Again, I suspect Yautan was the insider who facilitated their removal."

"Where is he now?" Governor Rikion asked.

"He is held by the King's Guard. The high judge agreed to retain the documented charges in confidence, pending this meeting. Are there further questions pertaining to Yautan?"

Danivid left a brief pause, but no one took advantage of it. "These extremely serious events are examples of the crime and corruption that can only be attributed to ambertrop. Due to the severity of the drug's damage to Welcia, I have prepared a motion to outlaw it. Turnin will distribute copies, then give the formal reading. Before we adjourn today,

I want the deciding vote to send the proposed law to the General Council of Welcia."

Governor Bayalkor drew his shoulders erect. "We must have time to discuss this in our provinces."

"There will be plenty of time for that before the General Council votes to enact it as law."

Governor Rikion took the paper Turnin handed him. "Permit me, for the sake of discussion, to state the argument that will be shouted throughout the city. As with every new advancement, problems can occur, but there are also benefits. There are those who struggle with anxiety and need the calming effects that ambertrop provides. I realize it is new. A different method to achieve calm than we were accustomed to. But just because it is new, does not mean it is bad."

"It makes no difference whether it is new or old," Danivid said. "Only what is *true* or *false* matters. I've heard it likened to the restful savoring that the Holy Writ advises, but there is no similarity beneath the surface. True rest is powerful because it enables one to set aside the chaotic voices, to discern and value truth, and to act with wisdom. Ambertrop's calm is false, for it causes one to believe lies, to make foolish decisions, and to take no useful action. It is particularly dangerous, for when a person is in the grip of the lie, they can no longer find true rest."

"Well," Governor Bayalkor said, shifting in his chair, "if it's the best calm someone can get..."

"Oh stop," Lenneth hissed. "Ambertrop lies until the agony returns worse than before, then demands that the lie be repeated." Her chest heaved. "Even if that were not so, my daughter is robbed of speech, my husband is murdered, and my king is hunted. Stop babbling your opinions as though they are truth and act on real truth."

Pretty much every council member had drawn back, unsure what to do as more tears gathered in her eyes.

Lord Wirth cleared his throat, breaking the uncomfortable silence. "We do have facts before us that must be acted upon. The murder and attempted murder of our kings are treason. Not only ending life, but also threatening Welcia itself. This is primary. We must find out who is behind these attacks."

"Until we know who that is," Allirae said, "protecting the king's life is the highest priority. The motive for murder is already known. To prevent the king from bringing the truth of ambertrop to center stage. To prevent him from creating the motion to outlaw it. Once the matter is advanced to the General Council, there will no longer be a purpose for killing another one of my brothers. Or me, after him."

Governor Varanaw turned to her. "Believe me, Lady Allirae, I do not wish either of you killed. But removing *a* motive is not enough, for there could be another. We must find whoever is behind it."

The opening of a door created a slight pause, but it was only Koriak returning.

"I agree," Danivid said, "though we won't find that person here today."

Lenneth's voice cracked. "I know who it is."

Her words brought a deathly hush. Every eye locked on her.

Heat rushed through Danivid. She looked like guilt personified. Could she have—no! Not her own husband!

"It's Shevnal," she squeaked.

Danivid almost choked in relief that she wasn't confessing. But Shevnal? Terrible Chief Former—absolutely. Devious thief—sure. But did she have proof that he was behind *everything*. Even the murder of the king?

Governor Bayalkor was already accusing Lenneth of slander, and Lady Katowau snapped, "Oh, so that's a crime again now, is it?"

Lady Trellian hissed a question toward Danivid's ear. "Can't a person state evidence against someone?"

"Quiet, everyone." He gave Trellian a faint smile with the words, "Of course, she can," before turning to Lenneth.

Her anguished eyes met his. "It has to be Shevnal." Tears traced down her cheeks. "I should have realized." She covered her mouth with her hands. "But I didn't. I really didn't."

"I'm sure that is true, my sister. But please tell me, what makes you certain, now, that it's Shevnal?"

"He supplied our ambertrop. Usually through Yautan, but sometimes he gave me some himself." She uttered a derisive sound behind the handkerchief she'd pulled from a pocket. "*Gave.* He never *gave* without taking." She wiped her tears. "You remember the shimmerstone table from the queen's chamber, Danivid?"

He nodded, still grappling with all that her words meant.

"Shevnal displays it in his entrance foyer. No one else would realize where it came from. But Vancent and I knew. Inviting us to parties—reminding us—what once was ours is now his."

Others looked confused, and one of the governors said, "Disturbing, perhaps, but if the exchange was agreed to…"

"It's an heirloom of great value," Danivid said. "It's also not the only such item now missing without record of a sale or exchange."

"Do you have proof of this?"

Danivid considered telling them of the mural gems that were replaced with glass and now graced the walls of Shevnal's formal dining room. "For now, I must protect my sources, lest they also become targets of murder."

"You cannot know that will happen," Bayalkor said.

Was he an idiot or complicit? The governor of Bonador Province would soon find his dealings investigated.

Lenneth's mournful voice saved Danivid from answering. "My maid bought ambertrop for me from Yautan, and she knew when Shevnal brought me some. She had noticed that when Yautan ran low, he'd pretend to deliver a note to Shevnal. That must be why they killed her."

She sniffed and crushed the handkerchief. "Vancent was so upset about the table, but I was out of money, and I was desperate for more amber." She managed to glare around the room. "Don't any of you *dare* say that addiction is some trivial thing, easy to escape. It is not! And Vancent wasn't careless. He always said we should just take it in the evening. Morning doses wouldn't have been his idea." She shook her head. "Every piece of property sold—no matter how—the decision was made in the morning, with Shevnal advising it."

Perhaps the skeptical looks bothered her, for she shouted, "I was there. I heard it!"

Turnin made a faint ahem sound and waited for Danivid's nod before speaking. "I would like to document all your evidence later, lady queen. It's important, but it seems to indicate coercive theft rather than murder. Is there something more pertaining to the king's death?"

Lenneth scrunched her eyes. "I...I told Shevnal..." She sobbed. "I told him that Vancent planned to outlaw ambertrop." She dragged out another handkerchief. "I didn't know he'd kill him." From behind the cloth, she uttered barely discernable words. "I didn't even realize he had. But after Vancent died—"

Her voice failed. Danivid ground his teeth in frustration. They needed to hear this!

Her father wrapped an arm around her. "Calm yourself, my dear. You are not at fault for what he chose to do. None of us blame you. Just go ahead and tell us anything else you know."

She wiped her face yet again and drew a few breaths. "Before the funeral—when Aneen was with me—he mentioned that she was now queen and started talking about confirming my regency. I told him about the will, and that Danivid was king."

She rounded her eyes. "Shevnal went completely livid. I've never *seen* him like that. He absolutely raved. Demanded that I get her crowned. No matter what I said, or how much I cried, he wouldn't listen. He fed me ambertrop, put the glass to my lips himself, and swore I'd never get another drop if I didn't get her crowned."

"Hmm," Governor Bayalkor murmured. "I assume no one else witnessed this conversation?"

She lifted her nose to him and looked down it. "You are like Shevnal, acting as though Aneen doesn't exist."

"She's hardly, uh…"

Lenneth's eyes narrowed. "Too damaged by ambertrop to know what's happening, you mean?" She sneered. "That drug you claim is safe. *She* never got to decide whether to take it. But she *does* know things."

"Indeed, she does." Allirae used her voice to defuse tension. "Aneen calls Shevnal 'bad man,' and when Danivid asked her why, Aneen said, 'made Mama cry' and quoted the phrase 'no money, no amber'. Her vehemence fits the scene that Lenneth described. And while we all know that no seven-year-old child can give evidence…" Allirae nailed Governor Bayalkor with a glare. "Queen Lenneth certainly can."

"We all saw the outcome," Katowau said. "Shevnal hovering like a bat over our queen during her darkest hour and trying to get Aneen crowned. The man should be arrested."

"And yet," Governor Varanaw said, "no one felt it warranted charges at the time. I do believe this needs to be investigated before we consider the motion about ambertrop."

Katowau instantly countered. "We didn't know the queen's information at the time. We didn't know Shevnal was in on the ambertrop trade, though I've wondered where he got money enough to buy up de Noviam land." She leaned forward to ask Trellian, "Would that vile trade give him enough money to pull that off?"

"Probably," she replied. "It *definitely* would if he is the major importer into Regissa."

Katowau turned to Danivid. "Lord king, I petition you to have one of your guards find him and bring him here before he can do more harm."

"He is already in the palace," Danivid said.

That got him some sharp looks. "Why?" Governor Rikion asked.

"Another matter on my agenda for today. Shevnal's gross neglect of his duties as Chief Former of Welcia."

"You may consider it so," Governor Rikion said, "but if you had asked the Formers' Guild for another vote this morning, they would have re-elected him. Accusation is not proof of murder, so it cannot be used to sway their vote."

"True. It would be interesting, though, to see who votes for him after I bring charges against him for assigning formers to perform theft on his behalf."

Governor Rikion spoke over the exclamations. "Do you have proof of that?"

"Do you think I make these things up?" Danivid waited for Rikion to shake his head, then continued. "There are other formers in the palace at the moment. Two of them participated in the quite significant theft, which I just mentioned. The other one could serve as an interim Chief Former until I convene a Formers' Guild meeting. Besides Shevnal's overwhelming bias toward projects on his own land, he has no mitigation plan for the recurring quakes that shake Regissa City."

Danivid leaned back. "Those reasons were adequate to question his role before. I cannot allow him to serve while he is a suspect for the murder of a king. Koriak, escort Formers Shevnal and Rebanak to this chamber."

Danivid stopped another comment with a lift of his hand. This was all happening out of the sequence he had planned. Arresting Shevnal should clear the distractions so he could get back to the ambertrop motion.

As Koriak departed, Burnie leapt to his feet.

"What's wrong with the dog?" Governor Katowau asked.

Danivid glanced at Burnie. "He senses tremors before people do."

The ground proved his words. Vibration flowed through his chair, and the water in glasses upon the table began to quiver. This had become so common that no one rose, but tension crept throughout.

Hands tightened on the nearest object, and jaws clenched. All interest in conversation evaporated.

It wasn't a hard tremor but long enough for Shevnal to arrive, followed by Koriak who said, "Rebanak had just stepped out to assess the situation. He will be escorted here soon."

"Do you need," Shevnal drawled, "yet another assurance that your palace is still standing?"

"No," Danivid said, "but since you raise the point, what is your plan for barriers to protect the port, palace, and lower areas of Regissa City in the event of a severe quake with high waves?"

Shevnal had the nerve to roll his eyes. "Since no one can predict the necessary height of the barrier you suggest—none. If the need arises, residents should proceed to the high ground. The new buildings would provide the best refuge from high waters, which, I must repeat, are the responsibility of streamers, not formers."

"Inadequate, as always," Danivid said. "Taken with your ongoing neglect of structures in the original city, allegations of inappropriate financial dealings, and recent discoveries pertaining to ambertrop dealing and the king's murder..." Danivid left a pause to judge his reaction.

"King's murder?" Shevnal scoffed, but his eyes flicked in Lenneth's direction. "Absurd beyond belief! If anyone accuses me of such, she is surely mad!"

"She?" Danivid said. "Have you spoken with Yautan recently?"

A few seconds ticked by. "Yautan? No. Why should I? We should vacate the building."

"Suddenly you find tremors a problem." Danivid stood as others jumped to their feet. "Or have you just realized a need of escape? You will exit under guard."

A fist hammered the chamber door. A voice shouted along with it. "Lord king, urgent message!"

Koriak clinched his fingers around Shevnal's arm as he jerked the door open. The wire operator ran in with a paper in hand, which he thrust at the king.

Danivid paused to take in the few words. The tremors beneath his feet seemed to spike to the top of his head. "From Velzain, the peninsula wind weaver. A towering volcano plume is rising from the sea."

CHAPTER 29

The chamber shook harder, and a portrait fell from the wall, its frame splintering on the floor. Lenneth whimpered, "Aneen!" Those nearest the double doors were already rushing out them, and the rest surged after.

Koriak snapped, "Lord king, the rear exit is the fastest way out."

"No! I must get to the harbor." Danivid gripped Trellian's wrist and snapped orders as he strode for the hall. "Lord Eavertin, tend Lenneth. Prentov, your family. Two guards on Shevnal. Bring him harborside."

Allirae reached the hall ahead of him and turned to run up the stairs. "Allie! Outside!"

Meroak hurried down the stairs with Aneen in his arms. He sent his wife a stern look. "Go!" The child's maids and tutor followed him. Prentov's family started down behind them.

Danivid couldn't keep track of anyone else, and Koriak was practically shoving him toward the main entrance. A vertical crack split the mural. Glass pieces shattered on the marble floor. Danivid gave in to Koriak's direction and emerged onto the terrace with Trellian. Soft clouds floated in the blue sky—a discordant calm above the rending land. An ancient tree beyond the garden crashed to the ground.

Too many voices shouted behind him. He needed to concentrate. What was the sea doing? Someone tugged on his arm. "Not now! I must sense." He crossed the terrace and ran down the steps into the garden, almost falling when the ground heaved. Only then did he realize that he still held tight to Trellian's wrist. He released it. "Forgive me."

"I didn't object."

Some portion of his mind heard that, but he was reaching with the fullest extent of his streaming gift. It allowed nothing else except a staggering, determined stride across the garden toward the colonnade.

Only when Trellian gripped his arm and said, "No farther," did he realize she had stayed at his side. She tugged downward. "Sit before we fall."

Better to comply than argue. Burnie nuzzled him and whined. Distant voices made no impact, for water engulfed his senses.

He must separate the motions. Normal currents, vibration driven from the quaking seabed...and was there another surge radiating from the volcano he could not reach? He sensed the shockwave first, then startled as the full mass charged into his awareness. "Oh, no."

"What is it?" Trellian hissed. Her fingers trembled against her parted lips.

Had he uttered that aloud? Must have. "A tsunami is coming." *Ellincreo! What do I do?*

Calm words formed within him. *Direction. Speed.*

Obviously. "Give me a minute," he said to Trellian, then focused again. No longer shocked, he studied the distant motion. The relentless power overwhelmed him, but the speed and distance granted a ripple of hope. "We have some hours."

She exhaled, then spread her skirt across her knees.

Danivid turned to see who had followed him. None of the High Council—just as well. Those dear or loyal to him clustered in groups on the grass between flowerbeds and bushes. Farther away, Shevnal—looking quite rumpled—sat on a bench between two guards.

Another guard and his chef approached, lugging containers. Where was Rebanak? Ah, there, drawing near at a careful pace across the inland side of the cliffs. Katowau emerged from around a corner of the palace, paused to look, then hurried toward him.

Time to get organized—act calmer than he felt. He was king, after all.

Danivid faced the small crowd, crossed his legs and rested an arm on each knee, so his hands dangled. He raised his voice enough to carry to the guards and staff drawing nearer from all sides. "A tsunami is heading for the harbor. It will be enormous, but we have a few hours to prepare."

He hated to address Shevnal but must. "Now that the disaster is upon us, will you take any action to create a barrier?"

"It's pointless to do so here. Higher up in the city, yes. I've sprained my ankle. Someone fetch that medic who was in the palace."

"No, her priority is preparing disaster aid. I hereby remove Shevnal from the position of chief former. No, do not speak again. Rebanak, I appoint you as interim chief former." Danivid looked around and found the face he sought. "Prentov, I need messages sent to announce this and summon the formers."

Prentov opened a notebook. How like him to have it even amid disaster.

An aide spoke up. "The wire system has failed, sir."

"The rails are down too," a guard added.

"There's quake damage at the nearest station," Rebanak said. He sat down in a bare spot, even though the quake had subsided to intermittent quivers. "There are likely magnery outages all over Regissa."

Someone vaguely familiar, with scratches across one cheek, came nearer. "I can carry your orders to my press, lord king." Ah, one of the press agents. "We still have an old hand-crank printer, and we can post things around the city."

"Thank you. Prentov, compile what needs to be said. Warn residents of approaching high water. Advise that they seek high ground with orderly haste. State that Rebanak is now chief former and summon all *gifted* formers to meet him on the palace grounds. Summon Chief Streamer Chardomeer and all streamers to the palace garden. I also need a runner to the port. It is urgent that all ships get out of the harbor and as far from land as possible. And we need horses and a carriage too."

Already, Danivid knew that runners on foot would never be fast enough. He needed the wires repaired *now*. Could the formers do that *and* protect the city? He looked at Rebanak, whose unfocused eyes revealed that he was using his forming gift. Danivid was loath to interrupt when his work could be crucial.

Someone in the crowd asked, "How will the ships sail without wind?"

A woman's voice carried to them from a distance. "Wind, they shall have." A tall woman with wild hair strode toward them, and a shorter one trotted to keep up with her. Wind weavers.

Danivid's chest expanded, and he jumped to his feet. Of course—the old ways, true to their purpose.

Chief Wind Weaver Cinnawa faced the port and arced her hands around an invisible tunnel of air. Her words sounded ordinary to him, but they would bellow across the port. "Orders from the king to the port. All ships depart the harbor immediately and sail far from land. Wind weavers will guide you out." She repeated her distinct message, then turned to the opposite side of the harbor and stated the names of weavers and their task.

She walked the rest of the way through the garden, listening with her own gift. Reaching Danivid, she said, "My weavers have responded. They'll get the ships out orderly. This is Peppi, an excellent voice lifter."

The girl—she couldn't be a woman yet—bobbed a curtsy. "At your service, lord king."

"My thanks, for you are both about to save many lives."

"Our honor," Cinnawa said. "What message next?"

"Send this one to the stable in the woodland. Bring all horses and every form of carriage to the palace."

Peppi's eyes rounded. "I don't know where the stable is."

Cinnawa patted her shoulder. "I'll do this one, while you sort out what's next."

She stepped aside, and Danivid said, "Prentov, give her the messages to the guilds." He pointed to the press agent. "I still want notices printed and posted."

"On it, sir!" The man darted away with a paper torn from Prentov's notebook.

Danivid took a moment to think as the weavers sent his messages. While several repeats of the *seek high ground* message resounded over the lower portion of Regissa City, he turned to his sister. "As soon as a carriage arrives, you and Aneen must get out of the city."

"I'm not going anywhere," Allirae said flatly. "You'll do something dangerous. I know it!"

"You are heir to the crown, and you *are* leaving. This quake has happened at the worst possible time, for word of our movement against ambertrop will spread before the critical step. Our adversaries will take advantage of the chaos. They have already murdered and will not hesitate to do so again. Meroak, get them to safety *outside* the city. Take Cam to check your food and drink, and a guard to keep watch for other threats. Get private word back to me of where you take refuge."

"I'll see to all of it." Meroak turned to Koriak, who was motioning for some of his men.

Danivid turned to Trellian. Why was it so hard to say what he must? "Lady Trellian, I believe you will be safest with them. Travel with Allirae." He read the argument in her steady eyes, but she didn't open her lips.

Trellian tilted her head. Arguing with the king in front of everyone who should *not* argue would only make his work harder. She walked over to listen while Koriak and Meroak hurried through plans with two assigned guards.

Allirae gave Aneen into the care of her tutor and rejoined the men while they discussed practicalities. Interrupting Koriak mid-sentence, she said, "Meroak, I understand why the king and his heir must be in different places, but one of us must be with him. He does dangerous things!"

Meroak reached out to her as Koriak said, "I will stay with him at all times."

"Of course you will, but you are honor-bound to obey his orders. We can talk him out of the crazy stuff."

Meroak's throat caught on a scoffing sound. "Do you really think so?"

"I will also stay with the king," Trellian said. "You may soon find Lenneth and her parents in your party, plus aides, Aneen's retinue, etc. You don't need another person who can do nothing but follow along." She looked at Koriak. "A person who can watch for all types of danger to the king *is* useful."

Koriak studied her with narrowed eyes. "You have a point." They both looked at the king, who was talking with Rebanak, Katowau, and some others who must be formers. "We'll tell him in a bit."

Trellian hid a smile, knowing exactly why Koriak wanted to wait. Something bumped her arm, drawing her eyes—a large sack, from which Chef Perkett pulled bread. He handed it to members of Allirae's party. She got his attention. "Please bring a pack of travel food and water for the king and me."

"Certainly, lady."

A former joined them. "The palace has some cracks but is *moderately* safe. I can escort a few people inside to get what is critical. You must promise to be quick and to exit fast if there is the faintest aftershock."

Perfect. Prentov and two others were selected to go inside. Trellian followed them without permission, earning a glare from the former, but no objection from the guard. She changed into riding clothes as quick as a spy and grabbed her pack, then met Prentov at the top of the stairs. He lugged a blanket with its corners tied in a crooked knot.

"I can take that to a guard," she said, "if you need to get other things." He passed it to her and ran down another corridor.

On the terrace, she left the bundle with a guard and surveyed the changed scene. Allirae and company were on the south side of the garden. The king stood amid a group on the north side. Chief Streamer Chardomeer was among them, so they must be streamers. Rebanak spoke to others, probably his Formers' Guild, on the grassy expanse beyond a branch of the colonnade.

Koriak strode to her side. "The horses have been spotted descending the road from the stables. They should be here soon. Can you ride?"

"Yes."

"Lady Allirae's group will need two carriages. We can have them full enough that there is no room for you—unless you change your mind."

She smiled slightly and shook her head. "Are those people with the king streamers?"

"Yes." Koriak growled, "Chardomeer is an idiot, insisting nothing can be done. The king has split the streamers, assigning some under Chardomeer to manage flood control throughout the city. He's keeping almost twenty under his command, calling them *wave* streamers. They are the more powerful, willing to take on the joint task of diverting the harbor current." His mouth held to a grim line. "Though I don't think even one of them believes it's possible."

The chef hurried up to Trellian with a stuffed drawstring bag. "Here's the food and water, lady." She slipped the looped end over her head and shoulder as he spoke. "I can't get the king to accept any food. Too busy giving orders." He handed her a bunch of grapes. "These won't travel well, but maybe *you* can get some into him."

"I'll do my best." She doubted he heard as he hustled away. Her sweeping gaze snagged on movement that was far too dignified for the event. "What is *she* doing here?"

Koriak swung around, then scowled at Lady Zendell. "I need to see if there's a gap in the guards."

All Trellian cared about was learning what she was up to.

Zendell reached the king just after he dismissed many streamers to follow Chardomeer. He saw who approached and waited for her with a stern look. Trellian found a bench partially obscured by a bush where she could watch their profiles while listening.

"Lord king, I am so relieved to find you unharmed!" Lady Zendell gushed.

Trellian rolled her eyes. The remaining streamers shifted a few yards away.

The king replied, "I'm busy, Lady Zendell. I suggest you go at once to high ground."

"It's because of that warning, I came. With your palace so near to the sea, I had to risk it. The lower floors of my building are complete, and I offer them to you for the safety of the royal household."

"I have made plans for my household. You may open your space to those in the city who have nowhere to go. The need for shelter will be great."

"Ah, but don't you see? In the days to come, you will need a new seat for your government. Even now, you could use it. You're holding meetings *outside*." Zendell pressed her hand to her chest as though some scandal was occurring. "I saw horses and carriages arriving on the far side of the palace. Please, let us take a carriage to my building at once. The people of Regissa will be reassured knowing that the kingdom's leadership is stable in that secure location."

"Will they? Am I not the streamer who just might be able to save their lives and homes? You think I should sit in spacious comfort, while their houses are swept away and they're lucky to find a spot on the street to sleep? Go and meet a real need!"

She lifted her chin. "I am. My offer remains open to *you*."

Two guards approached, and the king ordered, "Guard, see that Lady Zendell leaves the palace grounds."

"Yes, sir," one said. "This way, lady." Despite his courteous words, he gripped her arm.

The other guard said, "The carriages and horses are here, sir. We are taking Lady Allirae's party to them now."

"Tell Jonger I need the biggest wagon to carry streamers around the Harbor Circle Road."

"Yes, sir."

While Trellian smirked over Zendell's dismissal, the king turned and looked across the walkway toward the far side of the garden. His eyes searched. He nodded to someone but still searched.

Trellian dared not move, for she sat near his line of sight. He started looking more broadly. Still though she was, his gaze locked on her. He narrowed his eyes, and she knew he wasn't surprised.

He strode toward her and rounded the bush. "Lady Trellian, you must go now."

"Allirae's party has grown too large, and I won't take up a much-needed seat."

"I want you safe!"

"Then I will stay with you, for you have many guards." She tried a quip. "And Burnie."

"I don't have time to argue. I must get wave streamers deployed around the harbor."

"I hear you haven't eaten."

"I don't have time."

"I'm carrying your food supply. Have those streamers been provided food for the long hours they will be on duty?"

He scowled at her, then stepped a yard away to call to Koriak, who was approaching. "Get a food ration to each of those streamers."

Koriak returned a distinct nod and changed course.

"This means you have a moment to eat." Trellian handed him a grape.

He threw it into his mouth. "No, it doesn't. I need to let Rebanak know what we're doing with the waves."

She stood. "You can eat on the—"

An approaching rumble pulled both of their heads around to the source. An enormous vehicle rounded the corner of the palace, spewing steam. She gasped. "What—"

"A rock mover," Danivid said. "Designed for excavation where magnery has not yet been installed." A small tree in its path succumbed to iron treads. "There are only three—the other two are enroute to the port."

She matched the king's pace as he strode toward Rebanak.

A wind weaver's voice boomed across the area. "The formers are beginning intentional rock drops along the cliffs. Each will be announced." She paused, then intoned, "Rock drop."

Sharp cracks reverberated. A section of the colonnade dropped from view, and a shattering crash followed. Trellian cringed and covered her ears, slapping her cheek with the grape cluster.

Danivid stopped, too, and gripped her arm. One look at his face, and she knew. He grieved a loss. "Are you all right?" he asked her.

"Yes."

He strode forward again. "You should go."

"Have a grape."

He huffed and took it from her.

They neared Rebanak and turned to look at what the man watched. The earth mover, having pulverized more of the garden, reached the central walkway that divided it. The machine descended ponderously toward the palace dock, where part of the cliff had slid into a slope of rubble. Odd shape to have landed in, but of course, formers had guided it.

Looking at the king, Rebanak puckered his brows. "I am so sorry!"

"I told you to do it."

"I know. But that lovely colonnade—centuries old. Part of your home. You must feel it more than I do."

Danivid swallowed hard enough that his throat convulsed. "About the harbor…" He paused, looked at Peppi, then gestured to the gifted. "Can you spread my voice around all these formers and streamers?"

"Of course. Speak normally, please, in one direction."

He faced Rebanak. "As soon as the ships are out of the harbor, the streamers and I will begin a swirling current like so." He swung his arm overhead, completing two broad circles. "When the wave enters the harbor, we'll do everything in our power to maintain the circular motion. Water will rise up the cliff faces. If possible, we'll drive the force of the circling wave back out of the harbor mouth. My hope is that we can diminish inflow."

"Got it," Rebanak said, then turned to his guild. "Formers, when you make the arced walls, overlap them to match that current. The gaps for outflow will thus channel water into that same current, which will help suck the water out of the city. Expect strong current through the gaps." He paused. "Lord king, we will build them as high as we can, but if we reach thirty feet, I'll be surprised."

"That is thirty feet of water the city will not feel. For which we all thank you in advance. I'm going to station the wave streamers all along the cliffs surrounding the harbor. Decide the safest locations for them. Then we will need a guide, so we get them to all the right places."

Rebanak called a former over, and the king motioned Peppi to cease spreading their voices. "Where is Cinnawa?" he asked her.

"She went into the city to organize some wind weavers for communication. It's the only way to direct those who are fleeing, lest they choke the roads and get trapped."

"Are there enough of you to surround the harbor as well?"

She grimaced. "I don't see how. Now that we communicate better with the wire system, hardly anyone practices voice lifting. That's why you got me. I'm still training with weather, but lifting is my natural gift."

She squinted over the harbor as she spoke. "If I could be at a central point, I should be able to reach almost to each of the headlands. But I can ask Cinnawa, if you wish."

The king pressed the center of his brow beneath the crown, muttering, "Worthless wires! Failure-prone, so-called *better* method." He refocused on Peppi. "Tell Cinnawa the need, but getting people to safety is the highest priority. Tell her the king's woodland is an option as well as the upper city. Let her know you'll be coming with the streamers."

Rebanak interrupted. "Just a minute with that, if you don't mind. Can you announce another rock drop?"

The king turned his back on the cliffs and covered his ears. Trellian covered hers, too, but couldn't shield her heart against the look on his face. The colonnades—where he walked beside his beloved sea. They were more his home than the palace was. And they were being smashed into rubble. At his order.

CHAPTER 30

Danivid kept his back resolutely turned to the destruction. It must be done.

Lady Trellian pressed a small bunch of grapes into his hand. Any distraction was better than none. He consumed them on a slow walk toward a row of horses tied to magnery lamp posts. Katowau joined them. She'd been hovering around the edge of the formers.

A table and a few random chairs from the first-floor salon stood incongruously beside the road. Prentov motioned them over to join him there, then resumed stuffing Danivid's belongings into a saddlebag. He even had an open suitcase. The man never ceased to amaze Danivid.

"Sit down, sir. Your riding boots are under the table."

Weirdly practical—and just as weirdly comfortable. For a moment, Danivid would do what Prentov said, rather than telling others what to do.

Katowau made use of the nearest chair. "I've been following everything as close as I can," she said. "I'll be heading to the tunnel soon, to take word down. Before I leave, is there anything else I should know about the tsunami?"

"The wave streamers are aware of the dome over passage lake and the need to protect it. Which is comparatively easy." He shoved his foot into a boot and kicked off the other shoe. "The wave will strike the peninsula. Hard." He pulled on the other boot. "Give me a moment while I check the ocean again."

He stood and faced the harbor, closing his eyes so destruction would not distract. He felt his fellow streamers reach with him. Most dropped away beyond the harbor headlands. He passed the gaps in the water that marked the bases of distant islands. The last of his fellow streamers faded away. Only he remained when the relentless surge met him. Even though he knew what to expect, it still awed him. Compressed momentum reaching from wave crest to ocean floor. Was he doing enough?

Danivid withdrew. "We have about two hours before landfall." He looked over at the streamers who clustered nearby. "Those of you who reached past the islands, take note of how it strikes them. Learn what you can."

Peppi broke her rapt look toward the woodland. "Velzain has reported from the peninsula. She can feel the swell press into the air and sends good news. She says that it doesn't feel very high."

He shook his head firmly. "False hope. Tell the weavers not to spread that."

"Why is it false?" Trellian asked.

"Wind weavers can only sense where air meets the wave crest, which has plenty of room in the open ocean. I feel the depths, and that wave is immense. When its base reaches the continental shelf, it will be shoved upward." He reached through the near waters again and studied the island gaps. "Penn Island has the broadest underwater base, so it will give the best example of what we can expect." He addressed the former who'd been assigned as their guide. "That one is taller than our cliffs, is it not?"

"Slightly taller than the harbor cliffs. Most of the peninsula is also taller, but the end tapers lower."

The biggest wagon rolled to a stop near the table, and a groom ran to the team's head, allowing Jonger to climb down from the driver's bench.

"I have seats for sixteen," he said. "A few more will fit in the aisle if need be."

The streamers hid appalled looks behind forced stoicism, and the sole former squatted for a look underneath.

"Would you prefer a riding coat, sir?" Prentov held one over his arm, anticipating the answer.

Danivid unhooked the jeweled clasps of the coat he'd worn to the High Council meeting—which now felt like it occurred a week ago. He shrugged it off. "Lady Katowau, you'd best hurry to the tunnel mouth. Jonger, assign a driver to the smallest buggy to take her there. Oh—is anyone left at the stables?"

Jonger waved a groom over, as he answered. "Burdock and his wife are there. We were chewing ideas when the quake hit. They promised to stay till I return. I left them a horse."

Katowau touched Danivid's sleeve. "Should we seal the tunnel mouth?"

"No need. The wave will not surmount the peninsula. Get in the buggy and be off. Wagon driver, set out the instant you're loaded. The former will direct you. Peppi, did you learn where the stables are?"

"Yes, sir."

"Send a message there that refugees may arrive." He slipped his arms into the riding coat that Prentov held, then pointed at Allirae's horse. "Trellian, take that mare. Prentov."

"Sir?"

Danivid broke off what he was about to say to his aide, for Lord Eavertin approached. "Why are you still here? What delays your party?"

"The ladies are well away, lord king. All the governors and lords have fled, and not even Governor Rikion remains to assist you. If you go with the streamers—as I imagine you must—who stands in with your authority at the palace?"

A gap Danivid had realized but had scant means to fill. Loyalty in the face of danger was too rare to refuse. "I was about to dump that load on my aide and royal guard, for there was no other. Prentov, you know my ways. Lord Eavertin, you know Welcia above. You two share the duty until I return. Members of my guard, support them. But all of you must understand that the palace itself is not safe from the sea. I value your lives above a building. Leave it if you must, but stay together to maintain the rule of the crown." This reminded him of its physical weight on his brow. He took it off and handed it to Lord Eavertin.

Though he accepted it, Lord Eavertin said, "You should wear it, sir."

"If I return, I shall. But if I fall, it will be lost with me. You'll need it to crown Allirae." Danivid strode from them, lest they see his face. For the moment he spoke it, he realized that he may indeed fall.

Danivid reached his horse, which a groom hastily untied. He ran a hand down its neck—a moment to compose himself. To commit. If only hours remained to him, they must be spent on saving lives.

Danivid mounted and glanced around. The wagon rumbled away on the deserted Harbor Circle Road. Trellian was already in the saddle, and Koriak reached his foot to his stirrup. Danivid sensed the waters. A current flowed out of the harbor mouth. Wind teased the surface, and a string of ship hulls pressed divots into its flow. He loosened his reins and shifted his weight in the saddle. "Let's go."

He and his companions soon caught up to the wagon and followed it. If only it could attain a better speed. Precious moments were lost as it pulled to a stop to drop off the first streamer, then ponderously started again. At this rate, they wouldn't be ready when the last ship left the harbor.

"Let down the tailgate," Danivid ordered at the next stop. "From now on, the wagon will only slow and each of you will jump down from the rear."

They did so without mishap, although he called for a full stop at the central-most point. Here, Danivid would leave the wind weaver and the most elderly streamer, whom he could trust to direct others if he must leave. "Continue on," he instructed the driver. "Stay with the last streamer until an all-clear is announced. Then return, picking everyone up along the way."

"All night if I must," the driver replied, slapping the reins of his team.

Danivid dismounted. "Rest the horses." Only two ships remained, traveling at a smart clip toward the open sea. "Peppi, lift my voice to the streamers."

She gave him a crisp nod, turning to face those already in position. "One phrase at a time, please."

"Streamers," Danivid said, "when the final ship is out, we will start circling the current. As the circle passes the eastern headland, fling it outward." That, he would soon show them anyway. He waited while she repeated the message toward the wagon. What else needed to be said?

Ah. He checked with her first, then stated an order. "Peppi will listen, circling around each of you. Streamers who watch the islands, practice communicating with her."

She spread their voices, one by one.

Good. That worked. Now for the current. Danivid planted his feet and silently commanded. Instinctively, he extended his right hand and gripped, drawing in toward his shoulder as he summoned the current to follow the palace-side shore. He felt the wave streamers join in, rushing the flow around the harbor toward him. The crest reached him, and he flung his left hand out as he swept the current away. Another of the streamers had deployed and joined in to drive it farther. Seconds later, those in the wagon all flung it ahead of them.

Danivid's streaming sense reached farthest of all. He allowed not a single drop to shed its momentum. At the eastern headland, he flung it full-force out of the harbor, demanding that the ocean accept his counterflow.

Chardomeer's reprimand of old played in his mind. *You cannot stream an ocean!*

Oh, can't I? The ocean *would* obey him!

The harbor's circling current widened, sweeping up more of the central waters. Not a deep whirlpool, but he gave it an apex and demanded that the entire harbor follow the spin. The flow seemed lazy at the center, but at the edges, a rising wall of water thundered past the cliffs. Only where the formers still labored to raise barriers, did the waters pass in silence. The streamers he'd left to protect them forced the current to form a wall offshore, zipping past their structures.

Danivid sensed the entirety and confirmed that all streamers were now deployed. This was working better than he'd expected. He could spare a moment to assess distantly. Where was the leading edge of the approaching tsunami? He tapped Peppi's shoulder and announced, "Maintain this flow…"

She sent it, then stopped. "One of them is shouting back."

On the heels of her voice, another's voice spread from the distance. "The wave is fully cresting over Penn Island!"

Danivid had just reached that far himself. He stopped breathing. *No. No. NO!* A tumult crashed over the distant island. A small break in the overall force. Like a single rock breaking the surface of a river, its impact swiftly lost in the current.

He'd underestimated how much the rising seafloor would lift the wave.

Trellian gripped his arm. "What does this mean?"

"We're in trouble." His fault. "Let me think!"

He delved the waters and realized what was happening in the harbor. Dread flowed from the streamers as strong as the current. But their fear let water falter. He gripped Peppi's shoulder again and ordered, "Maintain the spin!" With his own command, he sent it high again. Then watched the tsunami approach another island. "Lead streamers, notice how the shoreline is drained before the strike. Make use of that when it reaches us." During the pauses that wasted too many seconds, he agonized. "I'm going to the peninsula. My horse, Koriak."

The lead streamer beside him turned in shock. "What? Why? We'll never hold it without you."

He grabbed the reins and reached a foot to the stirrup. "You won't hold it with me either. I must divert the primary wave from the harbor entrance. You keep the harbor spinning." He hit the saddle and snapped a demand at Trellian and Koriak. "Stay here." His horse surged forward.

Behind him, Trellian was shouting, "Tell the weavers to…" Her words were lost to him. Please, let her stay behind!

Pursuing hooves beat the road. Folly. They couldn't help him. But he could not stop to order them back. He probably wouldn't even reach the tunnel mouth in time. If only he hadn't told Katowau that the wave wouldn't surmount the peninsula. To protect Regissa, had he sacrificed Jourendia? He should have told Peppi to alert the formers. Could she even do so? He shouted the order over his shoulder but heard nothing back from her.

His only hope was to ride hard. Beat the wave. His chest shook with the impossibility of it all, driving silent sobs through him. He *was* going to die today. "Ellincreo!"

I am here.

"Please don't let my death be in vain. What should I do?"

I am with you. Ride on.

"Stop Trellian from—"

Ride on. Focus.

He could do that much. Better than heeding the panicked guilt that threatened him. He left the harbor road. Trees surrounded him—tighter the farther he rode. For a split-second he saw a mounted man in their shadows. Something hissed through the air. He knew that sound, but it made no sense. The hooves behind him altered from a steady beat to chaos.

His roan knew these bridle paths and devoured them. He leaned forward over its neck. Only one set of hooves still pursued. Farther back.

Whoever it was, they would die with him. The roan galloped like it knew a watery beast pursued them. No need to urge it faster.

Danivid delved the wave again. There, his awareness would remain until he went to ground beneath it. He summoned. The vast mass resisted him, but the leading rise curved ever so slightly toward the peninsula. Never had he streamed from horseback. The contrary motions of the water's flow and the horse's thrust made him sick.

A distant weaver's voice reached him. "Evacuate the retaining walls."

Someone had decided it was time. May they reach safety.

His horse was flagging. Down to a trot. Jolting his stomach worse. Still too far from the tunnel mouth. No speed would help now. Danivid drew rein to let it walk. He kept all awareness in the charging wave. Somehow...unbelievably...its flow angled from the harbor. Scant comfort, for that fed more energy into the mass. But if he had done that much...could he somehow do more? Protect the tunnel?

"Whoa," he murmured, then dismounted, mumbling, "Like a river? Make a gap...a wedge to part it." He tried it in the distance. It didn't last a second. Could he flip the wave over on itself? Impossible when he could barely turn its current. Even if some water obeyed him, the rest would sweep him from the peninsula. And if he somehow kept it from cresting over the peninsula, the full force would smash the cliffs. Worse devastation in Jourendia than if the tunnel was breached. Might even take out the entire province of Dirklan. Danivid groaned.

As though this wasn't bad enough, clopping hooves penetrated his desperate thoughts. He turned. Trellian.

"No," he moaned. One life mattered as much as another, but why did it have to be her?

She jumped from the saddle and ran to him, dragging the mare with her.

"You shouldn't have come."

"Don't waste time. What is next?"

"I've done all I can. Much of Regissa will survive, but we will be swept away."

Her clamped lips worked stubbornly. "Then why stand? Are these horses trained to lie down?"

"Yes, but—"

"Show me. Have you heard from the peninsula wind weaver yet?"

"No. Why would Velzain—"

"Try!"

He nudged his horse's foreleg and urged it back. The exhausted beast lay down on the first suggestion. He walked a few yards away and shouted, "Velzain!"

The wind tugged, then pushed. Distant words reached him, along with hoofbeats. "Coming to you, lord king. Where are you?"

"Not yet to the tunnel mouth. I cannot reach it before the wave."

"I am beyond it. What are you about to do?"

"I cannot stop the wave from washing over us. Lie down. Behind any shelter."

The hooves stopped. "I will make a wind tunnel over us." She paused as the wind buffeted him, then demanded, "Is that you standing up?"

"Yes."

"Well, don't! And stop yelling."

He hustled back to the horses and helped Trellian get the mare down. Was this actually changing anything? Trellian scrunched herself into an awkward position behind the mare's back. He dropped to his knees, covering her head and shoulders while bracing his hands on the saddle. Silently, he asked, *Ellincreo, I'll die for my own mistake, but I beg you to protect Trellian.*

Drop the self-blame. Regissa and Jourendia need you alive.

That felt like a snap-out-of-it slap. Well—if *he* said so. "Velzain, there are two of us here, plus two lying horses. They're our only shelter."

"I feel you within the wind. I've found Dirklan Tunnel's mouth. I'll cover that and us three. What will you do?"

As though he knew. "I'm out of options."

"You better think of something, because no wind weaver can support the weight of the ocean!"

Ellincreo!

It has all the power it needs for the leap.

Oh, of course! Let it do what it wants. He had no time to lose.

Danivid summoned the nearest water. Madness, for the wave was almost on them. A vast green wall ready to crush them all. He closed his eyes, lest terror betray him, and demanded that the crest rise higher. Higher! "Velzain, I'm arcing it over the peninsula. Twist the wind that direction."

"That's insane! I can't support that."

"You needn't. Just keep air over us like we are surfers in the barrel of a wave. No more words."

Thunder enveloped him. The tsunami had a voice. He wove his command into its raging throat and demanded it leap over them.

Trellian was tugging on him. "Lie down."

"Can't!" He snarled.

He was upright on his knees. Hands extended wide. Trellian's hair whipped his face, caught in Velzain's swirling tube. His lips parted. The wind chilled his teeth. A yell, impossible to voice, erupted through his streaming command and pierced every roiling channel of the wave. *Over!* A single demand that lasted minutes. Through the first seconds of the wave leaping airborne over the rocky slope. Through the half-light beneath its underbelly. Through timeless crashing as the wave cascaded down the far side. Not ending until trailing droplets fell like salty rain.

Trellian's breath came in a whispery pant. So unlike her. "Is it done?"

"Give me a minute to judge the next wave."

She halted her movement to sit up. "There's another?"

"Waves don't travel alone, my dear. The second is smaller, and I sapped some of its energy to lift the first." He studied it. "The next wave will die on the cliffs. Did you hear that, Velzain?"

"Yes. I must withdraw a moment to check the volcano area and report to Cinnawa."

Danivid's knees complained. He twisted around to sit on the rock, using the saddle as a backrest. He cradled Trellian's shoulders in one arm. "You can take it easy now."

"You covered me. When you thought the wave would sweep us away."

"So I did. Probably wouldn't have worked."

"No, but your final attempt did. Do you know that you look quite vicious while streaming an ocean?"

He chuckled. "Well...it was kind of big. One must intimidate a monster like that." He drew her closer. "Why did you follow me?"

"I...um...I promised Allirae I would stick with you, because she was convinced you would do something dangerous. She was right, of course, and I was supposed to talk you out of it. Meroak was right too."

"Right about what?"

"That none of us can talk you out of the dangerous things you do."

"At the moment, I'm a little tired of danger. What happened to Koriak?"

"I'm not sure. He was right behind me. I heard his horse veer aside, but I didn't look back."

"There was someone in the woods. Did you see him?"

"A bit of movement, but you were well ahead, and I couldn't risk losing sight of you. Why?"

"I think he shot a crossbow at me."

The breath from her rounded lips hit his cheek. "Full-sized?"

"I didn't see it but heard a bolt whiz past me. Could have been for small game." She would realize that could still be lethal. "I know of only one person nearby who has a crossbow." The bite of yet another betrayal tried to find purchase.

"One?" she asked. "They'd be common in any woodland of Felverland."

Fair point, though the image of such a weapon in Burdock's pack lingered. Please let it be someone else.

"Regardless," she said, "Koriak would only have stopped for a reason. He won't delay long."

"I hope he does. I doubt you'd let me hold you if he were here. Did you really only come because Allirae worried?"

She looked into his eyes. "No. I am with you no matter what. I just made up reasons for Allirae and Koriak. Who knows what people might say? I don't want to ruin things if you need to marry Lady Zendell."

"Zendell? Now, there is a danger you *ought* to save me from!"

Finally, Trellian laughed, and the tension left her shoulders.

In the distance, Burnie let out an exultant bark. Horses followed him. Danivid stood and pulled Trellian to her feet. Pity he couldn't do more, but another wave needed his attention. He churned some of it offshore to disrupt its momentum but let the rest strike the rocks. Its roar doused every sound. When words could again be heard, he shouted, "Velzain, if you hear me, try to get me a report from the palace area."

She must have reached Peppi, for soon the voice of a streamer near the palace was lifted to him. "Some water surmounted the protective walls, but flooding is manageable. There's pier damage at the port. Rebanak has sent formers through the lower city to assess buildings. The garden here is mud, but the palace stands."

They had succeeded. He let a surge of tingles wash through him.

Trellian still gripped his hand. "I predict a full-out party in the streets next Savoring Day."

"Rightly so. It will gladden Ellincreo's heart." He tilted his head. "And I have even more to savor, for this event gives me causes galore to restore both the Formers' and Streamers' Guilds."

"The master streamer is still king."

What did she mean? "I can't help but be king."

"Just so."

No time to figure her out, for the horses scrambled to their feet, and Velzain rode toward them.

She jumped to the ground, blending the motion into a curtsy. "Sorry the tunnel was so rough inside." She tugged at her dress and rummaged in a pocket. "I'm not used to spinning a water-coated wind tunnel. Makes eddies." She pulled out a comb and handed it to Trellian.

"Thanks!"

Trellian set to work on her tangles, as Danivid said, "Tell me about the volcano."

"Less steam now, but still pumping out vile air. I'd guess it has made itself into an island."

Might be a good thing. Less to worry about beneath the ocean surface. "I need a message spread over the city."

"That's why I'm here." Velzain's smile suddenly bloomed. "I'm sure they're waiting to hear from you specifically, so Cinnawa will spread it in relays." She faced the city and proclaimed, "Hear the words of King Danivid."

He spoke distinctly with pauses. "Take heart, Regissa. The severe waves have passed. We offer thanks—"

"Just a minute." Velzain held her hand up. "They are cheering." She dropped her hand after a bit. "Now, we should be able to get through again."

Danivid resumed. "We offer thanks to the streamers, formers, and wind weavers...who joined forces to spare us from the worst...and to Ellincreo, who gifted us. To those who are gifted with possessions and skills, please share now while your neighbors are in need. The lower city repairs will be the highest priority until you all rest in your homes again."

"They're cheering again. Do you have more?"

"That is enough. I assume they are getting specific instruction from others, yes?"

Velzain nodded. "Cinnawa passes it all on."

Danivid turned toward the dismounting men, but checked as Velzain spoke in the distinctive timbre of a lifted voice. "I, Wind Weaver Velzain, will share what I witnessed. The mightiest streamer of all, King Danivid, grappled the raging wave and cast it o'er top of the peninsula to spare Dirklan from destruction."

He frowned. "I didn't ask..."

Trellian stopped him with a grip on his arm as she said, "Well done," to Velzain. To him, she murmured, "Let them have their hero. They have needed one for years."

Velzain teared up. "Oh, how they cheer." She covered her mouth with shaking fingers as she drew the sound along the peninsula.

On and on it came. Never would Danivid forget how those myriad voices spread balm over his weary heart. Even Burnie joined in, licking his hand between a woof and several bounces.

Koriak approached, his uniform a complete mess with one sleeve torn and dark.

"Is that blood on your sleeve?" Danivid asked. "What happened?"

"Barely any. Worth it, for I captured Durki."

"Who? Oh, the saddle incident." Realization of the obvious sent a wave of relief through Danivid. It hadn't been Burdock.

Whatever his expression revealed, it wasn't what Koriak expected, for he scowled. "Do you realize he shot at you?" he demanded.

"Only that someone did—and I thought I had yet another enemy. Did you witness the actual deed?"

"I did. Then he saw me charging him and took another shot at me."

"Either he's a poor shot," Trellian said, "or he's not truly up to killing people."

Danivid rubbed his forehead. "I'm a hero on one side, and hunted on the other." Still. Did they not have the real perpetrators in custody? "Yautan couldn't have instigated this. Why would Durki try to kill me now?"

"I suspect he's been hiding in the woodland all this time," Koriak replied. "Few come here, but you would eventually return. He could have had instructions to kill you when opportunity arose. Weavers were spreading your orders, and he had a spyglass. Much of Harbor Circle Road is visible from higher ground. He could have easily seen you set out from there—alone at first. He had time to get into position. Besides all that, the chaos of hundreds arriving in the woodland would make it harder to pin the crime on him."

Made sense. More than mistrusting someone like Burdock, who loathed ambertrop. "I'm getting more paranoid by the day."

"Understandable," Koriak said.

"No, it's intolerable. It only makes me mistrust my friends. I will not live cowering from threats. Nor will I leave my people wondering who next will be murdered in the streets."

No one dared answer.

"We were so close this morning, but we lost the element of surprise," he said. "The queen's revelation shows that Shevnal must be behind all of it. Ambertrop, robbing the crown, regicide. But he has covered his tracks. I must have certainty. Proof."

He looked around the handful of people. They had no more proof than he did. Yautan wouldn't talk. Durki might, but such a blundering tool probably knew little. The corrupt police wouldn't talk, for they'd incriminate themselves. Short of Shevnal confessing—but he wouldn't. Or could he be made to?

"Where is Shevnal now?"

The guard who'd arrived with Koriak answered. "When I left the palace, he was held in one of the ground-floor rooms."

"Is it declared safe now?"

"Mostly. Everyone stays on the ground floor near exits. They couldn't take Shevnal to the cells because the quake jammed the door. Besides, no one was keen to let Shevnal and Yautan talk."

"Is Yautan at risk?"

"Nah. Somebody managed to shout through the ventilation to him. He's in the dark but not hurt."

An old story came back to Danivid. From the days when the substance gifts were valued. He looked at Velzain and smiled. "Will you come to the palace with me?"

CHAPTER 31

Velzain returned Danivid's smile. "I was hoping you'd offer, lord king. I doubt the old weaver's cottage at Land's End is still standing."

"Oh, no," Trellian said. "Have you lost everything?"

"Not all." Velzain patted her horse, which held an enormous duffle tied behind its saddle. "I live with Cinnawa half the year, so some of my things are there. I packed the important stuff from this cottage when I realized the ocean's threat."

Danivid rubbed his roan's muzzle. "Sorry, old pal, but I need you again. We'll walk, I promise." He waited for everyone to mount, then nudged his horse near Trellian's and whispered, "Do you still have water for me?"

Her somber expression lightened. "Of course."

If he wasn't mistaken, there was a hint of a caress in those simple words. The slow ride granted them relaxed moments for quiet words and a delayed snack.

Jonger met them with fresher horses and took charge of their overworked mounts. Thus, Danivid's party reached the palace before dark.

As they approached from the street side, light flicked on within a few windows. Magnery line repairs must be in progress. This side of the palace looked normal—except for a horse-drawn carriage standing ready at the curb. At least he didn't have to look at the ruins of the garden and colonnade.

He left his horse with a groom and strode inside, only to be confronted by the mural of wind, water, and rock. A crack ran down through the sky and pierced the tallest wave where it beat against a high cliff. Both the rock and water sides of the crack were pocked with gaps where glass replacements had fallen. The broken shards on the floor had been swept aside. Cracked like his kingdom. The false revealed.

He turned his back on it and interrupted Velzain's sorrowful awe of the treasure she beheld for the first time. "Come. We must plan." He led his little retinue into the salon where his proxies coordinated relief as best they could. Only Rebanak was with them at the moment.

Danivid gave the briefest possible answers to Lord Eavertin's questions and cut short Prentov's attempted report. "Well done. I appreciate all your efforts, but we have little time left for a critical task. Rebanak, repair the door to the foundation cells at once. Don't talk to Yautan. Figure out where the ventilation channel runs, then tell me where in the palace we can get closest to it."

Rebanak blinked, began a sentence, then changed it to, "As you wish, lord king," and left.

Prentov leaned forward, his gaze intent on Danivid. "What do you need?"

"A trap."

They crowded into the serving pantry. An entire wall held the royal dinnerware behind glass doors. Meant to be a busy place, the room had no chairs, but they carried some in from the dining room, placing a couple on either side of an ordinary window.

Danivid motioned Velzain to sit beside the window and opened it. Somewhere below, a narrow vent provided airflow to the foundation level. He sat across from her, while two more chairs were placed near them for Trellian and Lord Eavertin. Prentov and one of the judges' recorders opted for stools at the central table under the ceiling-mounted magnery light. Koriak, looking much better in a fresh coat, stationed himself by the door.

Velzain took a few minutes to sense. "I have the feel of the channel," she murmured.

"Hear anything?"

"Not yet."

Rebanak pushed his chair against a wall. "Hope you don't mind if I take a break." He stretched his legs out and closed his eyes.

"Ah, there," Velzain murmured. She drew the sound up into the room.

Scrapes and a clank preceded Yautan's voice. "It's about time!"

The guard said, "Be glad you got something. The palace kitchen had to feed all the gifted of Regissa today."

"Why? Because of the quake?"

"More because of the tsunami that followed it. And by the way, you should be thanking the king that you didn't drown today. If he hadn't taken charge of the streamers, that wave would have struck the palace and flooded this level." Another clank and footsteps ended the conversation.

It worked! Danivid kept excitement from his voice. "Any chance he can hear us?"

Velzain's braid wobbled with the shake of her head. "Whoever talked to him through that vent must have been shouting his lungs out."

They waited in silence despite her assurance. The guard stuck his head into the room with eyebrows raised in question. "Good?"

Koriak nodded and motioned him out.

Minutes ticked by. Then more scrapes and clanks reached them, along with two sets of footsteps, one of them halting. This prisoner would be placed in the adjacent cell, so he and Yautan could talk without fear of being overheard.

After the final slam of the door, Yautan croaked, "What are you doing down here?"

A shuffling sound and a grunt came next, then Shevnal's voice. "A charge that will not stick."

"What charge?"

"Theft of heirlooms. I'll just say that I paid for them and King Vancent wanted no receipts written."

Other sounds filtered through. Movement, perhaps. Strange to hear this well when separated from the source.

"I've been waiting for you to get me out." Yautan sounded accusing. "Why didn't you?"

"I didn't know where you were. The king went belowground, claiming illness. I assumed he'd discovered something, and you bolted. Only this morning did I learn that you'd been caught. How did you let that happen?"

"Let?" Yautan demanded. "I'd bet anything it was that meddling Felvarian woman. Her and that foul dog."

"Unfortunate, but they aren't witnesses. What can be proven?"

"They have my tea caddy. Rather incriminating." Yautan's voice trembled. "They're charging me with murder of the king!"

"A known risk. Please tell me you did not admit to it."

"Of course not!"

Another pained grunt.

Yautan asked. "What's wrong with you?"

"Sprained my ankle when the ground heaved."

"What all happened up there?"

"A significant quake followed by a tsunami. All of which gave our last-century king a chance to play the hero. I'll have to prove him a fool again."

"Except you won't, because you're down here. Theft can't be the only reason, or the regular police would be holding you. Admit it. You're in the same position I am."

"Not at all." Shevnal sounded as arrogant in that cell as he had in Danivid's study. "Unprovable theft is a far cry from the murder of one king and drugging of another. Also, Lenneth came back, so your lie that her maid supplied their ambertrop won't hold."

Shaky breaths reached them, and for a moment the scribes' pencils stopped. Danivid frowned. This locked down the case against Yautan, but he needed something more tangible against Shevnal.

At last, Yautan said, "This whole thing was your idea."

"Pretending you were unwilling now?"

"The money was one thing, but killing wasn't part of the plan. That was your idea too. You said you could keep the police from investigating."

"They didn't investigate, and they won't. I've taken care of you as promised. Your days in the palace are over, but why mourn? Your secret fund must be quite substantial by now."

"Hard to use if I hang. They're threatening to punish me for hiding an accomplice too. I won't bear it for you. If I go down, you will too."

"Enough drama. Neither of us will go down. I'll get you out tonight."

A long pause, then Yautan asked, "How?"

"I'm a *former*."

"No—really?" Yautan's tone held a sneer. "Have you noticed we're underground?"

"Two feet of the wall is exposed above the surface." Danivid envisioned the eyeroll inherent in Shevnal's voice. "Cracks will appear. The natural result of a quake. Also natural that you would pry the rock loose and escape. In the morning, the guards will find only the rubble in your cell."

There was a long pause. "I take it," Yautan said, "that you are not escaping tonight."

"I'd rather take my chances in court than running with a sprained ankle."

Another pause. "You want me away, so I don't testify against you."

"Mutual benefit, as always," Shevnal said. "Though I must admit, you have the greatest need and benefit this time. Not that I grudge you the use of my gift. Find some distant place to enjoy a well-funded retirement."

An even longer pause. "I can't, though. My stash is in Regissa. I won't be able to get to it."

"You know where to hide. I'll get it to you there."

A short pause this time. "Yeah. All right." Yautan sniffed. "Got to admit, I won't miss the new regime. He'll squelch amber use if he can. What will you do without that income?"

"A business that was bound to falter. Profit early, then abandon it. There's a reason I bought land with the income."

"I suppose. You own the Formers' Guild too. You're sitting pretty."

"In a cell, with my ankle feeling like it will explode, is not what I call *sitting pretty*. You'll have to excuse me from this fascinating conversation."

Though Danivid waited, nothing more was said. Prentov and the recorder compared their notes and wrote out copies of the formal statement, which required Lord Eavertin's and Danivid's signatures. He read through it, considering, then scrawled his name.

The recorder accepted the paper from him. "Do you want me to witness more tonight, sir?"

"No. Ensure that the high judge sees this as soon as possible."

Koriak closed the door behind the man. "What action do you prefer, sir? Prevent the escape or catch Yautan in the act?"

Danivid rubbed his chin. "Shevnal is playing Yautan."

"How so?" Eavertin asked.

"Yautan is a week behind on information. Shevnal pretends that little has changed, so Yautan will believe he can escape."

"He'd have to be a fool," Trellian said, "to take refuge in any hiding place that Shevnal knows of."

Eavertin scoffed. "Murdering a king is the act of a fool."

"Or of a desperate man," Trellian said.

Danivid paced between the table and glass doors. "Yautan is more desperate now, with fewer options. Tonight, that means escape or confess his *and* Shevnal's deeds."

Koriak said, "Yautan will turn on Shevnal anyway when we capture him on the far side of that wall."

"I beg of you, sir," Eavertin said, "that you do not risk any possibility of his escape."

"I won't." Danivid turned to Rebanak. "Watch for any changes to the wall."

He drew his legs in and straightened. "Sure, but the moment I sense Shevnal's presence, he will sense mine."

"Then Yautan will have a decision to make. We may have a long night."

"The moon will cast a shadow here starting around midnight." Rebanak made a slanting gesture toward the window. "If I were Shevnal, I'd wait for that."

Prentov stood. "I'll see about getting us food."

"Not everyone need stay," Danivid said.

Eavertin heaved himself from the chair. "Not as young as I used to be. I'll hear of your success in the morning."

"Ladies?" Danivid said suggestively.

"You'll need me," Velzain replied, "if they start talking again."

"Trellian?"

She smirked at him with raised eyebrows.

Danivid's chest shook with silent laughter.

They stayed awake by taking turns strolling around the table and by nibbling on the fruit and cheese that Chef Perkett provided.

The only speech they heard from the cells was a grumbled, "Dark as a cave," when the guard turned off the magnery light.

It was indeed past midnight when Rebanak jerked his head around toward the exterior wall. "Shevnal just started to split a crack, then halted when he noticed me. And now he repaired it."

Velzain ran back to the window, the half-eaten pear in her hand forgotten as she focused her gift.

When too many minutes had passed, Danivid asked her, "What's happening down there?"

"Two people are breathing."

Snark, he didn't need, but before he could rebuke her, she spread her empty hand and words drifted up.

"Yautan. Are you awake?"

"How could I sleep tonight? Is it time?"

Shevnal groaned. "Yes, but my leg is killing me. Can you reach through the bars and help me up?"

"Just a minute." The brush of groping hands and careful steps followed. Yautan's disgruntled voice demanded, "What does it take to get you up?"

"Stay near the bars," Shevnal whispered.

"Why?" Yautan hissed. "Let go!"

"We may be heard." Shevnal's breathy words were barely audible. "Get your ear near my mouth."

"How could anyone—" A gasp ended his words. Bars rattled, and Yautan croaked, "What—"

Velzain dropped her pear. "The breathing is all wrong."

"Sorry," Shevnal said, velvet smooth, "but you must hang yourself tonight. I'll do the hard part for you."

Koriak jerked the door open and bolted from the room.

Danivid raced after him, with more feet pounding behind him. The corridor stretched ahead of them. Stairs too. Would they arrive in time?

Koriak shoved the guardroom door open and bellowed, "Unlock that!"

The guard snatched up keys, his shaking hand costing them more seconds before he turned the key in the lock. The door swung inward as the magnery light flickered on.

An image locked into Danivid's mind. Shocked fury on Shevnal's face and Yautan tied by the neck to a bar, his tongue protruding below bulging eyes.

With a flurry of wordless action, guards opened the cells, floored Shevnal, and released the belt that strangled Yautan.

Velzain demanded, "Get him flat on his back."

Two guards stretched Yautan's limp body on the shelf that served as a bed, then backed away.

Velzain slipped her hand beneath Yautan's neck, positioning it as her gift drew air in and out. His chest rose and fell.

Trellian hovered beside him, resting her fingers against his neck artery. "He is alive."

Minutes passed. A guard tied Shevnal's hands behind his back, marched him to a more distant cell, and anchored his bound hands to a bar. "Not so arrogant now, are you?" he snarled.

But it was Yautan's face that Danivid watched. The color began returning to normal. The distortion easing. Eyes naturally closed.

Velzain stepped away. "He's breathing on his own now."

"Come out of the cell, ladies," Koriak said. He locked it and ordered, "Two guards present here for the rest of the night."

"Yes, sir." The guard on duty jerked his thumb backwards. "What about his forming gift?"

Rebanak stepped into the doorway of the guardroom. "I monitored. He tried to use it in the ceiling a few minutes ago. Clear intent to kill by means of his gift. He lost it while I sensed."

"I suppose there was no longer a point in trying to preserve it," Danivid said. "He is certain to be hanged now."

A raspy croak came from Yautan's cell. "Lo...lo'd ki..."

Danivid stepped near and leaned an elbow on a crossbar, watching.

Yautan struggled through a swallow and met Danivid's eyes beseechingly.

"Are you ready to tell me about your accomplices yet?"

"Shev...Shevna..."

"We know all about Shevnal. And others, but I want all of them. The dealers who hide. The corrupt police. I want every name, and I know enough to recognize a lie."

Yautan nodded.

Danivid addressed Koriak. "Get a medic for Yautan. See that he is comfortable and well fed. Record all that he says. If he cannot speak, give him paper and pen to write the names." He strolled partway down the aisle between cells and raised his voice. "Oh, and Shevnal, do you remember all that de Noviam land you so diligently built on? The crown will recover it. All of those leases you negotiated will fund the heirs of the House de Noviam. Have a pleasant night."

CHAPTER 32

With a murmur of thanks, Trellian accepted the wire transcript from a page. Even after the woman left, she delayed opening it, gazing instead around the elegant décor of her palace bedroom. She'd considered it overdone when she first arrived, but it had grown comfortable and home-like as the weeks passed. Especially the later ones. Who might be about to interfere?

She opened the paper enough to read the *from* line. Prime Minister Starroni.

Expected. She'd written him a lengthy report and sent it by mail. She'd waited as long as possible, sending only brief wires of hopeful news. Like when the full truth came out about the extent of Shevnal's and Yautan's amber organization. And when the enraged citizens of Regissa demanded that amber be outlawed in their province. It took Welcia's General Council a month to do the same for the entire country, and with that she'd lost all excuses to delay a full report.

Which she should have delivered in person.

Instead, she'd included a paragraph explaining that she was helping Welcia's police recognize amber trafficking strategies and helping the medics understand withdrawal. She'd sent similar letters to her parents, including references to court events. Exactly what her mother liked, so

Trellian's parents hadn't urged her return. But had she convinced the prime minister?

Enough dallying. She snapped the paper open and read the PM's brief message. Congratulations on accomplishing her mission...and a summons to report in person. No surprise. She refolded it, running her fingernails along the creases.

She knew it had to end. Leisurely breakfasts. Allirae and Meroak treating her like family. Teaching art to Aneen. Evening walks with Danivid...the rides in the woodland...their trip to Crysalan in Dirklan. Actually, it was the walks she liked best, even though they had to traipse over rough grass to reach the remaining section of the colonnade. He wouldn't allow replacement of the rest of it until every home in the lower city was repaired. Guards were farther away during the walks, so they had privacy. For talking, anyway. The sort of talks she'd never had in Felverland. It was hard for her to think they might end. Would he think so?

She should stop being silly and just go tell him.

He'd be in his study with Prentov, going through the morning's communiques. He might even have one from Starroni. Not how she wanted him to learn that she must leave. That got her feet moving, though she still wasn't sure what to say.

Voices reached her as she neared the staircase. Talk of the mural in the hall below. Was the king finally allowing work on it?

Someone said, "The best way to close the crack completely is to shift this side of the mural. We can seal it so no one can tell it was ever cracked."

"No." Danivid's voice. She reached the stairs and turned down them as he spoke. "Too many ancient reminders have already been lost. We aren't pretending this never happened. We aren't forgetting—or letting our children forget—how we escaped destruction."

The artisans among the formers began spouting ideas...how to make the crack through the cliff represent the quake...how to portray the swirling or high leap of waves while hinting at the wind tunnel. Trellian reached Danivid's side and stared up at the near vertical crack that split the ancient art—a couple inches wide at the top, tapering to a point at the bottom.

One of the formers said, "We'll have to fill the sky part of the crack, though, for stability."

Danivid shook his head. "Your ideas sound good, but I want the crack visible."

"How about filling it with gold?" Trellian suggested.

"Gold?" one of them murmured.

"We use gold to represent Ellincreo in Felverland. Isn't that used here?"

Danivid smiled at her. "Indeed. That's the part we were missing. Luminous gold."

The ideas started bouncing again, and she whispered, "May I have a moment of your time?"

"Of course."

He led her to a rear salon. "We won't be disturbed in here," he said, closing the door.

She faced him. "Prime Minister Starroni sent me a wire. He summons me to return to the capital and give him a report in person."

Silence.

His smile dropped, and his brow tightened. That could mean what she hoped—or something else.

"**A**h." Danivid cleared his throat. "Inevitable, though I wasn't expecting it quite yet. Do you know if he received the report you mailed?"

"He did. I assume that, with the mail and wire tampering only recently corrected, he wants to make sure all is confirmed." She rolled her lips. "I suppose I told you too abruptly."

His smile spread again. "You know I like it direct."

She only nodded. The tiny movements within the stillness of her face gave him a shred of hope that she was disappointed about leaving.

"I'll write to Starroni, commending your work here," he said. "Though if I tell him the full extent of your importance, it might sound too amazing to be true."

That got a bit of a smile out of her. "What a nice compliment."

As though commending her work was the point. "Listen, I don't know what your obligations might be, but…"

He left too long of a pause, and she said, "I do have to go."

"I realize that, but I'd like to ask him to send you back. If you are willing, of course."

She tilted her head. "Why?"

"It's been such a whirlwind month. The courts, the councils, finance, guild meetings, police restructuring—not to mention our first week. Life-and-death decisions on every side. I didn't get as much time with you as I wanted."

"It has been rather eventful." A trace of smile laced the understatement.

"What are you laughing at?"

"You forgot to mention the trip to Dirklan."

His voice lowered. "I was only listing the things that got in my way."

"You still haven't answered my question of *why*. You're not being very direct."

"Are you?"

She tilted her head. "Touché. Apparently, some things are harder to say directly."

His turn again—and time he got the right words together. "I must have been enjoying your presence too much between the chaos to realize how close I was to your departure. Frankly, being king is a real nuisance at times. I have to consider all sorts of ramifications and get the timing right. I won't commit to anything until I'm certain, but I *can* tell you that I want you to come back. *Very much so.*"

She gazed pensively past his shoulder. "Hmm."

Oh, sure...she was having fun with this while he agonized. Wasn't she? "May I ask your prime minister to send you back?"

"You may." She still sounded so matter-of-fact.

"What if he doesn't?"

"I can resign my job, you know." She finally smiled. "I'll be back."

A fountain sprang to life within him. He let it flow to his face.

"After all," she murmured, "Aneen is counting on me to teach her every last nuance of art."

Danivid laughed. "When you arrived, I didn't think there was a tease anywhere inside you."

"Someone taught me. I find I rather like it."

SHARE THE ADVENTURE

I hope that you found something in these pages that made your life a little richer. If you liked this story, maybe others would too. You can help them find it by leaving a brief review or even by clicking some stars wherever you like to purchase or review books. Those star ratings and reviews help me, too, and I greatly appreciate all of them.

Would you like to read more stories like this one? If so, I invite you to join my newsletter. I will send you some free short stories, share a little about life, and let you know about new books and an occasional sale. I won't overload your inbox or share your email address with others. You may unsubscribe at any time. Sign up at SharonRoseAuthor.com. I hope to hear from you!

BOOKS BY SHARON ROSE

FANTASY

Arts of Substance

To Form a Passage – Novel 1
To Weave the Wind – Novel 2
To Stream an Ocean – Novel 3

Castle in the Wilde

A Castle Lost — An Early Days Novella
A Castle Sealed — Prequel Novella
A Castle Awakened — Novel 1
A Castle Contended — Novel 2
A Castle From Ashes — Novel 3

SCIENCE FICTION

Diverse Similarity — Novel 1
Diverse Demands — Novel 2
Agents of Rivelt — A Novel in Short Stories

More titles are coming. Find the full list at SharonRoseAuthor.com.

ACKNOWLEDGEMENTS

There's so much to be grateful for, especially since my team always sticks with me through every project! So I will start with the little things, as I always do.

Small: That would be Sheba, the furball who keeps my lap warm while I write. She occasionally types, also, but that is less appreciated.

Difficult: That would be editing (shudder). Bridgett makes it bearable.

Typos: Beastly little things! Michael helped stomp them out.

Art: Once again, Kirk turned my imaginings into a book cover.

The long haul: This heavy work is supported by so many. Realm Makers, Write Now Writers Group, friends who know nothing about writing but still listen to me, and of course, my wonderful family.

Ideas and comfort: Father, Friend, and Spirit. Yes, I'm talking about God, but hey, I'm a writer! A single word is not enough for the one who loves me so deeply.

Readers: Yes, I mean *you*. Whether you read in advance, or you found this book long after I write these words, thank you for imagining with me. I hope you found some treasures to keep.

I appreciate all of you more than I can ever say!

About the Author

Sharon Rose has been weaving stories since her second-grade masterpiece, titled *My Life as a Flying Squirrel.* No publisher snatched it up, but her classmates loved it.

After creating home and family, Sharon pursued her dream of creating stories for people like you. To date, she has published ten books, with more in the works. She writes fantasy and science fiction because they offer vast spaces to explore the realities that we all face. Her stories blend cultures and characters into adventures with mystery, romance, and hope.

When not writing or reading, Sharon may be traveling, enjoying gardens, or searching for unique coffee shops with her husband. She lives in Minnesota, USA, famed for its 10,000 lakes and vibrant seasons.

To find out more, visit SharonRoseAuthor.com.
Follow me on:
Amazon, Goodreads, BookBub, Facebook, etc.
Find all of my links at: https://linktr.ee/sharonrose.author